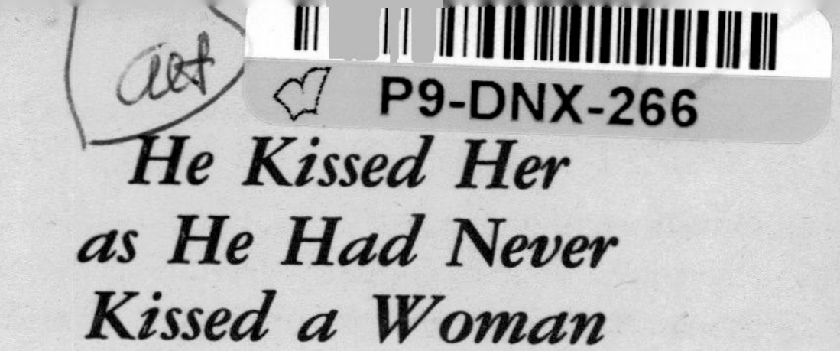


# *He Kissed Her as He Had Never Kissed a Woman*

He embraced her gently, surrounding himself with the heady essence of woods and snow and springtime that clung to her, cherishing her small warm body.

But soon he found himself, against all good sense, craving more.

"Open your mouth," he heard himself whisper. "Just a little." Her lips parted and his tongue brushed over hers. She tasted like the first fresh strawberry of the season, soft and ripe and unbearably sweet.

Her mittened hands grasped his shoulders and held tight. A murmur of longing thrummed in her throat.

Daniel yanked himself to his senses. He was a mercenary who had no call and no right to touch her innocence.

He pulled back. A slow, dreamy smile spread across her face. Daniel's stomach plunged. This was going to be worse than he thought.

* * *

**"Enthralling . . . a marvelous mixture of fact and fiction. Susan Wiggs is a superb storyteller."**

—*Kathe Robin*
*ROMANTIC TIMES*

Also by Susan Wiggs

*The Lily and the Leopard*

Published by
HarperPaperbacks

SUSAN
WIGGS

HarperPaperbacks
*A Division of* HarperCollins*Publishers*

HarperPaperbacks *A Division of* HarperCollins*Publishers*
10 East 53rd Street, New York, N.Y. 10022



Cover art by R.A. Maguire

First printing: November 1991

Printed in the United States of America

HarperPaperbacks and colophon are trademarks of HarperCollins*Publishers*

10 9 8 7 6 5 4 3 2 1

*This book is for my brother*
*Jon Klist and his family—*
*and no, Mom didn't make me do it.*

I wish to thank Barbara Dawson Smith, Arnette Lamb, Alice Borchardt, and Joyce Bell for their help and support during the writing of this book.

Pat Jones and Becky Hubert of the Houston Public Library and the staff of Fondren Library at Rice University offered assistance in procuring much hard-to-find research material.

I owe a debt of gratitude to Carolyn Marino, Karen Solem, and Chris Wilhide of HarperCollins. Their enthusiasm and encouragement have been invaluable.

Finally, a special warm thank-you to the Swiss National Tourist Office and particularly to Michel Clivaz of Martigny, Switzerland, for sharing his knowledge of the history of the Hospice of Saint Bernard.

Oft has a venerable roof received me;
But among them all
None can with this compare, the dangerous seat
Of generous, active virtue. What though frost
Reign everlastingly, and ice and snow
Thaw not, but gather, there is that within
Which, when it comes, makes summer.

—Samuel Rogers, *The Great Saint Bernard*

# Chapter 1

***Hospice of Saint Bernard***
***Switzerland***
***March 1800***

The urgent yelp of a dog broke through the frosty Alpine twilight. In the main building of the hospice, Lorelei du Clerc looked up sharply from the medical treatise she was studying. Across the lamplit room, Father Anselme dozed in a fraying horsehair chair.

She hated to disturb him. His evening nap was one of his few concessions to age.

Over the howl of the wind, more yelps echoed across the ice-crusted hospice compound. Lorelei snapped her book shut and hurried to the monk's side. She had to wake him. The dogs were never wrong.

"Father Anselme." She shook him by the shoulder.

The musty smell of old wool rose from his habit. "Father Anselme, wake up."

He straightened, blinked, and cleared his throat. "What's that? Er, we were discussing Corvisart's observations—"

"Not now, Father. The dogs . . . They never bark like this unless someone's out there." She took his hand. "But you needn't come. The rest of us—"

"Nonsense, child," he said, rising swiftly despite his age. Determination shone in his eyes. "I've been at this for more than thirty years. I'm not ready to be put out to pasture yet."

Recognizing his need and his pride, she nodded. They went to the outer chamber where scarves and cloaks hung neatly on a row of rough-hewn pegs. They dressed in silence, tense and listening for the deadly, swishing roar of an avalanche.

With steady hands Lorelei drew on her fur-lined chamois boots and an oversized jacket of thick merino. She tugged a brown wool hood over her head, winding its long end around her neck. Father Anselme's age-twisted fingers fumbled with the laces of his boots. She bent and tied them for him. Finally she shouldered a coil of belaying rope and tucked its knotted end into the waistband of her knee breeches.

"Is your kit ready?" Father Anselme asked, his voice muffled by the cavernous cowl he'd drawn over his white hair.

"Always, Father." She donned the rucksack containing her medical supplies while the canon went to the iron stove and filled a canteen with a mixture of wine and tea. "Still, I wish you'd stay here."

He held up a hand. "Don't keep me from my mission, Lorelei. Please."

Father Julian entered the hall. "It's not a likely night for travelers."

Lorelei regarded the spare, ageless face of the prior and chewed her lip. "But you'll ready the infirmary, just in case?"

"Of course." They walked to the door. There, Father Julian handed Father Anselme his alpenstock, then touched Lorelei on the shoulder. "The foehn is up," he said. "Watch your step."

She and Father Anselme left the main building and hurried across the shadowed compound toward the kennels. Apprehension shivered through her. The foehn, a treacherous southerly wind, whined through the remote canyons of the Great Pass and tore at her hood. She bent into the wind. The cold streaked across her face. Hurrying ahead, she led the way through the deep lavender twilight.

A lamp burned in the window of the kennels, and the yelps grew more frenzied. Lorelei heard a sharp command from Father Droz, the kennel master. The dogs fell silent. Like a desolate song, the foehn wailed in her ears.

Then came the sound she dreaded, the sound that never failed to turn her blood to ice. A bone-chilling swish, followed by a muffled thud and the hiss of ice crystals raining down glaciers into depthless gullies. She looked up, straining to see through the dusk.

High on the north face of Mont Vélan, a purple line split the field of white. She stopped walking and measured the time of awful suspense with her heartbeats.

One, two, three. . . . A giant portion of snowy ice glided downward, exposing a new field of purer white.

A crash like thunder exploded across the valley. The curtain of fallen snow disappeared behind a ridge. Trees bent and snapped and tumbled along with the avalanche. White dust poured like a cataract from a narrow defile. Echoes leaped across the range surrounding the Great Pass. A moment later, deathlike silence closed over the mountains.

Father Droz let a pack of six huge Alpine mastiffs into the yard. Framed by the glowing rectangle of the cellar door, the kennel master slipped a rucksack over his bulky shoulders.

Ordinarily the dogs greeted Lorelei with wet, playful kisses, but now the animals strained to be away. The white blazes of fur on their faces and chests flashed in the twilight as they ran to the gate, pawed the frozen ground, and whined with impatience.

"Someone's surely at the pass," said Father Droz. "Barry!" he bellowed at a half-grown puppy. *"Arrêtes!"* But instinct overrode obedience training, and the dog vaulted the gate before it opened. Father Droz hurried across the yard, shouting as he went. "Sylvain! Is the sled ready?"

"Yes, Father." Sylvain, a novice, arrived with pickaxes and a long sled padded with blankets. Lorelei bent to help him lash the supplies to the sled.

"Thanks," he said. His strong hands, chapped raw by the wind and the cold, swiftly secured the buckles. Though awkward and halting in the scriptorium, Sylvain was completely at home with the tasks that awaited him tonight.

Father Droz opened the gate. *"Allez-y, mes amis,"* he commanded.

In a pack, the dogs broke from the yard and fanned out across a vast sweep of drifts. Their huge paws padded through the snow, making paths toward ravines and precipices, gullies and glaciers.

Lorelei and Father Anselme hastened after Belle and Bard, the lead dogs. Barry scampered after them. Lorelei filled her lungs with painfully cold air that smelled of snow and nighttime. Already the chill had penetrated her mittens, and she flexed her hands to keep her fingers nimble.

"Who could be coming through the pass so early in the year?" she asked Father Anselme. "And so late in the day?" As she spoke, she followed the path blazed by the lead dogs. Their unique paddling stride packed the snow so the humans didn't flounder and sink.

"Only someone with an urgent need," said the canon, digging his cruciform staff into the snow. "These days it could be anyone. A royal duke fleeing the Jacobins. Italian refugees seeking the sanctuary of Switzerland."

One of the dogs set up a deep-bellied howling. The eternal snow cushioned the mastiff's voice.

"That's Barry," said Lorelei, feeling a surge of pride in the young dog Father Droz had given her. "He's found something."

Following a trail of canine footprints, they began to climb. The wind bit at Lorelei's face, and ice crunched beneath her boots.

She lost sensation in her cheeks and nose, and the thinning air froze her breath, but the discomfort paled against the vivid need of a traveler in distress. She climbed a hundred feet to a rocky shelf where the road from Bourg-Saint-Pierre snaked around the mountain.

From behind her came the steady thump of Father Anselme's staff stabbing into the snow, the tuneless whistle of air through Father Droz's teeth, the sliding hiss of Sylvain's sled over snow.

From far above, rocks and chunks of ice still rained down in the aftermath of the avalanche. Snow flurries, whipped up by the disturbance, pelted Lorelei's cheeks.

The icy twilight threw violet shadows over a rubble of boulders and giant mounds of snow. Bard and Belle dug furiously, the snow spraying behind them. Still untrained, Barry burrowed instinctively into the snow nearby. The dogs paused to howl from time to time, signaling to the rescuers.

Lorelei and the others clambered to their side and began digging through the mass that obscured the path. While her mittened hands worked frantically alongside huge furry paws, snow flew in her face. She wondered again who the victim would be this time. A refugee fleeing before Bonaparte's Army of Italy? A deserter or mercenary creeping behind it? Wayfarers, smugglers, and adventurers—all received the rescuers' most prodigious efforts. Such had been the mission of the canons for seven centuries.

"Think there's more than one?" asked Sylvain.

His hands sunk to the elbows in a snowdrift, Father Droz shook his head vigorously. "The dogs don't act like it. They're centering their efforts too closely.

"I feel something," he said a moment later, reaching until his entire arm disappeared. "A shoulder, maybe.

*Viens, Bard. Doucement.*" The dog came to his side and dug with well-schooled, delicate motions to avoid injuring the victim.

Father Anselme stood over them, his alpenstock in one hand and a hooded lamp in the other. The light swung wildly, buffeted by the wind. Behind him, Sylvain readied the sled.

Father Droz and Lorelei excavated the head, which was covered by a snug woolen cap. Lorelei burrowed her hand beneath, lifting gently. She brushed the snow from his face. A man.

An all too familiar sinking feeling enveloped her. In the yellow lamplight, the face had a curiously waxen, masklike quality. A few days' growth of dark beard sprouted from the cold, still flesh. The eyes were already sunken into their rims. If he wasn't dead already, he would be soon.

Grief sat like a rock on her chest. Another life, lost to the random caprice of the unforgiving mountains she loved and cursed.

Belle stretched out beside the victim's body, warming him with her own furry bulk as she'd been trained to do. Barry licked the motionless face, and Father Anselme explored the area with his staff, looking for other victims.

Lorelei dusted snow from the man's head. Father Anselme began to pray, and Lorelei's whisper echoed his words. The prayer of supplication came from hearts that had seen too much death, known too much grief.

The man groaned, then lapsed into silence.

"He's alive!" said Lorelei. "Monsieur!" She massaged the man's shoulder. "We're here to help you. Are you alone?" She repeated the question in Italian and German. He only groaned again.

After a few more moments of frantic digging, he was free of the snow that had swallowed him.

"I don't like the look of that arm," said Father Anselme. "Let's be easy getting him onto the sled."

Father Droz and Sylvain rolled the body to and fro as Lorelei spread a blanket beneath him. Her muscles strained, warming beneath her freezing flesh, as she helped move him to the sled.

*"Cherchez, mes amis,"* said Father Droz to the dogs. Belle and Bard obediently sniffed the area, and Barry raced about in clumsy circles. The mastiffs gave no indication of having found other travelers.

"Let's get him back to the hospice," said Sylvan, fitting himself between the projecting rods in front of the sled.

The unwieldy vehicle, bearing a large man in a cocoon of blankets, slithered down the slope, straining against the control of the men.

Half sick with hope and fear, Lorelei raced ahead to prepare for the patient. By the time the others arrived at the infirmary, she and Father Julian had a fire blazing in an iron stove and a bed warmed by copper pots of embers. A low table by the bed was spread with instruments, medicines, and vials. A metal lamp with a punctured hood threw stippled patterns on the wall.

Sylvain and Father Anselme brought the victim to bed. His damp clothes steamed in the heat as they thawed.

They worked quickly to remove a thick woolen coat, the knee breeches and vest and one tall chamois boot laced to the knee. The other, presumably, had been lost in the accident. Thick muscles shaped the body beneath the wet linen shirt and smallclothes, and yet the man seemed vulnerable.

"Mind his right arm," she said, eyeing the swelling limb. "I think it's broken."

Father Gaston, the almoner charged with welcoming visitors to the hospice, brought heated damp cloths from the stove. To warm the body, he and Father Emile, the sacristan, pressed the the cloths on the man's face, chest, hands, and feet.

Lorelei felt his throat for a pulse. A deep chill lingered on his skin, and she wondered how long he'd been traveling. "Faint and thready," she reported to Father Anselme.

"It always is in cases of chill." He glared in frustration at his stiff-jointed hands. "See to his injuries."

She examined the left arm by touch. Her fingers found the jagged break point of the bone.

"I was right about the arm," she said grimly, and glanced down the length of the body, peering through the frame of Father Emile's busy arms. "And I don't like the looks of that knee."

"Sprained, I think." Father Gaston pressed a cloth on it.

"Set the arm quickly, before he awakens," said Father Anselme. "If my hands were not so weak, I could help you myself."

Father Julian brought splints and rolled bandages. Sylvain returned from kenneling the dogs. "How can I help?" he asked, shrugging out of his woolen *bredzon.*

"Put some water into a bowl," said Father Anselme. "We'll need plaster to stiffen the bandages."

"Hold his other arm," Lorelei said to Father Gaston. "If he feels this, he won't stay still." The heat of several bodies and the roaring fire in the wood stove made her sweat. She took the man's large hand in hers, feeling the rasp of calluses against her skin. Then she braced her heel on the side of the cot and pulled.

The moment of resistance, of tendons and muscles straining, seemed to last forever. Lord God, if the man had been awake the pain would have brought him out of his skin.

With a dull click, the bone popped into place.

Shuddering with relief, Lorelei splinted the arm and secured the long, thin slats with plaster-soaked bandages. She moved to the head of the bed and carefully removed the man's cap. A dark, disturbing wetness seeped over the pillow.

"Blood." The faint, rusty smell of it rushed over her. Fear leaped up in her throat. Her hands began to shake. Head injuries meant danger, often death.

"Easy, child," said Father Anselme. "I've trained you from the cradle. You're well prepared to treat a head wound."

"It's here, behind the right temple," she said, feeling the bulge of the hematoma through a mass of thick hair, crusty with blood. She sucked a deep breath through her teeth. "Bring the lamp closer."

A robe swished and oil sloshed as the lamp was moved to the table. Yellow light glimmered over the victim's face, and for the first time, Lorelei gave her full attention to his features. She wanted, somehow, to know him as more than a stranger, for his life was in her hands. And if the wound proved fatal, she wanted to remember him as more than a lost cause.

A chilling vision of the hospice morgue stole into her mind. She didn't want to see this man laid out beneath a thin shroud, eternally frozen, waiting for his relatives to identify him.

Under a tumble of wavy black hair, a scar etched his right eyebrow to his hairline. Where the scar met the hairline, a blaze of white hair streaked through his inky locks, as if the old wound had leached the color from it.

"Who can he be?" murmured Father Gaston.

"And what the devil was he doing in the pass at this time of year?" asked Father Emile, leaning close, his bladelike nose outlined by lamplight. "Maybe he was outlawed by that cursed autocrat in Valais. The man never could abide commoners who value freedom and think for themselves."

"He may pay a heavy price for his freedom," said Father Julian wryly. The prior had a vial, and Lorelei caught the faint scent of olive oil. She fought an urge to snap at the canon for being so quick to prepare for last rites.

"A Swiss, surely," said Sylvain. "His clothes are Swiss-made." High color rose in his cheeks. "We must do our best to heal him. The Swiss will need all their able men to resist invasions from the French and the Austrians."

"Bonaparte's already invaded the Bern treasury," Father Julian muttered.

The unconscious man had prominent cheekbones,

the flesh below them slightly sunken. His wide, square jaw hung slack. His chin had a tiny cleft in the middle, and Lorelei had an inexplicable urge to put her finger there, beneath his pale lips.

Concentrate, she told herself. He needed her help, not her admiration. She pressed a folded cloth to the head wound, then placed her knuckles lightly on his forehead and, with her thumb, lifted one eyelid, then the other.

When the lamplight struck the pupils, they grew smaller. The irises were extraordinarily blue—bluer than the summer sky reflected in an Alpine lake.

"His eyes respond to the light," she told Father Anselme.

"That's good. He's probably only stunned."

"Sylvain," she asked, painfully curious about the victim, "did you find anything in his clothing to identify him?"

"No. Some money—Swiss marks, mostly, but he has Italian coin as well."

"Were any personal effects found at the site of the avalanche?" asked Father Julian.

"Just these," said Sylvain. "Barry sniffed them out." He rummaged among the blankets from the sled. The four friars pressed close to see. Sylvain held up a hunting bow and a quiver of arrows. "Odd, don't you think?" the novice mused. "The arrows are all fletched with raven's feathers."

Behind her Lorelei heard the hiss of an indrawn breath, then a thud as the lamp fell.

The room was plunged into darkness.

* * *

Deep shadows pulsed around him. He opened his mouth to speak, but the effort sent flames of agony through his head.

"Father Julian, light another lamp!" A female voice knifed like a blade in his ears.

Father Julian. Prior of Saint Bernard's.

So he'd made it. Fragmented memories tore at his mind: the fierce joy of standing on Swiss soil once again; the challenge of scaling its sharp-crested mountains, glaciers, and canyons; the cold purpose that had driven him to the remote, desolate Great Pass.

Those thoughts drifted away as he recalled the deadly hiss of the foehn, a vast whiteness smothering him, crushing him, squeezing the breath from him, his last thoughts a nightmare jumble of bitterness toward a powerful woman with a beguiling smile, and regret that the one man who desperately needed him was destined to rot in a Paris prison.

A door opened and closed. Smells of old stone and uncured native fir wafted to him. The flare of a torch slanted across a group of shadowy figures.

"Light the lamp," a man said, and suddenly the room glowed.

He narrowed his eyes to slits and lay perfectly still. It wouldn't do to reveal himself now, when he lay vulnerable as a wounded bird.

"You may all go now," said a male voice. "Father Anselme will see to the patient."

"Father Julian, no," said the woman. "He needs my care."

Who was she? he wondered. Some sort of servant? A lady traveler? A lay sister?

"She's right," said a third voice, this one thin with age. "My hands shake. I can no longer stitch cuts."

"Father Anselme, I've given an order."

"The prior's right," said a new voice, this one oily with a Parisian accent. "It's improper for her to minister to grown men. She should sew altar cloths, not torn flesh."

"If you please, Father Julian," the woman said, her husky tone edged with concern. "Grown men die just as easily as women and children. I must stay. This man could die if we don't care for him properly—and immediately."

A pause. Brief, but long enough to slice him through with suspicion.

Was it possible that Father Julian recognized Daniel Severin?

"See to it, then," said the prior in a clipped voice. "But have a care for propriety."

"You'll let them countermand you?" This was yet another voice, the accent also Parisian. Daniel discerned a slim figure licked by wavering shadows from the wood stove. "You're the prior."

"Yes, I am, Father Emile." Julian's tone made the other canon take a step back. "Father Anselme, is there anything else you and Lorelei require?"

"No, Father, thank you."

"Very well. In the morning, I'll expect a full report on his condition. Come along, then, Father Emile, Father Gaston. And, Sylvain, Father Droz will need your help in the kennels."

Through a charge of pain, Daniel listened to the shuffle of feet, the swish of woolen robes, the click of a closing door. Someone thumbed open his right eye, but shut it before he could see anything more than a flicker of lamplight.

"He's still unconscious. Hand me the shears. We'd best work fast." The woman had a low-pitched voice and spoke with the soft French-Swiss accent that Daniel often heard in his dreams when he was far from home.

Then her meaning caught him by the throat. There were things a physician would do to an unconscious man that he wouldn't think of inflicting on a conscious one.

Daniel braced himself.

Gentle hands touched his head and turned it to one side. The pillow beneath his cheek had a faint cedary smell.

Fingers probed at his skull. He suffered the explosion of pain in silence. Long ago he'd learned to endure agony, and his training didn't fail him now.

"I'll have to cut away some of this hair," said the woman.

Cold metal touched Daniel's head. Shears snipped loudly near his ear.

"My, it's awfully long," she said. "Thick, too, but not greasy like that Gypsy horse trader we stitched last year." Her tone reminded Daniel of a matron gossiping at a sewing circle. My God, he thought, he needed a surgeon, not a seamstress.

"This white streak in his hair fascinates me," she went on, her words punctuated by the click of her scissors. "I've never seen anything like it."

"He wears his hair in the style of Bonaparte," said Father Anselme.

"Do you suppose he's a follower of the first consul?"

*"Qui sait?* These days we get all kinds, eh? But by his clothes I'd say no."

Daniel felt the drag of a razor behind his right ear. Sharp torture unfurled from the wound and spread from the tips of his ears to the soles of his feet. He forced himself to lie still, his muscles tense, encountering stiff resistance in one arm and one leg.

Splints? God, was he wounded that badly? How the devil could he accomplish his task in this state?

A needle pierced his scalp. He felt the dull slide of silk thread through flesh. His thoughts dissolved into a single, all-consuming inferno of pain. *Oh God oh God oh God . . .*

A shuddering gasp burst from him.

The woman's hands fell still. "Merciful God," she whispered. "He's awake."

She brought her face close to Daniel's. The lightning bolts of pain in his head blinded him to her features.

"Can you hear me? I'm sorry I hurt you. Blink if you can hear me." She repeated the words in Italian, then German, then again in French.

Daniel blinked.

"Be very still. I'm finished stitching. I'm going to give you some medicine now. Laudanum. It dulls the pain."

Helpless, Daniel felt the narrow neck of a bottle at his lips, felt a thick, sweetish liquid slide over his tongue. Some of it dripped out the side of his mouth. The bite of alcohol lingered in the aftertaste.

Poison, he thought frantically. She *knew.*

No. The medicine spread like a languid tide through him. The strange woman couldn't possibly know. His imagination, stoked by unease, accounted for the wave of panic.

"I'll need to bandage your head now," said the woman.

"You're not going to cauterize the wound?" asked Father Anselme.

"I don't think so. The bleeding's slowed. And cauterizing leaves scars. Hurts like the devil, too."

"He'll thank you for that in the morning."

Somewhere close by, a bell tolled nine times.

"You'd best get to prayers and then to bed, Father." Genuine affection warmed the woman's voice, and something in Daniel responded with mild surprise. He'd rarely heard anything but falseness from a woman.

The drug swished through his veins, weighting him with lethargy. He moved his eyes to look around the room, but the images blurred and tripled themselves: small square windows, lines of wooden pegs on a stone wall, rows of empty cots.

"I'll sit with him," she said.

"Very well."

"Good night, Father Anselme."

"Good night, Lorelei."

The name nearly brought Daniel off the bed, but his injuries and the laudanum held him still. His heavy eyelids drifted shut. Before succumbing to sleep, he had one incredulous thought.

*By God, I've found her at last.*

# Chapter 2

He awoke to the smell of pine tar and woodsmoke. When he tried to lift his head from the pillow, pain shot like an arrow of fire through him. Abandoning his effort, he lay motionless. He tasted the stale tincture of opium on his tongue and felt the bristle of his beard in the folds of his neck.

His lungs fought for air. For a moment panic seized him; then he remembered the altitude. After that he recalled his injuries. His left arm and right leg. A gashed head.

He forced his eyes open. Bars of sunlight streamed through a small, high window and played across the rough stone and timber walls of the room. Several empty cots sprung with leather webbing lined one wall. In a corner stood a thick porcelain basin. By the door was a tiny bowl of holy water on a wooden stand, and over it hung a plaster Christ.

Somewhere in the distance a dog's deep bark sounded. An Alpine mastiff. The hospice was famous for its rescue dogs.

Gingerly moving his pounding head, Daniel let his gaze wander. He saw a table laden with a shiny curved needle, the razor that had scraped his scalp raw, and a brown bottle. Atop a pile of bandages lay a cylinder of whittled wood. He turned his head slowly, painfully, to face the other side of his bed.

In a carved wooden chair, a child slumped, asleep, his head pillowed on his arm. The lad had probably been assigned to watch over Daniel.

With his good arm Daniel propped himself up. His vision swam sickeningly for a moment, then cleared. He discovered that he was wearing a blousy linen nightshirt and nothing else.

The child stirred, arching back narrow shoulders and stretching like a cat, small breasts thrusting against the fabric of the shirt.

Daniel caught his breath in amazement. It wasn't a lad at all, but a woman.

*Lorelei.*

Tense with interest now, he examined her. Her curly hair—a rare chestnut color—was cropped short. She wore a heather *bredzon* vest over a shirt and breeches, and gray stockings. A pair of worn chamois boots stood on the floor nearby.

Her hands—small and scrupulously clean, the nails

pared—lay limp in her lap. The lapis beads of a rosary spilled through her relaxed fingers.

Good God, had she been praying for him, of all people?

With a queer tightening of his stomach, Daniel studied her face. Her eyebrows were strongly marked, her eyes set wide, her chin pointed. There was a fullness to the lips, a delicacy in the bone structure that hinted at a certain vulnerability. She had clear skin and high coloring. But aside from that, she little resembled the hardy folk of the Swiss highlands.

She wasn't beautiful. But then, Daniel hadn't expected her to be.

She was the image of her father, King Louis XVI.

Lorelei felt someone staring at her. Disconcerted, she opened her eyes and found herself looking at her patient, who lay propped on his elbows.

"Oh!" Spilling her beads to the floor, she came out of her chair and crossed to the bedside. "I must have dropped off for a nap." Even as she spoke, she examined him with a practiced eye. His coloring was sallow and lusterless beneath his dark stubble. He held his jaw tightly, and his nostrils thinned as he inhaled sharply, a sure sign of pain. The circles under his eyes bore the dark stains of suffering.

"How do you feel?" she asked him.

"Fine." His voice was gravelly with laudanum and disuse.

"Liar. You feel terrible." Dropping to her knees, she groped beneath the cot and retrieved her rosary.

"Are you a lay sister?" he asked.

"Not exactly." She placed the pads of her fingers on his wrist to feel his pulse. Racing.

He frowned at her hand, and she took it away. "A nurse of some sort, then?"

" 'Doctor' would be more accurate," she replied. "I have no certificate, but Father Anselme—he's my teacher—does. He's trained me for the last five years."

His blue eyes widened slightly, a common reaction in travelers through the pass. Yet there was a guarded look about him that she didn't understand.

"A lady doctor," he mused, sinking flat onto the cot.

"Doctor, perhaps." She grinned. "But a lady—I'm afraid the canons would argue with that, monsieur, most especially Father Gaston." She picked up her wooden listening device from the table and reached for the lace of his nightshirt.

He lifted his hand. "What the h—What are you doing?"

Annoyed at herself for alarming him, she drew back her hand. "I'm sorry, I should have explained. I must listen to your heart."

He blinked. "No one's ever listened to my heart before."

"I'm very good at it." She unlaced his nightshirt and parted the fabric. Her fingers brushed over the black curls on his chest, and she felt the warmth of him, smelled his scent of sleep and something she could only describe as maleness. She gazed at his half-bare chest. An odd tug, deep in her belly, slowed her hand, and she shook her head to recapture her concentration. "I use this to amplify the heartbeat." She held the trumpet out for him to examine. "May I?"

He settled back, his eyes still wary. "By all means."

She placed the wide end of the trumpet just to the left of his breastbone and pressed her ear to the other end. The regular ***lub-dub*** of a healthy heart pulsed reassuringly through the tube.

"What do you hear?" His voice vibrated in her ear.

"A very strong heart."

"That's a relief."

She moved the tube to his right lung. "Lift your arm, please." He did so, and she ducked under it, her cheek very close to his chest. "This is called auscultation. Breathe in." He did so, and she repeated the procedure, listening to each lung. The gentle swish of air, uninterrupted by crackling or bubbling sounds, lifted her spirits. Her patient was wounded but not ill, thank God.

"When can I get up?" he asked.

She set aside her listening device. "Monsieur, you've broken your arm, sprained your knee, and concussed your brain."

One corner of his mouth lifted the tiniest bit. She found herself wondering what a full smile would look like on that dark face.

"I never do things halfway."

"Indeed. I'm Lorelei du Clerc. You were buried in an avalanche, and now you're at the Hospice of Saint Bernard."

"And you patched me up?"

"Yes. I set your arm and stitched your head. Your knee will require hot herbal baths and massage." She rested her hand lightly on his shoulder. "Monsieur, you mustn't look at me so suspiciously. I'm nothing like my namesake."

"Your . . . ?" Now he looked confused.

"The Lorelei of legend."

"Ah." He nodded carefully. "The one who lured men to their death upon the rocks of the Rhine."

"Not a name to inspire confidence," she agreed. Lord, his eyes were rare. Blues within blues, each shade a different layer of a tense and guarded man.

He seemed about to speak again; then a knock sounded. He flinched as if the sudden noise startled him. She hurried to open the door.

"Sylvain! Good morning."

The novice's familiar grin brightened the room, and his shock of straw-colored hair fell over his brow. "I've brought breakfast." He set the tray on a chest at the foot of the bed.

"I'm famished. I haven't eaten since . . ." She paused, thinking. The toasty smell of coffee teased her nostrils.

"Since yesterday after Vespers," said Sylvain. "You ought not to skip meals, *chouette.* You'll waste away to nothing."

"And then you'd have no one left to tease," she said, feigning regret. "Look, our visitor's awake."

The novice brushed aside his blond hair and looked at the man on the bed. "Good morning, monsieur. How do you feel?"

"Mademoiselle says I feel terrible."

Sylvain grinned. "She's always been bossy. Unfortunately she's usually right."

"*Dommage.* Will you help me to sit?"

"You're better off lying down," said Lorelei.

"I'm bored lying down."

"Very well, but try not to jar your head." She and Sylvain each grasped an arm and slowly lifted. Beneath her hands she felt firm muscles. Good. He was young and strong. He'd heal.

She cushioned his back with a pillow and straightened the coarsely woven blanket over him.

"How's that?" she asked.

"Wonderful." Pain and dizziness glazed his eyes. "Bring on the dancing girls."

She didn't quite know what to make of him, his insouciance, his seemingly easy acceptance of his fate. Most men with traumatic injuries would be in a panic, peppering her with questions, begging for a prognosis. "Are you hungry?" she asked.

"Yes."

Sylvain walked to the door. "I'll tell the prior you're awake, monsieur."

The young man left. Daniel watched Lorelei pour coffee and add a generous dollop of thick cream from a jar.

"Here." She placed a plain white cup in his good hand. "Mauricio makes the best coffee in the Alps, and the hospice milch cow gives the best cream. At least I think so. Of course I've never been off the mountain."

Daniel gritted his teeth. His head spun with pain and surprise. A female doctor who'd never left the mountain? The novelty—the tragedy—of it added to his confusion, to his feeling that the plan was slipping out of his control.

Hiding his reaction, he sipped his coffee. She was right; it was excellent. "Never?"

"Not once, not even to Bourg-Saint-Pierre. In the winter, of course, it's impossible, for we're snowbound. In the spring and summer, I've always been too busy. No matter, Father Julian—he's the prior—says I wouldn't like it there." Taking two rolls from the tray, she handed him one and sat on the edge of the bed. She tucked one leg beneath her and took a huge bite of the roll.

Her unselfconscious lack of refinement deepened Daniel's shock. Good Lord, the bastard princess was nothing like what he'd expected.

He'd envisioned a nunlike young woman, silent and morose, schooled into obedience by the canons of Saint Bernard's. Instead he'd found a forthright girl, brimming with a vibrance and a quickness of mind that disturbed him.

"So," she said, chewing slowly, "what's your name, monsieur?"

Daniel hesitated. Could he manage the deception? He decided to try. Given his helpless condition, he'd need to buy some time. He looked directly into Lorelei's brown eyes and said, "I . . . don't know."

The bread dropped from her fingers, crumbs scattering over the coverlet. She fell to her knees by his side, her face taut. "Truly, monsieur? You truly don't know your own name?"

Her genuine concern took him by surprise. He'd inspired many emotions in many women, but never this. Never caring. An alien feeling of guilt slid up to him.

Mentally he slapped it back. Guilt had no place in a man like Daniel Severin.

"Truly," he stated, trying to sound bewildered.

"Sweet Mary, but this is rare." Deft and gentle, her hand came up and lifted his eyelids each in turn. Her face loomed close, and he noticed that she smelled of vague warm things, like a fire on a wintry night. "I've never observed a true case of amnesia before." She sat on the bedside stool and looked at him as if he were a laboratory sample.

It was yet another reaction he'd never inspired in a woman. "Amnesia?"

"It's a loss of memory due to trauma to the head. Soldiers wounded in battle have suffered amnesia, or so I've read."

Daniel had observed memory loss firsthand. He had a swift, agonizing recollection of a battle-dazed comrade wandering memoryless through the Tuileries in Paris, his mind empty of all save the horror erupting around him.

Daniel had seen a hell of a lot worse in battle. This affliction was one of the lesser ailments.

"Lavoisier described a case in 1786," Lorelei explained, "but wrote very little about it. He hadn't the time, for Marat ordered his head chopped off."

She spoke matter-of-factly, as only one who hadn't witnessed the Terror could.

"So you don't know much about my . . . problem?" Daniel asked, concealing his relief.

"Alas, no." She pursed her lips in an expression every exiled Royalist would recognize. Daniel tried not to recoil from the chilling resemblance.

Then the expression fled, and something else, a mixture of curiosity and excitement, danced in her eyes. "You can't remember anything about yourself?"

"No, I can't."

"Goodness." She took his hand in hers. "You'll feel lost, confused, maybe. But don't worry; you're safe here."

The irony of it struck him. "That's a relief."

"Now, although the person you are is locked away, you obviously remember general matters, how to eat and talk, what things are called." She let go of his hand and held up an instrument from the table. "What's this?"

"Scissors."

"And this?"

"A spool of thread."

She beamed. "See what I mean? You've retained a wealth of knowledge. It's just that the accident, the blow to the head, has wiped out part of your memory."

God, he thought cynically, she's helping me pull off this ruse. "I don't understand how a blow can do that," he prompted.

She locked her hands around one knee and rocked back and forth on the stool. "Let's see. . . . It's rather difficult to explain." She concentrated for a moment, ideas flashing like lightning in her eyes. "Now, imagine this. Imagine a basketful of ripe peaches."

He was in no mood for games. But the more she talked, the more he'd learn. "Yes?"

"What would happen if you dropped the basket?" Before he could speak, she rushed on. "The basket would probably stay intact, but the peaches would bruise. And that's what happened to your brain."

The image made him feel slightly sick. "Bruised like a ripe peach?"

"Exactly." She slapped her thigh. "And the part that was bruised contained your memories. When it heals, you'll remember."

"So it's temporary?" he asked.

"Oh, yes, in most cases." She frowned. "Perhaps something will trigger your memory. *Sprechen Sie Deutsch?"*

*"Es freut mich sehr, Ihre Bekanntschaft zu machen."*

She beamed. Her smile was rather lovely, a glow of warmth over her little Gallic features. *"Parla Italiano?"*

*"Sì, ma me sono perso."*

Her eyes misted. An errant curl, alive with ruby fires and rich browns, fell over her brow. Her lips opened slightly, full and unconsciously appealing, and the tenderness of her expression made Daniel's gut twist uncomfortably.

"You *are* lost, aren't you?" she said. "But your ease with languages proves you're properly Swiss, as I suspected."

She placed her hands on her knees and levered herself up. "Maybe I can jog your memory." From a line of pegs near the door, she plucked his clothes, his bow and arrows, and his belt with the hunting knife. He saw no sign of his rucksack and bit his lip against asking for it.

She held up his coat, *bredzon,* and breeches. "Do these look familiar?"

He'd bartered a figured velvet waistcoat and a silk

cummerbund to an astonished farmer for the mountaineering clothes. A pawnbroker in Geneva had gladly accepted Daniel's gold watch for the knife belt.

But he merely blinked at Lorelei and said, "No."

She picked up one boot. "You must have lost the mate to this in the avalanche."

Damn! The pair had cost him a plate snuffbox. He shrugged.

"Father Gaston—he's the almoner—can probably find you another pair."

He lifted one eyebrow in surprise. "The almoner keeps a cache of men's boots?"

"He gets them from—" She broke off, the corners of her mouth descending. "Not all travelers are as fortunate as you."

Daniel masked his reaction to the idea of wearing a dead man's boots. She brought the bow and arrows to the bed. "What about these? Few hunters use the bow and arrow these days. Sylvain thought the fletchings unusual."

He stroked one of the raven feathers. The arrows were his one conceit, his one concession to superstition, perhaps a reminder of the man he had been. An arrow like this had once saved his life; then his habit had given him his identity. He'd been sixteen then, fleeing the bonds of apprenticeship. He remembered the chill morning, his search for shelter in the Valais range, the bear suddenly rearing up before him. An arrow would have been a pinprick to the huge, thick-hided animal. But Daniel had aimed at a vulnerable spot. The black-fletched arrow penetrated the bear's eye and embedded itself in its brain, killing the beast in mere moments.

Now the midnight fletchings were his personal device, as dark and sleek as his identity as the Raven.

He shook his head. "I'm sorry. I don't recognize any of these things." He maintained a blank, baffled look. By God, what the hell was he doing? he wondered. She was obviously a skilled doctor. She could discover his ruse in an instant.

Yet her open, inquisitive expression said she believed him. It occurred to him that she wasn't accustomed to being deceived.

But her whole life was a lie. She simply hadn't found out yet—or had she? The possibility made him shiver.

"Anything else?" he asked.

"Just a hunting knife, and there's nothing unusual about it."

Relief drifted over him. He vowed to search for his rucksack as soon as he could move from the bed.

"But it was nearly dark," she added. "I'll take some dogs up to the site of the avalanche and see if they can find anything else."

"No!" Realizing he'd spoken too quickly, Daniel forced himself to relax. "You needn't go to the trouble. When I'm better, I'll go myself."

"It's no trouble, monsieur. I often go out on patrol with the dogs. Father Droz has given me a puppy, and I'm training him myself."

"I see. Er, if you do find something, I'd appreciate it if you'd bring it directly to me."

"Why?"

Fool, he thought, and his head began to throb. "I'd say it's only fair that I be the first to know who I am."

Her smile flashed again. She had a dimple in her left cheek. "You're right, monsieur."

He rubbed the bristles on his chin. "Thank you."

She watched his hand for a moment. "You don't know what you look like," she burst out. "Do you?"

Feeling like an idiot, Daniel shook his head.

She crossed to the washbasin, took down a small round mirror, and held it out to him. "You've a curious lock of white hair, see?"

Daniel peered at a thin, pallid face shadowed by several days' growth of beard and hard blue eyes overhung with long hair.

A bitter memory reared up, a memory of a woman's pampered hand running through his hair. He'd refused to cover the strange lock with pomade and had inadvertently created something of a sensation in Paris. Hoping to achieve Daniel's success with women, men of the Directory society had created artful white locks of their own. But while their ivory streaks came from powder pots, Daniel had earned his from the blade of a sword brandished by a man who despised him. The wound had healed, but that lock had lost its color forever.

"How very strange," he murmured.

"You don't recognize yourself?"

"No."

She gave him more coffee and a piece of buttery soft cheese to eat with his bread. He chewed painfully, for the movement of his jaw pulled at the head wound. They ate in silence for a few minutes, he awkwardly with his one good hand, she with the simple directness of a peasant.

"Do you need to use the chamber pot?" she asked when he finished.

"No, mademoiselle," Daniel said hastily.

"Liar. Your back teeth are probably floating." She brought a battered pewter pot to the bedside. "I'll leave it here, where you can reach it. If you need help, call for Sylvain."

"If I need help," he said wryly, "then I'm worse off than you think."

He steeled himself against her delighted expression. It was time to change the subject, time to draw her out. This simple, harmless girl was his opponent, and his best offense was to learn the lay of things. "Since I can't tell you anything about myself, let's talk about you. I might have met a female doctor before, but it's doubtful."

"You're probably right, but it seems the most natural thing in the world to me." The clarity, the earnestness, in her features struck him anew. "I never consciously chose to become a doctor. Something—call it a vocation—compelled me to help people, to heal them. Now that Father Anselme's getting on in years, I do most of the doctoring."

"Is there much of it to do?"

"No. I've pulled a few teeth, stitched a few wounds, lanced boils, and nursed fevers. Most of the travelers who come through the pass are quite healthy, thank God." Absently she made the sign of the cross, a gesture Daniel hadn't seen in years.

"What do you do with the rest of your time?"

"I work with the dogs. I study with Father Anselme, and sometimes Father Emile sneaks me books by progressive authors like Rousseau. My life is very busy."

He sensed a faint note of discontent in her voice. "Do you ever wish you could be somewhere else?"

"Of course not. This is my home." Her answer was too swift, too vehement. She obviously had a lively mind that she longed to use.

"Surely you've thought about it, just for a moment," he said.

She leaned close, a smile playing about her lips. "Can you keep a secret?"

Daniel's head ached with the secrets he kept. He nodded.

"Sometimes I long to study with the great men of medicine, to trade ideas with Jenner, Corvisart, Laënnec."

"So why don't you?"

She laughed and struck her thigh. Her mannerisms were open and frank, yet curiously appealing. "In the first place, the academies don't admit women. In the second place, I'd have no means of supporting myself. And in the third place, I'd be scared to death of going to a big city."

"Scared? Why?"

"Look at me. What do you see?"

He cleared his throat. "I'm not sure I have a basis for comparision."

"I'm different." She fingered a badly barbered curl. "Sometimes lady travelers pass through, and I can tell they're shocked by the way I look—as shocked as I am by all their lace and furbelows. I'm not sure I could face a whole city full of them."

Something about her simple, awkward statement touched Daniel. Willfully he swept away the sentiment.

"Well," she said, brushing the crumbs from her lap. "Enough about me. Until you remember your name, we've got to call you something." She picked up the quiver of arrows and took them back to the corner. "Have you heard of Wilhelm Tell?"

Daniel rubbed his chin. "Let's see. Apples and arrows?"

"Exactly. He united the people of Uri, and the first Swiss Confederation was born."

Daniel grimaced. "I'm not sure I should be likened to a national hero."

"Why not? Maybe you are one."

God, if she only knew. But for an accident of birth, he might have been. But that was not the case. Daniel Severin had embraced villainy long ago. Memories of an old horror held him in an iron grip, and a force beyond his control moved him like a puppet manipulated by soft, feminine hands.

"Probably not any more than you're the Lorelei of legend," he said. "It's presumptuous."

"It might be rather fun." Idly she began picking her teeth. "Just imagine shedding your identity, becoming a totally different person and not at all the man people think you are."

An intriguing fantasy. If only he could wipe away the past, start out clean and free and new . . . but the past clung to him like filthy, imprisoning clothes. Daniel felt a sudden chill, although the room was warm. Just how much did she know?

". . . much more than I should," she was saying.

His head snapped toward her. Pain from the sudden movement lanced through him. "What's that?"

She grinned. She had remarkably good teeth. "I said, I daydream about such things much more than I should."

Daniel sagged against the pillows.

"Here, I'm tiring you. I'd best give you your medicine and leave you to a lovely nap." She poured something syrupy from a brown bottle into his empty coffee mug. "Drink this."

"What is it?"

"Laudanum. You had some last night, and it didn't disagree with you. It'll dull the pain." She peered into the cup. "It's not enough to make you sleep. You should stay awake, because Father Julian will probably want to see you."

With some misgiving, he drained the cup. The drug left a strange, numbing sensation on his tongue.

"I wish you could remember," said Lorelei. "Perhaps something very important has sent you through the Great Pass. What would drive you here so late in the day, too early in the season for safety?"

"Perhaps I'm remarkably stupid."

"I doubt that, monsieur. There's something about you . . ." She gave him her unabashed scrutiny. "You're not an ordinary traveler. When I look into your eyes I don't see stupidity. I see . . . pain and uncertainty, but something good as well."

"Lorelei—" He didn't want her sympathy, her understanding. His eyes sought the weapons hanging in a corner of the infirmary. In his present state, he was powerless to retrieve them, much less to use them.

She gripped his hand. Hers was strong and warm. "Do try to remember why you came. It might've been urgent."

As the drug began to weave through his senses, Daniel let his gaze linger on her. Her image, surrounded by sunlight from the window, seemed to pulse with radiance. Her hair was a nimbus framing her face, the chestnut highlights flaring blood red.

She had an uncanny knack for hitting the target. Something very urgent indeed had brought him to Saint Bernard's.

He'd come to kill her.

# Chapter 3

"I don't know why you feel you have to take his belongings away," said Lorelei, eyeing Father Julian with dismay. "He's perfectly harmless. You never mistrusted travelers in the past."

His cheeks red from an outdoor walk between the infirmary and the chapter house, Father Julian crossed the room and stood before the stove. He held Wilhelm's bow, arrows, and hunting knife in one hand.

"The world is changing, Lorelei," the prior said. His hand closed briefly over hers. "Besides, we don't know the man."

"We don't know who?" His finger marking his place in a book of devotions, Father Gaston joined them by the stove. He, too, had been out recently, Lorelei observed, for snow clung to the hem of his habit, and a tracery of fine red veins stood out in his cheeks.

"Sound the bell, Gaston," Father Julian said. "We must discuss our visitor."

The almoner hurried off. Moments later the hospice bell tolled three times, the sound echoing through the pass. Canons and novices entered the chapter house, stomping the snow from their boots and brushing off their tall sugarloaf hats. Father Droz laid his gloves on the stove to dry. Sylvain winked a greeting to Lorelei.

Father Emile, his hands hidden in the voluminous sleeves of his robe, stood beside Father Julian. "Is the visitor going to recover?"

"Indeed," said Father Anselme, who had been dozing in a chair by the stove. "The rescue was a complete success."

"Not completely, Father." Lorelei was still disturbed by the prior's confiscation. "Those things"—she gestured at the weapons—"are all the poor man has. He may need them."

"And he'll get them," said Father Julian. "As soon as he explains himself."

"But he can't do that," said Lorelei.

Father Gaston's thick brows beetled. "He can't? But—"

"If you please," said Father Julian. "I'll explain if you'll give me a chance. Our guest has lost his memory."

Sylvain whistled through his teeth and jabbed a fellow novice in the ribs. "Odd turn, eh?" he whispered.

"It's a rare affliction," Father Julian went on, "but

Lorelei and Father Anselme tell me that a severe blow to the head can cause it. The patient can't tell us his name or anything about himself."

The men all began talking at once. "Maybe he's a brigand." "A scout sent by the Austrian army." "One of Bonaparte's spies."

"Silence." The prior held up his hand.

"Is there a cure for this affliction?" asked Father Emile, his hands moving restlessly within his sleeves. "A prayer we can say, or—"

"Not exactly," Father Anselme said. "There's no telling when his memory will return."

"I dislike the look of him," Father Gaston grumbled, tugging at a tuft of hair that grew from his ear. "Too handsome to be trusted."

Lorelei shot him a frown. "Father Gaston! It's not like you to condemn a man for his appearance."

He scowled back, but there was indulgence, not anger, in his regard. "You'd best look to your own appearance, child. When was the last time you combed that hair?"

Lorelei grinned apologetically. Father Gaston was forever trying to soften her appearance and correct her manners.

"Gaston has a point about the stranger," said Father Clivaz, the master of the novices. "I looked in on him this morning. There's something . . . sinister about that streak of white hair and those black-fletched arrows."

As the canons and novices continued to speculate about the identity of the mysterious visitor, Lorelei moved toward the door. The weapons weren't important, she decided. No one needed weapons at the Hospice of Saint Bernard.

"I'm going to take the dogs on patrol," she whispered to Father Droz.

The kennel master's eyes crinkled at the corners. "You feel it, too, then. The springtime."

She leaned up and kissed his cheek. He smelled comfortably of dog and pipe smoke. "I won't be long."

She slipped out the door. Knowing the dogs were free for their morning run, she put her fingers to her lips and whistled. Out of the trees bounded three dogs, paddling through the drifts toward her.

Lorelei chose a steep path through the woods. Barry frolicked with Belle and Bard, scrapping over a fallen limb, barking at the breeze, chasing rabbits. Bard made an amorous overture toward Belle, who snapped at him and sidled away.

Lorelei laughed, shaking her head. "You'll confuse the poor dog, Belle. Only last week you welcomed him—and bred a litter, I hope." She patted Bard's head consolingly. "I suppose males are easily confused."

Stopping above the tree line, she glanced back at the hospice. The buildings appeared doll-like, clustered above the half-frozen lake in the valley. Turning, she slapped her thigh to summon her companions, then headed toward the avalanche.

As she trudged upward over the heavy spring snow, she prayed she'd find some clue to the stranger's identity. Sympathy for Wilhelm throbbed in her chest. She'd always known, and rather liked, the person she was. The thought of suddenly having that knowledge stripped from her made her shudder. *Me sono perso,* he'd told her. I'm lost.

Lorelei kicked at a broken limb in frustration. She could heal his wounds, but she had no idea how to give him back what he desperately needed—his identity.

Her thoughts slipped to the scene in the chapter house. The canons all seemed so wary of the poor man. Why? Their mission was to aid travelers, not confiscate their belongings and question their character.

Perhaps Father Julian was right. Perhaps the world *was* changing. War, conquest, revolution. Somewhere far below, such events were taking place. With a stab of quickly denied discontent, Lorelei realized they'd never touch her life.

The night freeze had laid an icy crust over the surface of the snow. Slipping, she used spiny bushes for handholds where she could. The bowl of mountains threw the entire valley in shadow and preserved the chill of night. Darkness lingered in the deep, secret folds of ravines and defiles, scoring the range with mystery. But up here she felt she could touch the sun and clasp its warmth to her breast.

The surefooted dogs picked their way through the icy patches. Watching them, Lorelei banished her restive thoughts. Her life was full of delightful companions and people who cared for her. It seemed wrong to crave more.

At last they reached the site of the avalanche. Here the sun struck the ridge, and high clouds sailed past the rugged peaks. The foehn had dissipated, leaving peaceful silence in its wake. Beyond the deep, wooded cleft, filled now with debris from the avalanche, lay

Italy. If she climbed high enough on a clear day, she could see the shimmering plains of Lombardy. Mauricio, the cook, told her of the vineyards there and of orchards where apples and pears grew from April to October and of big, loud families of squabbling children and fiercely loving parents.

She stood with her hands on her hips, inhaled the crisp air, and surveyed the site. A spring avalanche. She could be thankful for that as well. The *staublawinen* of winter were far more deadly, great whirlwinds of loose, dusty snow that caused a chain reaction and turned the valley into a bowl of death. Yesterday's avalanche had been mercifully compact, striking only the narrow defile.

The dogs lumbered about the area where they'd found Wilhelm.

Belle disappeared over a snowdrift and gave a muffled bark. When she lurched back up the bank, she had a knee-high boot in her mouth.

"Good girl," said Lorelei, scrubbing the dog's ears. She stuffed the boot into her rucksack and eyed the other dogs with mock severity. "She's already humiliated you once today, Bard. Are you going to let her do it again?"

Bard snuffled loudly and trotted off. A few minutes later she found him pawing at a set of footprints. Barry sat on his haunches and watched.

Puzzled, Lorelei followed the trail for a few paces. The prints had been made by booted feet. They had to be fresh, for the wind had erased last night's prints. Odd, for none of the men in the chapter house had mentioned returning to the site.

Bard scrambled down a steep slope covered by grainy snow. At the bottom he stopped and barked.

Lorelei slid down to join him. She found two depressions in the snow. Her knees fit into them perfectly. In front of her, mittened hands had scooped out a large hole. In her mind's eye she saw a figure kneeling here, digging. But who? And why?

Thinking back to the meeting in the chapter house, she realized that nearly every one of the canons and novices had been out in the morning. One of them must have come here. But why hadn't he spoken of it?

She shrugged off the question. Despite her fitful sleep in the chair at Wilhelm's bedside, she felt invigorated. She always did after a successful rescue.

Filling her lungs with bracingly cold air, she stood and spun around. The mountains flashed past with dizzying speed, and she laughed at the sensation. The Alps were treacherous, but they could be conquered. A feeling of power surged through her.

"Come on," she said, patting her thigh. "If there's anything else to be found, it'll have to wait for the spring thaw." With the dogs bounding at her side, she traversed the ridge, heading east. The morning sun glanced off the snow and struck her face.

Several minutes of hiking brought her to the source of a spring. Crystalline water, pumped from some hidden place deep in the earth, burbled over ice-glazed rocks. Lorelei followed the spring down to its long fall into a pool.

A natural landing, scooped out of the face of the mountain, formed a level piece of ground bordered by huge rocks. Warm with exertion, she took off her scarf and fanned her face with it. The snow had melted here. Early snowdrops and wild Alpine roses had thrust out their first tentative leaf buds.

The dogs lapped noisily from the pool. Lorelei peeled off her mittens and drank the sweet clear water from her cupped hands. Spring waited to leap upon the Alps, and a feeling of restlessness spread through her. The new season quickened her blood, stirring half-formed plans and vague yearnings.

Prodded by the warming breeze, she crossed the dry, springy grass to an outcrop of rock. A grotto, gouged out of the mountainside by some ancient glacier, lay deep in cool shadows.

She often came here to think, to meditate, to dream. She'd never told anyone of it. Father Julian would say the proper place for meditation was in the chapel, God's house.

That was fine for the canons and novices. But because Lorelei was a girl, she'd always felt remote from the community of scholars. A deep, hollow loneliness came in secret to plague her, and this was her refuge from a need she could never confess to the men of the hospice.

She looked up at the billowy clouds scudding above the peaks. The sky was a brilliant, eye-smarting blue. A heathen thought crossed her mind: she was closer to God here, in the awesome cathedral of trees and rocks and mountains, than in the dim, musty chapel of the hospice.

She dropped to her knees. Years ago she'd been small enough to enter the grotto. But she'd outgrown the space and now groped among the dust and dead leaves for her box.

It was made of Alpine cedar, carved with arrow shapes and harts' horns. Some traveler had left it, empty, years ago. Lorelei had filled it with her dreams.

She walked to the flat grassy area where the dogs drowsed in the sun. She sat down, leaning against Bard's enormous bulk. His soft fur cushioned her, and his tail thumped gently in welcome. The grass, bent and sere from the spring thaw, smelled of last summer. Barry lay down at her feet. He was growing larger every day and would soon reach the weight of a man.

Lorelei opened the box. It contained copious penciled notes—observations about the patients she'd treated, commentary on medical texts she'd read, a long description of the typhus outbreak that had struck the hospice the summer before.

In addition to the notes, the box held trinkets and treasures collected over the years. She picked up a tortoiseshell comb given to her by Everard, the courier from Bourg-Saint-Pierre, and tried to push the ornament into her hair. It fell back into the box, and she shook her head in chagrin. There must be some secret to it that she didn't know.

"You try it," she said to Barry, and raked the comb over his furry head. He regarded her so dolefully that she removed the comb. "Sorry. Your dignity's been trampled enough today."

Her treasures included a broken watch a traveler had left; a translation of John Locke's works, a gift from Father Emile, who'd made her promise to keep the book of radical essays secret from Father Julian; and an interesting pamphlet from Father Gaston, a Royalist argument by Madame de Staël entitled *Reflections on Internal Peace.*

Lorelei's notes were no secret, of course. But at the hospice she was prey to interruptions, to Father Anselme's well-meaning but unwelcome criticism. Here she was free to think for herself.

She took out a stack of paper and the stub of a pencil and swiftly recorded a few thoughts on Wilhelm's condition. When she had more time, she would write at length about his rare, heartbreaking affliction.

The sun drew higher over the peaks. Her attention strayed to the typhus notes. Ideas too tantalizing to ignore hovered at the edge of her mind. She put away her papers, closed the box with a decisive snap, and tucked it under her arm. Spring had brought a mysterious visitor and a fresh purpose to her life. "Come on, *mes amis*," she said to the dogs. "I've been silent about this long enough."

Thirty minutes later she knocked on the door to Father Anselme's study. "Come in," he said.

She stepped inside and set her box on the floor. The room smelled of pine resin, musty wool, and old books. "Are you busy?" she asked.

He took off his spectacles, rubbed his eyes, and smiled. "Just reading."

She sat in a hide-covered chair across the desk from him. "I went to see if I could find any of Wilhelm's belongings."

"Who's Wilhelm?"

"That's what I'm calling our patient until he remembers his name." She shrugged out of her rucksack. "Belle found his other boot."

He blinked slowly. "Anything else?"

"Not really, but . . ." She pictured the fresh footprints, the carefully dug hole in the snow.

Father Anselme sat forward. She could almost hear his joints creak. "But what, child?"

"Someone was there before me. I saw footprints and signs of digging." She toyed with a button on her *bredzon.*

"We probably made the tracks last night."

"But we couldn't have—"

The old canon tapped the paper he was reading. "The post came from Bourg-Saint-Pierre while you were gone."

"Did Everard bring it?"

"Yes. You'll see him at supper."

Lorelei anticipated the encounter with pleasure. Everard, the bluff, hardy mountain courier, was always so cheerful, so full of improbable tales and news. He never failed to bring an entirely inappropriate bauble for her—a paste jewel, a sachet of lavender, a satin ribbon. They were items for which Lorelei had no use, but she treasured them just the same.

She looked across the desk at the broadsheet to see the date. "Second ventôse."

"Heathen revolutionaries," Father Anselme grumbled. "Why'd they tamper with a perfectly good calendar? I have to study a chart to discover whether it's Wednesday or Sunday."

"Something about nature replacing God." Lorelei shrugged. "The sansculottes tampered with everything else. Why not the calendar?" Her gaze moved down the broadsheet. "Any interesting news?"

Father Anselme handed her the paper. "Bonaparte's coming through Switzerland to march against the Austrians in Italy. It was supposed to be a secret, but once he carried off the gold of Bern for his Army of the Orient, it became clear he considered Switzerland his own territory." Father Anselme indicated a paragraph at the bottom of the sheet. "He didn't get all the gold from Bern's treasury."

Lorelei scanned the print. "It says here that some of the gold was stolen during transport."

"Not some. A lot. Let's hope it was a Swiss who did it—and that he got away with the deed."

"Father Anselme!"

"Now, don't get prissy on me. It was a theft in reverse."

She chuckled.

"Everard says Bonaparte is raising an army called the Reserve. They're coming by way of the Great Pass."

"Sweet Mary, Bonaparte's coming here? When?"

"As soon as the thaw bares the roads. Early May." He exhaled loudly. "We'll play host to an army of forty thousand."

Lorelei took a moment to digest this. The wars that raged throughout Europe had always seemed remote, had touched her only by way of occasional refugees and deserters. Now Bonaparte's campaign would bring the war to their very door.

"Well," she said, "it should be interesting. Do you think we'll have a chance to consult with the army surgeons?"

"Child, the visit will last mere hours, no more. And I'm not sure army surgeons are fitting company for you."

His caution frustrated her. She set aside the broadsheet. "Father Anselme, I've come to talk to you about my work."

"Your work? Is there a problem with the patient?"

"That's another matter. I don't think it was right for Father Julian to take his belongings."

"The prior must do as he thinks best," said Father Anselme. "But other than that?"

"No change. On my way here, I checked on him. He's playing chess with Father Gaston. I pray Wilhelm's memory will return."

Father Anselme nodded approvingly. "Sometimes prayer is a physician's best tool."

"But not always, Father." She flipped the box open. "These are my notes on the typhus outbreak. Father Anselme, I've prepared a treatise on the disease. I have some ideas on the recovery process and wish to pursue—"

"Lorelei."

"—further study, perhaps send to Bern or Coppet for—"

*"Lorelei."*

She stopped and looked down at her hands. "Yes, Father?"

"My child, you waste your time making theories. It grieves me that you stray from the course of healing into the realm of experimentation and speculation."

"But we must speculate if—"

"We're healers, my dear, not vivisectionists. Isn't my teaching enough? I've taught you to save lives."

She reached across the desk and grasped his gnarled hands. "Father, please. You act as if, in thinking for myself, I've somehow betrayed you. Don't you see? It's just the opposite. Thanks to your teaching, I'm able to think, to project—"

"Then think about this," he snapped. "Your so-called theory could prove false. It's certain to. The diocese would respond to the humiliation with strict censure."

"I'll take full responsibility for it, Father. I'll—"

"Enough," he said, withdrawing his hands. "Please abandon this course. We've given you more liberty than any academy would give a woman. You're doing God's work here, saving lives. That should be enough for you."

Very slowly she replaced her papers and closed the box. "Yes, Father," she lied. "I'm sorry I bothered you."

Leaving the study, she thought about presenting her thesis to Father Julian, but common sense warned her off. He'd rebuffed her previous attempts to correspond with physicians beyond this tiny piece of the world. The prior loved her in his remote way. But he shackled her with his protectiveness.

Dejected, she clutched her box and walked down a low-ceilinged corridor. Evening was coming on; the bell tolled the hour of Vespers. She decided to check on Wilhelm again.

* * *

Daniel looked up at the sound of approaching footsteps. He tensed, his nerves tingling with pain and suspicion.

After only a day here, he sensed undercurrents of danger and distrust flowing through the hospice. Father Emile had come to question him closely, his spare face hard and skeptical, his movements nervous as he polished a battered pewter monstrance studded with cheap paste stones.

Obviously preoccupied, Father Gaston had made foolish moves during their chess game. His gaze kept wandering to Daniel's lock of white hair.

Father Anselme, Lorelei's teacher, had come to check the injuries. His bedside manner, Daniel reflected wryly, wasn't nearly as intriguing as that of his student.

Father Droz and Father Clivaz had delivered wood for the stove, but they'd said little, as if Daniel's lack of memory made them uncomfortable.

And out the high window of the infirmary, Daniel had spied two figures meeting in the distance—one in a canon's robes and sugarloaf hat, the other in mountaineer's clothes. Their quick, furtive movements raised the hair on the back of Daniel's neck.

Which of them knew his identity and his purpose? Which of them suspected?

The latch clicked. Daniel stared implacably at the door.

Lorelei appeared on a gust of cold mountain air. Eyeing her tousled hair and windburned cheeks, he felt relief and, curiously, a vague pleasure. He trampled the pleasure with a swift jolt of resolution. It wouldn't do at all to get maudlin over King Louis's bastard.

With his supper tray on his lap, he leaned back and watched her walk between the rows of cots.

"Hello," he said.

"Hello." She set a weathered wooden box at her feet. "Is it still Wilhelm?"

"Still Wilhelm."

"You've remembered nothing more?"

"No." He looked at the barely touched plate. "I think I hated saurkraut and sausage."

"Oh, Wilhelm." The sweet sadness on her face made Daniel look sharply away. "I've been trying to imagine what it's like for you. Is it like being closed in a strange dark room?"

"No, it's . . ." He stared at the plaster Christ, the patch of snow and sky through the window, anywhere but at her intolerably sweet face. For some reason he had difficulty lying to her. "It's not frightening or painful." He forced himself to meet her gaze. "Sit down, Lorelei."

She sat on a stool at the bedside. Her eyes widened as she studied his face. "You've shaved your beard."

"It was hardly a beard. Just a few days' stubble. Sylvain brought me some shaving things and a mirror." Daniel reflected for a moment about the husky youth—his pale, watchful eyes, the way he hastened off the moment Daniel had finished.

"Well." She peered at him with an openness that was unnerving. "You look . . . rather agreeable."

Daniel fought an urge to laugh. Women had stared at him before. They'd called him beguiling, captivating, striking. But never agreeable. Then again, Lorelei was nothing like the women he'd known. Most had been conveniently bereft of minds and wills of their own and, less conveniently, of hearts.

"Thank you." He glanced around the room. Since he'd awakened from a fitful midmorning nap, a question had nagged at him. "Who took my bow and hunting knife?"

She shifted uncomfortably on the stool. "Father Julian took them off . . . for safekeeping."

Daniel's eyes narrowed. "Safekeeping? Have you thieves hereabouts?"

Lorelei chewed her lip. "Well, he's a cautious man, you see. He thinks you might be dangerous."

Daniel feigned surprise. "Dangerous? In what way?"

"In the way of a man who's lost his memory," she said simply. "None of us have any experience with this sort of thing."

Idly he stuck a finger beneath the bandage on his brow and scratched himself. "I see. So I'm a fugitive, a criminal?"

"I'm afraid the prior will treat you like one until you prove otherwise."

Daniel sipped from the mug of beer on his tray. "If he thinks I'm dangerous, why would he allow you to come here alone?"

She clasped and unclasped her hands. "Actually, he doesn't know I'm here. Besides," she added hastily, "I go where I please at the hospice. I always have. So I'm not really deceiving—"

Reluctant to hear more, he held up a hand. Her sincerity was getting on his nerves. "No one said you were, Lorelei."

She breathed a sigh of relief. "Don't worry, Wilhelm. You'll get your belongings back. Now, how do you feel?"

"Wonderful. Never better."

"Liar. You still have circles under your eyes." She glanced at the tray on his lap. "And you've hardly eaten any of your dinner." Without asking, she took a sausage and started eating it. The action was so unaffected, so childlike, that Daniel laughed.

She chewed slowly. "Do I amuse you?"

"You surprise me." The words came without forethought, and he knew her startled expression was reflected in his own face. "I've never known anyone like you."

She paused with the sausage halfway to her mouth. "You mean, you remember people? Who?"

Good God. He'd trapped himself in his own snare. "I . . . don't know. The thought just occurred to me that you're . . . unique."

She grinned. "I've been told that before. It's a polite way of saying I'm a freak. I'm not like other women." Wistfulness softened her voice, and she stared out the window.

He followed her gaze to the distant shore of Lake Saint Bernard, where he'd seen the two furtive figures meeting.

"Everyone's been speculating about your identity."

Apprehension blasted like a chill wind over Daniel. "And?"

"You might be a brigand, a spy, or an army scout."

*"Ça alors,"* said Daniel, trying not to reveal the tension that burned across his shoulders.

"But over dinner today the discussion took a different turn. You might be a drover on your way to Bourg-Saint-Pierre for the spring drive to the highlands. That was Father Gaston's idea."

She finished the sausage and licked her fingers. "Let's see. Father Emile considers you a chamois huntsman. I think Father Julian agrees with him, but he'd never admit to being in accord with Father Emile."

The explanations were safe enough, Daniel decided, his shoulders easing back against the pillow. He offered Lorelei a sip of beer from his tankard. "And what do you think?"

She took a long drink of beer. A mustache of amber foam clung to her upper lip. Wiping it on her sleeve, she said, "I think they're all mistaken."

He couldn't help staring. The bastard princess sat with her booted feet propped up on a crude bed, downing beer like a soldier on leave.

"You're much too intriguing to be a common drover or huntsman," she said.

Alarm jangled in his chest. "You find me intriguing? In what way?"

She set down the tankard. "You're not like anyone I've ever met, either. You have this odd way of looking at me, as if you're seeing someone else." Her brown velvet eyes, her probing doctor's eyes, seemed to peer into his soul.

Daniel felt, absurdly, as if his purpose were written on his face.

"It's very hard to explain," she said. "I see something

in your eyes, flickers of inner pain that have nothing to do with your injuries."

She saw too much, thought too much. He cursed the wounds that bound him helplessly to the bed. He questioned the sanity of a God who'd given woman a brain. "You've a vivid imagination."

"Maybe you're an exiled nobleman of the Old Regime. What if you're a Capetian prince? My, wouldn't that be something."

He froze. Was she playing cat and mouse with him? "That," he said, sick with the irony of it, "would be preposterous."

"True. Your speech marks you a Swiss."

"The romance of the exiled nobles is over," he reminded her. "They now have a champion in Bonaparte's court."

She leaned toward him. "How do you know?"

"I just know. Josephine Bonaparte has taken steps to restore titles and property. She's in favor of reconciling the Old Regime with the new."

"Is she? But her husband's first consul. Wouldn't she urge him to crown himself and make her a queen?"

"Not Josephine." The name tasted bitter in his mouth. She'd been Marie Josèphe Rose until Bonaparte, in the raging passion of new love, had dubbed her his "incomparable Josephine."

"You speak of her as if you know her."

"Everybody in France knows her." Daniel, unfortunately, knew her better than most. "If Napoleon becomes a monarch," he went on, "he'll worry even more about the succession. It's general knowledge that his wife can't seem to produce an heir, and she probably fears he'll put her aside."

The dilemma obsessed Josephine, but he didn't tell this to Lorelei.

"You know a great deal about the French court."

"So it seems."

"Well, if you're not an exiled noble, maybe you're an army scout, sent to reconnoiter the Great Pass. Bonaparte is going to cross with an army into Italy later in the spring."

Daniel knew of the plan. If sheer will alone could heal him, he'd have been well hours ago. The last person he needed to encounter was Bonaparte. "In that case, we'll find out soon enough."

"You could be a spy," she said with childlike fascination, "braving peril to infiltrate the Austrian forces in Italy."

Daniel looked away quickly. His head swam in the wake of the motion. He'd performed similar services in the past. Spying was a minor talent, but his greatest expertise lay in darker deeds. Did she know of the Raven?

Apparently not, for she continued blithely, "Perhaps something more personal drove you to the pass."

"Something personal?"

She nodded, her chestnut curls bouncing. "You might be fleeing an unhappy marriage or an affair of the heart."

"I have a feeling that, when I do remember, you'll be disappointed," he said carefully.

Lorelei finished the beer and set it down. "I'd best see to your injuries now." She folded back the covers.

Instinctively he recoiled. He disliked having people close to him, touching him.

"Oh, do stop," said Lorelei. "I've no patience with modesty." She pulled the nightshirt away from his splinted leg.

"Jesus, Lorelei!"

"Don't swear at me, please."

"But—"

"I'd half hoped your memory loss had wiped out any streak of prudishness." She sighed. "Apparently it hasn't."

An unwelcome thought sneaked up on him. "Who changed my clothes last night?"

"Sylvain, I think. Don't look so relieved. I was also present." She grinned impishly. "You aren't the first to be scandalized by my ministrations to men. Last year I lanced a boil on a man's backside. His wife nearly swooned." She shrugged. "Male doctors treat women every day. I don't know why people can't accept the opposite."

She returned her attention to his knee. Holding the hem of his garment high, she lowered her head.

"Very impressive," she murmured. "It's huge."

"What?" Daniel resisted the urge to slap the fabric back down.

"Your hematoma."

He began to sweat. "My what?"

"Your swollen . . . knee."

A sigh of relief burst from him. "Oh."

"Does it hurt?"

"No."

She squeezed it. He winced.

"Liar," she said. "Let's have a look at your arm."

This, too, was painful and swollen, pressing against the splints. She unwound the stiff bandages, gently brushing away bits of plaster. "I think the bone's properly set. It should knit."

"Will I . . ." He licked his dry lips. His life had depended on his shooting arm more than once. "Will it heal fully?"

She touched his shoulder in an absent gesture. "I think so." Then, carefully, she bandaged and plastered the arm again. "You mustn't move this until it's completely dry."

He nodded, then sat with his teeth clenched as she changed the bandage around his head. "I'll remove the stitches in a week or so." Finally she sat back, rested her feet on the box, and helped herself to a piece of cheese from his tray. "I went up to the site of the avalanche." She poked her finger through a hole in the cheese and twirled it.

He fought an urge to sit forward. "Did you find anything?"

"Just your other boot." She took it from her rucksack and set it by the stove to dry.

The tension began to slide away.

"And one other thing," she added.

Sweat popped out on his brow and seeped into the thick bandage around his head. "Yes?"

"Well, maybe I shouldn't mention it."

She almost seemed to be taunting him, for God's sake. "Go on," he prompted.

"I saw footprints and a place where someone had

been digging." She chewed thoughtfully. "I can't say who it was or if he found anything, but I'll ask around."

"Do that," he said, his heart racing. God, he had to finish his business and get out of this place.

"Of course." Now that her examination was over, she seemed distracted, nibbling the ring of cheese on her finger and frowning down at the box near her feet.

Daniel used the moments of her inattention to study her further. Some morbid urge made him curious about his quarry.

No one who had spent the night in a chair had a right to look so fresh. The day outdoors had agreed with her. Apple-cheeked, her short hair tousled, she had a healthy glow that made him reluctant to look away.

He yanked his mind from thoughts of mercy. Odious as his task was, he had little choice in the matter. Deep in the bowels of a Paris prison sat Jean Meuron, the man upon whose shoulders rested the security of Switzerland. Couched in the splendor of the Tuileries was a woman who knew what Jean meant to Daniel, and who could destroy the man with a single word. If Daniel failed, his own life, and Switzerland's only hope of avoiding complete domination by Bonaparte, would be forfeit.

One life for a nation. A life that would be mourned only by a handful of clerics and a pack of dogs.

Because of the loss of his rucksack, he'd have to change his plans. He'd intended to use arsenic followed by calomel to speed the process. But the deadly poisons were lost. He prayed whoever found the sack wouldn't recognize the substances—or discover the hidden documents that attested to his deadly mission.

The razor Sylvain had brought gleamed on the bedside table.

A cool hand touched Daniel's brow. He jumped.

"Easy," she said, smiling. "You're sweating."

He wished her little Gallic face weren't so appealing.

"I'm just checking for fever," she explained. "You grew flushed suddenly."

He sat there feeling her soft touch, absorbing her kind words, and wondering what she'd do if she realized he'd been plotting her murder.

"No fever," she said and took her hand away. "That's good, for a fever means something is putrid inside you."

Something was indeed putrid inside Daniel Severin, but it had been so for years, and he hadn't died of it yet.

She stared down at her feet. Melancholy glimmered in her dark eyes.

"What's in the box?" Daniel asked.

"My life's work." She picked it up. "I'd best be off."

He was suddenly reluctant to let her go. "Wait. You can't tease me with a statement like that and simply leave. Er," he fumbled, "something you say might jog a memory in me."

She sat back down. On his tray lay a withered apple from last year's harvest. She picked it up and took a bite. "It's a long story."

"I'm not going anywhere."

She put the apple down and stared at him for a moment, then opened the box and took out a stack of papers. Neat penciled handwriting covered the sheets of cheap foolscap. In the bottom of the box he spied trinkets—a doll's glass eye, a lady's comb, a book, and a pamphlet.

"Most of my notes are a journal of the cases I've treated—everything from birthings to boils."

"Birthings?"

"Just two. Lady travelers. Lord, it was thrilling, Wilhelm. To hold a brand-new child, to watch it take on the flush of life, to see the mother weeping with joy—"

"Am I in your notes?" he cut in, uncomfortable with her reminiscence.

"You will be. You're my first case of amnesia."

Damn, he thought. He'd have to take those papers, leave no record that he'd been to Saint Bernard's.

"But this"—Lorelei patted the papers on her knees—"is something different. It concerns an outbreak of typhus."

She changed as she outlined her ideas. Her small, gamin face lit with enthusiasm, her eyes sparkled, and she no longer looked so very plain. She had a curious way of speaking, her hands moving expressively to illustrate a point, her voice husky with a passion Daniel was hard-pressed to comprehend.

He knew the grim realities of typhus. He'd seen whole armies decimated, seen strong men reduced to feverish weaklings.

But Lorelei had insights he'd never considered. She understood the healing process. She believed she could use that knowledge to protect people from the disease.

Unease twisted through Daniel's mind. Louis XVI

had been fatally indifferent to the suffering of his people. His daughter had dedicated her life to healing.

She spread her notes on his lap. "What do you think?"

"I'm hardly qualified—"

"How do you know?"

"I just know. What does Father Anselme say of your ideas?"

The brightness left her face, and instantly Daniel missed it.

"He says I'm wasting my time. He believes in treating symptoms, not in experimenting with theories."

"You think he's a fool, then."

She scowled. "He's a knowledgeable man. In his day he was a skilled doctor. He simply differs with me on the value of discourse."

"What will you do with your notes and your theories?"

"Keep them. Add to them. Someday—" She broke off, bit her lip, and replaced the notes in the box.

"Someday?" he prompted, knowing with sick grimness that her somedays were few.

She shrugged. "Just one of my fantasies."

Daniel recalled that he, too, had once been full of dreams. Dreams that were drowned in a blood-red tide and shattered by a selfish woman. Lorelei would never live to see her dreams lying broken at her feet.

"I'd like to submit my theory on typhus to other doctors."

"Then do it." He spoke offhandedly of an event that would never come to pass. "Send it to the Academy at Bern, or"—a sudden thought charged into his mind—"to the baron of Coppet."

"But I could never—"

"Never is a long time for one so young." Daniel spread his hands. "Send it. Make a proper copy, and send it."

She laughed. "It's not that simple. My Latin's terrible."

"Mine is excellent." Christ, why was he offering to help?

Because working with Lorelei would bring him closer to her. He'd learn her habits, her vulnerabilities. A way to ease the completion of his task.

"It is?"

*"Felix qui potuit rerum cognoscere causas."*

She blinked. " 'Fortunate is he who has been able to learn the causes of things.' "

"Or 'she.' "

"How do you know Latin?"

He'd seen the trap coming and was ready. "I've no idea. I suppose that particular peach escaped bruising." Languages were easy for him. To please the harsh masters at the orphan asylum at Saint Gall where he'd grown up, he'd driven himself to excel at his studies.

"Extraordinary." Leaning forward, she put her hands on his. A healer's hands caressing the hands of a killer.

He recoiled inwardly, yet held his hands still. He had to get used to her closeness, her disconcerting touch.

"Would you really help me? It would take so much time."

He leaned back against the pillows and gently disengaged his hands. "Let's see. I'd planned, tomorrow, to count the ceiling beams, and the next day I was thinking of looking for constellations in the knotholes. But perhaps I can fit you in."

"Oh, Wilhelm." Her laughter was unaffected, unlike the brittle, modulated gaity of the women he'd known. Daniel found himself smiling.

She looked at him and sobered instantly.

"What's the matter?" he asked.

"You really do have the most remarkable smile."

Nonplussed, he pulled his hands from beneath hers. "Shall we get started now, or would you like to wait until tomorrow?"

"It's kind of you, but we mustn't. Why would a professor of medicine read the work of a female of my limited experience?"

"Because you won't reveal who you are. Use your first initial only, and make up a credential from . . . let's see. The Fredonia Lyceum."

She grinned, shaking her head. "I couldn't be dishonest. Besides, Father Julian would never allow me to send the paper off. He thinks I'm too worldly as it is."

Worldly? She was as naive as a nestling. "Father Julian. Is he very protective of you?"

"Oh, yes. He always has been."

"Always?"

"Yes. Since the day I was born."

"You're an orphan?" His mouth dried, and he waited. Now he'd learn her version of the truth.

"A foundling. Left by a traveler who stole away in the night." Reaching into a pocket of her breeches, she drew out a small leather pouch. "This rosary was all she left with me." The shiny beads trickled through Lorelei's fingers. "She never even gave her name. I used to pretend my mother was a fine lady, or perhaps an artist or a dancer. But I've a good head on my shoulders—Father Julian has always said so. Maybe I take after my father in that."

Not anymore, Daniel thought morbidly.

"Father Julian petitioned the diocese to keep me here."

The prior must have known she was the bastard princess. Why else would he have insisted on raising a female infant in this all-male community? Daniel wanted to question her further, but feared arousing her suspicion.

She nibbled the apple. "And that's the end of it, I suppose."

Daniel believed her utterly. She truly didn't know who her parents were.

"Your story or the treatise?" he asked.

"Both."

"Don't tell the prior about the treatise," said Daniel.

He could see by the look on her face that she hadn't considered this. Lord, she was naive. Deception was as alien to her as the manners of Josephine's court.

"But how could I go behind his back? He'd find out anyway, in confession."

"Surely you don't think a little fib will condemn you to everlasting hell. A lie for the greater good of mankind." A murder for the greater good of Switzerland. He wished he could believe it. "Your theory's too valuable to keep hidden."

Swift as a little bird, she sat on the edge of the bed and brushed his lips with hers. "Oh, Wilhelm, thank you."

His dark thoughts fled like clouds before a high wind. He found himself savoring the wild springtime scent of her, the flutter of her lips barely touching his, the faint lingering flavor of beer. There was nothing remotely sexual about her kiss. It was the impulsive gesture of an excited child.

A child whose very existence threatened two sovereign nations.

A child who had saved his life.

Sick with the battle that raged inside him, he drew back. Silent and blushing, she stared down at her knees. A lock of chestnut hair curled around her ear, and a pulse moved gently at the side of her pale throat.

The gleam of the razor on the bedside table caught Daniel's eye again. With a trembling hand he reached out slowly, gripped the handle. In one swift movement he could accomplish his task.

He lifted the blade.

Lorelei continued to stare at the floor.

He envisioned a ruby necklace of blood on that white throat. He wondered if he had the strength to drag her body outside in secret, to send it sinking to the bottom of Lake Saint Bernard.

He twisted his wrist, turned the sharp edge of the razor toward her.

She looked up, and his heart skipped a beat. Her smile was full of mystery, a cold wind gusting over his heart. She glanced at the blade, then at Daniel.

*Now!*

Her hand came up and cradled his cheek. "I think one shave a day is quite sufficient, Wilhelm," she said. "Wait until tomorrow." And then her smile changed, became open and guileless.

He knew then that he wouldn't—couldn't—kill her.

Not just because she'd kissed him, not just because she was a promising doctor, not even because she'd saved his life.

He wouldn't kill her because, buried deep in the dead ashes of his soul lay a spark of decency, and somehow, unknowingly, Lorelei du Clerc had fanned it to life.

But now he had a problem. If he didn't commit the murder as ordered, Jean Meuron, the stubborn Swiss patriot incarcerated in Paris, would die. And someone else, someone with even fewer scruples than Daniel, would come for Lorelei.

# Chapter 4

"Lorelei, you could drive a man to murder!" The cook shook a meat cleaver at her.

"I'm sorry, Mauricio. I tried to clean it, but . . ." She sheepishly regarded his best mortar bowl, now stained dark brown by walnut juice.

By the fire, a dog patiently walked a treadmill that turned a brace of chickens on a spit. Mauricio wrenched a leg from one of the birds and gave a tidbit to the dog. "I thought you'd outgrown pranks. What were you doing with my mortar anyway?"

"Making ink."

"Ink!" Mauricio's black mustache twitched. *"Ben trovato,* there's ink aplenty in the scriptorium."

"Not anymore. The advance quartermaster from the Army of Reserve sent orders that we're to provide fifty bottles."

"Oh. Buonaparte again." Giving the name its original Italian inflection, Mauricio raised his eyes and his open palms to heaven. "Next he'll have the potatoes from my pot. I thought the army was supposed to carry its own supplies."

"Apparently ink's in short supply." Impatient to be off, she kissed his cheek. "You'll forgive me, won't you, Mauricio?"

He folded his arms over his barrel chest. "It was my best bowl, *bambina.*"

"I'll tell Bonaparte he owes you a new one."

"He'll spit in your eye."

But she knew from Mauricio's smile that he'd forgiven her.

Lorelei entered the infirmary quietly in case Wilhelm was napping. From beyond the windows came the steady drip, drip of melting icicles. Wilhelm lay very still on his cot, his eyes closed, his good hand cradling his head. Afternoon sunlight streamed over him. He'd washed and shaved, she observed, for a basin and a damp cloth sat on the bedside stool. He was shirtless, a mat of springy black hair covering his chest, his stomach corrugated by hard muscle. His long midnight hair spilled out of the bandage around his head.

A queer sensation seemed to brush her soul. A week earlier she'd seen him as a victim half dead of an accident. But now that he'd begun to mend, her indifference to him as a man was slipping. "Too handsome to be trusted," Father Gaston had said. He was wrong.

The stranger's face was not merely handsome, but favored with a rare masculine beauty made up of equal parts arrogance and sheer splendor. Just looking at him infused her with a warmth that she knew must be a sin—one she despaired of disclosing in her weekly confession.

"Are you awake?" she whispered.

He opened his eyes. A smile spread slowly across his face, and the heavy, languid pulse in her chest rose to her throat.

"I was just resting," he said.

For a wild moment Lorelei fancied he saw her as a woman, not a gawky girl who knew only the ways of clerics. Perhaps his memory of females had been wiped clean of any notion of how a woman should look and behave.

She brought herself up short. How full of nonsense she was. The brilliant spring weather had, in the past week, descended like a perfumed blanket over the Great Pass. In the same manner, idiocy had descended over her.

"How do you feel today?" she asked, her movements brisk as she picked up her listening device. Her patient smelled of Father Gaston's lovely columbine soap.

He grinned. As one they recited, "Fine. Never better."

After a week he was familiar with the routine. He cooperated patiently while she listened to his heart and lungs and noted her observations on a sheet of paper.

She moved the basin from the stool and sat down. "Wilhelm, you must be honest with me."

A strange darkness shadowed his eyes. "What do you mean?"

"I don't think you feel fine, and I'd bet my green ribbon that you've been better. I can't treat you properly if I don't know where you hurt."

His expression eased. "Save your worry. I've been eating more than Father Droz's dogs and sleeping like an infant." He grinned. "If something starts to hurt, I'll let you know."

"Promise?"

"Word of honor." He propped himself up on his good elbow and looked around the room, his gaze fastening for a moment on one of the high windows. He could see the bank of the lake, she knew, and a short stretch of the road. In the distance, Sylvain and another novice labored with a sledge piled with split wood.

"Everyone's busy preparing for the arrival of the army," Lorelei explained. "Father Julian says there's to be advance deliveries of supplies. We'll start work soon on outdoor ovens."

"Have you discovered who explored the avalanche site?"

"No, and I did ask everyone, including Everard. Maybe the footprints *were* made the night we rescued you."

He nodded slowly, thoughtfully, then said, "I have something to show you. Help me sit up."

She placed one hand on his upper arm and the other on his shoulder. As she lifted him, she tried to ignore the sensation of touching his warm, clean flesh. But she couldn't. She loved the shape of his muscles, the texture of his skin. The human body was such a miracle. And Wilhelm's body—

"Would you like me to put on a shirt?" he asked.

Caught staring, she shook her head vigorously and arranged the pillows at his back. "There. Comfortable?"

"Immensely."

She bent to tuck the covers around his feet.

"Where did you get that hair ribbon?" he asked.

She touched the wisp of emerald satin clumsily tied around her head. "Everard, the courier. Father Julian told him to inquire about you. You might have relatives who are worried." His face paled a shade and she touched his cheek. "Maybe you shouldn't be sitting up."

"I'm fine," he said, his voice tinged with annoyance.

"Do you like the ribbon?" she asked, then immediately wished she could call back the words. She was pathetic, like a dog begging for table scraps.

"It's . . . becoming."

An unfamiliar fever touched her cheeks and ears. Looking away, she rummaged through the pockets of her vest and drew out a small section of polished horn. "Here's the ink you requested. I made it myself. You ran out of the first batch so quickly."

"I've been busy." From the bedside table he took the lap desk she'd brought earlier. Lifting the lid, he revealed a stack of neatly written papers. "Your treatise, Dr. du Clerc."

Certain he was teasing, Lorelei picked up the top page.

A Treatise on the Disease of Typhus
*Inventum novum*
L. du Clerc, M.D.F.R.S. &c.

"I'm not sure what all those letters mean," he said, "but I saw them after Jenner's name in his smallpox book."

"Oh, Wilhelm," she gasped. Here it was, her notes transformed into beautiful scholarly Latin. Her ideas were now explicated in a clear, concise dissertation. If every page was as perfect as the first, she'd have a polished work. Her eager gaze ran down the pages. At the bottom of the last he'd signed his name in the manner of a scribe: W. Tell. Above that, an inkblot caught her eye. Beneath the blot, three letters were scored into the paper.

Frowning, she held it up to the light. "What's this? You've written something—D. Se—"

He snatched the page from her. "An error," he said. "I'll recopy the page." He put it aside, saying, "The work's not done yet. I had a few questions." He motioned her to his side, and she looked over his shoulder.

"Here, on page three, you state that the typhus outbreak originated in Yverdon. I didn't quite understand how the epidemic reached the hospice."

"It's all explained on the next page, see?" Unthinkingly she settled herself beside him, leaning against his pillows. "Right here . . ." She frowned. "Now, that's odd."

"What?"

"One of the pages of my original is missing." She

shuffled through her notes, then dropped to her knees and searched beneath the cot. "I wonder where it could be."

His eyes narrowed with an emotion she couldn't identify. "You don't suppose someone's looked in the box, do you?"

"Certainly not. Why are you so suspicious?"

"It's not impossible. Several of the canons visit me each day, and your nightly doses of laudanum keep me sound asleep."

Lorelei sat down again. "Ridiculous. My work means nothing to the people here."

"You said the prior disapproved."

"He's not the sort of man who does things in secret. I suppose I misplaced the page myself."

"Can you remember what was on it?"

"Oh, yes. You see, Father Gaston, Sylvain, and Timon—he's another novice—traveled to Yverdon last spring to buy woven wool. The nuns there are known for the quality of their merino."

"The nuns?" he asked urgently.

Lorelei studied his hard, searching eyes. "Does that place mean something to you? Did you have a memory?"

"No." He relaxed against the pillow. "Do go on."

"They found the abbess on her deathbed. Father Gaston heard her whispered confession and administered last rites." She noticed that his grip on the inkhorn had tightened. "Father Gaston was already feverish by the time they returned. Father Julian wouldn't allow me near him." She glowered, remembering the row she'd lost to the prior.

"Because of contagion?" Wilhelm prompted.

"Yes. Father Anselme and Father Emile were in charge of the nursing." She wrapped her arm around her bent leg and rested her chin on her knee. "Father Gaston was delirious for days. From the corridor outside, I could hear him raving."

"Raving? About what?"

"I never could make out his words. Father Emile would know. He sat with him for days. In all, six men fell ill. We moved them to this ward. Father Gaston, Sylvain, and Timon recovered. That's what intrigued me, Wilhelm. On the fourteenth day, the fever drops. The body seems to produce something that kills the toxin. The parallel with smallpox is too obvious to ignore."

"So you think a vaccine could be developed?"

She nodded. "But by someone more skilled than I. That's why I want to write this, Wilhelm. Perhaps this work has been done long ago, but I want to be sure."

He turned a page. "And the other three died."

She shivered, remembering. "Horrible deaths."

"You wrote of that on page five. And very tenderly, Lorelei."

"Was I wrong to include my personal feelings?"

"I wouldn't know. If I've ever read a medical treatise before, I don't remember."

"Maybe we should take it out. I wouldn't want to sound amateurish."

"You're no amateur, Lorelei." He took out a fresh sheet of foolscap. "Now, about the missing page. You say it was Father Gaston who went to Yverdon?"

She nodded and spoke slowly while he made notes.

Heads bent, papers scattered over the cot, she talked and he wrote. He questioned. She clarified. She barely noticed the bell signaling Sext. Moments later Father Anselme shuffled in.

"How is our patient?" the old canon asked.

Lorelei snatched up a sheet of paper and hurried to his side. "Here's his pulse rate, and my observations. He's improving."

Father Anselme found his spectacles on a chain around his neck and put them on, but he hardly glanced at her meticulous chart. He was staring at the papers strewn across Wilhelm's lap.

"Here, what's all this?"

As calm as a clerk in a countinghouse, Wilhelm straightened the stack of papers and slid them into the lap desk. "Mademoiselle du Clerc has asked for my help."

Lorelei's stomach churned. Father Anselme opposed her treatise. But before she could form an explanation, Wilhelm went on, "It seems I'm good at Latin. I'm teaching her."

The lie spilled so easily from his lips, thought Lorelei uncomfortably. It seemed as natural to him as breathing. And unless she spoke up, she was a party to the deception. Yet she said nothing.

"That's fine," said Father Anselme. "Her facility with the language of the church has never been what it could be." He gazed longingly at the comfortable chair by the iron stove.

"Come sit," said Lorelei, guiding him to the warm, dim corner of the ward. "You need a rest."

"I can only stay a few minutes," he protested, but within minutes he was snoring gently.

Speaking in whispers, Lorelei and Wilhelm worked through the afternoon until the sunlight lay in long golden bars over the uneven floor.

The next visitor was Father Emile. "Ah, there he is," the sacristan said briskly, walking over to nudge Father Anselme awake. "We've a meeting with the prior." He turned to Wilhelm. "And how are you today, monsieur?"

"Better, thank you," said Wilhelm.

Father Emile tucked his hands into his sleeves. "We're all anxious for your recovery, so you can be gone about your business—whatever that may be."

Wilhelm drew a quick breath, but Father Emile didn't seem to hear. "Come on, *mon gars*," he said to Father Anselme, and helped the older man up.

After they'd left, Lorelei said, "I suppose you'd best tutor me a bit in Latin now."

"Give some truth to the lie. You don't like lying, do you?"

"No."

"I seem to be good at it."

"Yes."

They worked on until the dogs set up a howl for their evening meal.

Startled to realize that time had slipped away so quickly, Lorelei looked at Wilhelm. "You must be tired. I have to go. Father Gaston's lecturing at supper tonight, and I promised I'd be there. Will you be all right on your own?"

He gestured at the papers. "I've plenty to keep me busy."

Impulsively she took his hand. It felt firm and pleasantly large in contrast to her own. "Wilhelm, thank you so much."

He looked a little chagrined. "You're welcome, Lorelei."

After adding a log to the stove, she left by the door that led outside. From the corner of her eye, she saw a shadow beneath an overhang of the building. For the span of a heartbeat, a cold feeling touched her spine.

She willed it away even before putting a name to it. Never in all her twenty years had she had reason to feel insecure.

She walked toward the movement. The shadow detached itself from beneath the eaves and came toward her. Recognizing a familiar face, she smiled. "Hello, Sylvain."

With an irritated motion, he brushed a shock of straight blond hair from his brow. "You were with him all afternoon."

"With Wilhelm? Of course I was. Someone had to be. His affliction interests me. And he's helping me with my Latin." Repeating Wilhelm's lie gave her a strange, queasy feeling. She looked away from Sylvain's taut face and started walking toward the chapel. Her boots crunched over the snow.

Sylvain took her arm and swung her around to face him. "Lorelei, you know nothing about that man."

"I know he's wounded and needs my care."

"He could be a criminal. A thief or a murderer."

"He could." She disengaged her arm and started

walking again. "But he's not. He's been kind to me. Why are you so worried about a bedridden man? I've sat for hours with other patients and you never fussed at me about it."

But she thought of Wilhelm's rare, exquisite face and knew he was not like any other. Sylvain seemed to realize that, too.

He fell in step with her, slowing his long strides to match her shorter ones. The sweet, warm smell of the sacristy clung to him. "Father Emile claimed your services again," she said.

"Yes." Sylvain nodded.

"What was it today? Polishing candlesticks? Laundering altar cloths?" The sacristan was compulsive about keeping the hospice orderly; he was forever cleaning and rearranging things.

"You're trying to turn me from the subject," said Sylvain.

"True," she admitted.

"Lorelei, I want you to listen to me. You wouldn't be the first girl to be taken in by a stranger's kindness. Remember that gambler who came through and—"

"For heaven's sake, Wilhelm can't move. He's helpless." She formed a mental picture of Wilhelm, his face set, his blue eyes dark with inner anguish. "He's lost his memory. Do you know how frightening that must be?"

"Does Father Julian know about these long visits?"

"No." She put her hand on his arm and found the muscles tense. "Please don't tell him, Sylvain. Please."

"Why not?" He stopped walking, looked down at

her hand, and gently put it aside. "What are you hiding, Lorelei?"

"Nothing! Why are you questioning me like this, Sylvain?"

"Because I care. Because I don't want to see you hurt."

"Your suspicions hurt me."

"Oh, Lorelei." He gloved hand came up to cradle her cheek, the leather cool on her wind-bitten skin. "It's not you I don't trust. But there's something—" He hesitated, fumbling for words. "You may not even be aware of it, but a look comes over your face when you're thinking of him, and it scares me."

"Don't be foolish," she said, more defensively than she'd intended. "Wilhelm is important to my work. Father Julian wouldn't understand, any more than you do."

"I understand more than you think, Lorelei." Sylvain dropped his hand and strode away from her.

While the shadows of the mountains consumed the last of the daylight, Lorelei walked to the chapel. Never before had Sylvain spoken harshly to her. He'd been her friend since he came to the hospice three years earlier. Though gawky and poorly schooled, he had a heart made for caring and a body made for hard work. He used to take her fishing on the lake. He'd taught her wrestling holds and sometimes teased and tickled her mercilessly.

Last summer their relationship had begun to change, imperceptibly and unintentionally. An indifferent scholar, Sylvain had to spend extra time studying to keep up with his courses. The teasing and tickling became a thing of the past. Sylvain was maturing, moving along the path of the canons of Saint Bernard's. Lorelei became increasingly absorbed in her work. They were getting too old for childish games.

A nightmare sucked the air from Daniel's lungs. A strange force rendered him deaf, blind, unable to breathe. His heart bucked against his breastbone.

*Wake up, damn it!*

His eyes bulged open. The linen sheath covering the pillow scraped them.

He was awake. Someone held a pillow over his face.

The realization brought a gurgle of horror to his throat. Instinctively he tried to draw up his arms and legs. He met stiff resistance from the splints.

His attacker laid more weight on the pillow. Daniel's chest burned and convulsed, ready to burst. Panic clawed at his throat. The agony in his head scattered his thoughts.

Desperately he tried to reassemble them. *Think.*

With his good hand, he lashed out. Rough homespun fabric. Someone's arm. Strong as braided wire. His good leg came up, flailed in empty air.

The pillow pressed relentlessly. With a sickening tear, some of the stitches in his head popped free. The blood pounded a death knell in his ears. A seductive floating sensation came over him. The lassitude was dangerous, as much his enemy as the attacker intent on stealing his breath, his life.

But inside him lived a dark, determined creature. The Raven took flight on wings of rage.

Power rushed through him. Raw fury, stronger than

fear, renewed his will to survive. He coiled his good arm and leg. His foot pressed into his attacker's gut. Spending the last of his breath on a roar of anger, Daniel thrust his leg outward.

The weight left his face and chest. He heard a grunt, a muffled thud, then the sound of feet landing on the stone floor.

Daniel flung off the pillow and sat up. He groped blindly for his hunting knife but remembered the weapon was gone. While pain screamed in his head, he strained to see through the gloom.

Too late.

The door stood open to the black hole of the unlit corridor. The spicy scent of church incense and the smell of Daniel's own blood hung in the darkness.

Searing his lungs with gasps of fresh air, he stared at the door until the dizziness passed. He wadded up his sheet and pressed at the bleeding gash in his head.

The attack confirmed his worst fears. Someone at the hospice knew him, and likely knew his purpose. One of these holy men had no fear of mortal sin.

The bastard princess had a champion.

Sylvain's accusations the previous night lent caution to Lorelei's step as she approached the ward where Wilhelm slept. A mystery surrounded him, to be sure, and secrets haunted his eyes, but she could feel no fear of him, only concern and tenderness.

Gray ghosts of dawn wavered through the corridor and she quickened her step, for she was eager to log her patient's progress before morning devotions and breakfast.

The door to the ward stood ajar. Lorelei heard a thud followed by a groan. Gasping in fear, she ran into the room.

"Wilhelm!"

A curse from the other side of his bed singed her ears.

She raced over and found him lying on the floor. "Wilhelm?" Her hands moved over his bandaged head. Dried blood stained the gauze. "Did you fall?"

He glowered in self-disgust. "Help me up, will you?"

"I'll have you back in bed in a moment."

"I'm not going back to bed."

She bit her lip in consternation. He wore the breeches and shirt he'd had on when they brought him in. His coat was draped across his shoulders. The wrapping from his leg lay in a heap on the floor. "You're dressed," she said accusingly.

"Very observant, Professor du Clerc."

She ignored his rudeness. "You must go back to bed. You need a good dose of laudanum."

"No. No more laudanum."

"But you're not well enough to be up yet."

"That's your opinion." His scowl deepened. "Now. You may either help me up or stand by and watch me crawl."

She studied the hard, stubborn line of his jaw and sighed. "What's made you so angry?"

"Being confined to bed does get on a man's nerves," he retorted. His hand gripped the frame of the bed.

"Wait." She sidled close to him. "I'll help you, but you must let me mend your cut again."

He rolled his eyes heavenward. "Do what you must."

Five minutes later she'd removed the torn stitches and replaced the bandage. "There," she said, trimming the gauze. "I'm finished. Put your arm around me."

Breathing hard, he did so. The pulse in his neck raced. He smelled of sweat and determination.

"Ready?" she asked.

He nodded.

Bracing her arm on the side of the cot, she stood. His weight dragged at her, but seconds later they were standing. She gazed up at him in surprise. "My, you're very tall."

"You're very small."

"How do you feel?"

"Fine. Simply wonderful."

She tilted her head back and regarded his ashen face. The flickering movements of his eyes betrayed acute dizziness. "Liar," she said. "Get back in bed."

He regarded her implacably. Frustration closed around Lorelei's heart. This man, who was a stranger even to himself, wouldn't heed her, regardless of her intentions. He couldn't be the way she wanted him—warm, compliant, full of humor.

"Please," she said.

"No. I'm going to breakfast in the refectory."

She sighed. "You're being insufferable."

"Lying in bed is insufferable."

"You'll need a crutch."

"Have you one?"

She went to a cupboard and took out a stout walking cane. Father Anselme had cut it from an ash tree years ago, cured it with oil, and shaped the top into a curve.

She took the crutch to Wilhelm and fit it beneath his good arm.

"It's too short for you."

"It'll do." The church bell clanged. "Let's go."

"Put as little weight as possible on that knee. Let me bear the brunt of it." She put her arm around him. "You're so thin. Your ribs are sticking out."

"My ribs are fine."

"I know. I can feel every one of them."

Slowly they made their way outside. The day was crisp, the sky a panorama painted by rosy fronds from the rising sun.

He closed his eyes and inhaled deeply. The expression on his face startled her. Gilded by the morning light, his features softened into an expression of sublime rapture. He seemed to be absorbing the crystalline air through his pores.

Lord, he looked beautiful, even with the shadow of a beard and the bandage circling his head.

He opened his eyes and saw her staring. His face became a hard, lean mask of nonchalance. "Nice day," he commented.

"I didn't mean to stare," said Lorelei. "It's just that I've never seen you in the sunlight before."

He jerked his gaze from hers and stabbed the crutch into the snow. "We'll be late for breakfast," he muttered.

He had a vulnerable side, she realized. He didn't like her to see it. She pointed out the path across the yard. "The snow's packed, and Sylvain put pebbles down to keep people from slipping. You're sure you can make it?"

"I'll make it."

Many minutes later they entered the main door of the hospice and staggered toward the refectory.

"There are a lot of steps," Lorelei warned.

"The smell alone will get me there," he declared.

She inhaled the scent of yeasty rolls. "Mauricio's focaccias will make this worth your trouble." She was about to inquire about his knee. Knowing what his answer would be, she decided against it. Despite his claims to the contrary, she suspected that hellish pains were shooting up his leg.

They climbed the narrow stairs. The murmur of voices and the clatter of utensils greeted them as she pushed the door open.

Fifteen faces turned in their direction. A long table dominated the high-beamed room. At the far end, the shield of Saint Augustine, with its flaming heart, was carved in stone.

Lorelei recovered first from the awkward silence. "Wilhelm decided to join us," she said. "Against my orders, I might add."

Daniel trembled as she and a novice helped him to a bench that flanked the table. Lorelei seated herself beside him.

His head pounded and his knee flamed with agony. For the hundredth time, he cursed his blunder in nearly signing his own name to the bottom of Lorelei's paper. But last night's attack had honed the steel of his will. He wouldn't rest until he discovered who wanted him dead.

From the head of the table Father Julian presided over the meal. Though well into his middle years, he was a handsome man with long, stark cheeks, a blade-like nose, hard lips drawn into a severe line. His eyes were gray stones washed by an icy spring.

His nostrils thinned as he inhaled. "Welcome to our table."

"Thank you," said Daniel.

"It's good to see you're mending. You'll be leaving us sooner than we'd thought." Impatience underscored the prior's polite tones.

He wants me gone, Daniel thought. Would he attempt murder to speed the process?

Father Julian rose to read the lesson. Spare and stern, he stood behind a lectern and picked up a well-thumbed volume. Daniel noticed that he didn't open to the page marked by a long red ribbon, but turned elsewhere, as if he'd changed his mind.

" 'Who can say,' " the prior read, " 'I have made my heart clean, I am pure from my sin? . . . Take his garment that is surety for a stranger, and take a pledge of him for a strange woman.' "

Daniel glanced up sharply. The prior knew the text by heart. As he spoke, his cool gaze traveled around the room.

" 'The bread of deceit is sweet to a man, but afterward his mouth shall be filled with gravel. . . . The getting of treasures by a lying tongue is a vanity tossed to and fro of them that seek death.' "

The words were like arrows aimed at Daniel's heart. Furious at the prior's knife-sharp instincts, Daniel squirmed inwardly until the lesson was done. The Raven, squirming? Good God, was he was losing his mercenary soul to a conscience?

No. He couldn't afford to.

The canons, novices, and lay brothers of Saint Bernard's were simple men, healthy as Swiss peasants. The novices wore gray habits, their hair long, their heads uncovered. All were young and hungry. The pile of rolls and sausages dwindled quickly, as did the tankards of small beer and mugs of coffee. They snatched up food, raked sleeves over their mouths, and between bites discussed the new litter they expected from Belle. Searching the faces that lined the long table, Daniel couldn't find a hint of malice in any of them. But looks could be deceiving. He'd learned that painful lesson years before.

He sipped Mauricio's strong, nutty-tasting coffee and tried to eat a bit of sausage and focaccia. His stomach knotted like the scourges the canons wore around their waists.

Daniel wasn't afraid for his life, not at the moment. Whoever wanted him dead would do the deed in the dark. What he feared was that his deception wasn't working. Any moment he expected someone to jump up, point a finger, and denounce him as a fraud. Then what? Daniel wondered. Denials and more lies?

His gaze sneaked to Sylvain. Large and muscular, his head crowned by a shock of blond hair, his cheeks dusted with translucent whiskers, Sylvain typified the sturdy Alpine man. His blunt hands looked more suited to wielding a plow than to holding a prayer book.

Sylvain had been in Yverdon last summer when the abbess died. That was important. There was every possibility that he knew the secret the old woman had breathed on her deathbed.

Glancing up, Sylvain met Daniel's gaze. His strong-featured face flushed for a moment; then he looked away.

He's just a youth, Daniel told himself. What could he know of me?

Father Anselme had a cloud of snowy hair and a face lined by wind and weather. His deep-set eyes studied Daniel with an unnerving clinical detachment. A doctor's eyes. His hands were bony, the knuckles swollen and shiny. Daniel doubted the canon had the strength to hold a pillow over his face.

But all the others did. The harsh life at the hospice demanded the vigor of youth, and there was not another old man among them.

"More cream?" asked the canon across the table from Daniel.

Daniel took the pitcher. "Thank you, Father Emile." While pouring, Daniel surreptitiously watched the sacristan. Here was the man whose duties gave him charge of all ceremonial articles—including the incense.

Emile was thin and wiry, not yet forty. But his lips were full and sensuous and he ate slowly, savoring every bite in a way that seemed at odds with a canon's renunciation of worldly pleasures.

"How do you like our peaceful way of life?" he asked.

"I've been shown much kindness here," said Daniel. He sought a reaction, a look of irony, but Emile only smiled.

Beside him, Father Gaston nodded vigorously. The almoner was a cherubic, musclebound man with spiky brown hair. "That's our mission," he explained. "We help all travelers in distress as our founder, Bernard of Menthon, did in the tenth century. Smugglers and thieves haunted the Great Pass in his time, and his mission was to make it safe for travelers."

Daniel feigned interest in the legend, but it was Father Gaston himself he watched. Here was the man who'd heard the last rites of the woman who had revealed Lorelei's secret on her dying breath.

"The Romans had erected a statue of Jupiter at the pass," Father Gaston went on. "Saint Bernard destroyed it and founded the hospice. His motto was 'You who climb the Alps in safety under my guidance continue with me to the House of Heaven.' "

"You've a high calling indeed," Daniel commented. But like Father Emile, Gaston showed no response to the irony.

"An odd thing, your affliction," said Father Emile. "What's that you called it, Lorelei?"

She licked a crumb from her finger. "Amnesia. A partial loss of memory. I think it was caused by the head injury."

"Extraordinary." Daniel watched Father Emile's long, elegant fingers. He'd nursed Gaston through typhus. In delirium, Gaston might have revealed the secret.

Father Gaston sucked his tongue. "Imagine, having one's memory wiped out."

"It might be convenient," said Father Droz. "Think how little you have to confess, monsieur."

Daniel's gaze cut to the kennel master. He sought rancor and saw only bluff good humor. He forced a grin. "I'm afraid it makes for boring conversation. But not everything has been wiped out." He regarded Emile and Gaston. "For example, I realize that both of you speak like Parisians."

"Then you've been to Paris," said Lorelei, clapping her hands. She shot an impudent grin at Father Gaston. "You see, I told you he's no common drover."

Gaston sent her a smile of melting indulgence. Although his face was florid and bristles grew from his nostrils and ears, there was softness in his regard for Lorelei. "Mind your manners, *chouette,* or you'll overset your beer," he chided.

He alone seemed concerned about her manners. Was it because he knew who she was?

"We should make a wager," said Father Clivaz.

"Six marks says he's a huntsman," called Father Droz from the foot of the table. Like the stout German Swiss he was, he clapped his tankard on the pine plank until someone passed him the pitcher of beer.

"I'll put my alms on a traveler," said Father Anselme.

"Surely the man has children," added Father Clivaz. "How else does one develop that streak of white hair at such a young age, except by worrying about small ones?"

Laughter erupted around the table. Daniel glanced at the prior. With an intuitive sense of timing, Father Julian waited for the mirth to peak, then subside.

He held up his hand. "There will be no wagers," he stated. "It's not in keeping with our vow of poverty." Grumbles stole through the assembled canons and novices. Father Julian cleared his throat. His face was as bland as buttermilk. "Besides, what if he's from the diocese? We could face censure or be fined."

For a moment silence hung in the air. Then Father Droz began to chuckle, and was soon joined by the others.

"Our prior," said Father Clivaz, "thinks of everything."

Daniel sat listening to the laughter and feeling the bond of camaraderie that encircled this tiny community. Simple, pious men of God.

But one of them was a killer.

# Chapter 5

Lorelei bent over a steaming tub and cradled Wilhelm's knee in her hands. He sat on a stool, his leg submerged in a fragrant bath of comfrey steeped in springwater. She kept her head bent as she worked, the blood pounding in her steam-heated cheeks. Whenever she was with him lately a lassitude slipped over her, scattering her thoughts and making her a stranger to herself. Absurdly she wondered if amnesia was contagious, for surely the secret woman stirring inside her was no one Lorelei knew.

Father Anselme, who dozed in a chair in the corner of the ward, intruded on the moment with a snore.

"Does he always sleep so soundly?" asked Wilhelm.

She moved his knee deeper into the water. "He's been known to sleep through an avalanche. Tell me if I hurt you."

Wilhelm regarded her through the herb-scented wisps of steam rising from the tub. "You're not hurting me, Lorelei."

Disconcerted by the softness in his voice, she stared at her hand resting on his knee. Her thumbs circled his kneecap, which she'd lubricated with wintergreen liniment. The sharp, sweet fragrance teased her nostrils. Her gaze followed the motion of her hand on his bare leg, and her ministrations took on a new meaning. What she'd once considered clinical body parts suddenly became the flesh and blood and bone of a man who invaded her every moment, waking or sleeping.

He was a wayfarer, she told herself, destined like thousands of others to pass through her life, never to return. His wounds would mend, and he would move on. She was determined that he'd leave her heart intact. Resolutely she said, "The swelling's nearly gone. You're a fast healer."

"I always have been."

Her head came up quickly, her hair dancing about her cheeks. She knew that for a moment her expression was naked, revealing her thoughts. "You remember?" she asked quickly.

"No. You said the same thing when you removed the stitches from my head."

In a fever of confusion, she kneaded his injury, her thumbs gliding over slick skin. "You're sure this doesn't hurt?"

"I'm sure."

"It's been three weeks. I'm beginning to worry. Most of the case histories I've read say the patients recovered their memories within a few days." She chewed her lip. "Then there was that one Viennese fellow who never remembered. Imagine, starting over as an entirely new person."

"Being a new person might not be all that bad."

She turned his words over in her mind. Behind his eyes she saw secret pain and wondered what he hid from her.

"What if you've left a family behind? You might have a wife or a mother who's grieving for you."

"If I had a loving family, wouldn't I have told them where I was going? They'd have come looking for me by now."

Lorelei worked in thoughtful silence for a time. She had an unsettling sense that Wilhelm didn't wish to remember who he was. But why? Could his past have been so tragic?

"What do you mean, tragic?"

She blinked. "I didn't realize I'd spoken aloud. I was just thinking that maybe you're avoiding your memories."

He stared at her blankly for a moment. The steam from the tub moistened his face with a sheen of dew, softening the high sweep of his cheekbones, adding depth to the cleft in his chin. "What awful secret do you think I've locked away, Lorelei?" he asked, his voice rough with uncertainty.

Sensing his discomfiture, she shrugged. "You're probably very normal, and soon you'll recover from that blow to your head." Yet the glimmer of inner pain never quite left his eyes. She yearned to know what ailed him, for she wanted to heal him. She worked at his knee with deft tenderness, the pads of her fingers sliding over his warm flesh.

He flung his head back, closed his eyes, and said, "By God, that feels good. Don't stop."

His statement melted like warm honey through her. She tried to stop the flow with rattling conversation. "Some of my earliest memories are of tending the strained muscles of mountaineers. Perhaps it was then that I learned I wanted to be a healer."

He opened his eyes. "Why do you care so much?"

Flustered, she cleared her throat and worked vigorously at his knee. "It's my business to care for the ill and the wounded," she said. "It's the business of all doctors."

"But most perform their ministrations with a certain detachment. Don't ask me how I know," he added quickly. "I just do." He shifted on the stool. "You're not detached, Lorelei."

She didn't need him to tell her that. His nearness spawned feelings that were better left unexplored. She stilled her hands and rested them on the edge of the tub. Water dripped from her fingertips. The minty steam stung her eyes.

Wilhelm was absolutely correct. She didn't hold herself aloof from him, didn't regard his injured body as a tinker regards a broken gear. She cared deeply about this lost man with his empty memory, cared for him in a way that went beyond a doctor's detached humanity and delved into a realm of forbidden emotion.

She forced herself to hold his stare. What did those

deep, haunted eyes see when he looked at her? Did they hide memories of pretty women who spoke in soft, cultured voices? Someday would he compare her to dainty, beribboned beauties and find her lacking?

"No," he said.

For a moment she was terrified she'd spoken aloud again; then he repeated, "You're not detached, Lorelei." His large hand cupped her cheek, and his thumb drew slow, agonizing circles on her skin. The caress made her eyelids feel suddenly heavy. Looking down, she watched bits of comfrey float to the bottom of the tub.

"The water's getting cold," she said awkwardly.

"And you're avoiding the subject. You put your soul into your work, Lorelei." He grasped her wet hands. "I wonder, is that your way with all your patients?"

"No." Ducking out of reach, she grabbed the towel she'd laid to warm on the wood stove. She lifted his leg from the bath and buffed it gently with the towel. "You're special."

He looked beyond her. "Because of the memory loss?"

Because something in you calls to me, she wanted to say. Because when I touch you my heart leaps. But she held silent. Her confession would only confuse him more.

"Lorelei, look at me."

She stopped rubbing with the towel and lifted her gaze to his face. He was frowning, his face ruthlessly handsome.

"You've an excellent mind, Lorelei," he said. "But you're not using it."

"Why do you say that?"

"Because you're wasting your tender feelings on me. Father Julian's had no response to his inquiries at Bourg-Saint-Pierre. No one has reported me missing. Doesn't that tell you something?"

"Should it?"

"It should tell you I'm a loner, not fit company for impressionable young girls. Christ, the canons saw it from the first." He gestured at Father Anselme. His tall hat pulled over his eyes and his feet stretched out toward the stove, the old man slept on. "They don't leave us alone together, which is probably wise."

She eased a woolen stocking over his foot and calf. "Do you feel up to a walk today?"

"Yes. Do you agree with me or not?"

"No," she said simply. "Knowing you is good for me."

"What the devil do you mean by that?"

"My treatise, for one thing. Before you came, sharing my ideas with other doctors was only a dream. A hopeless dream."

"You'd have talked yourself into it eventually."

"Perhaps." Bending, she rolled down the leg of his breeches, buckled the cuff at the knee, and offered her hand to help him up. He waved her away. "But probably not," she added.

"Why not?"

She wouldn't meet his eyes. "You'll laugh."

He tucked a finger beneath her chin and tilted her face up. "Try me." His touch glided over her heated skin, and his dark blue eyes challenged her.

"I'm afraid."

"Of what?" he asked tautly.

Self-disgust rose inside her. "Of the world beyond the mountains. I've never admitted that to anyone."

"But you said you'd like to study at a university."

"It's safe to dream, knowing the dream won't come true. I've been sheltered here all my life. Beyond the hospice the world is so strange, so overwhelming."

Giving him a tremulous smile, she helped him don his boots and thick woolen vest, tucking up his shirt-sleeve so his splinted arm could rest on it. "But you forced me to act. You've given me courage and hope."

They walked to the kennels, where a dozen deep-bellied barks greeted them. The youthful, swarthy kennel master sat on a bench in the hay-strewn basement. Father Droz was a simple man of few words, and he was never more at home than when he was with his furry charges. Beside him sat Ivan, his huge paw in the canon's lap. Father Droz looked up and grinned. "Just trimming his nails," he said, and Lorelei heard the snapping of the shears. "Stella's coming into season, and I want to mate him with her."

Wilhelm cleared his throat. He turned to study a map tacked to the wall. Lorelei thought his ears seemed redder than usual.

"Wilhelm claims he's up to a hike," she said. "Can we take Barry and Belle?"

Father Droz's smile disappeared. He glanced at Wilhelm, then beckoned Lorelei closer. "I don't think so, *liebchen*," he said quietly. "The prior's forbidden us to leave you alone with our mysterious visitor."

She pressed her lips together in irritation. "Look at

him, Father." Wilhelm moved down the line of pens, pausing to pet each dog. "He's harmless. Besides, we won't be alone."

"The dogs are good protectors."

"And they like Wilhelm. You've always said they're better judges of character than any man."

"True." He rubbed Ivan's broad head. "I've learned more about humanity from these creatures than from any sermon or book."

"We won't go far. Wilhelm can't."

Father Droz gave her a grudging smile. "Brat. You knew you could talk me into it. But if anyone asks, I objected strenuously."

"Of course." Leaning over, she kissed him, then went to fetch the dogs. Father Droz stood at the door and watched them leave. Despite his good humor, he swiftly made the sign of the cross.

*You've given me courage and hope.*

Daniel stared at her sturdy legs as she climbed ahead of him through a forest of budding larches and fir trees. He was a fool to raise her hopes by helping with her thesis, for all hope had died in Daniel Severin long ago.

So why did he long to nurture a dream in someone whose every waking thought seemed to be a shining hope?

Because he wanted to manipulate her. He needed to win her trust, for he had to get her away—in secret—from the hospice. Soon, he told himself, inwardly cursing his weak leg, his broken arm.

Too many weeks had passed. In Paris someone

waited for news of the bastard princess's demise. If the news didn't come soon, another assassin would arrive.

His knee aching with exertion and his head full of half-formed plans, he tried to concentrate on the climb. The hospice lay a mile behind them, and two dogs bounded ahead. The trees grew sparse near the frost line. Daniel's breath came in quick, short puffs. Lolling in bed had weakened him, made him prey first to an assassin and now to the thin air of the mountains.

His untenable dilemma nagged at him. Very soon she'd discover that his motives were far from pure. A latent, long-hidden sense of decency reared up inside him. He wished he didn't have to be the one to kill all hope in the girl.

He wasn't accustomed to feeling responsible for people. But now, though neither knew it, Jean Meuron and Lorelei du Clerc depended on him for their lives. He disliked the weightiness of it. A responsibility that was as smothering as the pillow a murderer had held to his face. Daniel used people for his own ends. The last thing he needed was the burden of protecting a naive mountain-bred girl. But he couldn't kill her. He couldn't leave her. He wasn't free to walk away unencumbered.

He jabbed his walking stick into the melting snow on the mountainside. Damn! His own stupidity six years earlier had tangled him in this mess. Other men were guilty of youthful foolishness. Other fools had the luxury of living it down.

Yet Daniel's old indiscretion bound him like chains of iron. In refusing to murder Lorelei, he strained at the bond, but it was still there.

His gaze clung to Lorelei as if her unaffected sweetness could soften the discontent in his soul. She moved with grace and economy of movement, surefooted as a young chamois and nearly as quick as the two huge mastiffs leading the way.

He caught himself smiling. Straight-hipped, her short curls just brushing the collar of her jacket, she could easily be mistaken for a boy out for an afternoon of innocent adventure.

"It's beautiful up here, isn't it?" she called over her shoulder.

His eyes held her face. "Yes."

"You're taking care of your knee?"

"Of course. You're not going slowly for my sake?"

"For Belle. She's expecting." Lorelei started up a rocky path still damp from the recent melt.

"What will Father Anselme think when he wakes up and finds us gone?"

"He won't. You could set the church clock by his naps."

But the tension inside Daniel stayed tightly coiled. The canons had been watching him. He kept looking back to see if they'd been followed.

They reached the edge of a plunging defile. Grayish snow lay about in odd patches like frozen ghosts.

"This is the avalanche site," said Lorelei. The dogs snuffled aimlessly at a heavy, wet drift. "You can still see where we pulled you out, just there."

He studied the pitted, rock-strewn spot. The sharp metallic taste of fear pooled in his mouth.

"Are you all right, Wilhelm?" In a rush Lorelei was

at his side, her mitten peeled off and her hand on his forehead.

"It just struck me. This might have been my grave."

"Not likely. We're very good at what we do." She drew her mitten back on. "Do you remember anything about what you were carrying?"

"No," he lied.

They poked around the area, seeking items he might have lost in the avalanche. Lorelei couldn't have known it, but only one thing was missing. His rucksack, a brown canvas parcel with a tiny patch on the top flap depicting a sheaf of arrows. His gaze darted over fallen dead limbs and rocks.

"Nothing to be found," she said. "I must have been mistaken about those footprints."

She wasn't mistaken. Daniel knew it with cold certainty. Someone had returned to the site. Someone had found the rucksack with its lethal doses of arsenic and calomel, with its documents hidden in the lining. Someone had discovered the deadly secret of Lorelei, and of Daniel's purpose in coming to the hospice.

They sat together on a large flat rock warmed by the springtime sun. A breeze, perfumed by budding trees and evergreens, soughed through the ravine. There was a rarefied splendor in the day, a crystal clarity that dug at feelings buried deep inside Daniel.

He stared down at the distant hospice compound. Reflected in the surface of the glassy lake, the gray stone buildings appeared minuscule. Canons walked to and fro, some hefting tools, others carrying breviaries. A man, probably Mauricio, worked in a tiny garden behind the kitchen.

Daniel looked back at Lorelei. The wind stirred her chestnut curls, and between them he saw the pale flesh of her neck. Something warm and strange stirred in his chest, and he willed the feeling away. He was looking at a girl, a mere girl.

But this girl was many things. She was a daughter of the royal house of France. Some men would die to keep her safe; others would kill to see her eliminated. Her very existence polarized men and nations, threatened the one man who inspired something more than indifference in Daniel.

He should do it now. He should fling aside his noble intentions and choke her to death. The canons were too far away to hear her screams. The road was clear now. He could travel fast, be in Paris in a week with the deed behind him and Meuron's freedom ensured.

His hand came up, hovered inches from her delicate neck.

She turned to him and smiled. "How is your head?"

Inner conflict stormed through him, wrenching his gut. He didn't know himself anymore. He dropped his hand. "It's fine."

"No more nightmares?"

"Night—" He broke off. She thought a nightmare had caused him to fall out of bed, tearing the stitches. "No. No more."

She closed her eyes and turned her face to the sun. Her curls made a shining arcade around her cheeks, and the sun touched her eyelashes with flecks of gold. She wasn't beautiful, he told himself resolutely, but there was a purity, a chaste, unconscious appeal, about her that even he couldn't deny.

"Your life is rich here," he commented, wanting to draw her out, to find a clue to the identity of the man who'd tried to kill him.

She opened her eyes and followed his gaze to the valley. "From time to time a traveler will pity me because I'm an orphan. But I've never felt alone. Instead of two parents I have a dozen."

"The prior is very fatherly toward you."

Her face softened with affection. "Father Julian was young when I was left here."

"When did he become prior?"

"Eighteen, nineteen years ago. He's never spoken of it, but I've a feeling he had to fight the diocese in order to keep me here."

"Why do you say that?"

"It's not the mission of the hospice to take in orphans, especially female ones."

"But surely he can't expect you to stay here forever."

She hugged her knees to her chest. "Why not? I have nowhere else to go."

Daniel took a chance. "What about marriage?" he asked carefully. "Has Father Julian ever spoken of it to you?"

She chuckled as if the idea had never crossed her mind. "I wouldn't make a very good wife. I believe Father Julian means for me to spend my life here. He's always been so protective."

Or perhaps the stern-faced prior had a more selfish motive, Daniel reflected. Maybe, as guardian of Louis XVI's bastard, Father Julian expected a reward for himself.

But from whom? The Comte d'Artois, Louis's

younger brother, lived in exile. Daniel couldn't imagine that Artois would be pleased to learn of the existence of a bastard niece. But there was always blackmail. . . .

"You're sure Father Julian will be angry when he learns you're sending your treatise abroad?" Daniel asked.

"Oh, very angry," she said. "I shall be forced to sit through one of his lectures on obedience." She picked up a stone and pitched it far into the ravine. "And then I hope he'll be secretly proud."

Daniel wondered at her breezy insouciance. Despite her haphazard way of dressing and her lack of refinement, she'd led a charmed life. Nothing in her experience gave her cause to doubt her own security. And nothing in her experience had prepared her for the shock to which, very soon, Daniel would have to subject her.

She pitched another stone, and Daniel commented, "You've quite an arm for throwing."

She grinned. The bright sun brought out a faint bridge of freckles across her nose. "Father Emile taught me." She frowned in concentration and threw a third rock, and this time Daniel could see the training in each movement.

One of the Parisians, thought Daniel. "How long have you known him?"

"I was twelve when he and Father Gaston arrived from Paris," she said. "They'd escaped the bloody uprisings of 1792."

Daniel's stomach tightened. "They were Royalists?"

"Father Gaston believes fervently in the divine right

of kings. Father Emile is more a man of the common people, but he didn't favor the Reign of Terror. He said he'd seen hell and wished to devote his life to God."

Either man, Daniel realized, could have a stake in the future of the bastard princess. In whether she lived or died. "He sounds too pious to be teaching girls to throw stones."

"Father Emile loves to manage things. He's critical of the way Father Julian runs the hospice. Now, Father Gaston's the pious one. He's picky, too, forever correcting my manners."

Why? Daniel wondered. Because he had his own ideas on how a royal princess should behave? Daniel rubbed his hand over the lichened surface of the rock. So many lives, interconnected like threads in a delicate web.

"Tell me about Father Anselme," he said.

"I learned to read at his knee. I took lessons with the novices, but Father Anselme always made time to tutor me privately. He fancied I had a gift for learning."

Did he? Daniel wondered. Or did the old canon have a prideful desire to educate a Bourbon princess? "Did he teach you only medical arts?"

"Oh, my, no. He prescribed a full course of study—language and literature, geography, history, mathematics." She grinned. "Latin, too, but it didn't take."

"And is he right?" asked Daniel. "Are you gifted?"

She scowled, her brown eyes flecked with fire. "Father Anselme dismissed my skill as some divine gift, but he's wrong. I've worked hard. I've studied for years."

"Sorry. I'll never insult you by calling you gifted."

"Thank you."

Daniel continued to search out clues. "And Sylvain? How long have you known him?"

"Since he came here a few years ago. We used to be the best of friends." She pointed at the lake far below. "We built a tree house down there. We used to bring food from the buttery and meet there at midnight and tell each other ghost stories."

Daniel imagined the bygone days of her childhood. Equal measures of envy and wistfulness pulsed through him. He had no fond memories to savor, and for the first time in his life, he found himself wishing he had.

"But not anymore?" he prompted.

She shook her head. "He's changed. But I suppose I should have expected that. In another year he'll take his vows and become a canon regular of Saint Bernard. He's bound to become more serious about responsibility and faith." She kicked the toe of her boot at a chunk of snow. "We all are, I suppose." She glanced at Daniel, a smile playing about her lips. "You're full of questions today. Is it because we're the only people in the world that you know?"

"I suppose so, Lorelei." God, how he wished it were true.

The female dog, Belle, sidled over. Lorelei circled her arm around the mastiff's thick neck. The dog made a rumbling sound in her throat and rubbed her muzzle on Lorelei's thigh.

Torn between wistfulness and cynicism, Daniel watched. Genuine affection was rare in his experience. He'd had many women—too many—but with none had he shared a sentiment resembling affection. Having so many lovers, Daniel supposed, was a way to mask the man he was, to fool himself into believing he was of some worth.

Lorelei laid her cheek on the dog's thick fur, and Daniel was struck by the beauty that transcended her mild, unremarkable features. The light of pure love glimmered in her eyes. A woman couldn't find that sort of shining loveliness in a cosmetic jar.

Damn. She was so sheltered. What would the world beyond the mountains do to her?

She looked up and caught him staring. Daniel forced a smile. "They're amazing dogs."

"Father Droz says the ancient Romans used them as beasts of burden. About fifty years ago the canons started using them as rescue dogs. Belle's made fourteen saves." She picked up one of the massive paws. "They're perfectly suited to this life. See how the toes are webbed? It helps them paddle through the deepest snow. They can sense an avalanche before it falls and sniff out a human buried in the snow." She ruffled Belle's ears. "Belle did so just last year, didn't you, girl? A family got lost in a blizzard a mile away, and she found them."

Reaching down, she massaged the dog's underside, then grinned. "She's carrying a litter of at least six."

"And they'll be trained as rescue dogs?"

"Only the best of them. The rest will be given away in Bourg-Saint-Pierre. They'll be used as cart dogs or pets."

"Who trains them for the rescue work?"

"Father Droz."

A wry smile teased at Daniel's mouth. "With your help."

"Sometimes. Barry's my own project." At the sound of his name, the young dog ambled over and nuzzled her hand. "I do love them."

Daniel studied the dog's soulful, comically sad eyes. The mastiffs gazed at Lorelei with unadulterated adoration. "The feeling's mutual."

"The dogs were my playmates as I was growing up. My friends. Father Julian used to worry that I lacked other children to play with, but I was never lonely. I ran and climbed with the dogs, bandaged their hurts, watched them being born, and mourned them when they died."

She sent Daniel a gamin smile. "Want to see a rescue? Watch this!" She ran to the lip of the ravine, scaled a huge snowdrift, and disappeared over the other side.

"Jesus!" Daniel yelled, dropping his stick. With the dogs at his side, he scrambled up the wall of snow.

His heart rose to his throat, choking him. On a narrow ledge, Lorelei lay motionless, limbs splayed, her eyes closed and her face pale against the snow.

Wrenching his knee, he started over the edge.

The dogs were quicker. As if he were a rabbit rather than a giant dog, Barry sailed downward, landing at Lorelei's side. Belle followed close at his heels. The dogs burrowed into the snow beside Lorelei, licking her face and yelping.

Daniel slid down the embankment. His splinted arm came out of his sleeve. Pain flashed from his wrist to his shoulder. Loose snow crawled up under his shirt and *bredzon,* chilling his skin. He landed on his knees beside Lorelei and cradled her head in his lap.

"Lorelei?" he asked in a shaking voice. Christ. By killing herself she had completed his mission. He ought to be relieved.

She made no response even when Barry lapped at her temple with his long pink tongue. Her face was still, a death mask. Had the fall knocked her senseless? Glancing up, Daniel saw a rock jutting from the wall of snow.

"Goddammit," he snapped, his voice taut with frustration and fear. "Now what am I going to do?"

"For one thing, you can stop swearing." Her voice drifted like a song to his ears. "It upsets the dogs. *Bien fait, mes amis.*" With a wave of her hand she dismissed them, and they plowed their way back up the bank.

Relief and fury welled in Daniel's throat. "You were playacting!"

"Of course I was. It's how we train them. I told you—"

"Lorelei!" He gripped her shoulders and hauled her to a sitting position. His splinted arm ached with the motion, stoking his temper. "You could have killed yourself."

Her eyes shone with mischief. "No, Wilhelm. These mountains are as familiar to me as the Stations of the Cross. You need never worry that I'll make a fatal mistake."

He was amazed to find that his hands were shaking. He steadied them by clutching her tighter. "I could strangle you." By God, I ought to and be done with it, he thought.

She laughed and fell against his chest, then pulled back to stare at him thoughtfully. Snowflakes sprinkled her hair like fairy dust, and her smiling lips were moist. "I did give you a scare, didn't I?" she whispered, her breath warming his cheek. "I'm sorry, Wilhelm."

Wilhelm. It was Wilhelm who suddenly crushed her to his chest, Wilhelm who laid his mouth upon hers, Wilhelm who heard her quick gasp of surprise. He kissed her as Daniel Severin had never kissed a woman, with no other purpose than to show his desperate relief. He embraced her gently, surrounding himself with the heady essence of woods and snow and springtime that clung to her, cherishing her small, warm body.

But soon he found himself, against all good sense, craving more.

"Open your mouth," he heard himself whisper. "Just a little." Her lips parted, and his tongue brushed over hers. She tasted like the first fresh strawberry of the season, soft and ripe and unbearably sweet.

Her mittened hands grasped his shoulders and held tight. Her breasts pressed against him, and his hand came up to caress her softness, her warmth. A murmur of longing thrummed in her throat.

Daniel yanked himself to his senses. He wasn't Wilhelm, but a mercenary who had no call and no right to touch her innocence.

He pulled back. A slow, dreamy smile spread across her face. Daniel's stomach plunged. This was going to be worse than he thought.

"That was lovely," she whispered. "Simply lovely. I had no idea—"

"Lorelei, I'm sorry. I shouldn't have— It won't happen again. It's not like me to take advantage of young girls."

The misty glaze left her eyes. "It's not? Did that jar your memory? Do you remember who you are?"

If anything, he'd come close to forgetting himself altogether. He stood and helped her to her feet.

"Your arm," she said in dismay. Working carefully, she replaced it in the sling.

Lord, she was odd. "I didn't remember, Lorelei." His voice sounded thin and weary, and his knee throbbed.

"Then why did you pull away so quickly?" Her mouth gleamed with the sweet moisture he'd tasted.

He tore his gaze from the sight. "You and your guardians saved my life and healed my wounds. I'd be a bastard to return your hospitality by stealing your virtue."

She laughed and slapped her knee. "My virtue! I suppose I should thank you for saving me from—how does a lady put it?—surrendering to perdition."

Her amusement grated like iron filings over him. "You're a babe, Mademoiselle du Clerc. You understand nothing—"

"No, it's you who don't understand. Of course I have virtues, many of them. Children and dogs like me. I have cleanly habits, a whole list of virtues." Hurt flashed in her eyes. "True virtue is something no one—not even you—can take from me. Certainly not with a mere kiss!"

He held up his hand. "Enough, Lorelei. It's just a figure of speech. God, you *are* a babe."

"And you're a coward," she shot back. "You can't

even enjoy a perfectly lovely kiss." She snapped her fingers. "Unless you're married. Yes, you must be." Pivoting, she scrambled over the embankment and marched down toward the hospice.

Daniel followed more slowly, with plans churning in his mind and unexpected lust burning through him. Poor girl. Her life was a fairy tale. Surrounded by men of God and noble beasts, she lived an idyllic existence.

But he'd intruded upon her charmed world and brought to life a dark force that threatened to shatter her. Not for the first time he wished he were free to leave her alone, unspoiled by corruption, untouched by rivalry and hatred and fear.

But the game had been set in motion months ago, Daniel reflected grimly as he prowled the corridors of the hospice that night. He would have to search out every possibility. He needed to discover who knew the secret of Lorelei and who wanted him dead. He had no problem staying awake until everyone slept, for memories of kissing Lorelei played havoc with his emotions.

His shoulder bumped the rough stone wall. He'd reached a juncture in the corridor. To the right lay the office of Father Julian. To the left, silence shrouded the dormitory. Daniel turned right.

He wished fiercely that he could walk away from the whole affair.

But if he did, Lorelei would die by the hand of another hired killer.

One mistake could set off a chain of events that would rock the foundations of Bonaparte's ever-widening dynasty and lay waste to all hope for an independent Swiss nation.

It was incredible that a single person had the power to decide the fate of a nation.

But she did. Josephine Bonaparte did.

The very thought of the first consul's wife made his guts churn, for she owned Daniel's soul. She was privy to a secret so lethal that it hung like the blade of a guillotine over his neck.

One word from Josephine and the blade would fall.

He shivered, but not from the cold. The scent of old stone and uncured pine surrounded him. The texture of the wall abraded his questing fingers. He reached a thick wooden door with a curved lintel.

The prior's offices. Daniel tested the latch and found it locked. He paused to glance furtively down the hall, then fished in his pocket and found his penknife. Unlike his hunting knife and bow and arrows, this had been overlooked by Father Julian.

With well-practiced movements, Daniel inserted the small blade into the keyhole. The lock tumbled with a quiet click. He laid the flat of his hand on the ancient wood, opened the door, and stepped inside. He relocked the door and studied the room.

Daniel breathed a sigh of relief. A window let in a flood of grayish moonlight. He wouldn't need the candle he'd brought.

The room was as spare and neat as Father Julian himself. A massive pine writing desk, banked by locked drawers, dominated the furnishings. To one side stood a tall armoire, and on the other, beneath a crucifix, was a prie-dieu.

A footstep sounded in the corridor. Daniel froze, his eyes riveted to the door. Bobbing light and the shadows of someone's feet shone beneath the door. He melted into the gloom beside the armoire and flattened himself against the wall.

He heard a metallic click as someone pressed the latch. Then silence, punctuated by the pulse of blood in his ears. His hand tightened around the small knife.

The footsteps retreated. Daniel waited until his limbs ached with stiffness; then he opened the armoire.

Inside hung the prior's liturgical vestments, redolent with the scent of church incense. The smell reminded him so vividly of the attack that the hair on his neck stood on end.

He moved aside the vestments and discovered his hunting knife, bow, and arrows. No use taking them now. The disappearance of the weapons would only raise more questions.

He moved silently to the writing desk. The locks on the large drawers gave way easily to the blade of his penknife.

In a swift, methodical search, he shuffled through administrative papers, official and personal letters, ledgers, and inventories.

His hands like ice, Daniel examined the contents of each drawer. While searching the last, he heard a faint rattling hollowness. The drawer had a false bottom.

Fitting his blade under the edge, he pried up the thin, brittle wood and found a thick folio made of heavy, musty-smelling parchment. He carried it to the window and angled it toward the light. Written in the spidery script he'd come to recognize as Julian's was one word: *Lorelei*.

His fingers clutched convulsively around the folio. He opened it and knew immediately that he'd found more than official documents. This was a chronicle of Lorelei's life.

The first item was a childish drawing of a dog, its head huge and shaggy, its legs like sticks. Beneath that he found another drawing, this one more refined by perhaps a year or two. Again it showed a dog. A smiling human figure in a long black robe and round-brimmed hat stood nearby, and in the background the mountains were formed by inverted *V*'s. At the bottom was a scrawled inscription: "To Fr. Julian I love you."

Daniel had no experience with children. Until this moment he'd had no idea how powerful a child's simple, sincere declaration could be. Plagued by a strange, choking sensation, he couldn't swallow. He conquered the sentiment and leafed through the rest of the papers. There were sketches of plants and forest animals, a tracing of a little hand, a prayer copied from a missal, a poem or two. He discovered a note on brittle foolscap, written in large, childish letters: "I'm sory I wandered off and got lost. I'll never leave you again Fr. Julian."

Folded carefully in a piece of tissue, Daniel found a tiny tooth and a lock of chestnut hair. More recent items included an essay on Aquinas and one on Roger Bacon, and a paper concerning the Swiss nation. In this Lorelei praised the cantons where men through centuries had counted liberty more precious than life.

God. What would she think if she knew that the life

of Jean Meuron, who could check Bonaparte's plundering hand, depended on her death, for only when Lorelei was dead would Josephine authorize the release of Meuron.

An ache rose inside Daniel as he regarded the milestones of her innocent, untroubled past. The ache crescendoed to a throb when he contemplated what the future held for her.

From the bottom of the folio, a page slipped to the floor. Tensing inside, Daniel picked it up. The paper had yellowed, and the ink had faded to brown.

"My God," Daniel whispered, straining to read in the silvery dimness. He'd found a receipt: "A treasure of the realm, valued at half a million francs, to be held in trust for one Lorelei du Clerc . . ." It was signed by Louis Philippe de Bourbon, king of France. Two people had witnessed the document: the abbess of the convent and Julian Durand, canon regular of Saint Bernard.

Slowly Daniel put away the papers. So that was it. Treasure. Greed. At last he'd found a motive, a meaning for Julian's protectiveness.

His thoughts leaped ahead. Half a million francs. That amount in gold would be difficult to conceal. Unless the treasure was not in gold. Jewels, perhaps. Marie Antoinette had possessed so many that there were some she'd never worn.

Despite the revelation, dissatisfaction nagged at Daniel. Julian and the others lived in simple poverty. He'd seen no evidence of riches here. And Father Julian kept careful records and unexpected mementos. He loved Lorelei deeply.

But that didn't surprise Daniel. Only a man with a heart of steel could resist her clear-eyed innocence, her insouciant charm, her lively intelligence.

Thank God Daniel Severin had a heart of steel.

After returning the items he'd taken from the desk, he flipped through a large calfskin volume filled with Father Julian's writing. A light glimmered in his head.

He'd found a log of every visitor to the hospice in the past two years. Hands shaking, he turned back to the previous summer and scanned the entries that had been made after the typhus outbreak. One entry, dated 10 fructidor, made his blood run cold. An unidentified man had drowned in Lake Saint Bernard. "God keep his soul," Julian had written beside the entry.

Swiftly Daniel set the desk to rights and left the office. As fast as his flaming knee would allow, he hurried across the hospice yard toward a low, squat building of rough stone. A dog barked once, then quieted.

The building stood on the eastern shore of the lake. Gloomy shadows from a beetling cliff hung over it. Daniel opened the door, stepped inside, and hesitated. The barred windows kept wolves and bears away, but they were no proof against the icy wind that sliced, whistling mournfully, through them.

Daniel fumbled with flint and steel. It took a full five minutes to light his candle. He set it in a cobwebby corner shielded from the biting wind. The smell of dust and dry cold swirled through the small chamber. Drawing a deep breath, he turned to regard the eternal sleepers of the hospice morgue.

Several shrouded bodies lay side by side. They were travelers who had perished and now waited here, preserved by the everlasting cold, for relatives to claim them. The eerieness of it wrapped around Daniel. He glanced longingly at the door, wanting to bolt free of the spectral chapel.

He forced himself to lift the shrouds, one by one. "My God," he muttered, staring at a man's face. It was so full of life that the man appeared only to be sleeping.

It was the third face that Daniel recognized.

Henri Junot. He lay in motionless repose, this man who had once been a glittering ornament of Directory society. Now the devil kept his soul, for in life he'd belonged, like Daniel, to a dark, unyielding force.

Shaking, Daniel left the morgue. Junot had come to the hospice for the same purpose as Daniel. Junot had died.

The next evening Everard took a late supper by the fireside in the chapter house. Most of the canons and novices were present and waiting eagerly for news from beyond the mountain. His leg propped on a gout stool, Daniel sat beside Lorelei.

"It's good to see you at your needlework again," Father Gaston commented. "What are you making, *chouette?*"

"A surplice for Father Julian." Flushing, she avoided Daniel's eyes and concentrated on her embroidery. Daniel could tell, by her unaccustomed silence and by her dogged effort with the needle, that she felt awkward about the day before. He, too, found himself thinking of their kiss. Much more than was healthy, certainly more than he allowed himself to think of the chilling picture of Junot in the morgue.

He wanted to tear the fabric from her hands, to forbid her to transform herself into a lady for him. He wasn't worth it. She should save her dreamy-eyed looks for some other man. He had no idea what to do with a girl like Lorelei. He had no more place in his life for her than a raven had for a songbird.

He wondered if she realized what an incongruous picture she made, clad in her mountain clothes, one foot tucked under her and the tip of her tongue poking between her lips as she concentrated on her stitches. He remembered the damp satiny feel of her lips beneath his. Equal doses of lust and guilt drove through him.

He turned his attention to the visitor, who was making short work of Mauricio's *roesti* potatoes and salt-cured beef. Everard wore the traditional Swiss *bredzon* vest, the sleeves puffed, the lapels emblazoned with five-pointed stars. His breeches were patched with leather at the knees, and his sturdy boots bore scuff marks from miles of Alpine trails. He had the thick shoulders and thighs typical of mountaineers, and he guzzled beer as if it were water.

"Let me tell you about this Bonaparte," said Everard, wiping his mouth on his sleeve. "His captains in Lausanne say he'll drive the Austrians out of Italy."

"How will he do it?" asked Sylvain. The novice rested his lanky wrists on his knees and sat forward.

Everard pulled a stick from the hearth and stabbed the flame out. "Bonaparte's going to attack with three armies. Here are the Austrians in Germany." He made an X on the hearthstones. "The Army of the Rhine will act as flank guard. Here's Masséna's Army of Italy."

"The Austrians outnumber them and are forcing them toward the citadel of Genoa," Father Julian offered.

Daniel wondered uncomfortably where the prior came by his information. He found himself thinking of the two furtive figures meeting outside the infirmary window.

"Not for long," Everard replied. "The Army of Reserve will march south—right through the Great Pass, mind—and come up on the Austrians' asses." Everard snapped his fingers. "Just like that—a surprise attack."

Lorelei looked up from her needlework. "You make it sound so simple."

"Yes," said Father Emile. "To move an army and artillery through the Alps poses an immense risk."

"If the monarchy were secure," Father Gaston grumbled, "this problem wouldn't exist."

"Monarchy, bah," said Father Emile. "This is a conquest of the people."

The man obviously didn't understand Bonaparte, thought Daniel.

Everard took a gulp of beer. "Has Bonaparte ever failed?"

"He failed to get a son on his wife," said Sylvain, elbowing Timon in the ribs.

"Mind your tongue, boy," Father Julian snapped. The sound of barking dogs drifted from the kennels.

"The Lord is never on the side of a dictator," said Gaston.

"Bonaparte's no dictator," said Father Emile. "He's—"

The door burst open. In rushed a dragoon trooper and a soldier wearing a messenger's cuff.

Burning with an impulse to flee, to hide, Daniel clutched the seat of his chair.

Dirt and ashes smeared the dragoon's green coat. His eyes were round with urgency.

Father Julian approached them. "Welcome to Saint Bernard's."

The messenger's gaze flicked to the prior's chain of office. He nudged his companion. Carbines and sabers clanked as they bowed awkwardly.

"We need a bed for the night," said the dragoon. "And shelter for our horses."

Sylvain and Timon hurried outside. The dragoon swayed, grabbing the back of a chair. Blood seeped through his sleeve.

Lorelei leaped up. The needlework dropped as she rushed to the soldiers. "You're hurt! Come by the fire, and I'll fetch some bandages from the infirmary."

"Where are you from?" asked Father Julian.

"Army of Italy." The messenger accepted a cup of strong tea. Lorelei returned and set to work on his companion's arm. She'd handled needlework clumsily, but with living flesh she worked with infinite delicacy.

"What's happened?" asked Father Emile.

"April the fifth," said the trooper. "The Austrians split us in two." He winced as Lorelei began cleansing the gash in his arm. "We took the brunt of the attack. Masséna took his forces to Genoa. The rest have been driven beyond the river Var."

The messenger swallowed his tea noisily and looked as if he craved something stronger. "The two of us managed to break through a column of Austrian lancers and make for the highlands."

"A saber wound?" she murmured to the dragoon.

He nodded grimly.

"We've got to get the news to General Lannes in Lucerne," said the messenger. "Masséna needs the Army of Reserve *now*, or his troops will starve in Genoa."

Daniel realized that time was running out. The war and the risk of discovery were coming at him from all sides. He had to get Lorelei away from here.

His first plan was to end the game of cat and mouse. Wilhelm Tell would pass back into legend where he belonged.

It was time for the Raven to take flight.

# Chapter 6

High mass dragged as slowly as the spring melt on the mountains. Lorelei fidgeted, her restless gaze darting from the carved wooden pulpit to the scene of Saint Bernard fashioned in colored glass behind the altar.

She longed to be away, to find Wilhelm. The treatise was finished. They would send it to Coppet with Everard today.

Her hands clasped together convulsively. She despised the smallest deception, even by omission. But the lure of her goal tugged at her. Wilhelm said her pursuit hurt no one. All mankind stood to gain if her theory helped conquer a deadly disease. As to the kiss they'd shared, Lorelei told herself that the moment belonged to the secret woman inside her and was not to be shared with the clerics, who would never understand.

A chanted prayer rose from the canons. Father Emile, the sacristan, lifted a battered monstrance. Sunbeams from the high windows danced over the paste jewels set into the large vessel.

The service ended with a song. Lorelei rose and turned toward the back of the chapel.

His face and body painted by colored light streaming through the window, Wilhelm stood at the rear of the nave.

A jolt of pure desire struck Lorelei. Each day her awakening passion for the stranger grew stronger. The very sight of him rippled like a caress over sensitive flesh.

She started forward to greet him, but something in his stance and expression stopped her. Though he leaned on his crutch, he gave the impression of holding himself erect. Even in the soft jewel tones of the filtered light, his features appeared hard, unapproachable. Yet in his eyes she recognized unconquerable pain.

"My friends," he said in a flat, quiet voice that drew the attention of every man present, "your care and patience have healed me. I've regained my memory."

The news sent Lorelei running to his side. "You remember! Oh, Wilhelm—"

"Not Wilhelm." With a gaze as clear and cold as a winter sky, he took in the canons and novices pressing around to hear. "Daniel. My name is Daniel Severin."

No, thought Lorelei, unaccountably alarmed. You're Wilhelm. My Wilhelm.

"Daniel Severin," whispered one of the monks.

Lorelei stared. His image seemed to shatter before her eyes, then reassemble into a wholly new vision.

Daniel Severin. The sonorous name was as darkly enchanting as the man himself.

"At last the mystery is revealed." Father Julian's voice cut through the murmurs. "I confess, it was oddly unsettling to have a man wandering memoryless about the hospice. Come to breakfast and tell us about yourself."

Lorelei touched Daniel's good arm. The muscles beneath her fingers tensed. "We mustn't press him, Father Julian."

"I'm fine," Daniel said in a clipped voice, his eyes fixed on the prior.

The large, excited group started toward the refectory. The morning sun streamed over the valley and glinted off the lake. Clear, needle-sharp air stabbed into Lorelei's chest.

Daniel Severin walked with an even gait, although she knew his knee must pain him.

"What happened?" she asked. "Did the soldiers who came last night recognize you? Did your memories come to you in a rush?"

"I'm afraid it was nothing so dramatic. I simply woke up this morning knowing fully who I am."

"You don't sound terribly elated."

His lips curled in an ironic smile. "Perhaps I was taken in by your tales of exiled nobles and royal adventurers. It was a bit of a disappointment to discover I'm just an ordinary man."

He spoke so smoothly, so easily, she thought. As if his remarkable recovery meant little to him.

"Indeed," said Father Julian, who walked at Daniel's other side. "All the same, we're eager to hear what brought you to us." A chill glazed his pale eyes. "A man doesn't brave the Great Pass in March without a compelling reason."

At breakfast, Daniel related his story between bites of sausage and hard cheese. He wasn't sure why he felt so nervous; lying had been second nature to him for years. "I was traveling to Bern," he said.

"You have business there?" asked the prior.

"Yes. On behalf of Jean Meuron." He stopped, rested his palms on the table, and watched his listeners. To a man, each showed dawning recognition of the well-known name. Familiar envy stabbed at Daniel. Hidden deep inside him was a man who yearned to inspire even a fraction of the admiration the Swiss showered on Meuron.

"Are you a patriot, too?" asked Father Droz.

It was a question Daniel had often pondered, and he'd never been able to answer it. Instead, he said, "Meuron's being held in a Paris prison."

Outraged murmurs erupted down the length of the table. "Dear God," asked Lorelei. "Why?"

"He's been accused of stealing from the Bern treasury—gold that Bonaparte was transporting to Paris to finance his campaign."

"So," snapped Father Clivaz, "Bonaparte is spending Swiss gold on his conquests."

"What will he do next," Father Anselme demanded, scowling, "force his policies on the sovereign cantons of Switzerland?"

"Please God, no," said Lorelei fervently. "No true Swiss can abide foreign rule."

Daniel studied the bright flare of outrage in her cheeks. Her face glowed with compelling intensity. If her father had possessed a tenth of her will, he'd have triumphed over the Paris mobs.

The canons all began speaking at once. "Meuron is a man of honor." "He merely took back what rightfully belongs to Switzerland." "He's a patriot, not a thief."

Daniel held up his hand. "He stands accused of both theft and treason. The irony of it is, he's innocent."

Father Clivaz reached across the table and clasped Daniel's hand. "And you've come to clear his name."

"If I can," said Daniel, discomfited by the firm handclasp. The idea had occurred to him only the night before. He had little hope of success, for the evidence against Meuron was strong; a cache of gold had been found in his town house. *Damn you, Jean*, he thought for the thousandth time.

"We shall do everything we can to help," Father Droz vowed.

"Thank you," said Daniel. *But I'll be long gone.*

"Now," said Father Julian, his regard still skeptical, "continue your story, monsieur. We should like to know about the man who has braved peril for the sake of Meuron."

"I was born in Lausanne and orphaned shortly afterward."

"Oh, Daniel," said Lorelei, feeling a knot of sympathy in her throat. For some reason, she'd envisioned him as having a huge, loud family who yelled at one another constantly and loved one another fiercely. "What became of your parents?"

"My mother was a Romany horse thief, and not a very good one. By the time I was three, she'd been caught and hanged."

She watched incredulously as he sipped his coffee. He spoke with no more feeling than a man relating grain figures.

Daniel felt her wide brown eyes on him, but kept his attention on the men at the table. A practiced mercenary, he sought the subtle quick breath, the nervous blink, the too-tight grip on a utensil that would reveal the man who had tried to kill him. But so far even the smallest nuance had eluded him.

Sylvain shook the hair out of his eyes and nodded almost imperceptibly to another novice as if to say, I suspected he was of bad stock.

"And your father?" asked Lorelei.

"I don't know who he was," said Daniel. But he knew, all right. Trouble was, so did Josephine Bonaparte. "I grew up in the asylum at Saint Gall. They gave me an education and not much else."

"You're an orphan, like me," Lorelei whispered. "Oh, Wil—Daniel."

He forced himself to laugh. "Don't waste your pity on me. I was incorrigible and deserved every caning I got."

"No child should be made to suffer," she insisted passionately. "It's not fair. I was surrounded by men who love me, while harsh masters were caning an innocent boy."

He'd lost his innocence at so young an age that he couldn't remember ever having had it, but he let her comment pass.

"Have you any family?" asked Father Julian. "Brothers or sisters?"

"No," Daniel stated. "I do not." It was almost true. "When I was fifteen," he continued, "I was bound to an artisan—a fletcher."

"To an artisan?" Father Julian asked. "That's unlikely, considering your education."

"I was being groomed for the seminary," said Daniel. "Trouble was, I had no vocation, and my tutors finally gave up hoping I'd find one. My new master wasn't the least impressed by my scholarship, but he trained me in fletching and archery."

"Are you a fair shot?" asked Sylvain. Like every good Swiss, the youth had undergone the time-honored training in archery.

"I was before this." Ruefully Daniel indicated his splinted arm.

"Did you wish to become a master fletcher yourself?"

"No. My master was a superior teacher of archery, but I didn't care much for his manners."

Lorelei flinched, for somehow she knew Daniel would hide the worst of his life. She imagined him as a youth, skinny and not yet grown into his lanky form. Dear Lord, what hurts had he suffered? Did that account for the torment haunting his eyes?

"I left of my own accord." Unease prickled at Daniel. "I ran away," he amended, "lied about my age, and joined the Swiss Guard of King Louis of France. I made the rank of captain."

"Were you at the Tuileries in '92?" Father Gaston asked.

"Yes," said Daniel. Unwanted memories, slick with gore and stinking of death, leaped into his mind. "I was in the massacre." He could barely force the admission past a tongue suddenly thickened by horror and guilt.

Silence blanketed the refectory. Several people, including Lorelei, made the sign of the cross.

"I remember the day we heard," she said. "I was just twelve and paid little attention to news from beyond the mountains." She pushed her plate away as if the food had grown distasteful. "But I remember that Everard's father brought the broadsheets, and Father Julian called us to the chapel to read the news aloud." She shuddered, recalling the prior's harsh voice and the helpless rage that had risen in her. "We sat vigil for days. All those Swiss, murdered . . ."

"Nearly eight hundred of us," said Daniel. "In an ancient palace, at the hands of a mob summoned by the tocsins." God, his ears still throbbed with the sound of bells and drumbeats.

"But you survived," said Sylvain, his tone skeptical and faintly hostile. "What happened?"

"I did not desert," Daniel stated, his gaze piercing Sylvain.

Daniel touched the scar leading to his white lock. Like cold lightning, images flashed through his mind: the doddering *chevaliers du poignard* vowing to defend the Crown with their useless ceremonial swords, the irresolute king and his terrified wife frantically concealing their state jewels and their children, the Swiss Guards forced to stand like a wall, awaiting orders that came too late. And finally the hellish roar of the crowd shouting *'Vive la nation, à bas les Suisses!'* until Daniel's nerves had shredded like old hemp.

His voice brittle as ice, he said with complete conviction, "Believe me, my friend, I would rather have died."

"Daniel," said Lorelei, "you mustn't talk like—"

"Hush, let him speak," Father Emile cut in. "It was an important day for the Republic."

"You were there?" asked Daniel sharply.

Emile's full, smooth lips bowed into a smile. "Yes. I do not condone the slaughter of the Swiss, mind you, but the cause of liberty had to be served."

The righteous cruelty in Emile's eyes was familiar. Daniel had seen it a thousand times. Remembered horror surrounded him, and he couldn't beat it back. A forest of pikes and cutlasses had poured through the gates of the Tuileries and spilled across the courtyard. His throat had ached from bellowing at his men to maintain battle position.

"How was it that so many died?" Father Anselme asked. Beneath his nimbus of white hair, his face was pale.

Daniel struggled to conquer his emotions, for if he didn't, he'd never see his plan through. "We took a stand at the foot of the grand staircase. At first our martial bearing daunted the mob." His head throbbed, and he pinched the bridge of his nose. "We wore red livery braided in gold. Our muskets and swords gave the rioters a scare."

"Frightened men are often the most dangerous," said Father Julian.

Daniel looked at the prior sharply. He wondered if Junot had been a frightened man. "A few patriots promised us mercy, swore we'd be granted clemency if we laid down our arms."

"No one would have thought ill of you if you had," said Father Droz.

"We refused," Daniel said simply, loath to elaborate. *"We are Swiss,"* he'd screamed at the mob. He'd been young then, stupid enough to sacrifice lives for honor. *"The Swiss lay down their arms only with their lives."*

And so they did. A chill passed over Daniel. Halberds had hooked into Swiss men's chests, dragging them into the heart of the blood-crazed crowd. Daniel's pistol had come up, the curved trigger cold in the crook of his finger. A rioter's face blossomed crimson. Daniel had led a sortie, reclaimed the cannon, and retaken the gate. Chased by Swiss musket balls, the mob had surged back to the safety of the streets.

Daniel put his coffee mug to his lips and swallowed with difficulty. God. How long had he savored the sweetness of victory? Only moments, probably. He couldn't remember. The ensuing horror had blotted out all notion of time.

"We managed to turn back the riot," he said. "We were headed for the Riding School, an area of the palace still infested with rioters."

"The Swiss had everything under control. So what

the devil happened?" Sylvain demanded. His breakfast forgotten, he balanced on the edge of the bench.

Daniel glanced at Lorelei and let a terrible smile curve his lips. "King Louis the Sixteenth sent us our death warrant."

Your father, princess, he thought, sick with remembered rage.

"That's a lie," stated Father Gaston, his face florid, his features stubbornly set. "The king didn't want brave men to perish."

"Then he should have left us to do our job. But instead he ordered us to lay down our arms and retire to the barracks." Daniel's insides twisted as he recalled the humiliating retreat through the palace gardens. There the National Guardsmen fired on them at point-blank range. The Swiss who survived the retreat and reached the barracks met the shrieking mob. Not content with simple murder, the rioters hacked off limbs, stripped bodies naked, threw screaming men from high windows.

Lorelei touched his sleeve. Caught up in the nightmare, Daniel jerked his arm away.

"Please, you mustn't distress yourself," she said. "It's not—"

"Let him continue," Father Julian snapped.

"Less than two hundred of us reached the barracks. Some escaped by the Cour de Marsan and the Rue de l'Echelle."

"Were you among them?" asked Father Emile.

"No. There was fighting in the kitchens." Still Daniel heard the hoarse screams of the under cooks and scullions pleading for their lives. "I went to see if I could help." He stared down at a knot in the table. "I couldn't." His hands began to shake. "Is there some wine . . . ?"

Someone handed him a mug of rough monastery wine. He drained it quickly, willing the liquid to chase the demons from his head.

"I tried. . . ." Daniel wiped his sleeve across his mouth and held out his mug for more wine. "Any fool would have run for his life, but I . . ."

"What did you do, Daniel?" Lorelei asked softly.

A hiss of rage had risen in his ears. Like points of fire, an image of ruby earrings flashed in his mind. Hard little red eyes glaring from the ears of a monster. A piratical grin on his face, Chrétien Rubis had stood his ground beside a charred arm protruding from a brazier.

"I had an idiotic notion of avenging my comrades. I sent the rioters scattering," said Daniel. All but one. Rubis had a sword he'd torn from a chevalier, and he knew how to use it. The fight had been swift and brutal. Daniel remembered the stink of his own sweat mingling with the scent of blood and burning flesh, the tingling exhaustion creeping over him as he fought, the foolish parry, a reply, a blade slicing into his head.

"I was wounded and left for dead," he continued. "By the time someone discovered otherwise, the royal family had been chased to a press box in the Assembly. The mob's thirst for blood had been slaked. The members of the Commune imprisoned me at the Carmes."

"The Carmes," repeated Father Gaston, helping himself to the wine.

"What place is that?" asked Sylvain.

"It used to house the Carmelites, but it later became a tomb for some of France's noblest men and women," said Father Gaston. "I went there once, after the September Massacre. It was dark, dank, the walls dripping with moisture and smeared with noble blood. I remember stepping over the open latrine that ran down the middle of a corridor. Still I smell it. I had gone to pray with Madame d'Aiguillon." Tears started in Father Gaston's eyes. "But I could not pray. The rats and cockroaches and filth crawled over my robes, and I could not pray in that hideous place."

"Oh, Father," said Lorelei.

He waved off her sympathy and looked at Daniel. "How did you escape?"

Daniel didn't allow himself to be moved by the canon's emotion. Gaston knew the truth about Lorelei. He was obviously a Royalist. If, somehow, he'd guessed Daniel's mission, he could be the one who'd tried to smother Daniel. But would he kill to protect a bastard, a stain on the royal house of France?

"My execution should have taken place quickly," he said, "but somehow two years passed. Then one day I went free."

How simple it sounded to say it that way.

Lorelei clasped her hands. "Thank God. You were found innocent of any wrongdoing, then."

"Innocent?" He spat the word like an obscenity. "No, Lorelei. I simply made an influential friend."

"And who was that?"

"A fellow prisoner. Her name was Marie Josèphe Rose, vicomtesse de Beauharnais." He forced out the hated name.

"I've never heard of her," said Sylvain.

Daniel searched the group. He saw only avid curiosity—some feigned, some genuine. "She doesn't go by that name anymore. All Europe knows her as Josephine Bonaparte, wife of the first consul of France."

"Extraordinary," said Father Emile, his eyes narrow with interest.

"Is she as beautiful as they say?" asked one of the novices.

Daniel had once made the mistake of thinking her as beautiful as a goddess. Too late, he'd discovered that she was a serpent, a creature without conscience.

"She's a Creole," he said, "born in the West Indies on Martinique. And no, she's not beautiful." Daniel made a steeple of his hands. Only Lorelei was close enough to see how hard his fingers pressed against one another. "But she wears the illusion of beauty as other women wear perfume. An aura hovers around her and works on men like a drug."

"You know her well, then?" asked Father Julian.

An interesting question. Daniel ignored it.

Lorelei felt a vague stirring of dismay. How tedious he must find her compared to the incomparable Josephine. Vividly she recalled their kiss, and shame crept over her. He'd kissed her when he had no recollection of his past, no other women to compare Lorelei to. Once he had a chance to think about it, Daniel Severin would be appalled by Wilhelm's attraction to an unkempt mountain girl.

"I've always admired Madame Bonaparte," said Father Gaston. "She's dedicated to bringing exiled nobles back to their rightful positions in France."

"You admire a whore," stated Father Emile, his bluntness eliciting a gasp from the others. "The reason she's devoted to the French nobles should be clear, even to your thick head. She slept with most of them."

"That's a lie!" Father Gaston shouted.

Lorelei glanced at Father Julian. His mouth formed a grim line of displeasure, but he said nothing.

"It's the truth to any thinking man," Father Emile returned. "She's the topic of more published diaries and letters than Marie Antoinette ever was."

"Perhaps she's been indiscreet," Father Gaston conceded. "But she understands the divine necessity of restoring the Catholic kings to the throne of France."

"She'll need a miracle." Father Emile snorted and downed a tankard of small beer. "The blue blood was flushed out of the veins of France years ago."

"If anyone can restore it, Bonaparte and his wife can," said Gaston. "And they will."

Lorelei glanced at Daniel. Like a spectator at an archery match, he looked from Emile to Gaston. His skin had drained to white, and sweat ran down the sides of his face.

"You're unwell," she whispered, touching his shoulder. "Let me take you to the infirmary."

"I'll go with you," said Sylvain, shoving away from the table.

The refectory door swung open and three men walked in.

"Who are they?" asked Daniel urgently.

"Military contractors," Lorelei whispered. "I can tell. We've seen them before. They always have those sleek, greedy eyes and think they own the world."

Father Julian went to greet them. They spoke in low tones; then the prior returned to the table. "These gentlemen have brought a shipment of ordnance for the Army of Reserve. I'll need all able-bodied men to build shelters for storing it." Men rose from the tables and dispersed. The prior turned to Father Anselme. "You'll help Lorelei with Monsieur Severin."

As she made her way to the infirmary with Father Anselme and Daniel, Lorelei glanced without interest at the long mule-drawn sledges laden with barrels of gunpowder. Somehow the war still seemed distant, especially today.

Even the story of Daniel's troubled past hadn't made her completely forget her plans. Today was the day she would post her treatise to Coppet.

As they passed the kennels, she stopped at the yard gate to pet the dogs clamoring for her attention.

"Father Droz," she shouted over the yelps and whines of the frenzied pack. "Tell Everard I must see him before he leaves."

"Everard's gone," the kennel master yelled back. "Left at sunrise with the soldiers. Probably won't be back for weeks."

"Gone!" Lorelei's hands flew to her cheeks. A hot mist seared her eyes. To wait for weeks . . .

She sent an agonized glance at Daniel, but he was deep in conversation with Father Anselme, oblivious to her disappointment. Unnoticed, she lingered at the kennels, then fled toward the high meadows. An aching, depthless sense of loss gnawed at her. Yesterday "Wilhelm" had been her friend, her confidant. But Daniel Severin was a cold, unreachable stranger.

* * *

His lap covered by a thick shawl and his hands holding a book, Father Anselme took a maddeningly long time to fall asleep. Daniel yearned to go after Lorelei, to explain, but he wanted to do so privately. The sun was creeping toward noon by the time the old man had settled into a deep, snoring sleep.

At the kennels, Daniel won permission from Father Droz to take Barry afield. He'd wanted to take Belle, too, but Father Droz shook his head. "Too close to her time," he explained. "She'll be having those pups any day now." Father Droz laid his hand on Daniel's shoulder. "I'm glad you figured out who you are, Monsieur Severin."

"Daniel. It's Daniel." He felt sick for using Meuron's name to manipulate the canons.

Father Droz pointed to the yard, where men were erecting canvas shelters for the ordnance. "Keep him away from that gunpowder, Daniel. I don't trust the stuff."

Barry burst past the gate. Head lowered, he ranged across the hard-packed yard, cocking a leg at the hitching post outside the main building.

Once they were out of view of the hospice, Daniel whistled to summon the dog. "Lorelei," he said, hoping the young mastiff's training was adequate. *"Allons-y."*

Barry yelped and bounded off toward the slope of Mont Vélan. Though his knee protested sharply, Daniel followed.

As the dog led him through pine groves and over rocks, Daniel shot a wary glance over his shoulder. He hoped he'd revealed enough about himself to draw out the killer.

Much of what he'd told the canons was true—the awful remembrances, the theft of the Bern gold, Meuron's dilemma. He felt guilty for misleading them about his own role, but the deception was necessary.

Tension needled his shoulders as he recalled the questions about Josephine. Had anyone noticed, he wondered, that he nearly choked on his answers?

*Is she as beautiful as they say?*

The memories dredged up by the question tore at him, and he found himself wishing sincerely that his amnesia was real.

He could have told them much more about her. He could have told them that Josephine Bonaparte made the whores of Saint Denis look like schoolgirls in cotton socks.

God, he hated her.

Hated her with a passion that heated his blood and sucked at his reason. Hated her with the burning resentment of a slave for his master.

Hated her because she owned his soul.

The thought gripped him so completely that he nearly missed seeing Lorelei. Barry had taken him up along a streambed. The dog had already found her and lay at her side.

Daniel stopped walking and brushed a pine bough out of his line of vision. He needed a moment to collect his thoughts, to scrub his mind clean of Josephine before speaking to Lorelei.

She sat near a pool fed by a spring leaping over a rockfall. New-leafed trees and tender spring grass surrounded her. She held her knees drawn up to her chest and rocked back and forth in a curious self-comforting motion. Errant sunbeams fell over her, lending radiance to her cropped hair, igniting garnet-colored highlights in the curls.

She looked small and vulnerable, and the urge to protect her rose from the wasteland of Daniel's heart. Willfully he crushed the urge. He was no knight in shining armor, but an assassin who'd stayed in the game too long.

Still, a wholly new and unwelcome thought occurred to him. How had he ever thought he could take her life? It was like looking down a tunnel and seeing the ugliness he'd left behind.

Uncomfortable with the change in himself, he walked to her and sat down. The smell of loam and new grass surrounded them. Stubbornly she continued staring at the pool. For the first time she gave no welcoming smile, no chirrup of greeting.

He missed her warmth.

He thought about laying his hand on her shoulder, but stopped himself. Spontaneous gestures of friendship belonged to people like Lorelei—good people who didn't have the death of their comrades weighing on their conscience.

Which reminded him of Junot. How could he get her to speak of him without rousing her suspicions?

"I wish you hadn't run off," he said. "You'd have spared me a long hike."

"You didn't have to come," she snapped, turning toward him. Redness rimmed her fierce, angry eyes. "I know I'm being a baby about this. But I wanted to send my treatise today." Her speech came out in a rush, like wine poured from a bottle that had sat too long. "Now I'll have to wait for weeks, and you'll be gone by then. Alone, I might lose my nerve. I already have. Lord, what arrogance to think I have something substantive to say to—"

"I sent the treatise with Everard."

"—learned scholars who make it their life's work to—"

"Lorelei, I sent it."

"—listen to some girl's half-baked ideas—"

He touched her at last, and not gently. He took her by the shoulders and gave her a firm shake. Deep inside himself he knew it wasn't the treatise but his revelation today that accounted for her mood. Still, the treatise was a safer subject. "Damn it, girl, will you listen to me?"

She blinked in surprise. "You don't have to resort to violence."

He removed his hand. "At least I got your attention. Now, if you'll kindly listen—"

"Of course, Daniel." As quickly as the black mood had come upon her, it vanished.

"—without interrupting—"

"Sorry."

Exasperated, he enunciated each word with exaggerated clarity. "I sent your treatise with Everard this morning."

Her eyes grew big as pansies in full bloom. "You did?"

"Just before prayers. I found him as he was leaving.

Your paper's on its way to Coppet, Lorelei. I wouldn't be surprised if the baron awards it the Necker Prize."

She folded her hands into fists and pounded the ground. "You fool! Daniel, how could you? Now all the world will know what an idiot I am!"

"By God, is there no pleasing you, woman? First you run off and sulk because you think you missed your chance to send the paper. Now you curse me for a fool because I did exactly that."

Suddenly she was laughing, clutching her sides and rocking to and fro. Before Daniel could denounce her for a madwoman, she gave a squeal of delight and flung herself on him.

The impact sent them both sprawling, and then she was on top of him, laughing and covering his face with kisses. His body bolted to life with the shock of her sudden, sweet assault. The touch of her mouth was as soft as a butterfly's wing; her slight weight on his chest covered him like a satin blanket. He found himself responding to her pure, untutored affection. Slowly his arms came around her and he drew her close.

"Hush, be still," he whispered, his breath fanning her cheek. "You squirm like a puppy."

And then, in defiance of the vow he'd made the last time he'd held her in his arms, he kissed her—a long, heartfelt kiss with no other purpose than to taste her innocence, her affection. Her mouth blossomed beneath his like a bud in sunshine. She made a sound of pure delight in her throat. Her clever little hands caressed his neck, his chest, his—

"Lorelei!" He held her away from him.

She gave him a slightly dazed grin. "Yes?"

"We can't do this."

"We can't?" Bewildered, she sat back on her heels.

"No. I thought I explained all that—the last time."

"You did. But you forgot."

"I forgot?" he said scathingly. "You all but assaulted me."

Lorelei drew an uneven sigh and looked away to hide her disappointment. It wasn't fair. He brought her to the brink of passion, then shoved her back just as she was on the verge of discovering something mysterious and important.

"I'm sorry," she said simply. She studied his handsome, expressionless face. Daniel Severin. He'd known Josephine Bonaparte and no doubt dozens of other beautiful women. And now he remembered. He must be repulsed by an ill-mannered girl pawing at him.

"I suppose I should thank you." She started to reach for his hand, then stopped herself. "It was kind of you. I didn't expect you to remember my treatise in the excitement of recovering your memory."

"My memories," he said with grim amusement, "are morbid, not exciting."

She sighed again, and unexpected sadness stabbed at her.

"Why the long face?" he asked.

"I'm not sure. It's just that, when we were working on the treatise, each day was an event to look forward to. Now that it's over, I'm not sure what I'll do with myself."

"Write another paper."

She snorted. "On what? Lancing boils?"

He thought a moment. "What about that instrument you used to listen to my heart?"

"Oh, that." She shrugged. "It's probably common as edelweiss. Any tinker could devise one. Besides, you're healing. You'll leave soon, and the work won't seem the same without you."

She didn't know, until he touched her face, that tears were streaming down her cheeks.

"Don't, Lorelei," he whispered.

"Oh, Lord," she said in self-disgust. "Look at me." She dragged her sleeve across her face, rubbing it under her nose for good measure. "I once read," she said shakily, "that Josephine's tears could influence Bonaparte more surely than the entire Assembly of Five Hundred. But I'm certain she weeps very daintily, not all mottle-faced and snorting like me."

"You're nothing like Josephine," he said. He seemed in a hurry to make the distinction.

She could tell that her tears made him uncomfortable. He was the same man she'd known these weeks—but with an important difference. He knew who he was.

"Oh, Daniel. You must despise me."

"For God's sake, what gave you that idea? I don't despise you."

"You should."

"And why is that, professor?"

"Because I'm so selfish." She plucked a blade of grass and peeled it into strips. "When you were Wilhelm, you belonged wholly to me. You had no claims from the past, no memory. *I* was your past." She threw aside the blade of grass. "But now that you've remembered, I've lost you."

"Lorelei—"

"That's silly, isn't it? To think I've lost you when I never actually had you. I just had a moment of your life. And now it's over. You're Daniel again. You're the man you were before me. You probably have a sweetheart somewhere."

"You're wrong, Lorelei. I never—"

Barry barked and lumbered to his feet. Tail waving, he stared intently across the pool, into the shadows of the woods.

"Who is it?" Daniel asked, his voice taut. His hand strayed to his side as if groping for a weapon.

Lorelei patted Barry. "You're so suspicious. It's probably a rabbit or a chamois."

Barry whined and pawed the ground, but stayed at Lorelei's side. "We should be getting back." Daniel pulled her to her feet. "Father Anselme will be waking from his nap."

The note of urgency in his voice puzzled her. His eyes were watchful, moving to and fro. Lorelei observed the way he used his injured arm to grasp at handholds on the rough, steep descent to the hospice. His arm, like everything else, was healing. It was time to remove the splint.

It was time to draw the killer out. That evening as he lay on his cot and watched the light waning in the infirmary window, Daniel hoped he'd made his adversary sufficiently nervous. The next attack would come soon. Tonight, perhaps, after dark.

Who would it be? Father Gaston, still faithful to the royal house of France? Father Emile, whose eyes at breakfast had reflected the resentment of the citizens of Paris all those years ago? Perhaps the bastard princess's champion was Sylvain, who cared little about France but plenty about Lorelei. Daniel couldn't discount the prior or Father Anselme either. Both knew who she was; both had a stake in preserving her life.

He glanced longingly at the brown bottle of laudanum on the bedside table. The hike up the mountain had been a mistake, and he hadn't even come close to getting her to speak of Henri Junot. His muscles screamed with fatigue and his knee burned with agony. Twinges stabbed like needles into his shoulder blades. But he resisted the urge to dull the pain, along with his senses.

Damn, he shouldn't have gone chasing after that wild hoyden. He should have let her sulk.

But where Lorelei was concerned, he was not a reasoning man. He'd scaled a mountain just to dry her tears.

Why? Why did he feel responsible for her feelings as well as her life? He pondered the question until his head ached, but he could think of no good reason.

The square of light in the window faded to the dull purple of twilight. She'd said she would come after supper, but supper was long past. She must have forgotten, or perhaps Father Julian had set her to some task in preparation for the Army of Reserve.

His gaze darted around the darkening room to the squat silhouette of the iron stove, the armchair where Father Anselme often slept, the neat rows of cots, and the table by his bed. Something struck him as odd about the arrangement of the items on the table. There was Father Gaston's chess set, but the pieces were disarranged, as if someone had swept them to the floor and replaced them in haste. The inkhorn was missing, too. Daniel got up and checked beneath the table. The ink had spilled, a walnut-colored splotch spreading across the floor.

In an angry motion, Daniel sat on the side of the cot. The light faded from the window and the fire in the stove burned down to embers.

Someone had searched the room. Worse, Bonaparte was coming. Daniel and Lorelei had to get away before he arrived. Josephine would have spies in the army who'd report to her that Daniel had failed to carry out his task.

Uneasy, he lay down on the bed, pulled a blanket over himself, and stared into the thick darkness.

A faint footstep sounded outside the infirmary.

Beneath the covers, his hand tightened around the warm steel of his penknife, sharpened recently with a whetstone he'd stolen from the kitchen. Through slitted eyes he watched the door. The coals in the stove shed only a faint orange glimmer on the floor.

The door opened with a quiet swish. Damn, the light was low!

Daniel let his chest rise and fall in a semblance of sleep. Apprehension crawled like a snake over his skin, but he held still. The Raven had been trained to freeze the fear in his gut into rock-hard determination.

The footsteps tapped across the room, closer. . . .

He fought an urge to spring up. Acting too soon would frighten his attacker, and his weapon was poor.

Sweat drenched his chest and armpits.

The dark blur coming toward him was silent, ominous as death. It passed the window, blocking out the last fronds of dying light. The eerie shadow moved to the bed.

Fear invaded Daniel's mouth with a sharp metallic taste. His senses ignited with a burning need to act, to *know.* But he waited. Let the bastard come into the trap.

He didn't have long to wait.

The figure bent over the table by the bed. Daniel saw the dull gleam of metal. A blade.

*Now!*

Hissing a curse, he bolted up from the bed. He lunged, cracking his splinted arm against his attacker's head. Two bodies fell to the floor. The blade dropped with a clatter. Daniel flung himself on the dark figure and heard a harsh gust of breath rush from his assailant. He grappled the flailing arms and pushed his knee into the chest convulsing for air.

Something was wrong. There was wiry strength in the body beneath him, but something else, too, a softness. . . .

And instead of church incense, he smelled a clean springtime fragrance.

*Lorelei.*

Bitterness seared his throat as he shoved her away and stood, his vision red with fury.

She was the first person he'd ever believed in. Like

a fool he'd enshrined her false innocence in his heart and vowed to protect her from evil.

Her betrayal shouldn't have surprised him. She was a Bourbon, her father's daughter after all.

Finally she managed to drag in a breath, find her voice.

"Daniel, what—"

"Save it, princess," he snarled, his voice lashing like a black whip. "I just have one question. Blades are so messy. Why not use your medical skills to poison me?"

# Chapter 7

Lorelei's mouth dropped open in a perfect *O* of disbelief. Still winded from the fall, she shook her head and tried to reel in her thoughts. She could almost smell the danger emanating from Daniel. His hard-bitten rage, the fire in his eyes, the shock of his accusation, made her mind swirl uselessly. What did he mean, poison him?

She heard the rasp of flint and steel; then a halo of gold lit his face. He might have been a saint in a painted icon but for the deadly look glinting in his eyes. Fear jolted her legs into action. She rose and lurched toward the door. The instinct of fear was new to her, cold and unwelcome.

His hand shot out and sank into her hair. "Not so

fast," he said, yanking her to the center of the room. He forced her head back until her throat ached and she had no choice but to stare up into his handsome, deadly face.

"The game is up, isn't it?" He bit off the words like splinters of ice. His expression changed to a snarl of disgust and he thrust her away. She sprawled across the cot. "Christ," he mumbled, "I never thought it would be you."

Confusion tingled over her senses, heightening her awareness of a hundred meaningless details. The bedclothes smelled of the mountain woods, of liniment and sweat. She noticed the contrast of the thin white scar on his flushed brow, the tic in his jaw, the tenseness in his hands. The room felt icy cold, and absurdly she wondered why no one had added logs to the stove.

"Was it you that first time, too?" he demanded. "You went to great trouble to patch me up. Give yourself high marks for your performance. Were you at all sorry to ruin your fine work?"

Lorelei felt sick. Her lips moved, but no sound came out. What on earth was he babbling about?

"My, but you're practiced," Daniel went on, joining her on the cot. Instinctively she recoiled. "I thought I'd seen every female wile, but you've raised deception to the level of a fine art." The splint pressed on her shoulder. With his good hand he caressed her throat, his thumb flirting with the pulse there.

"Is this where you would have cut me?" he whispered. "Yes, the carotid, you once told me, one of the most important blood vessels in the body." His thumb slashed across the leaping artery, and she flinched.

"One cut, and death is almost instantaneous. Merciful even, you said."

She jerked away from him.

He hauled her back. "Say something, damn you!"

Tears of frustration and confusion stung her eyes. Finally her voice returned, rough and tortured. "D-daniel, please. I don't understand. You're frightening me—"

"Frightening you?" He gave an ugly bark of laughter. "I beg your pardon." His thumb continued to caress her throat in threatening, sensuous strokes. "But how would you expect me to respond to a conniving bitch who came to murder me in my bed?"

"M-murder you?" The alien idea howled like the deadly foehn through her mind. "Sweet Mary, why would you think I'd—"

"Surely you won't try to deny it."

"You're ill," she whispered. "You need help. Perhaps that concussion has affected your reason."

"No, it only blinded me for a while." Again his hand sank into her hair.

"Daniel, listen to me—"

"Yes, that's an excellent idea. You have a great deal of explaining to do."

She tried to wrench away, but he held her fast. Her temples ached from the tension of his grip on her hair. His heart thundered against her chest.

"Please, let me go. I—I can't think with you forcing yourself on me like this."

"Forcing." Low, humorless laughter spilled from him. "I never had to force anything. You were so pitifully willing."

Without warning, he shoved her back as if her nearness suddenly revolted him. She fell against the bed.

"Talk," he commanded.

"I—I meant to come earlier," she said, gingerly touching her throat. "But the lesson at supper went on and on. Father Emile and Father Gaston started arguing about the rights of man again. It was nearly dark before I could get away."

"Very well done, and I suspect the darkness suited your purpose much better."

Anger, as heady as a draft of fresh beer, pushed aside her paralyzing shock. She braced her arms behind her and sat up. "My purpose in coming here," she snapped, "was to remove your splint. I was hoping to find you awake so I could do it."

Uncertainty flickered in his eyes but hardened into accusation again. "That's how you would have explained my death, isn't it? The angel of mercy comes to succor the wounded patient. The slip of a knife—"

"I have no knife, damn your eyes!"

Her outburst silenced him. She savored the momentary triumph. Bending, she snatched up the instrument he'd knocked from her hand only moments earlier. Tensing, he moved back.

"Look at this, Daniel," she ordered. "Scissors. A pair of scissors." She flung them on the cot. "If I'm an accomplished conniver, why would I use scissors to do you in? I have access to opiates, razor-sharp scalpels, toothed saws. But I brought none of those things. Just scissors to cut a bandage."

Again the uncertainty crept into his eyes, and this

time it stayed. He sank onto the cot. "Oh, God," he whispered.

"Why on earth," she asked in a shaky voice, "would you think I—or anyone, for that matter—would try to kill you?"

"Lorelei, I've made a mistake."

The admission should have pleased her, but she felt only empty. Empty and betrayed. He'd insulted every ideal she held dear. He'd shoved her offering of friendship back in her face.

He sat at the foot of the cot, his splinted arm hanging at his side, his head cradled in his good hand. A tormented expression pinched his features.

Her anger retreated a few steps. "Answer my question."

"It was a foolish notion I had," he said, too quickly. "Probably the laudanum. Nothing more."

"Liar. I once told you that I can't heal you unless you tell me where it hurts."

"Some things can't be healed by splints and bandages." A bitter smile tightened his mouth. "Sit down, Lorelei. Please."

She lowered herself cautiously to the cot. The leather webbing creaked beneath her weight. Slowly and deliberately he held out the scissors, handles first. She took them.

"So you think I'm ready to have done with this thing?" With a nod, he indicated his splinted arm.

"Yes. The bone has had time to knit. I thought you should have the cast off so your muscles won't go to slack."

He brought the stool with the lamp closer. "I'm ready."

A little devil of stubbornness rose inside her. "Well, I'm not. Explain yourself."

"I'll talk while you work."

She accepted the compromise with a shrug and took his arm into her lap. Carefully she opened the scissors and slipped the lower blade beneath the plaster-stiffened bandage.

"I have enemies," said Daniel. "I was on the wrong side of a conflict that ripped France to shreds. In prison, attempts on my life became a common occurrence. I learned to distrust even those who claimed to be friends."

Lorelei glanced up from her work. "But you lived through a terrible massacre. If I'd had such a close brush with death, I'd spend the rest of my days savoring the sweetness of being alive, not suspecting people of murder."

"I suppose that's the difference between us, Lorelei."

The lower part of the bandage fell away. She studied the way the plaster dust clung to his damp, pale arm. "But you're safe here. None of us at the hospice had anything to do with events that happened in Paris eight years ago."

"How can you be sure? Maybe my presence opened an old wound. Father Emile and Father Gaston were both Parisians. Father Julian has an uncanny way of finding out about things that happen in distant places. If Bonaparte sneezed in Paris, Julian would hear about it in a matter of days."

The very notion made her laugh. "Are you saying

one of them wants to kill you? Oh, please. I know these men. Not one of them is worthy of your accusation. You're so distrustful."

"Untrustworthy men usually are."

She fought an urge to move away. "Oh, Daniel. What terrible thing have you done?"

"This time," he said, "it's what I didn't do."

"You speak in riddles."

"I've already said too much." Catching her expression, he gripped her arm. "Don't cry. By God, don't you dare cry."

She pulled away. "How in the world do you expect me to behave? I'm not used to this. I've never had to explain myself to you. I thought we were friends. I thought you trusted me."

"Lorelei—"

She cut him off with a wave of her hand. "I opened my heart to you, told you my dreams and my hopes. I've dedicated my life to healing." She stood and started to pace. The chill of the room penetrated her loosely woven shirt. She shivered. "I worked for hours to mend your wounds. I sat with you, bathed and massaged your knee."

He looked lost sitting there, a wary, battered stranger, his shrunken arm still half concealed by the remains of the bandage. Kneeling beside him, she peeled away the gauze and removed the two wooden slats that had served as splints.

"The canons are men of God, Daniel. They've taken in smugglers, outlaws, deserters, without asking questions. A man's deeds are never held against him at Saint

Bernard's. The canons are dedicated to saving lives, not destroying them."

"Father Julian took my weapons. Is that common practice?"

"No," she admitted. She kept his pale arm in her lap. He didn't seem to notice. Very gently she kneaded the muscles.

"Go away, Lorelei," he snapped, jerking from her grasp. "You're probably right; that blow to the head has affected my reason. Leave me."

His abrupt words should have hurt, but they didn't. For Lorelei understood now that his rage was that of a wounded animal lashing out from pain. Braving his temper, she leaned forward and brushed his scarred brow with her lips.

"Don't do that," he said.

She shivered again. The night cold had penetrated the room. She wanted to make it warm for him. "It won't work on me, Daniel," she said, walking to the stove. "For some reason you want me to think you're not worthy of compassion."

"I'm not," he assured her. "I've made enemies who crave my death. That's why I thought you were an attacker."

"What enemies? Is it something to do with the patriot Meuron?"

"Perhaps."

"You'll find no assassins at Saint Bernard's." Opening the stove, she added a log to the low-glowing embers. Vigorously pumping the bellows, she turned her face away from the heat and a strange sulfurous smell. "You're perfectly safe here."

A giant tongue of flame lashed from the stove. Thunder detonated in her face.

She heard Daniel's hoarse cry and her own piercing scream. A force lifted her up, up, hurling her backwards across the room. Something hot ripped into her leg. She landed hard on the floor. The ward blazed with shooting stars and terrifying noises. Something—someone—moved to encircle her.

Daniel picked her up and ran. She felt the jarring thud of each step, then the rush of cold air as they burst outside.

She clung to him, her ears ringing and her nose seared by a harsh acrid smell. Daniel spoke. She heard the rumble of his voice, but couldn't make out his words. Then he hugged her close and buried his face in her hair. She felt him shaking.

She blinked the grit from her eyes. The white flashes began to fade. Blood pulsed from the wound on her lower leg. Men ran toward them from all quarters. Deafened by the explosion, she could only make out snatches of conversation interspersed with yelps from the kennels.

". . . hurt?"

"Check her leg."

". . . happened?"

"Fire!"

Men formed a line stretching from the yard well to the ward, passing buckets with frantic speed. She stopped trying to listen, for her head ached as if a hot blade had riven it in two. She began to cry soundlessly, the tears pouring from her smarting eyes and washing tracks down her ash-smeared face.

Daniel wiped away the tears with his sleeve. His eyes were dark as midnight, and somehow she knew he was desperately afraid for her. "All in one piece, Doctor?" he asked.

She nodded miserably.

Huffing with exertion, Father Anselme arrived with a satchel of medical supplies. The old canon's hands shook violently, and he spoke a prayer through bloodless lips.

"I just have one question, Lorelei," Daniel whispered in her ear. "Now do you believe me?"

"Accident!" Hours later, Daniel slammed his hand on the blackened wall of the infirmary. "Do you mean to tell me you really believe that was an accident?"

Father Julian regarded him unblinkingly. Lamplight flickered over his stern face. They stood alone in the burned-out room. Twisted pieces of iron from the stove lay about their feet. The men had contained the fire and gone to bed; in the next few days they'd clear up the debris.

"It's the only reasonable explanation," said Father Julian. "Some sort of gases built up in the stove and ignited when Lorelei disturbed them with the bellows."

The wavering light slid over something green on the floor. Stooping, Daniel picked it up. Lorelei's ribbon. An icy gust of fear blasted over him when he recalled the roar of the explosion, her body flying doll-like across the room. He suppressed a shiver. He'd almost failed to protect her.

"You're not really fool enough to believe that," he

snapped. Or maybe the prior needed to have people believe it was an accident to remove suspicion from himself.

"Calm down, monsieur. Accidents happen. A wise man accepts them without rage. Be thankful that you and Lorelei were not seriously hurt. What was she doing in your room in the evening hours anyway?"

Daniel held up his arm. "Removing my bandage."

He thought of Lorelei, asleep now in her small tidy room, the gash on her leg bandaged, Father Anselme napping in the chair beside her bed. Daniel hated being away from her even for a short time, but the deadly game had gone too far.

The lamp hissed, and the light wavered over the prior's ashen face. He'd had a piece of paper in his hand, and he was slowly, methodically, ripping it into tiny squares. So, thought Daniel, Father Julian wasn't as calm as he appeared.

"No one was killed this time," said Daniel. "But what about the future?" He folded his arms across his chest. Gray ash smeared his nightshirt. "The whole damned ward reeks of sulfur."

"I'm afraid I have no explanation for that."

"I do." Daniel kneaded his arm. Weeks of disuse had rendered it thin and embarrassingly weak. "Someone put a gunpowder charge in the stove."

"That's mad, monsieur. A wild accusation."

Daniel took a deep breath to shore up his patience. "The powder was delivered this morning. Everyone had access to it. Someone took pains to fashion a bomb."

Father Julian betrayed no emotion. "Who here

would wish to cause an explosion? And why?" He shook his head. "You're mistaken."

Daniel crossed the room to a darkened corner. Bending, he picked up the length of splintered wood he'd found earlier. "Oh, no," he said softly. "See how it's been hollowed out. The powder stains are evident. The rest of the log was destroyed, but my guess is the murderer filled it with powder and replaced the top to resemble an ordinary log. Rather ingenious, no?"

Father Julian stepped back, shaking his head in denial. "You overvalue yourself, monsieur. We're men of God here. We wouldn't risk burning down the hospice at any cost. We don't steal, nor do we murder."

"Someone accomplished the first and attempted the second." And Daniel knew there was every possibility that the culprit stood here with him now, hiding his deed behind a sanctimonious facade. "I was away from the infirmary yesterday."

"I thought you returned here with Father Anselme after your rather startling revelation at breakfast, Monsieur Severin."

"I took one of the dogs for a run. And when I returned, I realized someone had been in the infirmary."

The prior regarded him coldly. "I'm well acquainted with the disturbing feeling that one's room has been searched."

With an effort Daniel concealed his surprise. "It is disturbing, isn't it?" he said, remembering the treasure, the body in the morgue. "Especially when one has secrets." He took a chance and plunged on, "Secrets such as Junot."

Father Julian took a sharp breath. "Who the devil is he?"

"The poor unidentified soul who drowned last summer in Lake Saint Bernard and who now lies in the morgue."

"You have been busy, haven't you?" The prior began brushing at his robes. "An unfortunate incident, to be sure. And the fact that you know him is extraordinary. What can Henri Junot possibly have to do with the accident tonight?"

Daniel leaned against the wall. He'd succeeded in making Julian nervous. "Interesting," he said. "I don't recall mentioning Junot's given name."

Father Julian's hands came up to his chest in a defensive gesture. "I had reasons of my own for keeping his name from our records," he said. "Reasons that are none of your concern."

Daniel shoved away from the wall. "What would you have done with my corpse, Father? Put the charred remains in the morgue, or left my body out for scavengers?"

"You're mad."

"You're hiding something."

"Not for the reasons you think. The only man of questionable character here is you. Think hard on what you say," the prior added hurriedly. "Men bring wood and carry out the ashes. They are hardly killers. Mauricio brings your meals—do you fear he'd poison you? Father Emile has been lending you his books. And hasn't Father Gaston played chess with you? You know these men, monsieur. Are they arsonists? Murderers?"

Daniel spread his hands. "I have to wonder. The opportunity was there."

"Suppose what you say is true. There would have to be a reason. And you haven't given me that, monsieur. Tell me why you believe one of my flock has tried to kill you."

Daniel glanced out the window. The jagged panes of broken glass framed a patch of the sky. Midnight had slipped past. He ached with weariness and shook inside with the underlying horror that he'd nearly lost Lorelei through his own negligence.

"You're an intelligent man, Father. I've told you enough about my past for you to realize I've made enemies."

"Did you recognize the army contractors who delivered the ordnance?"

"No, and they had no chance to arrange the explosion. They stayed only long enough to get your signature to present for their commission."

"So you're accusing someone at the hospice."

"I've accused no one. But I must suspect everyone."

The prior dusted his hands together. "It's late, Monsieur Severin. You'll sleep in the dormitory with the novices. Very soon you'll leave us. Within the week, I think."

"I think not."

"Don't make this difficult, monsieur. You've recovered from your accident, and I'm sure you're eager to be about your business . . . of investigating the treasury theft."

The prior's hesitation showed he doubted Daniel's story. "I'm not leaving until I discover exactly what happened tonight, and I want you to return my knife and arrows."

"I will not."

Daniel fixed him with a cold stare. "I left off questioning about Junot. But I could easily keep on probing."

Father Julian sighed. "You'll have your belongings in the morning. And you'll say nothing to anyone about your suspicions. I won't have rumors circulating about my hospice. Is that understood?"

"I understand," he said, and left the burned-out ward.

"You've been keeping too much to yourself," said Sylvain.

Lorelei stepped outside her room and inhaled the musty smell of the corridor. She blinked, but couldn't clear the fuzziness of sleep from her vision. Sylvain's face was indistinct, his hair a slash of bright yellow against the dark wall. "I was napping," she said vaguely. In the two days since the accident, unremembered but unpleasant dreams had plagued her.

"Is your leg all right?"

She glanced down. A thick bandage made a bulge in her stocking. "It's fine. Practically healed."

Sylvain turned slightly, showing her a quiver of arrows and a bow slung over his shoulder. "I'm going shooting. I thought you might like to come. If you're up to walking, that is."

She shook her head. She could walk fine but wanted only to crawl inside herself and try to forget that a killer roamed the hospice, that the peaceful place she claimed as home wasn't safe anymore. Someone wanted Daniel dead. Why?

"Please," said Sylvain. "I'm taking Bard and Ivan. You used to love coming on patrol, Lorelei. Besides, there's something in the kennels you'll want to see."

"Not today, Sylvain."

Anger pinched his features. "You've gone off with Severin twice," he said. "Am I no longer good enough for you?"

Resentment rose inside her. Sylvain had been watching them. But the pain behind his anger softened her. "All right," she said, and went back to get her boots. She'd have a chance to question him, to reassure herself that, despite his jealousy, Sylvain wasn't the one who'd tried to harm Daniel.

On their way to the kennels, they passed the ward. Drawn by the open door and the activity inside, she touched Sylvain's arm. "Just a moment." He waited while she went to the door.

Under the stern eye of Father Emile, a group of novices worked to clear the room of rubble. The twisted iron of the stove littered the floor, and window glass lay in shards all about. Smoke blackened the walls, but she could see few other signs of the terrible, hellish explosion.

Beneath the thick bandages, her leg stung. A monster had sneaked into her safe world. The ground seemed to shift beneath her feet—the very foundations of her life had been shaken. The outside world sucked at her, invading her mountain refuge.

She spied Daniel at the far end of the ward where his cot had been. Her heart pounded at the sight of his intent face, his midnight hair spilling over his brow. He could have died. She might have lost him forever.

She forced away the intolerable thought. On hands and knees, he swept with a fine-bristled brush. With chilling clarity she understood the reason for his precise work. He was looking for clues, trying to find evidence of the person responsible for nearly killing them both.

"He's bad luck," said Sylvain. "There hasn't been a fire at the hospice since its founding."

"That's nonsense."

"Come on." He touched her shoulder. "Let's go to the kennels."

Five minutes later she knelt in the straw, her lap full of squirming puppies, some still damp from the womb. The heavy, sweet scent of birth clung to them.

"Three males and five females," said Sylvain, offering Belle a morsel of dried beef. "Father Droz was up all night with them."

"I wish he'd called me." One by one, Lorelei returned the puppies to their mother. After the last litter, which had yielded Lorelei's beloved Barry, she'd leaped down the stairwells, announcing the arrival in a breathless, excited voice.

She shivered and wondered if she could ever run laughing through the hospice again.

She and Sylvain walked toward the lake. Bard and Ivan led the way. Chipmunks sprinted across the path and disappeared down secret holes. High in the spreading branches of the larch trees, robins and finches made their nests. The lake lapped at its banks, awakening sunbursts of yellow daisies and cornets of blue columbine.

They came to a rocky, level spot at the west end of the lake. Beyond the rise lay Italy and a war that seemed to grow closer every day. The dogs galloped to the water's edge and drank while Sylvain and Lorelei trudged across the field toward the target fastened with rawhide tethers to a tree.

Lorelei watched while Sylvain straightened the target. Made from a cask bottom, the painted wooden disk had hung there for years. The painting depicted Wilhelm Tell standing triumphant over his foe, the villainous Gessler, who pleaded for his life. At the top, Saint Sebastian, his body bristling with the arrows that had martyred him, held a banner bearing the words: "If you wander in harmony hand in hand, then bowered in blessings is your land." Lorelei had always thought it ironic that the scene was pocked by arrow wounds.

"Ready," said Sylvain, walking away in measured paces. "Gessler looks cocky today. I think I'll aim at his eye."

"Sixty thousand francs says you can't do it in three shots," said Lorelei, her heavy mood beginning to lift. Sylvain was her friend and decent to his simple soul. He couldn't have tried to harm Daniel.

"Ninety thousand says I blind him in one shot," Sylvain parried.

Lorelei looked at the mountains that thrust up in a jagged bowl around the lake and framed the vault of the sky. The very immensity of the mountains, their boundless duration, somehow comforted her. The Alps were a bridge between heaven and earth, changeless, a fortress against the loss of faith. The explosion had been an accident, she told herself. An accident.

Sylvain hadn't finished measuring off the paces when one of the dogs gave a sharp, questioning bark and pointed his nose to the south. Lorelei and Sylvain exchanged a glance. "Someone's about," she said. "Let's go see who it is."

Sylvain's pale eyes went hard with wariness. His bow slipped from his shoulder into his hand. He drew an arrow from his quiver.

"Really, Sylvain," Lorelei began, frightened and annoyed by his suspicion. "That's not the way we welcome travelers to Saint Bernard's."

"It is now." He struck off after the dogs up the narrow, winding road.

Lorelei followed. So Sylvain, too, had guessed that the explosion was something more sinister than an accident.

They hurried single file up the road to a boardwalk built into the side of the mountain. It was misty here, with low clouds gently wrapping the path and curling around their ankles. The thick, weathered logs echoed with their footsteps. The road bent sharply to the right, shadowing a narrow outcrop about twenty feet down. Below that yawned a canyon, its sides sheer and the bottom so distant that it was barely visible.

Around the bend, Sylvain came face to face with a stranger.

The man drew up short at the sight of the dogs. Lorelei saw a red flash in his ear. The man wore a ruby earring.

"Rescue animals," said Sylvain. "They won't harm

you." The mastiffs stood back politely as they'd been trained to do.

The traveler wore serviceable clothes of chamois and wool. He had a rucksack on his back. A pistol and hunting knife rode in a belt low on his hips. He looked like many other travelers who used the pass; yet something in his expression made Lorelei wary. Long, gaunt cheeks framed a hard mouth that looked as if it had never smiled. Flickering, watchful eyes took in the dogs and Sylvain and then fastened on Lorelei.

Sylvain's hand tightened around his bow. "Where are you from, monsieur?"

"About eight thousand feet below here," the man replied. He had a low, husky voice and panted slightly as he spoke. "I'm not used to the altitude."

"We'll show you the way to the hospice," said Sylvan, turning back toward the railed boardwalk. His natural, amiable nature broke through his caution. "Lorelei and I—"

A swift, rasping sound interrupted him. Lorelei whirled and saw the traveler's knife blade arc through the thin mountain air.

# Chapter 8

"She was here?" Daniel asked, reining in the urge to shake the novice called Timon. "Lorelei came to the infirmary?"

"Yes, a while ago." Timon glanced down at his sooty hands. "She only stopped in for a moment to see how the work was coming along. Then she went to the kennels to see the new puppies."

Daniel sagged against the wall of the infirmary. Father Emile and a few others still worked in the ward, sweeping and scrubbing, carrying away the rubble of a man's secret hatred.

"Father Emile," called a novice. "I've found something."

The sacristan raced across the room. "Yes? What is it?"

The youth held up a white shard. "What could it be?"

Father Emile snatched the object, turned it over in his hands, then flung it away. "A chess piece," he muttered. He seemed angry that the item was of such small significance.

"So she's still at the kennels," Daniel said to Timon.

"I don't think so." The novice wiped a smudge of ash from his whiskerless cheek. "I saw her go off with Sylvain. He had his bow and arrows, so I guess they were going shooting."

Daniel lunged away from the wall as if it had burned him. *"What?"*

Clearly baffled, Timon shrugged. "She's not a very good shot, but Sylvain is. He's been trying to teach her for—"

"Where did they go?"

While Timon gave him directions to the archery range, fear gripped at Daniel. Jesus, she'd gone off alone with Sylvain, and he was a crack shot, according to talk in the dormitory.

Armed with his own weapons, Daniel ran toward the lake. Leaping down the rock-strewn banks and following a curving path to the opposite shore, he found the archery range and spied the painted target. He saw no sign of Lorelei or Sylvain. He stood still, watching and listening. Where the hell were they?

In a fever of fear, he imagined Sylvain nocking an arrow, sighting down the shaft at an unsuspecting Lorelei. He had a sudden vision of Junot, laid out in the morgue, his frozen body further testament to the danger that haunted the hospice.

Daniel's gaze raked the area, finding no footprints in the frozen ground.

He heard the panicked barking of a dog, followed by a sound that turned his blood to ice.

It was Lorelei, screaming in terror.

He raced up the road, vaulting over rocks and crashing through underbrush. Branches lashed at his face. Warm pain shot up his leg, but he didn't slow his pace. He knew only the driving need to find Lorelei.

Deep in a gully below the road, he spied a dog, its body limp upon the rocks. Many feet above lay Sylvain, dead or unconscious. His hair blazed yellow against the dull stone of a slanting outcrop. Beside him another dog skittered and slid, trying to claw his way back to the road. The brindled pattern of fur on his flanks identified him as Bard. He barked furiously, saliva flying from his mouth.

Somewhere Lorelei still screamed, ragged, mindless shrieks. Daniel raced on, his thighs pumping as he climbed the steep, narrow road. A drapery of clouds shrouded the high peaks above the pass. The blinding green of spring whizzed by as he ran. Far below, a glacier crawled from its mountainous womb, dropping blocks of ice with a dull boom into the canyon. Vapor snaked through groves of pine and juniper, obscuring the road beyond.

Moving through the mist, Daniel rounded a bend in the path. He spotted two figures on a boardwalk built into the side of the mountain. In the space of a heartbeat he took in the scene. Lorelei struggled with a man. He had a knife in one hand. His other arm circled her waist. He pressed her against the rail, bending her backward so that the upper half of her body bowed out over the canyon.

Yelling her name, Daniel pounded toward them.

The knife stabbed downward.

Panic iced his bowels and the harsh taste of fear flooded his mouth.

Lorelei twisted to one side. The blade stabbed into dry wood. Daniel was close enough now to see her face, a pale oval of raw terror and uncomprehending shock.

*Hurry.* His heart slammed the message home. *Hurry.*

The brigand raised the knife again. He snatched at her shirt to hold her still. The fabric ripped, exposing the curve of her shoulder and a small rose-tipped breast.

An iron spike of rage embedded itself in Daniel's mind. You've done it now, he vowed to the attacker. You're a dead man.

He rushed across the boardwalk and caught the brigand's knife hand in mid-arc. At the same moment, he leaped on his back, his forearm pressing into the man's neck.

The brigand gave a bark of surprise. Daniel felt himself being carried back, slammed against the rough rock face of the mountain. The air rushed from his lungs. His chest seemed to freeze, unable to draw breath. The brigand rammed Daniel backwards again and again. The man fought well and thought quickly. A seasoned assassin. He twisted his thick wrist, trying to wrench it from Daniel's grasp.

Fleetingly Daniel saw Lorelei stumble forward.

*"No!"* he yelled. "Lorelei, get away!"

The attacker placed his foot on her midsection and shoved. She reeled back against the rail. Wood splintered. Her arms flailed. She crumpled to the planks.

Daniel cursed the weakness in his arm. Since the splints had been removed, he'd regained only a fraction of his strength. Light-headed from lack of air, he managed to slam his hand against the brigand's windpipe.

The brigand screamed, dropped the knife, and clutched at his throat. Wheezing for breath, he sank to his knees.

Daniel stumbled toward Lorelei. A shadow fell over him from behind.

He whirled to face an upraised hand wielding the knife. Daniel saw a flash of red, the glint of a jewel in the man's ear.

Recognition burst over him and freshened his rage. He dodged the slashing knife and caught the wrist. He heard the muffled click of bones breaking. The knife sailed over the edge, disappearing into the void.

The two men came together in a deadly embrace. The railing bit into Daniel's back. Behind him lay emptiness, the yawn of eternity waiting to swallow him. Before him loomed the nightmare face of Chrétien Rubis, the notorious Parisian murderer. Daniel knew why Rubis had come. Josephine must have grown impatient.

With a surge of strength, he lunged to one side and twisted, reversing their positions. The weakened wood cracked.

"Please," Rubis rasped through his shattered windpipe. "Please, let's talk."

Daniel pressed harder. The rail bowed out.

"Daniel, stop. He's giving up."

Lorelei's words drifted toward him as if from a great distance, but he barely heard. He saw only a murderer's face, remembered only a murderer's hand baring the breast of an innocent girl.

Daniel gave one final shove.

Rubis seemed to fall slowly. His arms and legs cartwheeling, he sailed backwards into the rock-walled canyon. For silent seconds he seemed to float; then he crashed to the bottom where he lay like a boneless rag doll.

Daniel rested his aching arm on the broken rail. Sweat blurred his vision. He stood waiting for the black emptiness that usually came after he'd killed, the darkness that masked the deed from his conscience and saved him from going mad.

Instead he found himself staring into Lorelei's velvety brown eyes, felt the gentle press of her hand on his arm. "Daniel," she said in a tortured whisper. "He'd given up. He was begging for mercy. You shouldn't have pushed—"

"Don't," he snapped, yanking his arm away, half expecting to see that her hand had been soiled from touching him.

She stepped back and gaped as if he were a stranger. "I don't understand you, Daniel."

"For Christ's sake, the man was trying to kill you!"

"But he was defeated. Yet you never even hesitated.

You made killing him seem so easy, so . . . unimportant."

It was possibly one of the most important things he'd ever done, but he couldn't tell her that. He reached out and grasped the torn edge of her shirt. "Cover yourself. We've got to do something about Sylvain."

A half hour later Lorelei watched in a daze as Daniel helped Sylvain and Bard back up to the road. Two hours after that, they managed, with a system of ropes, to recover the bodies of the mastiff and the brigand.

Groggy from unconsciousness, Sylvain regarded the corpses for a moment, then turned away, his bruised face contorted in horror.

Daniel stared at the dead man and looked as if he'd have liked to kill him all over again.

How easily and dispassionately he'd ended a man's life. He had the heart of a hunter. Lorelei forced her gaze to the brigand. His face, probably not even handsome in life, had frozen into an expression of surprise. Though she was not usually squeamish, Lorelei felt surprised to find bile pushing at the back of her throat. Gulping it back, she ran several paces down the road, leaned on a rock, and vomited.

A few minutes later someone pressed a cloth into her hand. "Here," said Daniel, his voice soft and expressionless. "Clean yourself up. We'd best get back."

She wiped her face with a trembling hand. "Why would someone want to kill me?" she whispered. "I have nothing."

Daniel seemed about to say something. Then he

glanced at Sylvain and seemed to think better of it. "Let's go," he said, taking her hand.

She pulled away from his grip and clutched at her torn shirt. "I feel . . . violated," she said. "This is my home, the place where I felt secure, and now . . ." For some reason she thought of the last time Daniel had kissed her, and she remembered how safe she'd felt in his arms. Safe in the arms of a man who could kill without blinking.

"It always hurts," said Daniel quietly, "when an illusion is shattered."

"My life is not an illusion. I won't believe it. I won't!" Almost against her will, she began piecing together the incidents of the past few days. "Someone tried to kill you and now me," she said, staring at Daniel with growing horror. His eyes were hooded, his mouth hard. "You know something, don't you?"

"I know," he said, "that you shouldn't have gone off without telling me."

"I've survived twenty years without you," she retorted.

"Leave off," Sylvain called to her. "For God's sake, Lorelei, the man saved your life." Grim-faced, he turned away and began constructing a sledge of long branches bound with ropes. From time to time he glanced at Lorelei, and when he caught her eye, his face flushed crimson.

She longed to reach out to him, to tell him there was no shame in what he'd done. Faced with the knife-wielding brigand, Sylvain had acted on purely logical instincts of self-preservation. He'd vaulted the railing to escape. What agony he must suffer, knowing he'd lain senseless while she struggled with the assassin. And what guilt he must feel.

"Lorelei," said Daniel, "we must talk."

She turned back to him, lowering her voice so Sylvain wouldn't hear. "This"—she gestured toward the brigand's corpse—"proves that no one at the hospice is responsible for the accident. That man must have come in secret and set the gunpowder charge."

"I don't think so."

"Then you're a fool." She started to walk away.

He took her arm and turned her to face him. "I understand how you feel. The canons are your family. It would shake everything you believe in to suspect one of them. But sometimes a man must act against his own will."

"You killed in cold blood. You can't explain that away."

He drew in his breath on a hiss. "I won't even try. But one thing hasn't changed. There's still a dangerous person at the hospice, Lorelei."

"How can you be so certain it wasn't the brigand?"

"He's a stranger. Don't you think someone would have noticed him?"

"If you're so convinced there's a killer at the hospice, then leave," she said fiercely. "Everything was fine until you came here. Only when you're gone will we have peace!"

"I can't leave."

"Why not?"

"Because you need me, damn it," he flung at her, and stalked off to help Sylvain.

* * *

"Ashes to ashes, dust to dust . . ."

Father Julian's voice mingled with the hum of bees outside the squat stone building that housed the morgue. Stirred by a sharp wind, the lake swished at its banks. The men of the hospice stood staring at the body stretched out on two pine planks.

Daniel inhaled the scent of loam and grass. Yesterday Chrétien Rubis had been an assassin intent on murdering a bastard princess. Today he was another nameless corpse.

Regret lay like a chunk of ice in Daniel's chest. Sending Rubis to his death hadn't bothered him at all. But the fact that Lorelei had watched him kill disturbed him deeply.

She'd seen his dark side. She'd looked upon his naked soul and seen the ruthlessness he struggled to conceal. Even now she stared at him across the supine body, her gaze full of pain and confusion.

Father Julian closed his missal. The chill of his stare settled briefly over Daniel; then he turned to walk back to the hospice. Father Clivaz and Timon moved to either end of the planks to bear Rubis to his resting place, his dark, icy hell.

Father Emile glared down at the body, his eyes intent, as if he were trying to resurrect the secrets that had died with the brigand. Father Gaston sniffed in disdain and lifted the hem of his robe. Could the Parisian canons have known Rubis? Daniel wondered.

Father Anselme spat on the ground—an old man's habit, or a gesture of contempt for the man who had attacked Lorelei?

She started after Father Julian, and Sylvain moved

to her side. She and Sylvain had stayed up late the night before. She'd been trying to coax him out of his misery, Daniel guessed. Obviously the novice felt himself guilty of an act of cowardice. Just as obviously Lorelei must have managed to salve his guilt. In one easy motion Sylvain settled his arm around her shoulders.

Jealousy hit Daniel so hard that he winced. No, not jealousy. It couldn't be.

Gritting his teeth, he looked away. In a field to the right lay a yard of rubble-built cairns reserved for the rescue dogs of Saint Bernard. A new pile of rough stones covered Ivan. Daniel shivered, troubled by the thought that the dog might not be the last victim in this dangerous game.

Frenzied baying from the kennels interrupted his thoughts. A moment later the hospice bell clanged through the pass.

"What is it?" Daniel asked, hurrying to Father Emile's side.

"Trouble." The sacristan headed for the main building.

The rescue party struck out for the road. Haunted by visions of Lorelei struggling with Rubis, Daniel joined them.

"This is not a carnival act, monsieur," Father Anselme said. "We need no spectators."

"But you might need help," Daniel stated.

The dogs led the way with sharp yelps that sounded almost human. At the edge of a rocky glacial morass, the rescuers found the travelers.

A woman knelt on the pebbled road. Two young

boys stood nearby, shouting in Italian for help. A man crouched on the lip of a steep defile.

The woman spied the dogs and gave a little shriek.

"We're here to help," Sylvain said in Italian. "They're rescue dogs." The sight of the canons' dark robes and sugarloaf hats seemed to calm the woman.

"My little Bianca." The man's voice trembled. "She fell."

Fear clutched at Daniel's stomach. About fifty feet down, a small child straddled a spiny bush. Her feet were jammed into a crack in the rock. Her face stared up at him in mute terror.

"It happened in the blink of an eye," the man explained. "I looked away for a moment, just a moment." He wiped his face.

Daniel threw one end of Father Droz's rope over the edge. It dangled a few feet above the child. Even if she could have reached it, she was too small and frightened to hold on.

"I'll go down to her," said Sylvain.

Daniel regarded the novice's pale face, the long scrape along his temple. "Let me," he said. Before Sylvain could argue, he added, "I need your strong arms to draw us up."

For a moment the two stared at each other, hard-faced and combative. If Sylvain was the murderer, Daniel was handing him a rare chance. The novice could simply loose his grip on the rope and send Daniel plunging to his death.

He made a harness around his body. Damn, this was all he needed. But he had a driving desire for Lorelei to see him do this. He turned and backed down the cliff, paying out the rope. Chunks of earth, ice, and stone rained down into the gully.

Daniel felt a sudden lurch. He fell freely, too quickly to react. Then the rope tightened, biting into his waist and thighs, stopping his fall.

He brushed the sweat out of his eyes and looked up. Jesus. Had Sylvain let go on purpose?

Flinging aside the suspicion, he looked down. An arm's length below, the child watched him with terrified unblinking eyes.

He cursed, then hoped she didn't understand French. Placing his feet against the rock face, he held out his arm to her. "Take my hand," he said in Italian. "I'll help you."

The child hugged the branch harder and shook her head.

"Jesus Christ," Daniel burst out in anger.

"Hush," called Lorelei. "Can't you see she's scared?"

"For God's sake—" Daniel began. Seeing the child flinch, he said, "Why not, sweetheart?"

"I'm scared," she said in a tiny voice. "You look funny."

"Of course I look funny," he snapped. "Anyone would look funny hanging down the side of a mountain."

"What's wrong with your hair?"

"My . . . ?" He took a deep breath for patience. "Look, sweetheart, can you keep a secret?"

She nodded.

"I'm a magic prince."

"You are?"

"Yes. This white in my hair proves I have a spell on me. Only the touch of a special little girl can save me."

"It can?"

"That's right. Just reach up. There's a good girl. . . ."

Slowly she stretched toward him. His large hand closed over the girl's tiny one.

"He's got her," cried the woman. "Thanks be to God."

His muscles trembling, Daniel hoisted the girl from the precarious perch. His barely healed arm smarted in hot protest.

Clinging like a monkey, she looked into his face. "You haven't changed into a prince."

"These things take time."

Within minutes they reached the rocky path. The mother's prayers echoed in the stillness. Daniel was suddenly filled with wonder at the feel of the child's warm, healthy body in his arms.

"Still nothing," she said gravely. "A spell can't be broken without a kiss." She planted a wet one on the tip of his nose.

And Daniel Severin, seducer of women from Paris to Geneva, blushed to the tips of his ears. He raised his sheepish glance to Lorelei. Her face was rapt with delight. The thought that he'd restored Lorelei's faith in him lifted his heart.

"Gregorio!" A thunderous shout exploded from the road below. "Goddammit, Gregorio di Lido, what do you mean by rushing on ahead of me?"

Bianca's father slapped his forehead. "Santa Maria! The baroness! I'd forgotten all about her."

Tense with apprehension, Daniel stared at the mist-wrapped road. Out of the vapors came a lone figure, stocky yet moving with a fluid grace. She wore a traveling cape, and her head was crowned with a turban.

"Baroness," said di Lido. "Forgive me. There was a mishap—"

"This whole damned trip has been a mishap, ever since you lost my traveling seat—oh." She stabbed her staff into the ground and regarded the dogs and canons. "I see we've reached the hospice." Her thick lips rolled back to reveal yellowed teeth as big as a horse's. In well-bred French she said, "I am Germaine, the baroness de Staël-Holstein."

That night in the chapter house, Germaine de Staël, the most outrageous woman of letters Europe had ever seen, described her adventures to a rapt audience.

"Bonaparte ordered me away from Paris again," she said. "It's been so long since I've seen Papa at Coppet that I decided to oblige the little Corsican worm." She held out an empty mug. "Fine stuff, that Aosta wine." As Daniel refilled the mug, she added, "I thought to meet with friends in Milan, but the city's an armed camp. I needed an escort, and Gregorio needed work."

"There's no work for an honest man anymore," said di Lido. He kissed his fingers in Germaine's direction. "You were a godsend, baroness."

Germaine threw back her head and hooted with laughter. "I've been called many things in my life, but never a godsend." Her uncommonly beautiful eyes seemed out of place in her homely face. The glint in those eyes hinted at a powerful intelligence, a wit as sharp as the nib on her famous pen.

Daniel watched her nervously. The last thing he needed was for Germaine de Staël to learn the truth about Lorelei.

"I only hope we'll find a place to settle after we get the baroness to Coppet," said di Lido.

"I'll write to the governor of the Valais," Father Julian told Gregorio. "He'll give you work."

"He's an old guard Savoy," Father Emile said. "Just be sure he doesn't cheat you."

Father Gaston scowled. "He's of noble blood. He's got fairness bred into him."

Germaine studied the Parisian canons. Her penetrating gaze seemed to discomfit both of them, and they lapsed into silence.

A howl from the kitchen broke the tension. Daniel ran to investigate, Signora di Lido and Germaine at his heels.

Lorelei was kneeling in front of the girl. "You have a little abrasion here, Bianca. I must clean it and dress the wound."

Bianca rushed to Daniel. "I'm scared," she wailed.

Bending, he inhaled her peculiar little-girl smell, one of soap and earth and sugar. "Be a good little *ragazza*," he said, "and let Lorelei do her work. It won't hurt."

"You lied about being a prince, and now you're lying again."

"It's for your own good," he replied. Lorelei rolled her eyes, telling Daniel clearly that adult logic made no sense to a frightened six-year-old.

"If I let her do it," said Bianca, "will you tell me a bedtime story?"

"I don't know any stories." He caught Lorelei's urgent look and added, "Well, maybe one."

Lorelei kept up a gentle patter as she wielded a cloth. Her face took on a soft glow. She was in her element, the healer cleansing a child's wound.

"Excellent," said Germaine. "Bianca, hand me my bag. I wish to give the signorina a gift."

"Please, no," Lorelei protested. "The alms box—"

"This will not fit in an alms box." From her bag she took a blouse cross-stitched in a rainbow of colors.

"I've never had anything so fine," Lorelei said. "I'll treasure this."

"Don't treasure it, for Christ's sake. Wear it."

"I will. I promise." Lorelei fingered the dainty embroidery. "What is this device? I've not seen it before."

"The staff and thistle emblem is a favorite of mine. I've done up a room at Coppet with the design."

As he regarded Lorelei with Germaine de Staël's device draped over her chest, a chill slid over Daniel. The web seemed to tighten. Exiled from France for helping Royalists flee the Republic, Germaine would be avidly interested to know Louis XVI had left behind a daughter.

"I'll take great pride in wearing this." Lorelei bit her lip, then added, "I hope to hear from Baron Necker soon."

Germaine rubbed her chin. "You know my father?"

"No. But not long ago I sent him an essay I wrote on typhus." She twisted her fingers into a nervous knot. "I hope he'll share it with the scholars at his salon at Coppet."

"Hope no longer," Germaine stated. "I'll see that he does."

Daniel watched, intrigued. In an odd way, the two women were remarkably similar.

The bell tolled. Madame de Staël went to join the canons for Vespers.

"I won't go to sleep until you tell me the story," Bianca said as her mother carried her out.

Daniel and Lorelei stood alone in the kitchen. The smell of woodsmoke and coffee mingled with the scent of disinfectant.

Lorelei wrung out her washcloth, looked up at Daniel, and broke into gales of laughter. For the second time that day, Daniel felt his ears redden. "What?" he asked, annoyed.

"You're good with children."

"I don't know anything about children. Nor do I wish to."

"You can't make a promise to a child and not keep it."

"Watch me." He stretched his legs toward the hearth and began absently massaging his knee. A cloyingly sweet picture of Bianca's face pushed into his mind. He scowled. "I suppose I'll have to think of a story. The September massacre?"

"You'll give her nightmares. Make something up. Something with a happy ending."

"I don't know any happy endings."

She bit her lip. "What an odd thing to say."

He saw it again, that uncertainty at the back of her eyes. She'd seen him save a life today, but she'd seen him kill a man, too. "Wilhelm Tell?" he asked.

"That's more like it." She covered his hand with hers.

He snatched his hand away. He was beginning to enjoy her touch, and that scared him.

# Chapter 9

After bidding farewell to Germaine de Staël and the di Lido family, Lorelei walked to the rear yard of the hospice. The brilliant light of late morning dappled the soft, ankle-deep grass. Beneath a spreading oak tree, Sylvain and Timon were splitting logs and laying them in for Bonaparte's army.

A few yards away, two lay brothers struggled with wheelbarrows full of stones for outdoor bread ovens. Shovels and pickaxes over their shoulders, still more men headed for the road to clear away the rubble from the spring avalanches.

She looked for Daniel but couldn't find him among the workers. Ever since the explosion she had worried constantly. Unbelievable as it seemed, a killer stalked him.

But who? Try as she might, she couldn't place any of the men of Saint Bernard's in the role of murderer. Murderers were men like the hard-eyed brigand who'd attacked her and Sylvain on the road. Men like Daniel himself, she forced herself to admit.

Unnoticed in the hive of activity, she sat on the sloping door to the root cellar. Sylvain and Timon had peeled off their shirts. Their bare arms, chests, and backs glistened with sweat. She studied the play of hard muscle beneath supple flesh, the way Sylvain's skin caught the sunlight, and the spill of dark brown curls over Timon's damp brow. Her heart pulsed in tandem with the rhythmic arc of the ax, the swift downward swing, the deep crack as the iron blade rived the wood. Suddenly she saw darkness in the ordinary task. The ax could be a deadly weapon.

Shrugging off the thought, she slipped into a strange lassitude. She became aware of the texture of the weathered wood beneath her palm, the warmth of the sun on her head, the scent of Mauricio's sweet basil and lemon balm in the air.

Despite her unease about the attempt on Daniel's life, she felt a magic in the morning, a spell that wove itself around her senses and made her mind move sluggishly, like a traveler floundering in deep snow. The new life of springtime invaded her body. Strange feelings tingled through her. It was like waking up from a pleasant but unremembered dream. Unbidden came the memory of kissing Daniel, the image so vivid she could taste him and feel the texture of his lips on hers.

A secret place in her body began to pulse, just as it had when he'd kissed her.

"Scientific observations, professor?" said a mocking voice.

Lorelei turned sharply. "Daniel!"

Chalky mortar dusted his hair, face, and hands, making him appear ghostly, not quite human.

"You've been helping with the ovens," she observed.

"I have." He propped his hip on the slope of the cellar door. His gaze tracked across the yard and settled on Sylvain and Timon. "And you've been daydreaming, professor."

He seemed to understand her better than she did herself. She turned defensive, praying he wouldn't get any closer to her actual thoughts. "I wasn't daydreaming. You've told me that someone here is a murderer. I'm trying to look at these men through new eyes, as if I'm seeing them for the first time."

Sylvain glanced their way and scowled, but went on working.

"I assume you've released *him* from your suspicions," she said.

"Should I?"

"He quite literally held your life in his hands when you rescued that child. I saw his face, Daniel. He would have died rather than lose his hold on that rope."

"That's true. But then again, perhaps he didn't wish to kill me in front of a host of witnesses."

She bit her lip, released it, and said, "I know of only one murderer here."

His hand slammed down on the cellar door. She flinched.

"Meaning me, I presume," he said.

"It haunts me, Daniel. I still hear that poor man begging for his life—"

"That 'poor man' killed a dog and nearly killed Sylvain as well. The scum intended to knife you, my dear. Sylvain saw it. Christ, even Father Julian believes my actions were justified."

She turned her back on him. He touched her shoulder. "I can't help what I am, Lorelei. Any more than you can."

Very slowly she faced him. "I know."

"Then we'll speak no more of it."

She nodded, wondering if she could ever accept what he was, and wondering why it was so important to her.

"Let's talk instead of what you were thinking just now, when you didn't know I was watching you. I'm sure I'll find that much more interesting."

She cursed her own transparency, considered denial, and settled on candor. "It's all your fault, Daniel." She hugged her knees to her chest as a shield.

He rubbed the mortar dust from his eyes. "My fault?"

"You put ideas into my head. You make me think things I have no right to be thinking."

He held his face impassive beneath the dust. Yet a glint in his eyes caught the sun and she had the distinct and unsettling impression that he was laughing at her.

"What ideas, Lorelei? And how, pray, did I manage to take control of your thoughts?"

"Why, by kissing me," she retorted. Her voice had risen, and she looked around to see if anyone else had heard. But the noise of hammers and axes drowned their conversation. She plunged on, "Did you think I'd forget about it, as if it were no more important than yesterday's breakfast?"

"I suppose that was too much to hope for."

"Just because you've forgotten doesn't mean I will."

He stayed silent for a long time. Wood splintered beneath axes; swallows battled the air currents among the rocky peaks. The mountain breeze blew some of the dust from Daniel's hair. Looking down, she noticed abrasions on his hands from the masonry work. She was furious at herself for mentioning their intimacy. Of course he'd forgotten. Daniel had been to Paris, to court, and he'd probably kissed hundreds of women. Why should he dream about her clumsy, unschooled embrace?

"I haven't forgotten, Lorelei," he said at last, his voice curiously thick. "God help us both, I haven't forgotten."

She saw it again, that flash of pain and regret deep in his eyes. Her hold on her knees fell away, and she covered his rough hand with hers.

"Then you understand why it's your fault," she softly confessed. "You understand what you've done to me." Her gaze cut briefly to the two novices. "I used to look at them during devotions. I'd watch how the candlelight bathed their faces, and I'd listen to the way they spoke their prayers, and I was filled with admiration for them. But when I see them like this"—she gestured at Sylvain and Timon—"I get a wholly different feeling. I'm afraid I experience certain . . . reactions."

Daniel put his free hand on the door frame as if to steady himself. Never had she seen him so startled—wide-eyed, gape-mouthed, blinking fast. He snatched his hand away and raked it through his hair, creating a shower of dust. "Jesus, Lorelei."

"Don't blaspheme, please. Did I say something wrong?"

"Most women simply aren't so frank about their desires."

"Why not?"

He touched her under the chin. "You have much to learn. Bald confessions of desire make you vulnerable."

"Vulnerable?" she asked. "Is it bad to be vulnerable?"

"It can be," he said. "You lay yourself open to hurt."

"As you did?"

Alarm churned in his stomach. He could never separate hard fact from her remarkable intuition. "I don't know what you mean," he muttered, dropping his hand.

"Yes, you do. Someone tried to kill you, and you won't tell me why. You've been hurt—badly, I think."

"Save your diagnosis for someone else. I don't need it."

"Daniel." Her hand settled on his arm, warming his tense muscles. "Talk to me. Remember what I said after you were wounded? I can't heal you unless you tell me where it hurts."

"I'll remember that, Doctor." He stared down at his hands. It was wrong to let her get so cow-eyed over him, wrong to light a fire he could never put out. He glared at her, using anger as a weapon, a wall, to warn her off.

"You're retreating into sarcasm," she observed, "because I know things about you that you'd rather keep hidden."

"I'm getting defensive," he said through gritted teeth, "because you meddle where you're not wanted." He jerked his arm away. The wounded look she gave him cut deep. "Lorelei—"

Just then Father Emile and Father Gaston rounded the corner of the main building. Even from a distance Daniel could see their reddened faces, the sharp movements of their gesticulating arms. The Parisian canons disturbed him. There was much they might know, much they might be hiding.

"Don't keep after me, Lorelei," he said, drawing his gaze from the canons. "It's better that you sit and sigh over Sylvain's physique."

She gasped as if he'd struck her.

"You asked why it's bad to be vulnerable." He whisked away the tear that tracked down her cheek. "That's why," he said, and stalked off to resume his work on the ovens.

For no good reason Daniel's throat felt tight. Lorelei du Clerc was a jumble of contradictions. The canons dressed her in knickers and kept her hair cropped short. They'd lectured her on subjects from mathematics to medicine. She had the manners of a peasant, the mind of a scholar, the skill of a doctor, and the heart of a child. Despite the canons' efforts to insulate her, despite their denial of her frankly sensual nature, and despite her own scruples, Lorelei was maturing. The desires of a woman bubbled up inside her, as inevitable as the spring.

Later that morning Lorelei sat in Father Julian's office and waited patiently as she had so many times over the years. In his usual manner he'd sent an urgent summons, but now he took his time getting to the point. A stack of letters covered his desk blotter. One by one he made meticulous notes on each.

Comfortable with the silence, she looked about the familiar room: the hard wooden prie-dieu, as spare and devoid of comfort as Father Julian himself; the recessed window alcove where as a child she'd sat and drawn pictures while the prior worked; the massive pine desk with a pattern of knotholes she knew by heart.

Not every memory of this room was a pleasant one. The office had from time to time been the scene of stormy arguments and serious discussions about the person she was and the person he wanted her to be. But not even during their most bitter quarrels had she ever doubted that Father Julian loved her.

She shifted on her seat and considered confiding Daniel's suspicions to Father Julian. Then she reflected on his cruel comments earlier and decided against it.

The prior tamped his papers into a neat stack and set them beside the inkstand. He had thin hands with tapered fingers, which he always kept scrupulously clean.

At last he looked up. "The di Lidos and the baroness have left?"

She nodded. "Just after morning prayers." She grappled with a wave of guilt. She should tell him about sending the treatise to Baron Necker and about her appeal to his daughter, Germaine. He was sure to find out soon.

"I was busy," said Father Julian, "and hadn't the time to see them off."

The truth was, Father Julian hated good-byes. It was as if he feared what the world held for people who left the mountain. "How was the child?" he asked. "Did she sleep well?"

"Very well indeed, Father." After Daniel spent an hour recounting the story of Wilhelm Tell to her. Lorelei's cheeks heated. How was it that Daniel could be so tender one moment, so cruel the next? "Father Emile took things in hand," she said. "He gave one of his speeches about the common folk rising up to seize their rights from the large landowners."

Father Julian raised one eyebrow. "And no doubt Father Gaston went on about their responsibility to their masters."

"Of course." She smiled fondly. "Those two do go on, but I think they enjoy their differences."

Skepticism flashed in his eyes, but he said nothing.

Impatient, she said, "What was it you wanted to see me about?"

He regarded her with a cool, clear stare. "Daniel Severin."

Alarm jangled her nerves. She struggled to keep her face as expressionless as the prior's. Oh, Lord, she thought, he must have suspicions of his own. Or perhaps he'd found out about the treatise. Inwardly she cringed as she anticipated his cold anger and, worse, his unspoken disappointment.

"I want you to stay away from him," he said at last.

"But he's my patient."

"He's strong enough to work. You needn't spend so much time with him. The man's a scoundrel, Lorelei. I don't trust him."

"That's not fair! He needs compassion, not suspicion. I can't believe you're insensitive to the pain of a tormented man."

"Tormented?" Father Julian scoffed. "As a bear in a trap, perhaps. I'm surprised you'd defend him. You saw him kill a man."

"But Sylvain explained—"

"He did. He believes the brigand's death was unavoidable. Still, Daniel Severin is a dangerous man."

"He's the one who's *in* danger. You must know that."

Father Julian clutched the edge of the desk. "Why do you say that?"

"Someone tried to kill him."

"The explosion was an accident," the prior insisted. "Don't you see what's happening? He's poisoning your mind already. Which is all the more reason to avoid him." His eyes never left hers as he put a letter into her hands. "When Monsieur Severin regained his memory, I made inquiries about him."

"Inquiries? But Everard hasn't delivered the post since—"

"Everard is not my only link to the outside world."

Inexplicably, his statement made her shiver. She was stunned to discover that Father Julian had secrets, that correspondence could come and go with her none the wiser.

She glanced down at the paper. It was signed by Joseph Fouché, minister of police in Paris. "What is this about?"

"It's all there in the letter. Severin told us the truth—up to a point. He was a captain in the Swiss Guard. He was wounded at the Tuileries and imprisoned at the Carmes. He turned mercenary, as he said. But he wasn't simply a soldier for hire."

Apprehension blew like a cold wind through Lorelei. She glanced down at the letter, but the words swam before her eyes. She looked back at the prior and whispered, "Tell me."

"He's known as the Raven. He hires himself out to perform deeds too odious for men of principle."

"Deeds?"

"Thief-taking. Espionage and subversion." Father Julian paused. "Murder."

The word dropped like a stone in her stomach. Had Daniel planted the explosive himself, knowing she'd put wood on the stove? Lorelei shook her head. It was ludicrous. Her unremarkable existence wasn't worth the trouble; a mercenary had no reward to gain from killing her.

"If it's true," she said, "if the head of the Paris police knows, then why does Daniel roam free? Why hasn't he been arrested and condemned?"

"There's no proof, only hearsay. But enough to move me to caution. Severin has also, the prefect points out, had numerous liaisons with women." He indicated a certain paragraph of the letter. "This one is particularly disturbing. Two years ago Severin was seen in the company of a certain Aimée de Ronsac. Not long afterward she was found dead of an overdose of laudanum."

Lorelei bit her lip. "A suicide?"

"Yes, according to the police ruling. Fouché says she grew despondent when he abandoned her for another."

Lorelei's heart rose up to her throat, then sank and shattered. The possibility had lurked at the back of her mind. Here was confirmation.

"I'm sure you understand why I must warn you away from him," said Father Julian.

She laid the letter on the desk and wondered about the man called Fouché. Was this an unsubstantiated indictment designed to ruin a man? Or was it the truth about a scoundrel?

"I've come to a decision about you, Lorelei."

The prior's voice made her look up. Never, ever, had she seen his face so pale, so strained. He seemed to have trouble looking at her. "You must leave the hospice, and soon, before the army reaches here."

Her stomach tightened. She rubbed a hand across her middle. "You mean stay somewhere else while Bonaparte's here?"

He shook his head. Still he would not look at her. "No. Permanently. You'll take vows at the Cistercian Convent of the Strict Observance. It's in Avila, Spain. I've not completed all the arrangements yet, but—"

*"A convent in Spain!"* Lorelei slapped both hands on the desk and stood so abruptly that the bench toppled over. "Those nuns aren't allowed to speak, much less to think!"

"But, Lorelei, the spiritual rewards—"

"I won't go there," she cut in. "I won't give up my life to years of silence and penance. I want to be a doctor." There. The words were out.

"You can't, Lorelei. But you can put your healing skills to work at the convent. It's the only way."

Lord, why had she been so transparent in her desires and ambitions? "The only way to what?"

Father Julian did a strange thing then. He rose from the desk, reached across, and took her hands. "The only way to keep you safe, my dear girl," he whispered.

"Father Julian, you're frightening me with this talk of banishment. I don't understand."

He dropped her hands, walked around the desk, and righted the bench. "You're a woman now. The other postulants will be your sisters. You don't need to understand. You need only to obey."

She backed away. She didn't know this man—this stranger—who meant to banish her from her home.

"Lorelei—"

"No! I'm nearly twenty-one. I can make my own decisions, Father Julian. I won't hear any more!" She bolted from the room, pounded down the dark vaulted stairway, and burst out into the sunshine. The hospice compound sped past in a blur. Fleetingly she saw Sylvain stop swinging a hammer to stare at her; faintly she heard Father Emile call her name. She ran until pain bit into her side, until her breath came in desperate gasps, until the noise of the hospice lay far behind and she was surrounded by the pine-scented woods and the soft chirrup of birds. Half running, half climbing, she went to the landing, the place that held a special kind of magic for her.

But today the magic was gone. All her life she'd loved and trusted Father Julian, and now he meant to banish her. The wrenching agony of betrayal was more than she could bear.

Without thinking, she tore off her boots and clothes, left them in a heap on the grass, and stood at the edge of the pool. For a moment she stared at her image, the reflection churning up, distorted by the narrow cascade from the mountain. Her neck seemed overly long beneath her close-cropped hair; her shoulders were slight, her breasts two negligible medallions on her pale chest. Her gaze traveled down to the dark patch of hair, the thin legs, the knees more prominent than her breasts.

She made a sound of disgust and plunged into the pool. Her backside met the pebbly bottom, and the icy water crawled over her scalp. The shock of cold was so great that she screamed soundlessly and then surfaced, dazed and gasping. She resisted the urge to leap from the stingingly cold water. Misery compelled her to stay immersed in the shallow pool and let the water from the secret springs of the earth crash over her. She welcomed the abrading pebbles, even scrubbed herself with handfuls of them until her flesh felt raw. She moved with wild, jerky motions, sobbing, wishing the numbing cold could freeze her heart, wishing the liquid thunder of the cascade could drown the clamor of betrayal in her head. She wanted to clutch the mountains to her chest and hang on for her life.

But the harder she fought, the more real the truth became. Father Julian intended to send her away. Daniel Severin was a profligate and a murderer.

"Damn," she said through chattering teeth. "Damn, damn, damn!" She picked up a rock and threw it as far as she could. But her fingers were blue from the cold and the shot went awry, dropping a mere dozen yards away.

Finally, her fury spent, she stepped from the pool and pulled on her shirt. It was a castoff from a traveler, and she hadn't bothered to alter it. The hem fell past her hips, nearly to her knees, and the sleeves hung several inches below her hands. But at the moment she was glad for its size. She buttoned the shirt and sat down, letting the garment envelop her.

Shivering, she pondered her absurd behavior. Disillusionment couldn't be washed off, no matter how hard she scrubbed.

With a groan of despair, she tried to shut out the world. She sat until her back cramped and the roar of the falls numbed her ears.

From the corner of her eye she spied a movement.

Large rocks, draped by budding Alpine roses, obscured the path. Something moved through the shadows of the larch trees. A trembling started in her belly. At first she didn't recognize the sensation; then she came to the sick realization that it was fear.

Her secure world had been shattered. Now she knew what it was to be truly afraid.

She sprang up to flee.

"Lorelei!" A tall man moved from beneath the canopy of trees.

Daniel Severin. The Raven. Murderer for hire. Slayer of innocent girls. She watched him closely to see if her perception of him had been changed by what Father Julian had told her.

The prior's recent words warned her off, but the look in Daniel's eyes held her still. Doubts and speculations swirled through her mind. Perhaps Father Julian had been exaggerating. The prior expected her to abandon her life's work, but Daniel had supported her. She owed him a chance to speak for himself.

He walked with a slight limp, his hands swinging at his sides, his expression one of concern. The hunting knife rode in its sheath upon his hip, and a quiver was slung over one shoulder. Deep, tender grass swayed in his wake, and Lorelei sat spellbound, drawn to him, afraid of him, wanting desperately to make sense of her feelings for him.

He stopped a few feet from her. Dappled sunlight picked out the layered blue depths of his eyes. His gaze traveled over her legs, her bare feet, her rolled-up sleeves. His throat worked as he swallowed. To her astonishment, she realized her appearance made him uncomfortable.

"I was bathing," she explained, making a vague gesture toward the pool.

He nodded. "I came to talk to you. I don't want you to be angry about what I said this morning."

She laughed bitterly. After all Father Julian had told her, she'd forgotten Daniel's cruel remarks. She took a step toward him. The grass tickled the bottoms of her feet. "Never mind that, Daniel. Father Julian had a message from Joseph Fouché in Paris." She watched his face closely, seeking a look of guilt or fear.

He regarded her mildly and prompted, "Go on."

She edged her tongue along her lips. Stupid of her to expect a man like Daniel Severin to betray himself. Her blunt speech could never disconcert a practiced mercenary.

"You know of Monsieur Fouché?" she asked.

"He's prefect of police, and not a very savory character. During the Revolution he was known as the Butcher of Lyons."

"He sent Father Julian a letter about you. He claims you're a spy, a womanizer, and a murderer."

Daniel lifted one eyebrow.

"Well?" she asked. "Is it true?"

He drew in a breath, let half of it out, and said, "Yes."

Lorelei blinked. She hadn't expected a simple, unadorned affirmation. She suddenly realized that, deep in her heart, she'd hoped fervently for an angry, self-righteous denial. She could think of nothing more to say except "Oh."

"Any more questions?"

"Yes. Tell me about Aimée de Ronsac."

He seemed to stiffen. The mountain wind whipped a lock of black hair across his face, and he raked it out of the way. "She was the daughter of a friend. I knew her only slightly."

"Fouché claims she poisoned herself on account of you."

"In that, at least, he lied. The girl was disturbed. She was seeing a doctor who treated her with large doses of opium, and one day she took one dose too many."

"What of his other charges?"

"No doubt there's some truth in each."

Her shoulders sagged. "You're an educated man, probably a good soldier. Yet you chose to live as a criminal. Why, Daniel?"

"Because I was tired of living with guilt and disgust, Lorelei. It was best to forsake all morals. That made it easier, somehow."

"I don't understand."

"The massacre of '92. I was their captain. The slaughtered Swiss Guards were my responsibility."

"But the king refused to let you defend yourselves."

His stare pierced her. She wondered what he saw when he looked at her. "True," he said. "But the mob was just a group of angry citizens, ill armed and poorly organized. We could have kept order." He kicked at a small rock. "I watched my men slaughtered like pigs."

"There was nothing you could do."

He glowered. "Damn it, you wanted to know why I became a mercenary."

"I'm certain," she said at last, "that Fouché doesn't understand your side of the story."

"Don't make excuses for me, Lorelei. The massacre, and then prison, turned me bitter. I saw things that drove my ideals into the mud. After that, I did what I did for money."

"Surely you acted the mercenary only when you knew you were serving justice."

"I have no sense of justice, after what I've seen. I was available for anyone's hire, so long as the employer met my price." His voice took on a cruel edge. "Shall I go into detail for you, Lorelei? I maimed thieves, murdered traitors. Or perhaps they weren't thieves and traitors at all. They never had the benefit of a trial.

They were convicted by those who hired me. I merely carried out the sentence."

"Daniel, tell me you regret what you did." She bit her lip. He admitted crimes that could take him to the gibbet. She desperately needed to hear that he had changed.

"At first, my activities were a matter of survival. Paris in 1794 was a dangerous place, a place of secrets and deeds done under a cloak of darkness. Men were in power one day, and the next, their heads rolled. Only those who had no scruples, no dearly held beliefs, survived. I had been two years in prison. When I was released, I was destitute and suspected of Royalist sympathies. I needed money and I needed to prove my political indifference. And so I accepted . . . a task."

"What task?"

He thought a moment, his face hard, his eyes distant. She wondered if his crimes were so numerous that he'd lost track of them all. He said, "It was a matter of a large debt, that first time. A man who owed a great deal of money to my client had refused to repay the debt. My client petitioned the Committee of Public Safety to no avail. At that time Robespierre's partisans were too busy massacring dissenters to bother with debt enforcement. My task was to induce the debtor to settle, and I did so very quickly."

A chill crawled up her spine. "How?"

"I broke one of his fingers. He swore he lacked the means to repay, so I broke another. After the third finger he capitulated, paid the amount in full, plus interest and my collector's fee."

Shock broke over her like a cold sweat. Most chilling

of all was that he showed no emotion. He seemed as calm and amoral as a cat killing a songbird.

"Don't look at me like that," he said curtly.

"After that first time," she said quietly, "I take it your reputation grew."

He nodded. "I had more offers than I could accept."

"And what about your affairs with women?" she forced herself to ask. "Did you do that for money as well?"

His gaze never wavered. "Sometimes."

"And the other times?"

"Other times it was simply a way to remind myself I was still alive."

She bit her lip and kept her eyes lowered. "Why didn't you just leave Paris? You had money. You could simply have left and returned to Switzerland."

"No, I couldn't." She caught a glimmer of pain in his eyes. "Being the man I was then, I couldn't have left Paris."

The women, she thought, suppressing a shudder. His notorious love affairs kept him in Paris. "But you did leave," she insisted. "Because of the patriot Meuron?"

He turned away. "You ask too many questions."

"You obviously didn't come to help me write a treatise on typhus."

"True. But neither did I come to bare my soul to a girl who understands nothing."

"I understand more than you think, Daniel," she said. "You're away from Paris now. Surely it must mean you've disavowed your past career and embraced Meuron's cause."

"Believe that if it comforts you, Lorelei."

Her fist shot out and thudded against his upper arm. His flesh felt solid, but she'd struck him hard and she saw him flinch. "You're infuriating," she snapped. "You treat me like a child too stupid to comprehend anything."

He gripped her shoulders and squeezed hard. "You *are* a child, Lorelei. Stay that way."

Suddenly it was all too much for her. Daniel's odious past, Father Julian's intolerable plan, touched the shortening fuse of her anger. Something burst inside her head, and she hurled herself at him, fists flying.

"You don't know anything about me. You call me a child and tell me to stay that way as if that will solve everything!"

He caught her wrists and hugged her hands to his chest. She felt his rapid heartbeat and saw the chill of contempt in his eyes.

"You don't wish to be a child any longer?" he inquired. "Very well, be a woman, then, Lorelei. Show me how a woman behaves."

Her mind cast about for an answer; her heart told her what to do. Very slowly she uncurled her fingers and laid her palms against his chest. The heat of him spread through her, and she let her hands slide upward, to the sides of his neck and then into his long, wavy hair.

He gave her a little push. "Lorelei, no. I didn't mean—"

"I don't care what you meant." His challenge had freed her, made her bold. "I don't give a damn what you meant."

He was far too tall. She rose on tiptoe, bringing his head down toward hers. She gave him a long, fervent kiss on the lips. The inside of his mouth was a dark, moist secret, which she explored with slow thrusts of her tongue.

He groaned, but not with pain. His arms circled her and drew her closer so that she felt the entire length of him, his chest crushing her breasts.

The cascade thundered in her ears. The sheer pleasure of being close to him filled her with hot, urgent sensations.

His hands rubbed up and down the length of her back, and the motion should have been soothing, but wasn't. She drew the nameless taste of him into her, breathed in his scent of mortar dust and sweat, and suddenly she wanted to be consumed by him, surrounded by him. It was right, wholly right, this wantonness that possessed her.

*It was simply a way to remind myself I was still alive.*

His words echoed in her mind and she understood fully. She wound her arms more tightly around him. Her shirt rode up, and his hands grazed her bare flesh.

He reared away from her then, backed up, and stared at his hand as if he'd burned it. "Jesus, Lorelei."

She put her fingertips to her moist lips. "What's wrong? Did I do something wrong?"

"You're damned right you did."

She took a step toward him, and he stepped back.

"Stay away from me, for God's sake. You have no idea what you're doing."

"I know exactly what I'm doing, Daniel," she flung at him. "You said I should behave more like a woman."

"And you misunderstood. You want me to believe you're an adult? Fine. Start acting like one. Get your clothes on."

She knew then that her appearance disturbed him in a deeply primitive, sensual way, and the knowledge filled her with a heady sense of power.

A wild plan took hold of her. He seemed to dread the thought of compromising her. Selfishly, and with a shocking lack of scruples, she realized that if he did, he'd have to marry her, thus keeping her safe from banishment.

She studied the hard, angry lines of his face. On second thought, she realized that a notorious womanizer would never be bound by honor. She didn't want a husband anyway. She hadn't the first idea about being a wife. She only wanted her freedom.

He picked up her clothes and handed them to her.

She laughed, took the garments, and dropped them. "You're afraid of me, aren't you?"

"No." He touched her beneath the chin. "Something's disturbing you. And it's not what I said to you this morning, probably not even Fouché's letter."

She tried to look away, but his hand held her steady. She gazed into his face—a face too handsome to be trusted, Father Gaston had once said. For the first time in her life she felt a need for caution.

"Father Julian plans to send me away," she said.

"I'm not surprised." Yet his jaw tightened almost imperceptibly.

"Why not?"

"He's about to play host to an army. He'll have

enough problems without having to worry about protecting a pretty girl from forty thousand soldiers."

She pushed his hand away. "I'm not a—"

"—pretty girl?" His gaze traveled lazily to her breasts, thinly covered by the shirt, to her bare legs and feet. "You do a fair imitation, then. God, Lorelei, you know so little about yourself. Have you never tried to see yourself through a man's eyes?"

She chafed beneath his stare. "No. Why should I? When the army comes, my capacity will be that of a physician, not a—a lap ornament. I was hoping to consult with Bonaparte's surgeons."

"And just what do you suppose they'll tell you?"

"Never having met one, I wouldn't know."

"Well, I know. Bonaparte's surgeons regard the sick and wounded as nuisances. They slow the march, clutter the roads, and eat into supplies. A man who can no longer be a soldier ought at least to have the grace to die." He took Lorelei's hand and held up her little finger. "You have more skill and compassion right here, my dear girl, than a whole host of army sawbones. They can teach you nothing."

Snatching her hand away, she folded her arms over her chest. "If that's so, I'd rather find out for myself. But Father Julian doesn't trust me after all these years."

"*I* don't trust you after that kiss."

A smile broke over her face. "Was it wonderful, Daniel? You must tell me."

"Lorelei—"

"Just answer the question."

He scowled. "Yes. It was wonderful."

"I *knew* it. Everything felt just right, didn't it? It was

just as I imagined, only better. As if some magical force picked me up by the feet and flipped me over. But I was thinking, you're so much taller than I, so—"

"Lorelei—"

"—it's hard to keep my neck tilted at that angle—"

"Lorelei, stop."

"—ever so much more accommodating if we were to lie—"

His hand pressed on her nose and mouth, muffling her words until she fell silent.

"Do you mind?" he asked tautly. "I thought we were having a serious discussion."

She took his hand away, holding it in both of hers, studying his long dusty fingers and squarish nails. "I'm sorry. My mood has been so unpredictable today."

"Now," he said, gently extracting his hands from hers, "where does Father Julian intend to send you?"

"To . . ." She shook her head. "It's all some great foolish secret. He wants to send me to a convent and force me to become a bride of Christ."

He crossed his legs, the toe of his boot pointing to the ground. "I take it you don't find the prospect appealing."

"Correct."

"It's not such a foolish idea. It could work."

He did an odd thing as he spoke. He began helping her into her clothes as if she were a child, holding out trousers for her to step into, smoothing her stockings up her legs and lacing her chamois boots, buttoning her *bredzon* over her shirt. Amazed by his ministrations, she didn't resist.

"It could work?" she repeated. "What do you mean by that?"

"Nothing. But if Father Julian thinks sending you away is in your best interest, it probably is."

Furious, she jerked away from him. "You're as hateful as Father Julian. I thought you admired my ambition."

"I do, Lorelei. Oh, I do. But it was a dream, don't you see? Wanting something badly doesn't entitle you to it."

She turned her back on him. "Go away, Daniel. You've no more right than Father Julian to meddle in my life."

Clenching her fists, she stood and listened to the sound of his receding footsteps and didn't look around until she was certain he was gone. The moments stretched into an hour, but no solution came to her. She'd find no help from Daniel. The other canons would surely support Father Julian's decision.

Lorelei realized, with a sudden wave of apprehension, that for the first time in her life, she had no allies.

Beneath the crashing noise of the waterfall she heard an unfamiliar sound. A cry of pain? An animal in distress? She listened, but heard no more.

She rose and wandered through the sharp cold evening toward the hospice. She was still a good distance away when she spied a large, brindled form streaking up the mountain.

"Barry!" she called, slapping her thigh. The dog bounded to a stop near her, but then plunged on, up the mountain. "Oh, Barry," she said in annoyance, *"tu es méchant.* Do come back."

But something in the young mastiff's actions intrigued her. His manner was purposeful, his muzzle low and his tail high, the posture of a dog on a search. She jogged to keep up with him and was surprised when they came to a spill of large rocks scattered by ancient glaciers.

Scratching her head, she realized the rocks gave way to a clear view of the landing.

Barry stopped. His legs stiffened, and the hair on his back bristled. The sound in his throat began as a growl, then crescendoed to a fearful whine.

"What is it, Barry?" Lorelei asked, gripping the largest rock and boosting herself to the top of it.

She looked down through the shadows and saw the body.

# Chapter 10

At supper, the prior said a hasty prayer and the men attacked Mauricio's *roesti* potatoes and succulent spit-roasted chicken. Uncharacteristically, Sylvain picked at his food. After a few minutes he murmured something about the essay he was working on for Father Clivaz and quietly left.

Daniel caught himself worrying about Lorelei, then chastised himself. Father Julian had provided a solution to the problem. Lorelei would be sent into safe obscurity.

Unless the prior. . . . No. Watching Father Julian over the rim of his mug, Daniel took a long pull on his beer, savoring the yeasty taste. Julian had kept Lorelei—and her treasure, if indeed it existed—safe for twenty years.

Even so, Daniel decided to see that she arrived safely at the convent. Then he would be free. Free. No longer responsible for the bastard princess, no longer indebted to Josephine Bonaparte.

He'd have to lie to the first consul's wife, but the prospect didn't bother him. He would tell her he'd taken the daughter of Louis XVI away from the hospice and that, during their travels, she'd died in a long fall.

Josephine would demand proof.

Her "proof," he'd tell her contemptuously, lay at the bottom of a lonely canyon, or perhaps in a deep crevice of the ancient glaciers that snaked through the mountains. That should satisfy Josephine. That should keep her tongue still about their past, and her lethal influence out of Swiss politics.

Yet inside, Daniel felt a little tearing sensation that hurt more than it should have. His encounter with Lorelei that afternoon had caused a strange eruption in his soul, blasted him through with a sense of newness, of wonder, that felt alien in a man who used to think he understood—and intensely disliked—the nature of females. He'd seen beneath her scruffy surface and discovered a beauty so light and clear it took his breath away. He'd gazed into her guileless brown eyes and confronted an affection and trust that shattered his notions about women.

He imagined Lorelei torn from her mountain home, stripped of her work and of the dogs and the men she loved, thrust into the bonds of strict convent life.

She's strong, he told himself, draining his beer mug and pretending to listen to the lesson Father Julian was reading. Her ebullient spirit wouldn't be chained by mere vows. He had to believe that. He had to believe she'd survive. He had to believe she wouldn't do anything rash.

The refectory door banged open. Heads turned toward the entrance. In the wavering lamplight, Lorelei's eyes were as large and dark as twin bruises. She had a stunned expression on her face and a raven-fletched arrow in her hand.

The men in the room fell silent. Father Julian's book closed with a thump. Instinctively Daniel knew that none of them had ever seen her in this wild-eyed state.

Without looking left or right, she walked to Daniel and slapped the arrow on the table in front of him.

He smelled a coppery odor and looked down. Blood slicked the tip and several inches of the shaft.

"Curse you," she said in a tortured whisper. "Curse you for a cruel, despicable murderer."

Daniel shot to his feet and grasped her shoulders. As the others closed in around them, he searched her body for the wound.

"What happened, Lorelei?" he demanded.

"Where are you hurt?" asked Father Anselme, coming forward with a haste that belied his age.

Ignoring Father Anselme, she flung off Daniel's hands. Her face was as pale as sun-bleached bone. "Don't you touch me."

Shock streaked through him. He was no stranger to hatred, but Lorelei's rejection contained a special kind of sting.

"Where did you get this?" asked Father Julian. He picked up the arrow gingerly. Gasps rose from the others.

Lorelei's furious, grieving eyes never left Daniel. "I tore it from the body of an animal slaughtered by this man. He killed Belle, you see. Monsieur Severin has killed our Belle."

A groan of anguish sounded behind Daniel. One of the younger novices began to weep.

"Monsieur Severin." The prior exuded a blast of anger so tangible that Daniel could feel its heat on his skin. "I suggest you explain yourself."

"It's a mistake," he snapped, furious and confused, more frightened than he cared to admit. "I never—"

"The arrow entered beneath the fourth lateral rib," Lorelei said in a curiously flat voice that drove home the horror more poignantly than histrionics. "The tip penetrated the aorta—I could tell because there was so much blood." She folded her arms around her midsection, a mindless gesture of self-protection. "Can we go get her, Father Julian? Can we go get her and bring her home?"

An urge to embrace her seized Daniel, but he thrust aside the impulse. She believed him guilty of a hideous, senseless murder. His touch would sicken her.

He faced a sea of accusing faces. Protestations of innocence would get him nowhere. But he'd find the culprit. And serve his head on a platter. Shoving through the crowd, he went out into the cold night. Sounds of protest followed him, then Father Julian's voice: "Let him go. Perhaps we're rid of him at last." The prior began organizing a detail to fetch the body.

A hunter's instinct sent Daniel to the kennels. One person had been missing from the refectory. Daniel knew with inexplicable certainty where to find him.

The dogs whined when he entered; their uncanny senses told them something was wrong. In a far corner, bathed in bluish moonlight streaming through an unglazed window, Daniel found him.

He sat on a bed of straw with Belle's puppies, speaking in mindless soothing whispers and feeding one of them from a flask.

Setting his jaw to drive away a wave of nausea, Daniel seized the culprit's collar and hauled him to his feet.

"Let's go, Sylvain," he stated, batting away the younger man's flailing fists. "You've got some explaining to do."

Large and brawny, Sylvain could have given Daniel a formidable fight, but he didn't. Stepping carefully to avoid crushing any of the puppies, he left the kennels with Daniel.

Men hurried through the compound. Daniel drew Sylvain into the shadows and shoved him down a path toward the lake. They came to a rickety landing where, Lorelei had told him, she sometimes sat and gigged for trout in the summer. An upended rowboat lay on the pier, and a night mist hung over the lake.

With swift, economical movements, Daniel twisted Sylvain's arm behind his back. He laid his own forearm across the novice's throat and pressed until he heard Sylvain's breath stop.

"Why did you kill that dog?" he asked calmly.

Sylvain made a gurgling sound in his throat. Daniel

eased the pressure so he could speak. "I—I didn't!" he gasped.

Daniel clamped his arm back down. It was the one he'd broken, and it had started to ache. Sylvain could best him if he weren't so crippled by fear. "Look, you're wasting my time. I'll have the truth from you even if it means breaking your fingers, one by one."

Sylvain's eyes rolled. In the dim twilight Daniel could see they were rimmed with grief. "Christ," he muttered. "You must have some explanation. Let's hear it." He lifted his arm.

"I didn't mean to shoot the dog."

"Lorelei described it as a clean kill, not an accident."

"I was aiming at some—something else."

"You're Swiss; you're a marksman. You don't make mistakes."

"The dog has such instincts. She leaped in front of him—"

"Him?" Daniel's stomach tightened. "Who? A brigand?"

Sylvain's lips moved, but he made no sound. Daniel realized the young man was praying.

"Tell me," he ordered. "Quickly. It's important. Who were you aiming at?"

"A . . . a canon. God help me, it was one of the canons." Tears gathered in Sylvain's eyes, and the trembling of his body shook them loose.

"Which one?" Daniel demanded.

"I—I couldn't tell. His cowl covered his head, and I was twenty paces away. It could have been any of them."

"For Christ's sake," Daniel exploded, "you were going to murder a man you couldn't identify? Why?"

"He had a musket, one from the army's ordnance supply. He was hiding near the landing and aiming at Lorelei."

Astonishment blazed across Daniel's face. He could feel his features and his limbs slacken. He released Sylvain and stepped back. He'd left her vulnerable. He'd thought he was through making stupid mistakes.

"Jesus," he said. "Sit down, Sylvain."

The young man slumped against the rounded hull of the boat.

"Did you give chase?"

"No, I—I couldn't. I . . . ran. I turned coward, just as I did when the brigand attacked me and Lorelei."

"You don't have time for self-recriminations," Daniel snapped. "The man you were aiming at knows what you saw. You've got to leave here."

"But Lorelei—"

"I'll keep Lorelei safe."

Sylvain hesitated. He moistened his lips. "Why should I trust you?"

"Because I'm not going to give you a choice."

Lashed by Daniel's harsh tone, Sylvain flinched. "After the explosion, Father Julian told me to keep an eye on her."

"Did he say why?"

"No. He just wanted me to watch over her in case of another . . . accident like the one in the infirmary. This morning I saw her dash off. I knew she had a place she liked to go on the mountain, so I decided to check there."

"She said no one knew about that place."

An odd look flashed in his clear pale eyes. "I knew. And so did you."

And in that instant, in the soft tenor of Sylvain's voice, Daniel realized that the miserable youth loved her.

He swallowed his shock. It could hardly matter now. "You armed yourself with my arrow. Why?"

"You know that, too."

"You were jealous. You wanted to discredit me."

Sylvain nodded.

"Well, it fooled her. She accused me. Exactly as you'd intended." Daniel's mind raced. The killer had obviously taken the dog to track down Lorelei. "I have to question Father Droz," said Daniel, thinking aloud.

"Father Droz didn't realize Belle was gone. He hasn't kept her penned because he knew she wouldn't stray far from her pups." Like moondrops, tears pearled on Sylvain's smooth cheeks. "The bastard must have told her to stay by his side. She—she looked right at me. You've got to understand, these dogs have a protective instinct that's completely selfless. Belle saw what I was going to do, and she leaped in front of him to protect him. To protect the murdering bastard."

Who? Daniel wondered feverishly. Lorelei said the dog had bled a lot. He resolved, though without much hope, to check the laundry for bloody garments. But the killer was probably too clever to leave behind such an obvious clue.

Sylvain scrubbed his sleeve across his face. Daniel wanted to look away. Away from the wide-eyed pain of shattered innocence. It wasn't right that this good man had killed and that he had to live with what he'd done.

"I'll go now," said Sylvain.

"Not yet," said Daniel. "You've got a confession to make."

"No," said Sylvain, shrinking back. "I couldn't face them."

"You will. You'll say nothing of the canon, only that you were out shooting and made a tragic mistake." Daniel intended for the confession to take place publicly, for if the killer got Sylvain alone, the novice's life wouldn't be worth a prayer.

"Why are you making me do this?" Sylvain demanded.

"The assassin might betray himself." And I don't want her thinking I killed that dog, Daniel admitted to himself. "After that, I want you to go to Paris."

Sylvain stared at him in surprise. "To Paris? Why?"

"Because of Meuron. Some Swiss partisans are trying to help him gain his freedom. They could use your help."

The grief began to clear from Sylvain's eyes. "You really think I could make a difference?"

"Possibly." Daniel was surprised at his own compassion. He made the youth memorize an address in Saint Denis.

"But what about Lorelei? I'd like to know your intentions."

Daniel almost laughed at the youth's self-righteous expression. "I said I'd keep her safe."

"That's not good enough. There's a lot more to this problem than—" Sylvain clamped his mouth shut.

"What are you trying to say?" Daniel asked.

"Nothing. Never mind."

Daniel took a step forward. "Tell me what you know."

Distrust and suspicion clouded Sylvain's face. He said no more.

Like a striking hawk, Daniel's hand clamped around Sylvain's wrist and tightened until he heard the bones begin to give. "Tell me."

"She's not what she seems." Sylvain licked his dry lips. "She's an important personage."

Daniel took a chance and loosened his grip. "Because of who her father was?"

Rubbing his wrist, Sylvain slumped back against the boat. "You know. I thought so." Realization broke over his young, handsome face. "She's the reason you came here, isn't she? You came to protect her."

"Never mind why I'm here," said Daniel, sick with the memory of his true purpose in invading the hospice and Lorelei's life. "How the devil did *you* find out?"

"Last summer." He let out a long helpless sigh. "I was with Father Gaston at Yverdon. He—he didn't realize it—the cell was dark—but I was there. I heard the abbess make her last confession."

"So you think Father Gaston was the one with the musket?"

Sylvain shrugged. "He's not the only one who knows about her. There's Father Anselme and the prior. And Father Emile. He nursed Father Gaston through the typhus and heard him speak of her in his delirium. Oh, sweet Lord, I can't imagine any of them . . ." Sylvain leaned forward, his face full of pitiful hope. "Maybe it was a stranger in disguise."

"The dog trusted him," Daniel reminded Sylvain.

"They're men of God," Sylvain choked out.

"They're men. As susceptible as anyone else to games of greed and power."

"You understand, then, don't you? You realize she must leave?" Desperation tore at Sylvain's voice.

"I'll see to it."

"You'll get her away from here?"

"Yes."

"And then what?"

"I'll take her to a place where no one knows who she is."

"That's what Saint Bernard's was supposed to be. And how will you force her to stay where she's safe? Your plan's not good enough, Daniel. You have to make sure."

"Any suggestions?" Daniel snapped, his patience dwindling. Shouts carried across the surface of the lake.

"Marry her." Sylvain's whisper drifted on the cold wind off the lake.

*"What?"*

"I said marry her." He spoke as if someone were behind him, prodding him with a knife, forcing the words from him.

"That's crazy—"

"No, just listen. I saw the two of you together today. She probably doesn't even realize it yet, but she's going to love you, if she hasn't started to already. And when Lorelei loves, it'll be forever."

"You're mad."

"I know her. In ways no one else does. I have four sisters. I know what a girl looks like when she's falling in love."

Daniel was struck with the realization that Sylvain, a novice who'd pledged his life to God, had fallen victim to the most lethal earthly affliction of all. He was no murderer, but a misguided boy who'd had the misfortune to fall in love with a bastard princess.

Sylvain took a deep breath and rushed on. "I've seen how you treat her—you won't hurt her. Marry her, Daniel. It's the only way you can be with her day and night, protecting her, always."

The yearning in Sylvain's voice raised a knot in Daniel's throat. He thought he'd forgotten how to feel the pain of loving. But Sylvain's broken admission brought all the anguish rushing back at Daniel.

"I'll see that she's safe. Believe it." He could say nothing more, and he knew it wasn't enough to salve Sylvain's wounded heart. The shouts grew louder, and an owl hooted in the woods. "You'd better go. Make your confession and leave."

"But my vocation—"

"You can serve another worthy cause in Paris."

Sylvain nodded miserably. "Just keep Lorelei safe." The words flowed like a prayer off his lips as he began trudging up toward the main building. "For the love of God, keep her safe."

*Marry her.*

The idea thrummed like a headache in Daniel's brain. He lay wide awake in the dormitory with the novices slumbering innocently all around him. As he'd anticipated, everyone had been shocked by Sylvain's admission of guilt. While the youth bundled his few belongings and started down the mountain, Daniel had watched the canons' faces. He'd seen grief, anger, even compassion in a few. But no one showed relief or malice. The assassin kept his counsel well.

Lorelei's choked-out apology to Daniel still echoed in his head and mingled with Sylvain's quiet statement.

*She's going to love you . . . and when Lorelei loves, it'll be forever.*

Daniel punched his pillow. What the hell did Sylvain know? He was an innocent, barely a man. But complex in his way, with a marksman's eyes that saw too much, with ears that had heard too much.

*I know the look of a woman who's falling in love. . . .*

Lorelei couldn't be falling in love with him. She was too sensible to let a man like Daniel Severin darken her heart. Still, he knew he fanned a fire in her that blazed hotter each time they spoke or touched or kissed. From the depths of her innocence a woman was emerging, a woman of passion and heart.

*Marry her.*

He pictured himself asking her. He'd proposed to a woman one other time, years ago. Would he go down on bended knee before Lorelei as he had with the first one? Fill her ears with pledges and promises? The image brought a curl of disgust to his lips. He was an accomplished liar. He could make her believe him.

And then what? Would he skulk off to some isolated Alpine hamlet and bury them both in obscurity for all time? He found an amusing irony in that—the bastard princess wed to the bastard son of a horse thief.

No, he decided firmly. He was the Raven. He wouldn't—couldn't—be caged. She'd have to settle for a convent.

But somehow he couldn't picture Lorelei chained by vows of obedience, silence, chastity. He couldn't see her spending hours in mindless meditation. She was a brilliant girl with dreams and ambitions and desires, none of which could be fulfilled in a convent.

Another picture drifted into his mind. He saw her nursing her child at her breast, patching a scraped knee, bent over her studies in the quiet of the night. *That* was Lorelei.

Yet mortal danger poisoned every breath she took. The murderer had been watching them, had seen them kiss like lovers.

Once again Daniel pounded his pillow into submission. Through a high, small window in the dormitory, cold stars glared at him. He was a fool where Lorelei was concerned. His weakness for her had made him vulnerable. He had to act, and soon.

He turned the problem over and over in his mind. Defy Josephine and risk their necks. Lie to Lorelei and break her heart.

As dawn broke in a spectacular spray of color over the mountains, Daniel came to a decision.

"I must speak to you," said Daniel.

Lorelei glanced up from her perusal of medical supplies, delivered that morning by an advance party from the Army of Reserve. Cases of bottled laudanum, bales of bandages, and crocks of antiseptic filled a temporary shelter made of canvas.

"Of course," she said. "I was just inspecting the medicines. How odd to see them stacked right here beside the gunpowder."

"Lorelei—"

"So much of it." The laudanum crates reached her chin. "They must be expecting many casualties. I hope the presence of all this medicine will prove you wrong about army doctors."

"Lorelei." He gripped her shoulder. How easy he found it to touch her these days. "Will you please listen?"

She saw it then, the look in his eyes. An intensity, an urgency she'd never seen in him before. Oh, Lord, she thought. He's too wonderful to look at. "I'm sorry, Daniel. I do go on, don't I? I've been so grieved about Belle, and—strange as it sounds—I miss Sylvain. On top of that, Father Julian won't change his mind about sending me away. What is it you want to speak to me about?"

He glanced over his shoulder, and she followed his gaze. In the week since Sylvain's departure, the hospice had come to resemble an armed camp. Soldiers worked alongside monks, building pens for horses, raising tents to house officers and supplies. Her stare focused on a long field cannon, the first to be dragged up the mountain in its huge log sledge.

"It seems a sacrilege," she murmured. "This is supposed to be a place of peace."

"Every corner of Switzerland is Bonaparte's personal property," said Daniel.

"Is that what you came to tell me?"

"No."

"What, then?"

He looked from side to side. Blue highlights flashed in his midnight hair, contrasting with the single blaze of white. "Not here. Meet me somewhere private."

Frowning, she fingered her lower lip. Her first thought was the landing by the pool, but the very idea made her shudder. It was too close to where she'd found Belle.

"There's a place by the lake—a huge alder tree. Sylvain and I used to . . ." She bit her lip. For a moment her thoughts drifted back to days of sunshine and openness. "We used to climb it." She described the location of the alder tree.

"Go there and wait for me." Father Julian enforced his restrictions without mercy these days.

"You'll do it, won't you, Lorelei?"

She studied his face and realized she'd do much more for him, if only he'd ask.

Daniel had no trouble finding the appointed spot by the lake. A giant alder spread its branches, laying black shadows over the water.

"Lorelei?" he called softly.

"Up here." She sat on a platform made of sticks lashed together with fraying rope. Her feet, ridiculously small and shod in chamois boots, swung just above his head. She was surrounded by new leaves and an aura of innocence that made his stomach knot.

He found a handhold in a crook of the tree and

hoisted himself up. He moved gingerly for fear the weathered structure would crash to the ground.

"Hello," she said and touched a lock of hair that had strayed across his temple.

He wished fervently that her smallest touch didn't have this weird, melting effect on him.

"Yes. Well." He cleared his throat. A green youth with his first girl couldn't have been more tongue-tied. He half expected his voice to break. "I want to ask you something. And I want you to think about it very carefully."

"Yes?" She blinked her huge brown eyes, a trusting doe who had no idea she faced a predator.

He scowled and looked away. This was harder than he'd anticipated. "Lorelei, have you ever thought about the love between a man and a woman?" It was a subject he knew nothing about, but he needed to sound convincing.

Her hands closed over his. "Love?" Her face was startled, her smile as joyous as a sunrise. "Are you saying we're in love?"

"Actually, I—"

"Oh, I knew it!" She lifted his hands and clasped them to her chest. He felt her heart beating, rapid and curiously fragile, beneath her delicate bone structure. "I just knew it!"

"But wait, we—"

"I'm so glad we can talk openly. I've been thinking about it for weeks, wondering why I get all strange and warm inside when I look at you."

"Don't be rid—"

"For a while I ached so much I thought I was coming down with something."

"The only thing you're—"

"You know, when Father Julian showed me the letter from Fouché, I feared you had many lovers in Paris. Well, you did, of course. But obviously they mean nothing to you now, because you're here with me."

He couldn't bear to hear the happiness burbling like a mountain spring from her. With no other thought but to silence her, he took her face between his hands and kissed her hard.

For a moment he lost his purpose, lost it in the unbearable sweetness of her, the passion she never bothered to disguise as she pressed against him and opened her mouth beneath his.

The ominous creak of the platform brought him back to his goal. He lifted his head. A chestnut-colored curl had fallen across her cheek. He had an urge to touch the soft lock, much as she had touched him a few moments ago. But unlike her, he resisted.

He was about to deceive her—monstrously. At the very least, he owed her a chance to turn away. "Lorelei, you've misunderstood. Men like me don't fall in love."

He expected disappointment or even tears; instead he got laughter. She fell against him and giggled into the lapel of his *bredzon*.

Jesus, even his one attempt at honesty had misfired. Didn't she realize he offered her a chance to see that he couldn't give her love?

"Oh, Daniel, what an absurd thing to say." She pulled back, put her fists to her hips, and mimicked,

" 'Men like me don't fall in love.' " She laughed with pure delight. "Of course you do. You have!"

"Lorelei, it's not like that for me."

"It is." Sobering, she laid her hand on his cheek. "I'm naive because of my upbringing. But I'm neither stupid nor insensitive. I feel your love when you hold me. When you kiss me." She put her lips to his, then drew back. "Sweet Mary, I can taste it!"

"Lorelei, don't—"

"I can so taste it. It's like honey and wine and buttered Jamaica water—Father Clivaz's brother sent him some from Louisiana once, and he gave me a taste."

"Damn it, will you listen to yourself?" Daniel drove his fingers through his hair. "Love isn't some exotic taste or a little flutter in your breast."

"I know." The smile left her face and was replaced by a simple, devastating solemnity. "It's not. It's the most complicated, most glorious, of all human emotions, so deep and shattering that it's foolish even to attempt a description."

"Oh, Christ." He looked away.

She put her hands on his face, touching him with a fire he despaired of smothering. "Just accept it, Daniel. You're a hard man. You've been hurt. But you can be healed."

He couldn't bring himself to tell her that there was nothing left of his heart to be healed. He couldn't bring himself to draw away from her feather-light touch.

"So, Daniel." She moistened her lips. The sight of her tiny pink tongue unnerved him. "We've fallen in love. So what shall we do next?"

He knew an argument would only subject him to more of her circular logic. Besides, she'd saved him the trouble of lying. He blew out a sigh and said, "So we get married."

# Chapter 11

Lorelei's hands shook with equal measures of fear and excitement as she packed her few belongings in a rucksack. Working in the darkness of her cell at midnight, she let her hands linger over each item.

An extra set of sturdy clothes. Sylvain had outgrown the woolen breeches the year before. Father Gaston's patient hands had made them over to fit her petite form. She brushed her finger over the waistband, where a pattern of roses adorned the fabric. Gaston had endured some teasing over his needlework, but he'd been adamant about giving her clothing a feminine touch.

She stuffed the garments in the bottom of the sack

and picked up her missal. The book had been a gift from Father Julian at her confirmation into the Catholic faith. The prior's own hand had tooled her initials in the calfskin cover. Lorelei had been bursting with love and gratitude for the stern man who'd raised her from infancy.

The memory tugged at her heart. Her elopement with Daniel would hurt Father Julian. But what choice did she have? She couldn't stay here, torn apart by the knowledge that someone at the hospice was a murderer. Nor could she accept banishment to a convent. She had to go with Daniel, had to follow her heart.

Next she packed the notes from her box along with a few precious medical instruments given to her by Father Anselme. The true gifts he'd given her couldn't be packed up in a bag. She carried them in her heart and in her mind. He'd taught her humanity, an appreciation for the preciousness of life; he'd given her dedication and the skills to go with it.

She added a hairbrush to her parcel. Father Emile had chiseled the handle from mountain ash and added bristles from a wild boar they'd feasted upon last Easter. Carved into the back of the brush was a small spreading tree. She suspected he'd retained the image from his days in Paris, when the tree of liberty symbolized the revolutionaries.

The men who had murdered eight hundred Swiss Guards.

She crossed herself, haunted by the connection. One man had lived to tell the tale, and no doctor could heal the scars he carried. Perhaps, she thought determinedly, a loving woman could.

Working more quickly, she finished packing. Every item carried some memory of the men and the home she loved: a little figure of a dog carved from horn by Father Droz, a mouth harp from Father Clivaz, a knife and fork from Mauricio.

She carefully folded the blouse from Germaine de Staël. The sheer whisper-soft fabric caressed her fingers. Filled with trepidation, Lorelei stood on the brink of a world where women dressed, thought, spoke, and behaved differently from her.

Finally she dropped in the velvet bag containing her rosary, her only legacy from the parents she'd never known.

Squaring her shoulders, she pulled on her jacket and muffler and slung the pack on her back. It was time to go.

She opened her cell door, stepped out into the corridor, and took a deep, shaky breath. She'd long since ceased to notice the familiar smells of the hospice. But now she paused to savor the sweetness one last time. The odors of old stone and church incense drifted through her senses, and her nose began to sting. Very quietly she shut the door behind her, closing off her room, her childhood, and the only life she'd ever known.

Yet happiness blotted out her regrets as she tiptoed from the monastery and down to the landing by the lake.

Daniel saw her coming toward him, a lithe form slipping through the dark ribbons of shadow cast by the trees. He still couldn't quite believe she'd accepted his outrageous offer and had agreed to leave with him.

Guilt scratched him like a hair shirt. She'd made his ruse easy. Too damned easy. The lamb of Saint Bernard's had put her complete trust in Josephine's wolf.

She ran silently down the bank. Even burdened by a bulky rucksack, she moved with the surefooted speed of a chamois doe.

"Hello, Daniel." Breathless, she stretched up to kiss his cheek. The adoring look in her eyes brightened the gloom of midnight and darkened his heart with regrets.

"Ready?" he asked, glancing over her shoulder. No lights burned in the hulking hospice buildings; no movement stirred the stiff reeds at the edge of the lake.

"Yes." She put one foot in the boat.

"Lorelei, are you sure you want this?" God, say no, half of him pleaded, while the other half was terrified she might change her mind.

"I'm very sure, Daniel."

"We could find some other way to—"

"No. I want to marry you."

"But—"

"I've thought it all through very carefully." She settled into the boat. The skin of ice crackled; then ripples slapped hollowly at the hull. "If I don't marry you . . . Do you know that a person can actually die of a broken heart? I read of a case in Padua. A woman was spurned by her lover, and she simply lay down and died. A perfectly healthy woman, with no symptoms." She watched him pick up the oars and begin rowing. "I'm sure that's what would happen to me if I ever lost you, Daniel."

"For God's sake, Lorelei—"

"Daniel, I know it must be hard for a man like you to speak of his true feelings. You're much like Father Julian in that." She hugged her knees as the boat lurched with Daniel's long oar strokes. "Each time I'd go off on a rescue, he'd say to me, 'Watch your step, Lorelei.' Just that, nothing more." A wistful smile curved her lips. "But what he was really saying was 'I love you, Lorelei.' "

Was he? Daniel wondered, listening to the quiet plash of the oars in the water. His bad arm ached; he was glad for the gloves he wore to prevent blisters. Or did the prior hide a murderer's mind behind his cool, intelligent facade?

Lorelei's talk of love and yearning made Daniel uncomfortable. He used to believe in love and honor; he used to have a grand sense of his own worth. But that was before war and subterfuge and massacre. And Josephine.

Shunning the dark remembrance, he concentrated on the present plan. He'd come here to kill her. Now he was taking her to safety. His plan was to take her to the Château Coppet near Geneva. There, in Baron Necker's unique salon, she would be free to discourse with scholars and pursue her vocation. Necker and his formidable daughter, Germaine, could be counted on to safeguard her secret and her life.

By crossing the lake they'd leave no trail. The dogs would eventually pick up their scent, but they'd have a small lead.

As the boat bumped the opposite shore, he caught the look on Lorelei's face. With wide, misty eyes and slightly parted lips, she stared at a point over his shoulder. He turned to look.

Framed by the purple night sky sat the monastery, its solid, boxlike buildings dark against a glittering sweep of stars. It was a picture of peace, serenity, security. It was the only home she'd ever known.

"It's not too late to go back," he whispered.

She blinked. "I wasn't thinking of going back. But do you remember, I once told you I was afraid of what lies beyond the mountains?"

"I remember." He braced himself. He could hear it before she spoke: You'll take care of me, Daniel.

"I still am. But it's a good fear, one to make me strong. I'm glad to be taking this step."

Daniel resisted an urge to take her in his arms. Once again she'd surprised him. She was no clinging, dependent female, but a woman of courage and heart.

He helped her out of the boat, placed his foot on the bow and gave it a great shove. They stood watching it drift away.

Finally he pivoted and started into the woods. And didn't look back.

For six hours they trekked northward, passing strange crags that pierced the starry sky, crossing deep tracts bridged by fallen firs, hurrying beneath spring cataracts that misted the night air and froze their skin.

"Army's been here," Daniel muttered, studying a series of tall masts set up to guide travelers. Nearby, a bear rooted indolently around a rotting pine tree.

Lorelei stabbed the toe of her boot at a rutted track. "Within the past few days, I'd say."

They came to a vast glacial morass, ancient ice scored by deep chasms they had to leap over. Daniel stopped at a wide crevice, its lip mounded with snowdrifts. He tossed her the end of a rope. "Gird yourself with this. It's a long jump."

She whispered a prayer and made the sign of the cross. Daniel gripped the rope in his gloved hands. She felt no fear. Her faith in him ran deep, deeper than the chasm that gaped like a black ditch in front of her. She paced back a few steps, then hurled herself forward, sailed over the crevice, and landed in a heap on the opposite side.

"Take off the rope now," said Daniel.

"Oh, no. Not until you're safe, too."

He glowered at her. "Look. I'm the leader. You're the follower. Surely you understand the basic principles of mountaineering."

"Fine. You lead, I'll follow."

"Good."

"But I won't take off the rope."

"Damn it, woman, if I fall, I'll pull you with me."

"Then you'd best take care not to fall." She regarded him stubbornly across the chasm.

Daniel swore again, took the leap with an inborn grace that left her breathless, and landed on his feet. "You're a sorry excuse for an underling," he grumbled, untying the ropes.

She adjusted the straps of her rucksack. "And you're an outstanding commander. We're a perfect match."

The narrow path wound down in a dizzying snail-shell pattern flanked by steep precipices and sheer drops. To keep from slipping, they strapped on iron pattens with sharp prongs that scraped loudly in the silence.

"Tell me about where we're going," she said over her shoulder. "Tell me about the Château Coppet."

"Jacques Necker bought it—and the barony—almost twenty years ago. It overlooks the lake about ten miles from Geneva."

"And you're certain we'll be welcome there?"

"I'm not certain of anything, Lorelei. But Germaine seemed to like you."

"I liked her, too."

A shadow seemed to pass over his face, and she suddenly realized he was still a stranger to her in many ways. As his betrothed, she felt she should ask about his thoughts, but she hadn't the courage. Someday she would, though.

"You don't think the baron of Coppet will think me . . . odd?"

The corner of Daniel's mouth lifted in a half smile. "With a daughter like Germaine? You'll be as welcome as springtime."

Lorelei hugged the words to her heart. She envisioned life at the château as an unceasing feast where she would be free to pursue her work, where Daniel would be safe from the past that hounded him.

The sun peeked over the rim of mountains. Boneweary and exhausted to the point of numbness, she blinked at the fronds of lavender light that struck the snow-dusted meadow below them. Although the terrain was still much like that which surrounded the hospice, the world seemed strange and new here.

The world hadn't changed, she thought in bleary introspection. She had.

"Let's rest," said Daniel, brushing snow off his collar and lowering himself to a fallen log. Gratefully she sank down beside him. She thought it uncanny that even after a night of hard travel he could still look so blessedly handsome. The soft morning light gilded his strong, angular features and settled like a mist over his long hair.

"Your knee's hurting you," she said.

"Yes." For once he was too weary to contradict her. "And you're about to fall on your face."

"But you're here to catch me. Now that we've diagnosed each other's ailments, why don't we eat something?"

He rummaged in his rucksack and produced a pair of rolls filched from Mauricio's kitchen. Lorelei whispered a prayer of thanksgiving, then looked up to see Daniel already eating.

"Sorry," he muttered. "I forgot to wait."

His look of chagrin endeared him to her anew. Leaning over, she kissed his cheek. "Daniel, you don't have to change your habits on my acc—"

An urgent baying broke the morning quiet. Daniel's knife snicked from its sheath. Seconds later a large animal appeared on the rise above them and hurtled downward.

Lorelei's throat closed around a flood of sentiment. "It's Barry." Then he was upon her, covering her face with warm wet strokes of his tongue. "Barry," she murmured, *"tu es méchant.* You shouldn't have come."

She glanced up to see Daniel studying the upper

trail. His every muscle tense, he waited to see who followed the dog.

"He came on his own," she assured him. "If he were searching, he would have given a yelp when he found us."

"I don't like it." Daniel jammed his knife back in its sheath. "We've been away for only a few hours, and already we've been found."

Bending on one knee, Lorelei linked her arms around the dog's thick neck. "He's always been an escape artist. I should have chained him, but I hadn't the heart." The look on Daniel's face chilled her. "What are you going to do?"

"You've got to make him go back."

Her arms tightened around Barry's neck. "But—"

"I said, make him go back. Isn't there a command you can give to send him to the hospice?"

"Yes, but . . ." How could she explain? How could she tell him how it felt to leave everything behind? She studied the uncompromising line of his jaw and the firm set of his lips. She tried to think like him: a huge dog would be too much of a burden on the path they'd set for themselves.

She willed her arms to loosen and let go of Barry. *"Vas-y,"* she said. "Go back to the hospice." She made a shooing motion with her hands. Barry walked away a few steps, then turned to regard her with his drooping, velvety eyes. *"Vas-y!"* she repeated desperately. "Go on, Barry!"

The dog hung his head, tucked his tail, and plodded up the path.

"He saved you," she said to Daniel.

"What?"

"Barry was the first to find you in the avalanche. I just thought you'd like to know." She didn't look at Daniel but continued staring after Barry. The dog slunk away as if she'd beaten him.

Daniel's low voice rasped behind her. "You are the most aggravating—"

"He *does* belong to me. Father Droz gave him to me personally."

"—manipulative—"

"I thought you'd like to know that, too."

"—whining little piece I've ever lost an argument to."

She paused, letting his words sink in. "Lost? You mean—"

"Call him back."

Lorelei gave a squeal of delight and spun around to wrap Daniel in a fierce hug. "You dear, sweet man!" She ignored his look of self-disgust, kissed him hard on the mouth, cold lips and warm breath mingling. "Barry!" she called, clapping her hands. "Barry, come!"

Daniel endured the second reunion in silence, tapping his alpenstock on the crusty snow. Common sense urged him to abandon the dog. But as he watched Lorelei burying her face in the shining brindled fur of Barry's neck, common sense ceased to have meaning. He'd come to the hospice with murder in his heart. He was leaving with a bastard princess and a giant dog.

"God help us all," he muttered under his breath.

How easily he gave in to her. How dangerous that

was for them both. The lie he'd told her gnawed at him. He didn't intend to marry her; he'd tell her so once they reached Coppet. By then, Daniel told himself with an uncomfortable lack of confidence, he'd have found a way to convince her that they didn't belong together. She'd have her work and Necker's protection; he'd have the task of finding out exactly what had happened to the Bern gold and clearing Meuron's name. It would be enough. Damn it, it had to be enough.

He leaned back against a tree, intending to close his eyes just for a moment. A loud cracking sound brought him instantly to his feet.

"Musket shot!" he said, making a lunge at Lorelei. "Take cover!"

They dived behind a large hollow log, the mastiff huddling with them. Lorelei's face paled. "Daniel, what . . ."

Daniel saw a flash on the ridge above them, then a puff of smoke drifting skyward. Another shot rang out.

"It's coming from the ridge."

"Bonaparte's soldiers? But why would they shoot at us?"

A third shot thundered from a lower section of the ridge. The ball thudded into the ground, spraying up ice and dirt, perilously close to them. Rocks rained down from an overhang above the road, loosened by the musket shots.

"He's coming toward us," Daniel said through gritted teeth. "Jesus, he'll set off an avalanche." As he spoke, he twisted around and whipped an arrow from his quiver. He'd have to stand to get off a shot, making a target of himself.

"Stay down," he said to Lorelei. He stood, flexing his bow and then nocking the arrow. At this range, he had the more accurate weapon. But he stood in plain sight while the sniper was still concealed by the lip of the road.

Sweat broke out on Daniel's brow and the wind turned it to ice. A shadow moved high on the ridge. A figure clad in a long brown robe appeared, shouting, aiming the musket at Daniel. A deep hood obscured the man's face.

"It's one of the canons," said Lorelei. "Oh, Daniel—"

Yet another shot exploded; the ball thunked into a tree trunk somewhere behind them. More ice and rocks crashed down the mountain.

His heart full of cold fury, Daniel aimed and loosed his arrow.

"No!" Lorelei screamed.

The arrow sprang forth with a sibilant whine, made a perfect arc through the morning sky and lodged in the assassin's chest. With a horrible cry, he pitched over the edge of the road. Echoes of the avalanche reverberated through the canyon. Barry whined, an animal warning sound.

High above the road, an overhang of ice-clad rock came loose, falling slowly, pouring into the narrow gully and burying the body. The sound of it crashed like close thunder, raising a cloud of cold, dusty smoke. Stinging bits of debris cut into Daniel's face.

Slinging his bow over his shoulder, he turned to

shield Lorelei from the flying earth and snow. Her face was pale and disbelieving, her eyes wide with fright.

"We found our killer," said Daniel over the roaring echoes, "only to lose him again."

She leaped up and started toward the ridge. "We've got to get down there and see if he can be saved."

"Don't be foolish," said Daniel. "If the arrow didn't kill him, the avalanche did."

She stared at the hopelessly steep sides of the chasm. "Then we must go back to the hospice and tell Father Julian."

"Unless he's the one buried down there," Daniel stated coldly. He sat down on the hollow log. Wearily he rubbed his jaw. Killing the canon seemed to have sapped his energy. Lorelei gazed at him, torn between sympathy and horror.

She wanted to leave the area as quickly as possible, to dodge the idea that one of the canons was a murderer. Yet equally strong was the driving need to know the truth. "I'm going down there to see who it was," she vowed, and started marching back up the trail.

Daniel grabbed her arm. "Lorelei, you can't—"

Barry growled low in his throat. Daniel's body went rigid as the crackle of breaking underbrush sounded behind them. His hand tightened on her arm. Very slowly, they turned.

Six razor-sharp bayonets, wielded by six uniformed men, pointed at their hearts.

# Chapter 12

*The valley of Aosta, Italy*
*May 1800*

"This simply must be illegal," said Lorelei. "We're private citizens—Swiss citizens! How could these men drag us along on their march as if we were prisoners of war?"

His arm resting on Barry, Daniel glowered across the muddy, crowded encampment. Seated around smoky fires, soldiers wrapped musket cartridges in waxed paper, did laundry, played cards, and traded yarns. In the distance the slate rooftops of Aosta nestled among the Alpine crags.

"Why the hell did you tell them our names and our plans?"

The four days since their capture had not been long

enough to cool Daniel's temper. Luckily for her, Lorelei had been under separate guard during the grinding trek southward, covering leagues of frozen valleys, crossing ramshackle bridges, skirting avalanches and rockfalls, and traversing roads littered by army waste and animal dung. If he'd been allowed near her sooner, he'd have taken great joy in throttling her.

Weariness and lack of adequate food had thinned her face and stolen the color from her cheeks, but when she smiled, he had a glimpse of the old Lorelei. "Why?" She handed a piece of stale biscuit to Barry. "They asked."

"You should have left the talking to me."

The smile disappeared. "I'm used to speaking for myself."

He jerked his head toward the octagonal tent across the compound. The Bruxelles canvas flaps were drawn back to admit a steady stream of aides and messengers. "When we meet with Bonaparte, would you mind keeping silent?"

"Why? General Lannes has already told him our names, and that we were going to Coppet to be married. There's really nothing more to keep secret, is there?"

"Bonaparte has a way of using even the smallest scrap of information against a man," said Daniel, glowering. "And he's been through the Great Pass, spoken to the canons there. Who knows what lies they might have told him about us?"

They sat silently in the cold spring mist. Ever since they'd been seized, frustration had dogged Daniel's steps. General Lannes's scouts had brought them well into Italy—Italy, of all places—to the very feet of Napoleon Bonaparte.

Lorelei dragged her sleeve across her dripping nose. "I'm sorry I gave the lieutenant our true names."

"So am I," said Daniel. Though they'd never met, the first consul probably knew of the Raven through Fouché, who seemed to know the business of every last mother's son in the Republic. Daniel glanced to the south. Though masked by the mountains rimming the spring-flooded river, Fort Bardo lay beyond.

A trio of light cavalrymen led their horses past in the direction of the fort. The soldiers were followed by men carrying a heavy trail rope, probably for pulling transports past the Austrian-held fort. Barry started toward the horses, but Lorelei grabbed his collar and held him back.

An aide-de-camp hurried over from the first consul's tent. "General Bonaparte will see you now."

Daniel stood and offered his hand to Lorelei. Though unkempt and grubby, she gave him a look that caught at his heart. Round-eyed, her chin held high, she tried to smile. By God, she was afraid for him. The novel idea closed like a knot inside his chest. The foolish girl still cared for him.

In a parody of courtliness, he bowed at the entrance to the tent and motioned for her to precede him. With Barry at her heels, she edged uncertainly inside.

Bonaparte rose from behind a field desk littered with maps, letters, and a plumed bicorne.

The first consul appeared as calculatedly formidable as his reputation. Beneath a mane of shining dark hair, he had a wide, clear brow and penetrating blue-gray eyes. Though he stood motionless, his stance suggested a strange, tremendous energy that could uncoil at any moment.

His dress was impeccable despite the mud and the stinking weather. The blazing white of his stockings and breeches contrasted with the deep blue of his coat. A nick in his chin indicated a recent shave. Yet beneath the refinements, Bonaparte was as powerful and unpredictable as a gunpowder charge.

Unsmiling, he bowed to Lorelei. "Citizeness du Clerc. How do you do?"

"General—I should call you General, shouldn't I?"

"I'm not one to stand on titles."

Daniel's mouth twisted in an ironic smile. Bonaparte had taken pains to erect a legend around himself, to polish his image with the patina of success. If he lacked a title, it was only because he hadn't yet discovered one lofty enough.

Daniel kept a close eye on Lorelei. He had no idea how she would conduct herself. Her hands folded in front of her, she perused Bonaparte slowly from the top of his comb-furrowed hair to the toes of his gleaming cuffed boots.

The first consul returned her bold gaze with a penetrating stare that raised a prickle of apprehension on the back of Daniel's neck. How much? he wondered feverishly. How much did Bonaparte know?

"Monsieur Severin," he said curtly. "I knew it was only a matter of time before we met."

"Fouché told you about me?"

Bonaparte laid his palms on the desk and leaned forward. "Fouché tells me everything."

Daniel held the first consul's stare. *Everything? Even what I did with your precious Josephine?*

Barry barked for attention, severing the tight moment. Bonaparte jerked his gaze from Daniel. "The mastiffs of Saint Bernard's," he said. "The canons demonstrated their extraordinary skills when we crossed the Great Pass."

"The canons?" asked Lorelei. "Which ones?"

Daniel waited as eagerly as she for Bonaparte's response. If the first consul revealed names, they might be able to deduce which man had come after them.

"I spent less than a day with them," said Bonaparte. "Regrettably, I didn't speak to each one personally." He gestured at a salver of sweetmeats and candy ices on the desk. "Would you like one?"

Daniel shook his head, but Lorelei stepped forward. "Are these licorice?" She began picking out the shiny black lozenges.

"I take it you're fond of licorice, mademoiselle."

"Not particularly." She held open the pocket of her outer coat and dropped the candies in. "It's an excellent expectorant."

Daniel suppressed a smile at Bonaparte's baffled expression. Lorelei said, "Many of your men are sick with the croup, sir. The medical supplies seem to be delayed with the main body."

"Indeed. Thoughtful of you."

"Their diet is poor, sir. They sleep in the wind and rain, and march through the mud during drills. If conditions don't improve, you won't *have* an army to lead against the Austrians."

Daniel blinked. They'd been in camp only a few

hours, and yet she'd already evaluated—with uncanny accuracy—the state of the army.

"I daresay, mademoiselle, that my expertise has been proven from France to Egypt. These men are soldiers. They're accustomed to harsh conditions."

Her gaze flicked over the toile de Jouy lining the tent, the gleaming silver service, the thick wool rug. "I see."

Bonaparte yanked out a folding field chair and sat down. "Now. As to your situation. General Lannes tells me you were traveling to Coppet."

Daniel said nothing. No use denying their plans now.

The first consul picked up a daggerlike letter opener and tapped it on the desk. "I've no objection to Necker, even though he stole the French people blind when he was minister of finance. It's his daughter I can't stand."

Bonaparte feared few things. But Germaine de Staël, a woman whose strength of character equaled his own, he seemed to have found intimidating enough to banish from Paris for long periods of time. He set down the letter opener. "Are you aware, Monsieur Severin, that you stand accused of kidnapping?"

"Kidnapping?" Lorelei demanded. "Who says he kidnapped me?"

"The prior of Saint Bernard's."

She drew in her breath quickly. So Father Julian wasn't the killer—unless another now served as prior in his place. "Well, it's not true," said Lorelei.

"Nonetheless, I must return you to him. It's the

least I can do for the canons who were so gracious to me."

"You can't send me back," said Lorelei, glancing desperately at Daniel. He shook his head, warning her to keep silent, but she plunged on. "I'm twenty-one years old now, and no one's ward. I can go where I please. Daniel and I plan to be married, and the prior can't stop us."

Bonaparte made a steeple of his hands. "But I could, if I so chose. On the other hand, we could form an arrangement."

"What sort of arrangement?" Daniel asked.

"You wish to marry?"

"Yes," Daniel lied. He knew better than to reveal his true plan to the first consul. Bonaparte was too unpredictable; it was part of his genius as a strategist. He couldn't be trusted.

"Then perhaps you shall. Provided you perform a small service for me."

Daniel shuddered to think of the huge numbers of men who had perished in Bonaparte's service. "Go on, sir," he said.

Bonaparte swept the hat off his field desk, revealing an intricately drawn map. "My plan is to sweep down toward Genoa, smash through the Austrian forces, and reclaim the Italian territory. I've poured forty thousand men through the Alpine passes. But there's only one road down into the plains of Piedmont, where I plan to engage the enemy."

Lorelei peered out between the tent flaps. "This road?"

"Yes. But thirteen miles from here is a garrison called

Fort Bardo. It's manned by three hundred Prussians of the Kinsky regiment, and they refuse to surrender. I've not been able to get enough heavy artillery past that fort." He jabbed the letter opener at the map, then drew it in a sinuous line along the river Dora. "The destiny of Italy, and perhaps of the Republic, depends on the taking of Fort Bardo."

"So what do you want from me?" asked Daniel. But he already knew. With gut-chilling certainty, he knew.

"I want you to destroy the magazine there."

"You agreed!" said Lorelei, snapping her fingers. "Just like that, you agreed." They had left the first consul's tent. Shadowed by two privates of the Consular Guard, they walked across the encampment.

"What would you have had me do? Refuse?"

"It has to be illegal for him to force you into service."

He stopped walking and gripped her arm. "Switzerland virtually belongs to Napoleon. The patriots and moderates have chosen him to formulate a new government. If I refused, I'd be condemned as a traitor."

"Then leave. Let them think you're going to do as he asks, and leave. Lose yourself in the mountains, Daniel. You don't owe Bonaparte anything."

"You're forgetting one thing."

"What's that?"

"You."

"Me?"

"Bonaparte will keep you to ensure my cooperation."

A soft warmth rose in her heart. "You won't leave me?"

"Of course not."

She flung her arms around him. "I love you, Daniel."

The Consular Guards chuckled knowingly.

Lorelei felt Daniel's heart thudding against hers. Then he eased back, his hand cradling her chin and his thumb skimming lightly over her cheekbone. "I have work to do."

"Are you going to fetch the men Bonaparte has assigned to you?"

Daniel nodded and glanced at the written order he held in his hand. He and Lorelei walked to a circle of wagons.

"But, Daniel," said Lorelei, eyeing the wagons flanked by guards. Small barred windows and stout locked doors gave them an ominous look. "This is—"

"The brig." His face taut with anger, he approached a guard and showed him the order. The guard led them to one of the wagons and opened the door. Lorelei's heart sank. *Criminals* were going to help Daniel steal into the citadel and destroy Fort Bardo's munitions.

Heads down, shoulders hunched, three men sat on a bench in the gloom of the wagon.

"I have orders from the first consul," Daniel said. "Two of you are to follow me on a mission into the fort. Toussaint and Charon."

One soldier, an older man with a scraggly beard, looked up. "I'm Charon. And I'm not interested in any mission."

"I'm afraid you have no choice. Besides, you'll be rewarded with your freedom"—Daniel paused and fixed him with a cold-eyed stare—"and fifty thousand francs."

Charon gave a low whistle. "So, who the hell're you?"

"My name's Daniel Severin."

Another of the men stood quickly, bumping his head on the roof of the wagon. Strawlike hair framed a pitifully boyish face. "Y-y-you're the R-raven?" Each word clogged his throat and was forced out with explosive effort.

"That's correct." Daniel didn't seem surprised that the soldier knew of him. "As of this minute, I'm your commander."

The man exited the wagon and snapped a salute. "P-private Michel Toussaint, at your s-service." His cheekbones stood out beneath sallow flesh. His uniform hung on him like rags from a scarecrow.

"What was your offense, Private?" asked Daniel.

Michel stared at the ground. "C-c-c—"

"What's that? I can't hear you, Private."

Lorelei flinched at the harshness in Daniel's voice.

"C-cow—" Michel drew a deep breath. "C-cow—"

Daniel thrust his face closer to Michel. "Speak up, damn you."

Furious, Lorelei stepped forward. "Good heavens, can't you see he's—"

"Hold your tongue, Lorelei," he ordered.

Michel's mouth contorted. "C-c—"

"Cowardice," said the old soldier in the wagon. "He turned tail and ran when we met up with snipers at Saint Gotthard's Pass."

"Is that true, Private?"

Still staring at the ground, Michel nodded miserably.

"Look at me, Private."

Slowly Michel's head came up. His nose was running, and his chin trembled. He was too young to raise a beard.

Daniel appeared unaffected by Michel's youth. "That's it," he said. "Look me in the eye. In the eye, lad. And not like that—you look like a whipped dog. Make me flinch!"

Michel's eyes narrowed, and his chin stopped trembling. A flush of red misted his cheeks. His obvious effort broke Lorelei's heart.

Daniel gave a very small nod as if to show he was only nominally satisfied; then he peered into the wagon. "Front and center, Charon. What was your offense?"

The old soldier shouldered past the other man who sat slouched in the shadows. "Pinched a bottle of General Lannes's best brandy." He grinned unrepentently.

A tic started in Daniel's jaw. "Come with me, please."

"Wait," said a voice from the wagon. "You need me, too."

Moving with careless grace, the third soldier jumped to the ground in front of Daniel. His height, the supple beauty of his dark skin, and the gleam in his obsidian eyes caused Lorelei's jaw to drop. His brutally handsome face shone like polished blackthorn.

He shifted his weight to one hip. "I'm Emanuel," he said in a curiously melodic voice. "From the isle of

Martinique. Same as Bonaparte's wife, eh?" He threw back his head and laughed. Sensing something sinister in his laughter and in the graceful way he moved, Lorelei stepped back and put her hand on Barry's head.

"My orders call for only Charon and Toussaint," said Daniel.

"You can change your orders." Emanuel leaned forward and hissed, "You must."

"Why are you here?" asked Daniel.

"For murder. Ah, and thievery, too, but I'm not supposed to talk about that." Again he dropped his voice, but Lorelei heard his raspy whisper. "But I *will* talk, if you get me out of here."

"Who did you murder?" Daniel demanded.

Emanuel regarded him through lazily slitted eyes. "A Bern treasury guard."

Daniel stiffened and sucked in a breath. Lorelei's eyes grew wide. She knew what he was thinking. Emanuel knew something about the theft of which Meuron was accused. In exchange for his freedom, he would tell Daniel.

"You're in," said Daniel.

A guard stepped forward. "But this man's under a death sentence. You can't—"

"As commander of this mission," Daniel snapped, "I certainly can."

"But General Bonaparte—"

"Has the security of all Italy to attend to. Only a fool would bother him with such a minor detail."

The guard backed off. Daniel began to explain the plan.

With outrage boiling inside her, Lorelei listened.

Bonaparte had given Daniel an impossible task. Then instead of assigning able men to the detail, he'd provided a boy, an aging drunk, and a murderer.

Why? Why would Bonaparte assign men of questionable character to this exploit? They were outcasts. Disposable men.

The answer hit her like a fist to the belly, and she gasped aloud.

The raid was a suicide mission.

The next day she followed Daniel and his three men along the road to the fort. Apprehension built in Lorelei's chest as she listened to the clinking of Daniel's gear and eyed the bulges of dynamite concealed in his coat. Barry loped ahead of them, and an armed guard paced behind.

"That's far enough, mademoiselle," called the captain of the guard.

She and Daniel stopped walking. The road wound downward into a misty river valley, then rose in the distance. High on a promontory loomed the garrison of Fort Bardo. The sun hadn't quite risen, and the citadel lay in ominous shadow.

"There'll be action soon," said Daniel, pointing to a company of gunners guiding their wheel-mounted twelve-pounders toward the fort.

Lorelei shivered. The men had rejoiced when the big guns arrived by way of the Little Pass. "Now that the guns are here, why doesn't Bonaparte change his mind about sending you?"

"He needs an early prize," said Daniel, "for morale." He slid an ironic glance at his surly faced men.

"So you'll be trying to enter the fort in the middle of a bombardment?"

"No. The four of us won't move until nightfall." He pointed at a tall slope creased by glacial rock. Lofty firs sprouted along a ridge. "We'll wait out the attack there."

Lorelei touched his arm and said, "I'm scared."

"I can't do anything about that." He reached into his pocket and took out a scrap of paper. "Here's an introduction to Baron Necker. If I don't come back, I want to you go to him."

She crushed the note in her fist. "How can you speak so casually of this?"

"Whether I choose to be hysterical or calm changes nothing. Just promise me you won't try to go back to the hospice."

She pressed close to him. "There's nothing there for me now except a trip to a nunnery." The soft leather of his chamois jacket cooled her cheek. "I can't bear to talk about losing you."

"Then let's not," he whispered. "Kiss me good-bye, Lorelei."

It was the first time he'd actually invited her embrace. She stood on tiptoe and their lips met, softly at first. Muttered comments rose from the men, but she ignored them. The taste of Daniel flooded her, and she cherished the unique scent and texture of him.

"I love you, Daniel," she said.

"Keep well, Lorelei. I'll be back."

The whistle of an ascending missile split the air. Sitting in her moldering tent back at camp, Lorelei cringed and buried her face in Barry's neck. The bombardment had begun an hour before, and the noise jangled her nerves.

Her conception of war had been a fairy tale nourished by Everard's fireside tales. The reality turned the fanciful stories into bald lies. Everard had said nothing about the strain of waiting, the pain of not knowing, the discomforts of camp life, and the raw horror of battle wounds.

Another gun fired in the distance. She burst from the tent and began to pace. A Consular Guard watched her every move. She was nothing but a marker, she realized bitterly. Insurance that Daniel would carry out Bonaparte's orders—or die trying.

A clatter of hooves distracted her. Two horsemen, both wearing messengers' cuffs, arrived from the direction of the fort. Mud spattered in their wake as they galloped to Bonaparte's quarters and hurried inside.

Hungry for news, Lorelei crossed to the large tent. Men had already clustered around the first consul's chief aide.

". . . very little progress," he was saying to his eager listeners. "The fort's still strong, and our casualties are heavy."

She chewed her lip. Daniel's work hadn't even begun. "What happens to them?" she asked. "The casualties?"

The aide shrugged. "There's a surgeon and two assistants. They do the best they can."

"Do they need help?"

"They always need help, mademoiselle."

"Then I shall go to them." She marched off toward the road, the dog trotting in her wake.

"Mademoiselle!" Private Foissy, the guard assigned to her, followed. "You're not permitted in the combat zone." He coughed and spat into the mud.

She quickened her pace while digging into her pocket. "I'm an experienced physician. I can help." She handed him a licorice drop. "Here. This will soothe your throat."

"If you don't cooperate, I'll have to restrain you."

"I wouldn't try that, Private. Barry wouldn't like it."

"Barry?"

She indicated the huge dog. "He's very protective of me."

The private reached for her arm. Instantly Barry drew up short, hackles raised and lips rolled back to reveal his long, sharp teeth.

Foissy reached for his pistol. "The first consul will forbid it."

"Then the first consul is a fool who cares nothing for saving lives."

"And you, citizeness," said a familiar voice behind her, "make free with your criticism."

She whirled to see Bonaparte approaching, his hat held under one arm and his sword slapping his thigh.

"I heard the report," she said, undaunted by his thunderous scowl. "With such heavy casualties, your surgeon would welcome my help."

"Surgeon Major Larrey is no second-rate army sawbones," Bonaparte stated. "He's a wounded soldier's best chance."

"But he's only one man." Tamping back her frustration, she decided to appeal to Bonaparte's practical nature. "A dead soldier is no use to you, sir. With my help, perhaps more of the wounded can be returned to battle."

Nearby, men began to murmur among themselves. Lorelei realized that the first consul didn't often conduct arguments with strange women. He seemed to take a keen interest in her, an interest that was chilling in its intensity.

"The canons did say you were a headstrong female—but a skilled healer." With the quick decisiveness he was famous for, Bonaparte addressed Foissy. "Accompany her to the field, Private." He scribbled an order. His wink at the soldier indicated that he expected her back very soon, sickened and terrified.

He didn't know her. Leaving Barry tethered at camp, she followed an escort of three soldiers along the road to Fort Bardo. Injured men needed her. She tried not to think about the possibility that Daniel might need her, too, before the night was over.

The road looped southward and down to the valley. Rounding the curve, she spied the company of gunners. Shielded by a natural wall of rock and earth, they trained their artillery on the fort. From a distance they resembled little lead soldiers in a mock battle. Tiny puffs of smoke blossomed, followed by a deep boom she could feel in the pit of her stomach. The guns reeled back after each shot, only to be shoved into position again by more scurrying toy soldiers.

But as she drew nearer, the impression of a child's game disintegrated. She saw where the gun carriages had crushed the spring flowers blooming at the roadside. She smelled the sharp odor of gunpowder and recalled the explosion at the hospice, and when she inhaled, she could taste sulfur on her tongue. She heard the frantic, hoarse calls of soldiers.

A body lay in the ditch beside the road. Ignoring her escorts' warnings, she rushed to investigate. The man was dead, his gut neatly opened, his slick entrails alive with a swarm of flies.

A hand touched her arm. "Saber wound," Foissy said, his eyes scanning the area. "Do you want to continue, mademoiselle?"

Fear buzzed in her ears, but she nodded. A group of infantrymen erupted from the trench and ran toward the fort. A cannon on the garrison wall swiveled toward them and angled high.

"Christ, that's a howitzer," said Foissy.

Lorelei frowned. "What's a—"

"You'll see, mademoiselle."

Sparks flashed from the big gun. An explosion detonated in the midst of the soldiers, scattering them like ants in a hill disturbed by a giant foot. One soldier was tossed into the air, his body wheeling loosely before he fell in a heap.

Waves of sickness shuddered through Lorelei as she followed her escort to the rear of the battleground. Wounded men lay on the trampled grass. Some stared at the sky; others wept and prayed; a few joked and called encouragement to the gunners.

"Dr. Larrey's over here." An orderly led her to an area sheltered by a stand of tall trees.

The surgeon major knelt beside a supine soldier and probed with a pair of long tweezers. Moments later he held up the instrument. Pinched between the slender tongs was a small lead ball. He dropped the bullet on the man's heaving chest. "A keepsake," he muttered. "Bandage him."

The doctor paused to drink from a flask. He was wiping his mouth on his sleeve when Lorelei handed him Bonaparte's order.

"I'm Lorelei du Clerc," she said, "from the hospice of Saint Bernard. I've come to help."

The surgeon read the message. Looking up, he gave her a glimpse of his handsome face which, despite the current situation, made her think he was a happy man, probably married, probably a father. From his long, flowing hair to the toes of his mud-caked field boots he was the image of the man she imagined whenever she wondered who her father was.

"I'm Dominique Larrey." He offered the flask. "Brandy?"

"No, thank you. What can I do?"

He shrugged. "Patch them up and pray."

Incredulous, she asked, "You'll accept my help?"

"Yes."

"Because Bonaparte ordered you to—or because you believe I'll be useful?"

Larrey blew out his breath. "Either you're genuine or you're crazy. I'll find out soon enough."

An explosion ripped through the air. Lorelei flinched. Soldiers arrived bearing three stretchers. Larrey rushed forward to the first one. "Shattered knee," he muttered, regarding a young soldier's leg. "Let's see the others."

The second man lay silent and pale as new snow, his

eyes round and glassy. He held both hands firmly over one side of his throat. Blood seeped between his fingers.

"Get the cauterizing irons," Larrey ordered.

The third man lay covered with a rough blanket. He wore a soft, dreamy expression and smiled vaguely at Lorelei.

Larrey lifted the blanket. "Gutshot," said the surgeon. "Don't waste any laudanum on him. He's beyond pain."

"You won't try to help him?" Lorelei demanded. "But perhaps we could—"

"Perhaps we could indeed. But in the meantime the others could bleed to death."

"That's not f—"

"No, it's not fair. It's war."

A moment later he held the glowing iron. Lorelei laid her hands on the soldier who was clutching his neck and pried his fingers away. An arc of blood spurted from the wound and streaked over Lorelei. She dragged her sleeve across her face.

Larrey laid the tamped end of the iron on the wound. The man bucked off the stretcher.

"Hold him steady, damn it!" roared Larrey. He repeated the procedure three more times. The flow of blood stopped.

Shaking, Lorelei turned to plunge her hands into a basin. As she washed, she noticed a silent detail of men bearing the gutshot soldier away. She dropped to her knees to pray.

"Dr. du Clerc!" Larrey's impatient voice jolted her.

"See to this man's thumb." He jerked his head toward a man huddled on the ground.

Hours passed in a frenzy of activity. Lorelei no longer cringed at the thunder of guns, no longer recoiled at the sight of corpses, no longer turned from the odor of burned and torn flesh.

Red to the elbows, her shirt resembling Mauricio's apron after he'd butchered a pig, she stitched wounds, despaired over the hopeless cases, and exulted when a man survived.

At sunset an order to withdraw rang through the ranks. Columns of men formed and started along the road to Aosta.

Dr. Larrey looked up from his examination of a man whose arm had been peppered by canister shot. "Sixty casualties," he said. "And we've barely made a pockmark on the walls of that fort."

He finished his work and put a carved whistle to his lips. The shrill note summoned a horse-drawn conveyance that resembled an elongated cube with small windows and double doors. A pair of orderlies opened one end, and the floor slid out on rollers.

"What's that?" she asked.

"My own invention." Pride stiffened Larrey's drooping posture. "I call it a flying ambulance." Orderlies loaded two unconscious men into the ambulance. The inside was equipped with leather-covered mattresses. Pockets with bottles and instruments lined the sides. "The old fourgons move too slowly," Larrey explained. "We were losing too many men in transport."

He was wonderful, thought Lorelei. Not callous, as

she'd first thought him, but driven by a passion to save lives.

"Will you come, Dr. du Clerc? I could use you."

She cast a worried glance at the fortress. "Bonaparte gave me leave to help only in the field."

"My dear, following orders is not always as wise as following your heart."

She tore her gaze from the cold walls of Fort Bardo. She could do nothing to help Daniel. She stepped onto the running board of the ambulance and clung to the side. But as the vehicle leaped forward she looked back at the ridge of trees leading up to the fort.

"The tables will turn tonight," said Larrey. He was inside the ambulance, peering through the tiny window. "The Raven will blow away their magazine, and we'll be halfway to Ivrea by noon tomorrow."

She welcomed the cool rush of the wind through her hair. "Why do you have such faith in him?"

"I've heard he's good at what he does." Larrey tucked a bandage neatly around the unconscious man's arm. "Good at subterfuge and murder."

She wanted to deny it, wanted to insist that Daniel was different now. He was no murderer, but the man she loved.

But her love couldn't protect him tonight. He had to steal into a fortress on full alert. What would happen if Kinsky's men captured him?

# Chapter 13

"We'll never make it." Slumped in the shadows of a rockfall, Charon scowled up at the distant hulk of the fort. Below them the river rushed past like a dark satin ribbon. Charon put a goatskin flask to his lips and sucked it flat. "Man'd be a fool to try."

Daniel clenched his teeth in frustration. "Your drinking won't help matters."

"True." With a grimace, Charon flung the empty flask away. "Awful stuff, that green Italian wine. Not fit for a goat."

"Kinsky's men'll serve us up for breakfast, eh?" Emanuel's deep, melodic voice drifted from the shadows. He fingered the pistol he'd been issued. "I say we desert."

A tense silence drew out among the men hidden in the gloom. The sweet warble of a *passero solitario* rippled through the night, the lone bird's mournful notes playing over Daniel's nerves. Emanuel's idea might have tempted him at one time. But now he had Lorelei to think about. What would become of her if he simply disappeared? In the hands of the first consul, she would be as helpless as a rose in a windstorm, for Daniel knew with cold certainty that Bonaparte understood who she was.

"I can't force you to stay," Daniel said. "But take care. Bonaparte's sentence for desertion is death. Besides, I've a hankering to spend the gold he'll owe us when we succeed."

"I-I-I—" Michel began. "I'm s-s—"

"Scared?" mocked Charon.

"I—I'm staying. I'm with you, s-sir."

Daniel felt the sheaf of arrows pressing against his back. He almost wished the lad had elected to desert. "Thank you."

"Hell, I'm no good at running," said Charon.

"I can't be shamed into cooperating," said Emanuel. "But a man could live very well on fifty thousand francs."

"Idiot," said Charon. "He offered that sum because he doesn't expect to have to pay us."

"I've gambled before," Emanuel said. "Sometimes I win, sometimes I lose."

Daniel handed a cheap watch to Charon. "Take Toussaint up the ridge and time the sentries."

The Frenchmen crept off into the night. "Ah, gold," said Emanuel, his mouth a twist of irony. "It's brought me bad luck."

"It's time you told me about that, my friend."

The burly islander regarded him through slitted eyes. "I thought you'd never ask."

"How did you know the information would interest me?"

Emanuel chuckled. "One look at that face of yours, and I knew."

Daniel's jaw tightened. Emanuel was not the first to note the resemblance. "I've held up my end of the bargain, gotten you a chance to win your freedom. So talk."

Unhurriedly Emanuel crossed his legs. "Bonaparte sent an armed convoy to transport gold from Bern to Paris. Just outside the city we set upon the convoy and stole some of the gold." His grin slashed through the darkness. "The guards didn't even pretend to resist. They'd lined their pockets as well.

"I was to plant some of the gold in Meuron's Bern town house so he'd look guilty." His eyes gleamed with anger. "The guards were supposed to seize only him, but they arrested me as well. Damn her," Emanuel whispered, ramming his fist into the ground. "The bitch never intended to keep her part of the bargain."

"I presume you mean Madame Bonaparte."

Emanuel spread his broad hands. "Who else?"

"Where's the rest of the stolen gold?"

"You'll have to buy that secret from someone else, my friend. I don't know."

Toussaint and Charon returned from reconnoitering

the fort. "Six minutes," said Charon, "if the pattern holds."

Daniel glanced up. Bruised by torn masses of clouds, the sky glowed dully with diffuse moonlight. He took the watch from Charon. Thumbing it open, he said, "It's nearly time."

On the riverbank below, a squadron of infantry waited in the reeds. When the magazine blew, they'd storm the fortress and subdue the Austrians. The plan allowed no room for mistakes.

Daniel stood. "Let's go."

Armed to the teeth and crouching low, they traversed the hill and headed for the west guard tower. During the day, French guns had pounded a hole in its base. Austrian masons had repaired the breach.

But the mortar was still wet.

Michel bent to loosen a stone. Sentries patrolled the high battlements, their shapes bobbing against the night sky.

Like the wings of a dark bird, a shadow passed over Daniel's heart. He stood a moment, suspended between surprise and confusion, wondering at the trickle of sweat that crawled down his back and the almost forgotten rhythm pulsing in his ears.

The Raven was afraid.

He'd faced death a hundred times. He'd embraced pain and torture without blinking. He knew better than to call it courage. He simply hadn't cared.

But he cared now. In a cell in Paris sat the one man who could unite the warring parties of Switzerland and ensure fair treatment from Bonaparte. In the camp at Aosta waited the one woman who had breathed life into a man dead to feeling. Both depended on his success, his survival.

Stone by stone, they dismantled the wall, and Daniel led the way inside. Pools of moonlight coasted eerily across the yard. Few lights glimmered in the barracks. After a long day of repulsing the French assault, the soldiers had earned a rest.

At one end of a building Daniel spied a dim glow. Groans of pain drifted through the open door. The infirmary, he guessed, no doubt crammed with casualties. The sounds of suffering reminded him so poignantly of the Tuileries that he shuddered. Fighting the recollection, he turned his attention elsewhere. Twenty yards to the front, in the middle of the yard, sat a squat, square structure with a low tiled roof.

"That's the magazine," Daniel whispered.

A lone guard slowly paced its periphery. The orange spark of a cigar brightened as the guard inhaled its smoke. Daniel consulted the watch again, timing the sentry's route.

Emanuel drew his pistol.

"Put that damned thing away," said Daniel. "The only advantage we have is surprise."

They edged through the shadows toward a narrow flight of steps made uneven by generations of soldiers' boots. A harsh smell wafted to them.

"The latrine." Daniel jerked his head at a row of wooden stalls beyond the steps. His gaze stalked the pacing guards. A deadly calm settled over him. Reaching behind his shoulder, he withdrew three arrows from the quiver and stuck two of them in his belt.

"Sh-sh-shouldn't you t-take one more?" asked Michel. "In case you m-miss?"

"I never miss."

"You Swiss," said Charon. "You're so smug."

The yew bowstave, molded to the curves of Daniel's hand, felt smooth. The sharp raven feathers, fletched for perfect flight, brushed his knuckles. Like a musician tuning a harp, he ran his thumb along the taut bowstring.

"W-w-w—" Michel began.

"Wait," said Charon. "Someone's coming from the barracks."

"Oh, G-god. He'll see us."

"Don't move." The curved blade of Emanuel's knife gleamed like a terrible grin. Knees bent, he coiled like a steel spring. As the big dark man prepared to kill, Daniel recognized the cold intent in his eyes that signaled the emptying of the mind, the momentary retreat from humanity. The fact that they were brothers in this sent a chill slithering up Daniel's spine.

The soldier reached one of the latrine doors and opened it. A harsh stench fouled the air. Swearing, he turned his head to one side and spotted the intruders.

He opened his mouth to call an alarm.

Like a bolt of black lightning, Emanuel's hand shot out. The snakelike blade flashed across the soldier's neck.

With a soft gurgle, the man sank to the ground. The pace of the sentry at the magazine didn't alter. Michel's lips moved silently. Daniel wondered if he stuttered when he prayed.

Furtively they mounted the steps, cringing as dirt and stone crumbled beneath their feet.

A musket leaning against his shoulder, one of the sentries approached.

The tapping of the guard's footsteps grew louder. *Turn around,* Daniel pleaded silently, even as he nocked an arrow. *Turn around. Don't make me do this.* But the man came heedlessly on. He saw the intruders and stiffened. Daniel's arrow buzzed, then thumped into the man's chest. A quick, clean kill.

Daniel swallowed hard, then turned to let four ropes hang down the outside of the wall. "Dynamite ready?"

Charon and Michel nodded. The younger man carried a few oblong bundles, and Charon had a glowing slow match, the orange tip hidden in a loose case of hopsacking.

"You know what to do," said Daniel.

A burst of laughter rippled from the officers' quarters. Someone struck up a tune with a mouth harp.

"Now," said Daniel.

Charon removed the match from the sack, cupping his hand around the glowing tip. Daniel aimed an arrow at the sentry who patrolled the magazine. Emanuel drew his pistol. With shaking hands, Michel held out the sticks of dynamite.

The fuses ignited with a soft hiss and a shower of sparks.

Michel gasped and threw the first one. It landed with a thud on the roof of the magazine.

The guard stiffened and came away from the building. The barrel of his musket dropped into his hand. "Who goes there?" he yelled in German. Fuse glowing, another charge arced toward the magazine. "Intruders!" he bellowed, taking aim.

Daniel's arrow embedded itself in the guard's stomach. The man screamed and squeezed off a wild shot as he fell.

Soldiers burst from the barracks. Nightshirts flowing, muskets at the ready, they poured across the compound.

The third sentry raced toward them; Daniel dispatched him with his third arrow. "Let's go!" he shouted as the last charge found its mark. He turned to lead the way over the wall.

A shot rang out. Behind him he heard a bowel-chilling slap like a rock hitting a bag of mud. Daniel turned to see Emanuel cartwheeling, grasping at air, falling backwards over the wall.

"Damn!" Charon snatched a rope and disappeared over the side. Michel stood frozen except for his mouth moving in silent prayer. Several yards away a soldier raised his musket.

Daniel whipped another arrow from his quiver and jammed it against his bowstring. The raven fletchings whirred as it flew. The razor tip slammed into the soldier's throat.

The youth bolted into action, grasping another rope. Bullets spattered the wall around them.

The roar of detonating explosives filled the compound. There was a moment of stunned calm. Daniel felt the thunder in his gut. The wall began to crumble beneath his feet. Men and horses screamed. Nightshirts aflame, soldiers darted in every direction. Sparks shot heavenward on plumes of sulfurous fire.

The rope burned Daniel's palms as he let himself down. He and Michel tumbled out onto the rocky hill in time to see Charon disappearing down the embankment. The French infantrymen scrambled up the hill.

Leaping over rocks and debris, Daniel searched for Emanuel. Despite the danger, he felt he owed the man a search. The outlaw from Martinique had given him, at long last, a weapon against Josephine—and possibly proof that Meuron was innocent.

But Daniel found no sign of Emanuel amid the rubble or on the bank below the fort. He darted into the woods.

On the rock-strewn slope, two men faced each other. One was an Austrian armed with a bayoneted musket. The other was Michel.

Daniel drew out his bow and an arrow.

"Surrender," the Austrian commanded.

"N-n-n—"

Daniel nocked the arrow and aimed. Michel moved heedlessly between him and the Austrian.

"Come now, give up, lad. I don't want to have to kill you." Even as the soldier spoke, Michel labored to force out a word.

"Never!" he finally said on a burst of air. "I'll never surrender. The French have won Fort Bardo."

The Austrian jabbed with the bayonet. Daniel put away his bow. He'd have to fight hand to hand, for he couldn't get a clear shot.

Michel's foot flashed up and out. The Austrian stumbled back. Michel wrested the weapon from him. Without hesitating, he jabbed the bayonet into the man's gut.

Then, retching, he stumbled off into the darkness.

Daniel opened his mouth to call to the youth.

A footstep crunched on the rocky ground behind him.

Daniel turned in time to see the butt of a rifle swinging toward his head.

Orderlies scurried to and fro, bearing stretchers and loading the wounded into ambulances. Working alongside Dr. Larrey, Lorelei forced herself to concentrate on her task, but with each new arrival her heart lurched: Would this man be Daniel? Would she find him with an arm or a leg blown off, a gaping hole in his chest?

"Casualities?" Bonaparte's voice cut in on her thoughts.

"Just a small number now, sir, and none require surgery," said Larrey. He wiped his hands on his apron, taking advantage of a lull.

Bonaparte turned to one of his aides. "Any news of the Raven?"

Lorelei didn't hear the reply, for just then cheers erupted from the soldiers crowding the road below the stronghold. Leaping up, she gazed at the dark, distant crags crowned by Fort Bardo.

Exultant cries filled her ears. Bright as noontime, sparks and flames shot skyward.

"They've blown the magazine!" a man screamed. "The Republic triumphs again!"

Men clasped one another and danced crazy jigs. Barry stayed close to Lorelei and whined in confusion. Bonaparte's field glasses stayed trained on the exploding fortress. The thunder reached a bone-crushing crescendo, then subsided to the roar of a steadily burning fire.

Bonaparte lowered his field glasses and turned to his second-in-command. "Now the Piedmont can be ours." His deep, cold eyes never blinked. His mouth was pressed into a stern line.

"Now we wait," said Larrey. He reached down and patted Barry's head.

She drew a shuddering sigh. "Yes."

"The casualties have slowed. We'd best get back to the hospital." He murmured instructions to an orderly, then led Lorelei back to the public building that served as a hospital. Terror squeezed Lorelei's chest, but she clung to the chores of nursing as a way to keep her sanity.

An aide held a lamp to light their way through the darkened ward. Most men slept on, though a few moaned and prayed, their sounds of pain twisting through Lorelei. This was so different from doctoring at the hospice. There were so many men here. She couldn't cope with all their needs.

She tried to drive the frantic worry from her mind. Like a sponge she absorbed everything: Larrey's technique of debriding a wound, his insistence on using clean bandages to prevent infection, his method of keeping written charts on the progress of each patient.

One grossly obese soldier was having trouble breathing. His great belly strained at the buttons of his nightshirt, and his face was flushed red. Pursing his lips, Larrey opened the man's shirt and pressed his ear to the massive chest. "By God, you're well insulated," said Larrey. "I can't hear a sound."

Lorelei frowned. "Have you no trumpet, doctor?"

Larrey looked up, rubbing his chin. "A trumpet?"

"For auscultation. I find mine most useful for listening to the heart and lungs." Turning, she rummaged in her rucksack and drew out the hollow wooden trumpet.

"I'm not familiar with this," said Larrey.

"But it's so simple." Lorelei bent to the man's chest.

His beefy hand shoved her back. "Get her away from me. She's some kind of witch."

Lorelei bristled. "I just want to show Dr. Larrey—"

"I'd sooner die than let a woman treat me."

She looked to Larrey for support. He regarded her impassively. Scowling, she turned to the sick man. "We'll know better how to treat you if we can listen to your heart and lungs."

"It's not right, not natural—" The soldier broke off and began to wheeze.

"Monsieur, did you slap away your mother when she nursed you as a child?"

His eyes narrow with distrust, the man submitted. Lorelei found congestion in the right lung and invited Dr. Larrey to use her trumpet. He listened, his face registering curiosity, amazement, and finally admiration. He ordered an expectorant for the patient and vowed to acquire a trumpet of his own.

An hour later Larrey rotated his head wearily. "Barring a plague, I don't think we'll lose too many more tonight. Let's get some air."

Outside, he sat astride one of the stone lions that

flanked the entrance. He tapped the trumpet on his wrist and peered into it. "Remarkable instrument. Where did you get it?"

Lorelei shrugged and craned her neck toward the road. "Father Droz carved it for me. At first I used a rolled-up book, but the trumpet works better."

He regarded her with interest. She couldn't savor his attention, for the question of Daniel's safety claimed her mind and her soul.

"May I keep this?" Larrey asked.

"Of course It's just a piece of whittled wood. I can always make another."

A volley of shots cracked from the darkness.

"Snipers!"

The cry jolted Lorelei to her feet and sent men scrambling for their weapons. Bonaparte's orders rang across the encampment. Officers organized men to seek out the hidden enemy.

"Probably escapees from the fort," said Larrey. "They'll have revenge on their minds. And we'll have more casualties on our hands. Go inside, Lorelei. The black flag protects the hospital from attack."

She stood in the doorway and watched the flashes of bursting powder in the woods. The idea of men killing one another, even in pitched battle, still baffled and sickened her. Daniel. Like an unending song, his name drifted through her mind.

"Casualties!" someone yelled.

Out of the woods came a man holding a limp form beneath the arms and dragging him toward the encampment. Disregarding Larrey's warning, Lorelei ran to meet them. She recognized Charon's mud-caked face. The limp form was that of Michel Toussaint.

"Where's Daniel?" she demanded.

Two orderlies rushed forward with a stretcher.

"Don't know," said Charon. "Emanuel's lost, too." He jerked his head at Michel. "Leg's nearly shot off, poor lad."

A stunning realization struck Lorelei. Michel lay in peril of his life, and yet her first concern had been for Daniel. It was frightening to have to admit that he had a stronger claim on her heart than doctoring. Her stomach jumped in panic. She pressed her hands to her middle as she followed Larrey into the surgery.

The stretcher sped past in a blur. Larrey's aides scurried in with lanterns, instrument trays, basins, and jars of medicine.

"Tourniquet," said Larrey. "Quickly. Lift his leg a bit."

She slid her hands beneath his upper thigh. Larrey tied a cord around Michel's thigh and knotted the ends.

"Cut away his trousers," said Larrey.

Despite her frantic fear, she grasped a pair of scissors.

Michel, eloquent with agony, let a moan escape his lips.

"Hush, you're safe now," she said. But when she peeled the blood-soaked fabric from his knee, doubt slid over her. The knee was shattered.

"Get some laudanum in him," Lorelei said to an aide. She reached toward a basin for a cloth to swab the ruined leg. The aide poured liquid through a paper cornet into Michel's mouth.

Lorelei glanced at his bare foot. Already it looked as pale and cold as dead flesh. Catching Larrey's eye, she bit her lip in an unspoken question.

The surgeon nodded grimly. "We can't save the leg."

"What?" Michel's eyes flew open. Suddenly lucid and terrified, he tried to writhe off the table.

"We've got to have that leg off, lad," said Larrey.

Michel fought the aides. The look on his filthy young face broke Lorelei's heart.

"It's your leg or your life, my friend," said Larrey.

Michel imbibed more laudanum, and his eyes glazed over.

An hour later, her mind filled with the wonder and horror of the amputation, Lorelei stepped outside, not surprised to see Bonaparte entering the hospital, not even resentful of Foissy, who still shadowed her every move.

Barry trotted to the edge of the encampment, barked sharply, and returned. He repeated the behavior three more times.

The dog's purpose penetrated the worry and fatigue fogging her mind. "Good Lord," she whispered, running back to the hospital. "Why didn't I think of that before?"

Pale and haggard, Larrey stood over a basin of water, his face and hands dripping. Michel lay on the table, blood seeping through the bandages. Bonaparte had entered, his face sallow, his throat working as he swallowed hard.

"You earned both clemency and the reward," he said quietly to the young man. Michel lay as still as death.

"Damn," said Bonaparte. "The fifty thousand won't buy you a new leg."

"General," said Lorelei, "I know a way to find Daniel."

He seemed to welcome the chance to look away from Michel. "Do you, mademoiselle?"

"My dog can find him."

Bonaparte pinched the bridge of his nose. "Then let him do so. Foissy, see to it."

The night had begun to pale. Barry led them up the wooded slope and past the smoldering fort. The mastiff bolted ahead and stopped at the top of a ridge. Lorelei and Foissy hurried to join him, and came up short.

"It's him," whispered Lorelei, her heart convulsing with terror and love. "It's Daniel."

His hands clasped atop his head, he trudged toward the valley of the Dora, a bayoneted musket prodding him from behind.

Foissy raised his musket, but Lorelei shook her head. "You might miss. I've a better way." Leaning down, she took Barry's head between her hands. *"Vas-y,"* she whispered. *"Vite!"*

The dog bounded down into the valley, streaking through the fir and chestnut trees. Moving with inborn grace, he sailed toward the Austrian. Canine jaws closed around the soldier's forearm and overbalanced him. Daniel whirled around and grasped the musket. Lorelei was too far away to comprehend the slight dipping motion he made before turning toward the ridge.

"Daniel!" Love and despair roughened her voice. She squeezed her eyes shut and choked out his name again.

She opened her eyes to find him standing a few feet away, grinning rakishly. The white streak in his hair glowed in the predawn light. Blood smeared the side of his face. "It's about time," he said. "That was not a restful night."

She touched his cheek. "You're hurt."

"I'm fine."

"Liar." With a cry of joy she placed a long, heartfelt kiss on his lips.

"Remarkable," said Foissy.

Blushing, she stepped away from Daniel. "It was only a kiss."

"I was speaking of your dog," Foissy said.

She craned her neck toward the valley. "Daniel, the Austrian. Is he . . . ?"

"Dead," said Daniel. His eyes went hard and blank. Something in Lorelei hardened, too, in defense of what, she did not want to know.

As they walked back toward Aosta, Daniel explained what had happened. "Emanuel was shot, but we found no sign of him. The rest of us broke free. Someone hit me from behind." He touched the side of his head. "It dazed me just enough to be captured."

"Charon and Michel made it back," said Lorelei. "Charon's fine. Michel lost his leg."

Daniel's face went taut. "Will he live?"

"They usually don't," said Foissy. He started down the slope. Lorelei hung back a moment and took Daniel's hand. His dry, callused palm brushed her fingers, and she shivered. He'd killed again.

"I almost wish," she said, "that I didn't love you so much."

He snatched his hand away. "For Christ's sake, don't go on about that."

"I do love you," she said resignedly. "With all my heart. I just didn't expect it to feel like this."

"Like what?"

She moistened her lips and studied the trampled grass beneath her feet. "When Charon brought Michel in, I asked about you. I didn't think like a doctor. The news that you were missing hurt so much, Daniel."

"Think about it, then. It won't be the last time I'll hurt you."

"Because you've killed people?"

"That's part of it."

"But you won't have to be a mercenary anymore. Bonaparte promised you a fortune for destroying Fort Bardo. We can live on that until I set up a practice at Coppet."

"Bonaparte never gives a gift with no strings attached."

"But he said we'd be free to go."

"So long as it's on his terms."

"He said—"

"Damn it, Lorelei." Daniel stopped walking, grasped her by the shoulders, and regarded her fiercely. "You can't be fool enough to take a man like Bonaparte at his word. Not everyone's as forthright as you are. People lie. Get used to it."

She found herself studying his lips, the play of morning light on his face, his bone structure, clean and beautiful beneath muddied, haggard skin. In his eyes she saw the pain, familiar now, yet still unfathomable.

A havoc of desire, distrust, and pure love swirled through her.

"Hold me, Daniel," she said. "Please hold me a minute."

He brought her close, and she laid her cheek on his chest. She had the fleeting impression that he clung to her as desperately as she clung to him.

Back at Aosta, they went directly to the hospital. Charon lay in a drunken stupor beside Michel's cot.

"Oh, Jesus." Daniel stared at the thickly bound stump. "God damn it to hell."

"You won't help him by swearing." Lorelei touched Michel's forehead and drew her hand back sharply. "He's feverish."

His eyes fluttered open, and he smiled. "You're Daniel's woman," he said through dry lips. She offered him water from a flask. He swallowed with difficulty. "He told us about you. You're a wonderful doctor."

Lorelei felt a flash of gratitude, quickly snuffed by Michel's next words: "You saved my leg, didn't you?" She laid her hand on his burning cheek. "No, Michel. God forgive me, I did not."

"Of course you did. I can feel it. I can wiggle my toes. It's getting better." His gaze darted to Daniel. "Glad you made it back, sir. We weren't sure about you. You should have seen me. I took on a man with a bayonet."

"I did see you, *mon gars*. You fought well. A true soldier."

"Yes. At last."

For the first time Lorelei realized Michel wasn't stuttering. But neither was he breathing.

*"No!"* Her anguished protest ripped through the ward. "No, please God, no!" She nudged his arm as if to stir him from sleep. His eyes were wide open, unseeing, staring at a mystery too deep to comprehend.

Grief and fatigue dragged Lorelei to her knees. She pressed her fist to her mouth in a vain attempt to hold back the sobs.

Daniel's hand clamped like a vise around her wrist. With his other hand he brushed Michel's eyes closed. "Come on," he said. "Let's go get some breakfast." He half dragged her from the hospital, past men awakened by her weeping.

"Breakfast?" she demanded, trying to yank free. "How can you think of food?"

"Because life goes on, Lorelei. One's stomach doesn't cease to growl simply because a man has died."

"You call this life?" she demanded, gesturing around the muddy camp. "Michel is dead. Today Bonaparte will march into the Piedmont and thousands of others will die. Tell me, Raven, where's the sense in that, the honor?"

"Hush," he said. He looked oddly helpless. "Where's my optimist?"

"She's dying, too, Daniel. Life is cheap to most of the world. I wasn't prepared for that." His face, blurred by hot tears, swam before her eyes. "Too much killing has made you callous, Daniel."

"I don't deny it." All around them, men prepared for the march to Ivrea. A few stopped to clap Daniel on the back and congratulate him on his success. He pulled her aside, into the shadow of a transport wagon. "You want to be a doctor, Lorelei. Your business is healing and life, but the other side of that is death. If you let a piece of you die with each loss, before long there won't be anything left of you."

She rubbed her eyes with her sleeve. "You'll understand me better in time, Daniel. After we're married, you'll change."

A strange smile curled his lip. "I wonder how many unhappy women have gone blithely into marriage with that assumption."

"I'm right. After I set up a practice, you'll help me with my work, just as you did with the typhus treatise."

"You think I'd be content to scribble scholarly documents all my life?"

"It's preferable to killing."

"You shouldn't marry me, Lorelei. It was a foolish idea."

"You said—"

"I did. But have you forgotten what I told you? People lie."

Shock drove through her. Over the sick thud of disbelief in her ears, she said, "You mean you lied about marrying me?"

"I'm afraid so."

"Daniel, why?"

"It was the most expedient way I could think of to get you to come away with me. Father Julian wouldn't let you stay at Saint Bernard's. You found the idea of a nunnery abhorrent. Look, I'll stay with you as long as it takes to get you settled at Coppet, and then—"

"You simply must marry me, Daniel."

"Oh? Why?"

"You promised—"

"Don't take on about honor and promises wrought. Since I have no honor, I'm not compelled to keep my promises."

"It's not that." The morning breeze, ripe with the smell of mud and bruised grass, tossed a lock of raven hair across his cheek. Reaching up, she smoothed it back. "You have to marry me because you love me."

"I never said that."

She shrugged. "It doesn't matter. I *know*."

"Your intuition is wrong this time." Daniel stifled a foul curse. Her steady, wide-eyed regard unnerved him. Why didn't she dissolve into tears, plead with him? Why didn't she make it easy for him to put her aside? He meant to be brusque but his hand was gentle as he touched her under the chin.

"Lorelei, listen to me. I can offer you nothing but my own peculiar hell, and you wouldn't like it there. Believe it."

She shook her head, turning it to one side to place a light, yet shattering, kiss on his palm. Exhaustion made him vulnerable to her sweetness.

"No," she said gently. "There is goodness in you, else I wouldn't love you with all my heart." She smiled. "We'll be married, Daniel Severin. Believe that."

# Chapter 14

"Citizen Daniel Severin, do you swear to abide by the laws of the Republic, to render your service to the Consulate, and to honor this woman as your wife?"

Daniel's stomach flopped over. He stared down at the stone surface of the church porch, then looked up. Before him stood the first consul of France and an Italian country priest, his wide-brimmed hat catching the breeze off the mountains. Behind him stood an army of thousands, all curious about the novelty of witnessing a marriage on a battlefield. And beside him, garbed in muddy trousers and wrinkled shirt, stood the bastard princess.

She jabbed her elbow into his ribs.

"I . . ." Daniel's voice grated, and he cleared his throat. This wasn't supposed to be happening. He was supposed to take her to Coppet, invent a new identity for her, and leave her to pursue her studies in genteel obscurity. But Bonaparte—at Lorelei's insistence—had taken that option from him. The fools. How could Daniel care for her? He was no fit husband. Promises to honor and protect a woman had no meaning for him.

But he finally spoke his response: "I so swear."

Her face shining with sincerity, Lorelei listened to the first consul's next words. Head up, shoulders straight, she faced marriage like a crusader pledged to convert the infidel. Her stout "I so swear" rang loudly across the plaza of Aosta, causing a ripple of amusement in the ranks.

While Bonaparte clutched his book of civil codes, the priest conducted mass in broad Italianate Latin, and Daniel struggled to bear up under a suffocating sense of certain doom.

Fool that he was, he had failed to seize the opportunity to steal away from the encampment. Instead, he'd let Lorelei go off to pray for Michel. Daniel had succumbed to the fatigue of the eventful night and stolen a few hours' rest.

Bonaparte's aides had shaken him awake. The first consul, they informed him, considered the marriage an excellent idea. It was the least he could do for a man who had destroyed a key enemy emplacement and for the woman who'd labored to save men's lives.

Daniel's protests had fallen on deaf ears. His flat refusal had been met with an outright threat. Still he heard Bonaparte's smooth, low voice: "Marry the girl, or I'll pursue a course of my own choosing for Louis's bastard."

The first consul had known who she was all along.

The country priest began reciting the Credo. Daniel sent Bonaparte a sidelong look. In dress uniform, his dark face shadowed by a plumed bicorne hat, the first consul glared back. The figured brass hilt of his ceremonial épée, embellished with a silver sword knot, glittered in the light of the lowering sun. He exuded domination and self-will from every pore.

Just how much did he know? Surely Josephine wouldn't dare tell her husband of her own black plan for the Bourbon princess. Then why was he so intent on this marriage?

There was only one answer to that.

What better way, short of murder, to dilute Lorelei's royal blood than to wed her to a commoner? If the Royalists ever discovered her identity, they wouldn't be able to use her in an alliance with the enemies of France. Unless, Daniel thought uncomfortably, they killed him and made her a widow.

With a discernible chilling of his blood, he mouthed the words to the final prayer. A long silence drew out. He stared straight ahead. Deep golden fronds from the setting sun bathed him with light. He could feel Lorelei's presence beside him, waiting, wanting, trusting.

"Why do you hesitate to give your new bride a kiss?" said Bonaparte, a challenging grin flashing beneath the bicorne. "I always thought the Raven a man of action."

Chants and clapping rose from the soldiers. Daniel

took her hands in his. He stared into her eyes and saw in their deep amber facets more joy and pride than he'd felt in a lifetime. Christ. The girl only fancied she loved him.

Her tongue flicked out to moisten her lips. The unconsciously seductive gesture disconcerted him. In a very short while she would expect him to make love to her. And Daniel Severin, smooth seducer that he was, felt terrified. The priest's words were real to her. Didn't she realize even a papal soliloquy couldn't make a good husband of him?

The wind skirled down from the high peaks. She had washed her hair and rinsed it in something herbal-smelling. He pressed his lips to hers. Her mouth was soft, her lips moist and cooled by the mountain breeze. She parted them, and a taste sweeter than forbidden fruit flooded him, purling through every vein. He suffered an impulse to consume her, to possess her, to bury himself in her and never emerge.

Ribald remarks erupted from the men. They shouted with a heartiness unique to soldiers on the eve of battle. They were going to conquer the world. Bonaparte had convinced them of it. But for many of them, this celebration would be their last.

"A room has been prepared at a house across the plaza," said Bonaparte. "Take your wife away for the night, Citizen Severin."

Lorelei flitted like a magpie around the freshly scrubbed room. She alighted on a chair beside a round table. "Just look at this feast," she cried, plucking a black olive from a bowl. She lifted the domed lid from a platter and inhaled the steam. "Pasta with pine nuts. Delicious."

Barry shambled forward to investigate. A long string of saliva dropped from his mouth onto the pine-planked floor. Taking pity, Daniel tossed the dog a crusty roll.

Her appetite forgotten, Lorelei jumped up and ran to the window. "Lace curtains," she exclaimed, fingering the delicately worked fabric. She draped the curtain around her head like a church veil. She looked ridiculously, impossibly childlike. "We've a view of the gardens. How terribly grand."

Keeping his distance, he peered outside. The tiny courtyard, centered by a weathered well sweep, was anything but grand. Straggly roses climbed the pitted plaster walls and geraniums in cracked pots lined a pebbled walkway.

"Very nice indeed." He went to the table, poured wine from a heavy clay jar, and drained the goblet in one swig.

"Goodness, look at this bath," she said, peering around a folding screen. He moved the screen aside. A long copper tub, its edges draped by snowy linen, occupied the small space. Steam, scented with rosewater, wafted from the surface. He remembered the crude half-barrel hip baths at the hospice and realized she had never seen the like.

"What in the world is this?" she demanded, lifting a painted porcelain vessel.

He cleared his throat. "It's for . . . privy purposes."

"Oh. It's grand, too, isn't it?"

This simple room with its sturdy furnishings might

have served as a linen closet for ladies Daniel had known intimately. Yet to Lorelei it seemed a veritable palace. And this was but a taste of the changes she would face as his wife.

"Why did you beg Bonaparte to force this marriage?" he demanded in the softest of whispers.

She tossed her shining curls. "You were getting cold feet. I couldn't risk losing you. And you might not know it yet, but it would be a disaster if you lost me."

He looked away, struck dumb by the irony of her statement.

She walked back to the table. "I love it here, Daniel. It's perfect." She tasted the wine, closing her eyes while a smile of pure delight curved her mouth. She looked rapt, beautiful, and all too tempting. "You know what makes it so perfect?" she asked.

The way your body looks beneath that thin shirt, thought Daniel. "I couldn't guess," he said.

"It's our nuptial chamber."

His mouth dried. He hastened to fill his glass with more wine. "Lorelei, sit down."

They sat across from each other, separated by a simple peasants' feast and a gulf of misunderstanding.

"We were too hasty in getting married."

She laughed and slapped her thigh. "Hasty! My goodness, Daniel, I'd have gone crazy if we'd waited any longer."

He took a bracing gulp of wine. "I think we should dissolve the marriage. I'll take you to Coppet. You can make a home with Germaine and Baron Necker—"

She cocked her head to one side. "Excuse me, did you say dissolve our marriage?"

"I did."

Her lower lip trembled. She chewed it into submission. "But why would you change your mind?" Her finger traced the rim of her goblet, then tracked a drop of wine down to its base.

He drew his gaze from her finger. "I told you, I never meant to marry you in the first place. Divorce is permissible under certain circumstances."

"Not in a union sanctified by the church." She caught another drop of wine and slid her finger into her mouth.

He shifted uncomfortably in his chair. "Annulment, then. The church permits that."

"Only in cases of consanguinity. And we're not relatives."

She couldn't know how true that was. She, with the blood of a dynasty of French kings; he, the son of a common horse thief and a man who'd never known he existed. Fascinated, he watched her hand, still moving absently over the wine goblet. She had the most sensitive fingers—quick yet gentle, soft and knowing. A healer's hands, a lover's hands.

"There's another way," he said, steeling his emotions. "A marriage that hasn't been consummated—"

"If you think for one minute that I'm not going to consummate this marriage, Daniel, think again." She hooked one leg over the arm of the chair and bounced her foot up and down. He found the motion mesmerizing.

"I see," he forced out. "So you're determined that I should have you on your back."

"Delicately put." She smiled, but he could see the hurt behind her eyes. "Why must you be so crass?"

"I'm a crass man. And any woman will tell you that the pleasures of the marriage bed are overrated."

"Not our marriage bed." She took a noisy gulp of wine and stood, her movements lithe and graceful. "You'll see to that."

"You're quick to put the burden on me."

"Why not? You're experienced. You won't let me forget that."

"Which is how I know it's overrated." He thought suddenly of Josephine, her full, smiling lips and milk white body, a body he'd once worshiped like a heathen before a stone idol. Never again, he told himself, rising from the table. Never again would he fall prey to a woman, let his heart be trampled beneath her dainty feet.

Lorelei is different, whispered a voice at the back of his mind. You know she is.

He spun toward the door. "I'm going below to wash up."

"But you can use the bath here."

His present state demanded an icy sluice of mountain-chilled water. He grasped the door latch.

"Daniel, wait." She stood gripping the back of a chair and regarding him with fierce intensity. "I'll hear no more about divorce or annulment. You want me, you *need* me, and nothing you say will convince me otherwise."

Without another word he stomped downstairs.

A quick check of the front and back doors of the house confirmed his worst suspicions. Soldiers wearing the dark blue and red coats of the Consular Guard stood sentinel at each exit and lined the alley below. Bonaparte had laid the trap well. Daniel had no chance of stealing away with Lorelei.

Cursing under his breath, he walked toward the courtyard. The owner of the house, no doubt paid by Bonaparte to provide discreet service, gave Daniel a shaving kit and towel.

At the well he stripped down to his trousers and drew water. He poured it over himself, willing the burningly cold water to wash away his craving for the bastard princess.

Only after he'd repeated the gesture ten times and shaved his face nearly raw did he come close to succeeding. The chill of the water left him shivering, a bluish cast to his skin. Feeling sufficiently numb, he made his way back to the room.

The sound of off-key singing drifted through the door.

He knocked once and stepped inside. Spread like a rug near the stove, Barry lifted his head, sneezed, and placed his chin between his front paws. A lamp glowed through the fabric stretched over the screen divider.

"Back already?" Lorelei called from behind the screen. The lamplight threw a detailed silhouette against the thin cloth.

"Yes," he choked out, his attention riveted on the shadowy image of a leg extended high in the air, the toe pointed, a hand drawing a sponge slowly down its slim length. The trickling sound of perfumed water rose to a roar in his ears.

"I'll just be a minute." Humming tunelessly, she repeated the process with the other leg, her movements languorous and self-indulgent. He imagined soapy hands caressing smooth flesh, and the image was intolerable.

"Take . . . your time." With his gaze still trained on the screen, he groped for the wine and drank straight from the carafe. She lowered her leg and stood, revealing her entire body in sharp profile.

Whispering a curse, Daniel turned away. Too late. All his efforts to cool his lust had, in less than a minute, been burned away by the furnace that raged out of control inside him.

He set down the pitcher and glared out the window. Two soldiers lounged in the courtyard now, sharing a cigar. Spying Daniel, they aimed a mocking salute at him. He pulled the shutters closed. He was Bonaparte's prisoner, but Lorelei's hold on him was stronger and far more mysterious. He didn't like the way she made him feel—raw and aching, too crazy with need to think straight. He listened to his own heartbeat, trying to drown out the sloshing sounds as she exited the bath.

He was completely out of his depth. Were her needs only physical, he could have satisfied them, but Lorelei harbored dreams he couldn't begin to answer. He knew he should turn away now, while there was still time. If he claimed her body, he risked subjecting her to a slow, lingering torture to last a lifetime. One day she would learn the truth. One day she would learn to hate him.

"All finished," she said. "But the water's still warm if you'd like to use it."

"No, thank you."

She stepped from behind the screen and shook her head like a damp puppy, chestnut curls flying loose and then springing back to crown her head. Germaine's gauzy embroidered shirt covered her—inadequately—from neck to mid-thigh.

Her long slim legs gleamed with perfumed dampness. The shirt outlined her torso, the dusky peaks of her breasts just visible through the fabric. "It's not a proper nightgown," she confessed, "but it's the only feminine garment I own."

If she managed to appear any more womanly than she did at this moment, he'd fling her on the bed and give in to the rampant beast inside him. A long silence drew out. Words couldn't capture what he felt, his frustration and—he admitted it—terror at the inevitability of this night. She stirred restively under his regard, a tiny questioning pucker in her brow. "Daniel," she whispered. "I need to know . . . if I please you."

An unbearable tenderness welled inside him. "Too much," he confessed, his eyes drinking in the play of light and shadow over her body, his lips hungering to taste each part. "Too much."

She blushed, and the color in her cheeks reminded him of the first flush of dawn, the first unfurling bud of a wild rose, the first shade of ripeness on a peach.

"Daniel," she whispered, twisting her fingers together in front of her. "I don't know what to do."

God, she was a babe, unschooled, untried. Unspoiled. Yet the yearning in her eyes reached out to him. The new tenderness curled through him, and thoughts chased one another through his head. This proud, unique girl was not one to be bedded like a whore. He didn't doubt his ability to give her simple, fleeting pleasure. But she deserved—needed—more. She needed love, contentment, a man worthy of her devotion, and Daniel didn't have it in his power to give her that.

Then she touched him, laying her hand on his forearm, and he felt a rush of emotion as blinding as lightning, yet as enduring as Alpine rock. His surrender started as a pulse of yearning that crescendoed into sharp need. He yielded to his craving, to the wordless pleas that haunted her eyes. The marriage might ruin both their lives, but this night could be perfect.

"You'll know what to do," he said, cupping her chin in his hand. "Don't worry, you will." He took her hand. He felt none of the awkward discomfort that had plagued him when he'd touched her in the past. This time was different. She was no longer forbidden to him. He pulled her against him. She sighed, her breath stirring the hair on his chest.

"It's about time this moment arrived," she confessed. "I thought I'd go mad wondering what it would be like."

Never had he heard that sort of unfettered honesty from a woman. A feeling he refused to name rose inside him, and he rested his chin on the top of her head. The perfume from her bath mingled with her own unique scent. Lord, if the *parfumiers* in the Rue Saint Honoré could bottle that wild, fresh fragrance they'd create a craze.

She lifted her face to look at him. "You shaved."

"So I did."

Her warm hand cradled his cheek. "You feel nice."

"So do you," he replied, a ridiculous understatement.

"But you're so solemn."

"I've never been married before. I'm told it's serious business."

The sweet shape of her lips beckoned him. He bent his head, catching her gust of breath and brushing his lips against hers, tantalizing himself with the light contact. A sound of impatience burst from her, and she flung her arms around his neck. The hem of her blouse rode up, and his hands encountered smooth flesh, still damp and silky from the bathwater. The pressure inside him built unbearably. Suddenly he was a youth again, out of control, frantic with desire and a richer emotion, a tenderness that felt alien, yet perfect and right.

She came into his heart like a breath of springtime into the dead of winter. For some reason he felt like thanking her, and his throat went numb with the unspoken words.

He stepped back, lifted the hem of her blouse, and drew the garment over her head.

He was used to pale, doughy forms shaped by corselets and stays, or the limp, wistful nudes of the painter Gérard. Once again Lorelei's uniqueness shone before him. She was a David heroine, a woman Daniel had thought existed only in the master painter's mind. She had firm flesh shaped beautifully by muscle and bone. Though compact and sturdy, she had an ineffable air of fragility about her, in the stillness with which she held herself, in the sweep of her eyelashes over her cheek.

For once Daniel was glad the canons had kept her ignorant; she didn't understand lust, but she didn't know shame, either. His gaze slid from her small breasts to the subtle flare of her hips. Hunger blazed like wildfire over him.

"Lorelei," he said, "you make a man crazy. You should have become a nun."

She stepped forward, a flame-tipped curl drifting across her cheek. "I would have made a terrible nun. I love the feeling I get when you look at me like that."

"If you knew my thoughts at this moment," he said roughly, "you'd run screaming for your rosary."

She tossed her head, curls nodding enticingly around her slim neck. "Nonsense. Shall I help you out of your trousers?"

"Do you want to?"

She stepped back, eyeing him with unabashed interest. "The boots first," she stated. "Sit down."

Incredulous, he lowered himself to the arm of a chair. She gripped his knee with one hand, his boot with the other, and pulled. It slid off, followed by his stocking; then she moved to the other foot. In a daze of dread and yearning, Daniel stood.

So long. It had been so long. Yet it had never been like this.

Her teeth worrying her lower lip, she hesitated, eyeing him not with fear but with uncertainty. Then, seeming to come to a decision, she slipped her fingers into the band of his trousers, brushing his belly with fire.

He suppressed a gasp. He'd always suspected that women, even innocent ones, possessed instincts for driving men mad. Slowly, so slowly, she loosed the side buttons. He was certain of it now.

"It won't be the first time I've disrobed you," she reminded him, stepping close to slide his trousers and small breeches down his legs. "We had to undress you after the aval—oh, my."

He tried not to smile at her shock. "I daresay it's different now."

A flush colored her skin from waist to hairline. "Yes . . . quite."

"I'll dim the lamp," Daniel offered.

"Must you?" she burst out, then clapped her hand over her mouth. "Of course you must, if it's customary."

"Nothing about us is customary, Lorelei."

"Then leave the lamp." She subjected him to a frank appraisal until he nearly blushed as well. The heat of him, the tingling awareness of every nerve ending, brought his senses to full awareness and crushed the last of his reservations to dust.

He reached for her, stretching out his hand as if his heart were in it. She placed her hand in his, her eyes brimming with innocent trust. They moved to the bed. She sank with a sigh into the billowy eiderdown coverlet. She looked fragile lying there, cushioned on a summer cloud.

"This is lovely," she said. "So much nicer than the rough blankets we had at the hospice."

He lay beside her, the eiderdown rising around them, a cocoon against the world, against all good sense. He stared into her face and was glad he'd left the lamp burning. In her wide, solemn eyes lay every hope he hadn't dared to dream of, every tender feeling he'd kept buried for years.

Yet keeping pace with his rampant lust was an urge to protect her. He touched his lips to her brow. His cause was lost. His task lay before him like a lavish banquet. *Please God don't let me hurt her.* . . .

As Daniel's hands traveled over her, Lorelei felt herself shiver with anticipation. She knew textbook anatomy to the letter, but the experience of lying beside the man she loved surpassed words. No book had warned her of the fire that brushed her skin each place he touched her. Hot, liquid sensations surged through her, opening a hunger inside her, burning away all awareness save that of him. She combed her fingers into the midnight silk of his hair. They kissed deeply, and she sensed a newness in his embrace, a letting go, a willingness to give.

Awash with love and awe, she ran her hands over his shoulders and downward, encountering ridges of muscle and ribs. Here was the human body as she'd never encountered it before—vibrant, brimming with vigor, heated by passion. There was a magical luster to his skin, a silkiness to its texture, and a warmth like a fever.

He propped himself on one elbow and gazed down at her. The blue irises of his eyes came into clear focus. She found herself studying the sharp crystalline spears of light that imprisoned, even now, the mystery of him, the pain.

"Oh, Daniel." Her whisper drifted against his ear. "This is right, wholly right. We're husband and wife, bonded forever. You don't have to hurt anymore."

Her words shot him through with a dizzying mixture of guilt and tenderness. Resting on one elbow, his free hand playing over her warm, responsive body, Daniel saw himself reflected in the dark pools of her eyes. On her upturned face, sweetly gilded by the lamp glow, he saw an expression of fierce, unconcealed yearning. Never had he been so sure of a woman's desire—and of her trust. Always before he'd seen question marks and unspoken demands in their eyes. Lorelei wanted him, but she didn't know that he was incapable of giving her what she needed: love, security, happiness. Notions as alien to him as prayers to the damned.

I'll take what you have, her wide eyes said to him.

If only you knew how little it is, he answered silently.

His mouth skimmed the rapid pulse of her throat, and he imagined he could feel the thick swish of passion-heated blood swimming through her. His fingers traced the delicate skin of her inner arm, lingering at her wrist, where the pulse echoed that in her throat. In a smooth motion he parted her pliant fingers and slipped his own between them, closing their palms together like hands clasped in supplication.

He forced back the urge to bury himself in her. Her pleasure had to come first; that was one trust he wouldn't shatter. God knew he had little else to offer.

"Lorelei."

"Umm?" She lifted her gaze to his face. Adoration shimmered in her gold-flecked eyes.

He wanted to look away, to hide the cold-blooded, corrupt man he was. "I assume, since you're trained as a doctor, that you understand the way . . . things work." Tongue-tied by her innocence, her vulnerability, he cleared his throat. "That is, do you know how—"

"Yes."

He blew a sigh of relief against her flushed brow. "Then you understand that the pain—"

"Pain?" She went rigid in his arms. "Daniel, I swear I won't hurt you."

"Damn." He sat up and leaned against the pillows. "You just said you understood." His hand came up to cradle her soft cheek. "It's not I who'll feel discomfort, but you."

"You said pain, not discomfort."

"I believe the degree varies."

"But I never read anything about pain, for heaven's sake."

"Most women experience it the first time."

"Why?"

He exhaled loudly. "I've never had to explain this before."

"Just tell me." She folded her hands on his chest and rested her chin on them. Her curls framed her brightly flushed upturned face, and for a moment Daniel was lost in memory, wondering how he could ever have thought her plain.

"Make an analogy or something," she said. "I like analogies."

He rolled his eyes. "This from a woman who once likened my brain to a bruised peach." He moved a stray curl from her forehead. "Love, if you consider what takes place . . ."

A gamin smile lit her face. "I confess I have considered it. More often than is probably healthy. But do go on."

"Then you realize our joining is bound to be—" He broke off, frowning at his clumsy way with words. "Damn," he said again.

Before he could continue, she raised her head from his chest and subjected him to a long, empirical perusal. "Oh," she said. "I think I see." She settled back and curved her body into his. "How bad is the pain, and how long does it last?"

"It's an individual matter. Lorelei, maybe we shouldn't—"

"We should. We must. And thank you for being honest about the pain." Her mouth softened in a thoughtful smile. "Father Julian once gave me a new pair of boots, and they pinched awfully. But after I walked a few miles in them, they became quite comfortable." She grinned at his thunderstruck expression.

A strange sense of unreality enveloped him, a sense that this could not be happening. Yet here he lay, imprisoned from without by soldiers and from within by an impossible girl who likened lovemaking to ill-fitting boots. An awful tenderness took hold of his heart.

"I'm a grown woman, Daniel." She stirred against him; the satiny ripple of her flesh felt like a sweet lash of torture. "Don't worry about hurting me."

His hand came to rest on her knee, his thumb circling the supple flesh on its underside. "I'll always worry about hurting you, Lorelei. But there are certain things I can do to make it better for you."

She smiled brilliantly. "By all means, do them."

His hand skidded northward, the silk of her brushing his callused palm.

"You know, I'm glad you were honest about—"

"Lorelei—"

"—always much better to be truthful—"

*"Lorelei—"*

"—respect for each—"

He besieged her mouth with a long, deep kiss, his tongue plunging out her unceasing rush of words. When he lifted his head, she drew in a sharp breath.

"Oh, my."

"Lorelei," he said, his patience in shreds, "some things are better accomplished in silence."

"I agree completely. In fact—" Seeing his expression, she broke off. "Yes. I'll be quiet."

There was willing submission and an adoration he didn't deserve in the way she lifted her arms and curled them around his neck. She rose up slightly, her breasts stirring against his chest. Blessed silence drifted over them.

An enormous responsibility dragged like a yoke at him. With one exception, he'd always chosen his women carefully, selecting only those who were independent in every way—emotionally, monetarily. He didn't know if he had the strength of heart to bear Lorelei's burdens—burdens she didn't even know she had.

His only hope lay in lifting them one by one. And right now she needed gentleness and understanding. His hands moved over her, into her, trembling slightly in awareness of her fragility. She wrung from him a patience he didn't realize he possessed, a conviction that his own needs were unimportant. His lips traced the delicate line of her jaw and moved lower to the rise of her breast. She tasted of the scented water she'd bathed in and another mysterious flavor that belonged solely to her. An invisible bond thrummed like a waxed bowstring between them.

He drew back to see if she, too, felt the magic. Wreathed in chestnut curls, her face was rapt, soft, her eyes closed and her lips parted. His finger came up to trace her mouth and penetrated slightly to the sweet curve of moistness that lined her inner lips; then his hand moved downward, trembling still, to skim her belly and thighs, to find her warm and ready.

He felt her press against him, heard the sharp intake of her breath. He caught her mouth with his and found himself drowning in her pleasure. An alien feeling thudded through him, and he fell still, trying to find a name for what he felt.

"I think," she whispered against his mouth, "that if you don't get on with it, I shall explode."

"Hush," he said, his thoughts crumbling beneath waves of desire. "Don't rush a man with a job to do." His kisses skimmed her face, her throat, her breasts; his hands introduced her to an irresistible rhythm, and she clutched at him as if she feared dropping off the edge of the earth. Tiny gasps built in her throat and made soft explosions against him. "Let it go, darling," he heard himself say. "Let it take you."

She relaxed with a fluid movement like water settling in a pool, but then she tensed and cried out. He felt the eddy of her response, the long sigh of surprise and delight, the kittenlike grasping of her small hands.

And through it all, a feeling of unspeakable joy rose up inside him.

The honest purity of her pleasure humbled him, made him long to sweep aside the secrets between them and start anew with her.

With a twist of guilt, he reflected that he'd gone to the hospice to kill her. What if he'd succeeded? The notion sent a chill down his spine, and he infused his embrace with more gentleness, more generosity, than he had known he possessed.

"Goodness," she said at last. "Why don't the scholars put these things in their books?"

Casting aside the urge to confess all to her, he nuzzled her curls. "They'd be burned as heretics."

She clasped him to her, surprising him as always with her wiry strength. "Daniel, I love you." And then her hands were on him, caressing the tightened muscles of his stomach, touching him with innocent fire.

"Lorelei."

"Some things are better accomplished in silence," she mimicked, and shifted on the cloud of eiderdown. "I wish to touch you. I assume it's allowed."

"Yes," came the rough whisper. *"Please."*

Lorelei buried a secret smile in the warm curve of his neck. His hoarseness betrayed emotions he wouldn't admit and convinced her utterly that his earlier talk of divorce had merely been an attack of nerves. She loved the feel of his skin, alive with a healthy fever, and she felt a pounding surge of anticipation. What had begun as an exercise to solidify their marriage had grown into a celebration of beauty and joy. She meant to leave no inch of him untouched and applied herself lovingly to the task.

Much later he pressed her back against the coverlet. The faint rustling of goose down grated in her ears. "Father Anselme was right," he said. "You are a quick learner."

Nodding solemnly, she drew him against her, embracing him with her legs and pressing her mouth to his.

Their joining started as a deep, secret probing that startled Lorelei with its force. Dazed by an excess of sensation, she could manage no more than mindless sounds of yearning in her throat. Her flesh stung, resisting him even as she strained to draw him closer. His shoulders shook, and she knew it was from the effort to take her slowly, to minimize her pain. If she could have spoken she would have told him it didn't matter, that what they were doing made pain unimportant, insignificant. Instead she clasped him tighter, sliding her lips from his neck to his shoulder, tasting him, tasting dreams and joy and hope.

She couldn't identify the point where discomfort slid into pleasure, and pleasure to a nameless drifting that swept her in circles like petals on windblown water. She rose upward, teetered dangerously, and willingly plunged. Like a flood of sunlight, his warmth flowed through her. His outrush of breath wafted against her cheek, which was cool and damp.

"You're crying." His expression wavered between shock and self-disgust.

She touched his cheek. "And you look as if you need to."

From outside came the sounds of soldiers' voices as they passed through the darkened streets of the village. A breeze slipped past the shutters and buffeted the pretty curtains, and Lorelei felt, very strangely, that she and Daniel no longer belonged in the world that moved around them.

The second time he made love to her, she was sure of it.

Although the day was clear, a soft pink mist seemed to envelop Lorelei. Waiting beside Daniel for Bonaparte to appear, she ignored the frenzied preparations in the encampment and let her thoughts linger on the night before.

Daniel's love had transformed her. She'd learned that marriage was more than a legal state, more even than vows sanctified before God. It was a spiritual state of being, lifting her to soaring heights, filling her with heady power while making her weak with the intensity of it.

A spasm of remembered pleasure stirred inside her. All through the endless night, he had done things to her body that should have hurt, yet instead bathed her in unspeakable pleasure; that should have been sinful, but felt more like an act of grace.

Dizzy with memories, her body feeling pleasantly raw, she reached for his hand. He squeezed hers briefly, then let it go. He wore a vague, distracted look. His eyes hid a host of nagging worries and fruitless regrets.

"Daniel?" she asked. "What do you suppose Bonaparte wants to see us about?"

"We'll find out soon enough." His expression told her he expected nothing good.

Still cushioned from the world by the fine, soft of mist of newness, she gazed across the compound. The hospital, protected from attack by a black flag, was empty of all save the most infirm. Dr. Larrey wouldn't hear of her making rounds the morning after her wedding.

She saw a posting chaise with fresh horses. The lacquered vehicle was surrounded by six heavily armed outriders. Elsewhere, wagoneers sang while lading supply carts; soldiers joked as they strapped on canteens and muskets, preparing to march out to meet the Austrians at Ivrea.

"They seem so confident," said Lorelei.

"Because Bonaparte's leading them," Daniel replied in a taut voice. "Men say he's worth forty thousand on a battlefield."

Movement erupted at the command tent. The Bruxelles canvas flaps drew back. Clad in battle regalia, the first consul emerged. Napoleon Bonaparte seemed to soar in stature with innate confidence. The luster of his achievements clung to him like a mantle of silk. His gaze took in the activity, then settled on Daniel and Lorelei. One hand resting negligently on the hilt of his sword, he approached them.

An aide handed Daniel a heavy purse and a thick packet.

"That contains your safe conduct, special orders for Dr. Lorelei du Clerc Severin, and a message to my wife," said Bonaparte. He smiled coldly and straightened the finger seam of his glove. "You're going to Paris."

# Chapter 15

***Paris***
***June 1800***

The posting chaise, coated with six days' worth of road dust, passed beneath the triumphal arch at the gate of the Tuileries. Inside the coach, Daniel leaned back against the banquette and stared at his wife. As she had throughout most of the hectic trip, Lorelei knelt on the velvet seat, the leather window flap drawn back, her head thrust out into the open air. Similarly occupied, Barry barked at statues, horses, and passersby.

The sight of her firm backside, bobbing with the motion of the coach, had an unsettling effect on Daniel. In a blur of memories he recalled the trip—a few hours of sleep snatched at posting inns, meals of bread and cheese in roadside fields ablaze with poppies, curt conversations with the outriders who watched their every move, short of monitoring their privy stops.

Daniel tore his gaze from Lorelei, but the recollections lingered. Their first night as man and wife had uncorked in her an explosion of feelings. Never had he known a woman to be so frank in her lust, so insatiably curious about lovemaking. One moment she'd be hanging half out the window, exclaiming over her first glimpse of a château. The next she'd be in his lap, her legs wrapped around his waist and her body doing things he wouldn't have thought possible in a moving vehicle. Making love to her was a celebration, full of adventure, tenderness, even humor. Her delight, her wide-eyed wonder, sparked in him a mixture of passion and protectiveness.

Still, he held certain things back from her—dark pleasures he'd indulged in with women who thrived on danger, women who were not satisfied with simplicity and gentleness in the act of passion . . . women like Josephine.

He had another reason for holding back, and that, he reluctantly admitted, was fear. Already his concern for Lorelei bordered on obsession. He could no longer trust himself to act rationally where she was concerned.

Restive, he glanced out the coach window. Few trees remained in the Place du Carrousel save two slender poplars stripped of their skeletal branches. The rough wooden fence around the Tuileries had been replaced by an iron grille with guardrooms at either end. A plaque on the southern guardroom bore a chilling reminder of the day he had lost his soul: "On August 10,

1792, royalty was abolished in France. It will never be restored."

The inscription hurled him into the past. Here Daniel Severin's ideals had crumbled to dust. Instead of a well-kept public square he saw a courtyard strewn with bodies, a detachment of Swiss Guards desperately sweeping the square with musket fire. Instead of the quiet Italianate symmetry of the palace he saw a building overrun by howling madmen bearing the standards of the Swiss to the Assembly, to flaunt them in the face of the befuddled, inept monarch.

The familiar nausea crept over Daniel. His chest tightened painfully. A fusillade of grape and musket fire crashed in his ears; the stench of Swiss corpses, hacked to pieces and burned by the rioters, made him ill.

"Daniel?" Lorelei's low, clear voice rescued him from the darkness. "You've gone quite pale. Are you all right?"

Her effortless assessment of his mood was jarring. He forced a smile. "I was just struck by some reminiscences."

She held his hands tightly in her own. Her strength, as always, took him by surprise. "We'll make good memories here, Daniel. You'll see."

He wished he could believe her. But Bonaparte's orders boded ill. Daniel had been stunned to read, as the chaise had lurched down the mountains from Aosta, the first consul's plans for Lorelei.

"Oh, my," she called, interrupting his thoughts, "Look at those women, Daniel. They're in their nightgowns."

Near the south wing of the palace a group of women

walked toward the Seine, visible through the arches of a covered walkway. The ladies wore diaphanous tunics, their trailing skirts draped over bare arms to reveal the openworked Roman-style buskins on their feet. The overall impression was a calculated and tantalizing suggestion of nudity.

"They're fully dressed," he said, trying not to smile. "It's the new mode of costume."

She drew her head in. "Well, it can't be very practical in cold weather."

He looked at the river again. Between barges and bathing houses, sunlight glinted like coins off the river. Unease jabbed at him. Everything—*everything*—was new to her. She was as out of place in Paris as a wild rose in a hothouse.

Half of him couldn't believe he was accompanying the bastard princess straight into the hands of the woman who sought her death. The other half understood that, for the time being, Lorelei was safe at the Tuileries. The death of a healthy young woman under the first consul's protection would create a scandal even Josephine couldn't explain away.

Still, Josephine had it in her power to crush Lorelei's enthusiasm, to poison her gentle, naive spirit.

Daniel didn't relish her reaction when she discovered herself playing hostess to a Bourbon princess and her mercenary husband. He steeled his resolve to keep Lorelei safe, to conclude the business with Meuron and to leave Paris for good.

The coach rattled to a halt at the grand entrance to the Tuileries. Lorelei wrenched open the door and leaped out before the footman could get his box in place.

Catching the man's chagrined expression, she gave him a self-deprecating grin. "Oh, I've done it again, haven't I?"

Barry sailed out behind her and immediately lifted his leg to mark one of the gray stone risers flanking the entrance.

Whirling, Lorelei scanned the vast palace wings. "Bonaparte and his wife *live* here?"

Two of the outriders snickered while a third hurried beneath the arched portal and disappeared through a massive doorway.

Noticing the snickers, Lorelei placed her hands on her hips. "I suppose you think a Swiss girl is born knowing city etiquette?"

Chastened by her forthright remark, the outriders dismounted and turned away. "When will I get to meet Madame Bonaparte?" she asked Daniel.

He took her elbow and guided her through the large door. Barry's nails clicked on the floor behind them. Cool air rushed through the high, vaulted corridors.

"Soon enough," he said tautly.

She gaped in wonder at the sinuous sweep of the grand staircase, the endless galleries sprawling out to right and left, the high sheen of polished marble beneath their feet.

Sweat slithered down Daniel's back. His hand came up to touch his scarred forehead. He didn't want her to guess that ghosts leaped out at him—halberds hooking at his chest, hatred burning in a thousand pairs of eyes.

God, he thought, why couldn't Bonaparte have moved into a place less fraught with horrors, a building not consecrated by human blood?

There were damned few places like that in Paris.

Paris, City of Light, City of Blood.

Bonaparte understood the symbolic value of living in the splendid palace that for two centuries had housed the kings of France. Under different circumstances, Lorelei might have grown up here in genteel splendor. Daniel was suddenly glad that she hadn't, but he feared for her now that she was here.

Virtually uninhabited since the massacre of '92, the palace was undergoing a massive refurbishment. In the left wing, a team of glaziers installed panes in the tall, narrow windows while laborers sanded the walls.

"Why are they sanding off those designs?" asked Lorelei.

"Those were Phrygian caps, painted by the sansculottes," said Daniel. "Bonaparte apparently doesn't care for them."

"Oh." She pulled him down the north gallery where large new paintings in thick gilt frames graced the walls. At their heels, Barry skidded on the sleek floor. She stopped in front of a picture. Her jaw dropped to her chest. "Oh, my," she murmured, her voice echoing down the corridor.

Daniel bit back a grin. "Like it?"

She swallowed audibly. "Cupid and Psyche?"

"Yes. By the painter Gérard."

"I never pictured them quite like this." Her astounded gaze traveled over Psyche's breasts to the curve of Cupid's naked hip to the erotic bow of his lips as he bent to kiss her. "It's a most interesting depiction."

In spite of himself, Daniel swallowed a chuckle. "I'm sure Monsieur Gérard would be gratified by your opinion."

Her cheeks blooming, she moved down the gallery, passing scenes of ancient heroism and mystical legend. She stopped before a scene filled with muscular warriors in improbable poses, their expressions ecstatic as they fought and died. "Surely they didn't actually do battle in the nude."

"Probably not. But the human form is a great challenge to a painter, and Bonaparte is an avid student of ancient Rome."

She pointed to a magnificent man wearing nothing but an iron shackle around his neck. "Who is that?"

"Regulus. His name's synonymous with honor. The Carthaginians captured him, and he begged to be allowed to warn his people of the invasion. In return, he promised to come back to his captors."

"Very noble," said Lorelei.

"For all the good it did him. He came back and the Carthaginians beheaded him. Seen enough?"

"Not remotely. And don't you dare tease, Daniel. The human form is of great interest to me, too."

"There's plenty more to gape at across the Place du Carrousel at the Louvre. Bonaparte has stolen quite a collection."

"Stolen?"

"Spoils of war. He brings back art treasures from every campaign. Obelisks from Egypt, stone lions from

Venice, paintings from every grandee foolish enough to oppose him."

"But that's wrong. Those things don't belong to him."

"The day is fast approaching," Daniel said softly, "when no one will tell Bonaparte he's wrong."

They returned to the foot of the grand staircase. A small man in a livery of blue trimmed with silver lace hurried toward them. "Monsieur Severin?"

"Yes?"

"Pardon the delay. I was overseeing the drapers. They're dressing the windows in the first consul's study." The man's nose twitched above a neat little mustache. "I am Louis François de Bausset, prefect of the palace. Welcome to Paris, monsieur." His gaze darted to Lorelei, taking in her breeches and rumpled shirt. "Madame," he added, pursing his lips.

*"Enchantée,"* Lorelei murmured, her gracious reply and engaging grin taking some of the starch out of the self-important official.

Bausset cleared his throat and aimed a glare at Barry. "Well, er, I'll send a groom to take your pet off to the stables."

"That won't be necessary," Lorelei said, her speech as smooth and cultured as any courtier's. "Barry stays with us."

"No, no, no," said Bausset, looking as if he was about to stomp his slippered foot. "Quite impossible, madame."

A high-pitched yapping echoed from the upper galleries. Sherry-colored fur flashed between the marble railings. "Christ," muttered Daniel. "It's Josephine's dog."

Barry lunged up the staircase to give chase. Swearing, Daniel followed with Lorelei and Bausset close behind.

They reached the top of the stairs to see the dogs careen around a corner.

"Fortuné!" a maid shrieked. Skirts hiked above her knees, white-stockinged legs pumping, she joined the chase. At the end of the gallery, the lapdog came up short against a bank of closed doors. Howling, it darted beneath Barry's legs. The terrified creature bolted past, paws scrabbling on the marble floor. Yelping with high delight, Barry galloped after it.

Daniel slumped against the rail. Bausset and the maid shrieked for help. Lorelei lunged for Barry and missed, her arms grasping at empty air. Her feet came out from under her. She skidded, belly down, into a plant stand. A potted fern toppled to the floor with a resounding crash, scattering clumps of damp brown soil.

Daniel stood watching, shaking his head as he murmured under his breath, "Welcome to Paris, princess."

Sitting in the bath wing of his opulent guest suite, Daniel scowled at Barry over the rim of the copper tub. "Never again," he said sternly. "Do you hear me?"

Barry's tail swished against the inlaid floor.

"You'll behave, or you'll find yourself warming the straw in the stables."

Barry started to nibble at a gilt tassle hanging from the draperies, then looked at Daniel and stopped. He laid his chin between his front paws, his jowls pooling on the floor.

"No more terrorizing Josephine's lapdog," Daniel repeated, opening the steam geyser to subject himself to a hot fog. Barry stood, pricked his ears, and cocked his head to one side. Like warm fingers of unspeakable luxury, the steam entered Daniel's nostrils and lungs. Suddenly he wished he hadn't been so hasty in sending Lorelei off shopping with Madame de Remusat. This was one luxury he wouldn't mind showing her.

"Bonaparte doesn't like the rodent any more than we do," he continued, "but his wife spoils it like a child, lets it sleep in her bed and eat off her plate."

Barry lifted his head and sneezed.

"And no prowling about the city, you," Daniel admonished. He took a shaving cup and plunged a brush into the ambergris soap. "Paris is different. The females here are all sluts."

"I beg your pardon." A languid female voice drifted through the fog.

Daniel's bathwater turned to ice. A slim, pale hand parted the draperies surrounding the tub. He fought to keep a bland, uninterested expression on his face. "Josephine."

She stepped into the chamber and blinked lazily through the steam. Her full lips parted in a sultry smile. She wore a pale, wispy gown that left her arms and most of her bosom bare. Gossamer and lace encasing a will of steel, thought Daniel.

"Clever man," she said. "I see you remember my voice."

"Who else but you would barge in on a man's bath?"

"Who else but you would, in a word, insult the entire female population of Paris?"

Idly he twirled the shaving brush and waited for the steam to clear. "I do apologize. I shouldn't have said they were sluts. It's too kind a word for some." Giving her a humorless grin, he said, "You'll pardon me if I don't stand."

All oversized paws and lapping tongue, Barry cavorted around her gown. Josephine wrinkled her elegant nose in distaste and lifted the hem of her dress away from the dog's wet nose.

"This must be the monster who terrorized my poor little Fortuné," she said. In a quick, neat motion, her foot lashed from beneath the hem and kicked Barry in the ribs. With a yelp of surprise and pain, the dog scurried to safety outside the draped area. "Beast," said Josephine. "I ought to have his neck wrung."

With studied insouciance, Daniel lathered his whiskers and picked up a razor. He eyed the long, thin blade. "Madame, it's only fair to tell you that if any harm befalls that creature, you'll find your own little carpet louse gutted and turning on a spit over the kitchen fire."

She shuddered delicately. "You always did have a cruel streak." The gauzy gown wafted against her beautifully rounded figure as she stepped closer. Pretending not to notice, he began to shave.

"Where is your wife, Daniel?" she asked softly.

He suppressed a chill. "Lorelei is quite safe in the hands of your good and compassionate friend, Madame de Remusat."

"Claire?" Josephine's nostrils flared. "She's with Claire?"

"Is your hearing failing?" he asked, drawing the razor along his lower jaw. "Ah, yes, I've heard it's the first faculty to go in women who've reached"—he paused to rinse the razor—"a certain age."

"Bastard."

"Whore."

She braced her hands on the foot of the tub and leaned forward. Steam dewed her flesh; her breasts resembled a pair of pale, exotic fruits.

"When, pray tell, did you become so charming?" she inquired.

"Since you sent Chrétien Rubis to the hospice," he replied, studying his face in a hand mirror.

She stiffened very slightly. "I have no congress with that thug."

Daniel decided to let the lie pass. "What do you want, Josephine?"

"Where has Claire de Remusat taken the chit?"

"Shopping. Your husband sent us here with no more than the clothes on our backs." He lifted one eyebrow. "Oh, and a reward of fifty thousand francs. You did read the first consul's letters?"

"Of course." She dipped her hand into the water, half closing her eyes. "We've much to discuss, Daniel." His name was a drop of honey rolling across her warm tongue. Leaning down, she ran a delicate finger up the calf of his leg. "Not the least of which is your little midwife, who impressed my husband so. I'll wait for you in the outer chamber."

Like a striking eel, his hand burst from the water and

snared her wrist. "Oh, no," he whispered, his voice taut with hatred. "I'm quite comfortable right here. Just say what you came to say."

Her face paled. She tried to wrench from his grasp. "I am the wife of the first consul," she said, her bosom rising and falling rapidly. "I do not conduct audiences with men in their baths."

He chuckled and loosened his grip. "Audiences, is it, now? How very royal that sounds, madame."

She managed to slip away from him. But Daniel's other hand was quicker. He grabbed a handful of her artfully tousled sable curls and held fast. Slowly he brought her face down to a level with his. Nose to nose, they glared at each other. He used to drown in the sparkling pools of her eyes, used to be entranced by the lyrical lines of her facial structure. Now he felt sickened by this faithless woman.

"Let go of me," she commanded.

"Oh, no," he said, twisting the lock of hair. "You came into my bath like a whore, thinking to find me defenseless."

"The Raven, defenseless?" she inquired, a tiny tremor in her voice. "You speak of our association as a battle."

"A battle I intend to win," he stated, warm with the confidence of the knowledge Emanuel had given him. "I won't dance to your tune anymore, Josephine."

She gripped the razor, which he'd laid on the bath stool. "Be careful how you treat me, Daniel. Citizen Marat was murdered in his bath."

"You're no Charlotte Corday, my dear." He knocked the razor from her hand.

To her credit, she showed no fear or pain. "I paid you well to do a job," she said. Her breath smelled of honey and wine, her body of an unmistakable musk that turned Daniel's stomach.

"You misjudged me," he said, his voice nonchalant but his grip like iron. "Rubis is dead."

Her long lashes swept downward. "You killed him."

No question, but a statement. He said, "The cleric is dead, too." He held her with his gaze, willing her to reveal the name of the assassin he'd killed.

"I know nothing of any cleric," she said.

He searched her face but found no evidence of the lie. She was good, too good; he couldn't be certain whether or not the dead canon had been her accomplice.

"Why did you marry her, Daniel?" Josephine asked suddenly.

He released her hair. In an unhurried motion, she levered herself upright. "Why?" she asked again.

A hundred complex reasons sprang to mind, not the least of which was the fact that Bonaparte hadn't given him a choice, but Daniel would have died before he confessed that to Josephine. "She needed me," he said simply.

"I needed you, damn it!"

He laughed huskily. "Oh, you are desperate, aren't you, madame? Terrified that Bonaparte will divorce you and that barren womb of yours." Her mouth worked in silent rage. "But you should know your husband better. When he decides he's had enough of you, he won't settle for a royal bastard. I've done you a favor, dear Josephine. By marrying Lorelei, I've neutralized her. No one will use her as a political pawn now."

"You betrayed me," she said. "You'll pay for that."

"Empty words, darling. Your husband's taken a liking to Lorelei. More than that, he expects her to consult with your physicians on the matter of your childlessness. If she so much as breaks a fingernail, you'll have some explaining to do."

Her lips thinned in a vicious smile. "Pity no one cares as much for Jean Meuron. He's still mine, to dispose of as I will."

Jean Meuron. Daniel's other Achilles' heel. Hiding his concern, he propped an elbow on the rim of the tub. "Your husband is knee deep in debt to the Swiss after this last campaign. You'd be a fool to upset them."

"How tenderhearted you've grown, Daniel," she drawled, her voice like warm molasses. "A husband *and* a patriot. I'm impressed."

He decided to play his trump card. "Not half so impressed as I was when Emanuel told me the truth about the Bern gold."

She gasped sharply, nostrils flaring. "How do you know about Emanuel?"

"It hardly matters now," he said easily. "I *know.*"

"You've no proof."

"Perhaps I have," he bluffed.

"But tell me, does your little wife know about us?"

"You're skirting the issue, Josephine."

"Perhaps we should tell her," she replied viciously.

"Tell her what? That you whored your way out of prison, used me to decorate your salon—"

"You're pitiful," she snapped. "As pitiful as you were the day we were released from the Carmes and you begged on your knees for my hand in marriage."

It took all his restraint to keep from strangling her. Her laughing refusal echoed across the years, filling his head with a clamor of rage. He'd been full of dreams then; but now he knew the price of dreaming.

"No more pitiful than you, sweet Josephine," he said. "You come in here reeking of your lover's sweat—"

The blaze of rage in her eyes confirmed his guess. "How dare you—"

"How dare I what, madame?" He laughed softly. "How dare I mention that while your husband is off facing peril, you are keeping his bed warm with Hippolyte Charles?"

She drew her arm back to slap him. He caught it in mid-arc.

"It is still Charles, isn't it?" he inquired. "Or have you added another stud to your stable?" Slowly and deliberately he loosed her arm. He made a great show of washing his hand. Even more slowly he rose from the tub.

Her eyes devoured his slick form. "That's none of your concern."

He couldn't believe there had been a time when he was afraid of her. He'd actually believed she owned his soul. She still had a power he respected, but during the cold weeks of an Alpine springtime, Daniel had learned that fears could be faced. Wrongs could be righted. Cold hearts could be warmed.

Josephine, apparently, had learned nothing. She

stepped close, coming between him and the pile of fresh towels on the bath bench. She loosed her beautiful curls, the pins dropping with tiny pinging sounds on the floor. Her hand brushed his outer thigh, tracing its muscled structure upward.

"We shared something special, Daniel," she confessed, her voice as heavy and sweet as treacle. "Perhaps I was wrong to throw it away. But it's not too late for us."

Stepping out of the tub, he trapped her wrist in a steely grip. "Oh, but it is, sweet Josephine. You see, I've already had my bath"—he bent toward her; her tongue darted out to moisten her lips—"and you're still soiled." He gave a gentle push. The backs of her knees bumped the rim of the tub. In an eruption of white batiste, she fell backwards into the tepid water.

Ignoring her sputtered threats, Daniel picked up a towel, slung it negligently about his hips, and walked out.

Mademoiselle Tournon, master dressmaker of L'Ornement des Grâces, raised a gold-rimmed lorgnette to her eyes and walked in a slow circle around Lorelei.

"You say you're a guest of the first consul?" she inquired.

"Yes. My husband and I are lodged at the Tuileries."

Mademoiselle Tournon and Claire de Remusat exchanged a long look. Although she was the same age as Lorelei, Claire had the knowing air of sophistication of a much older woman. Her beautiful mouth, beneath a rather long nose, curved into a smile, a pair of dimples adding a piquant quality to her regard.

"Daniel Severin performed an important service for Bonaparte," said Claire. "Lorelei needs dresses for every occasion."

"I take it he was adequately compensated," said Mademoiselle Tournon, her nostrils flaring delicately.

"Indeed," said Claire, reaching over to finger a bolt of rich Lyons silk.

Lorelei blushed with awkwardness. She had no idea of the value of things; she wasn't certain she could afford what Claire had in mind.

"Does Madame Bonaparte know you've come to me?" asked Mademoiselle Tournon.

"She does not," said Claire, and the two women shared a look of conspiratorial delight that baffled Lorelei. She submitted to the dressmaker's perusal and wished Daniel had better prepared her for life in Paris.

"Where the devil did you get these clothes?" Mademoiselle Tournon asked, gingerly touching the lapel of Lorelei's *bredzon.*

"From the Hospice of Saint Bernard." She glanced down at her vest and breeches. "It's all I have. Can you help me?"

"Help you?" Mademoiselle Tournon fingered Lorelei's curls. "Small hair," she murmured. "But adequate. You've good bones, my dear, and a certain air of wistful romance that will work well with the Grecian style." At last she smiled, some of the severity softening from her features. "My dears," she said, "we three are going to have some fun."

* * *

"You did what?"

Through the dim, dust-filtered light of the wineshop in the Rue de Valois, Daniel regarded a ring of shocked faces. All were familiar to him—rugged men with hard mouths and determined eyes. They were Swiss patriots, gathered in Paris to support their imprisoned leader, Jean Meuron.

Daniel took an unhurried drink of his wine. The cheap vintage burned his throat. "It's as I said," he explained. "I called Josephine's bluff."

"And signed Meuron's death warrant," snapped Nathaniel Stockalper. His father had been killed during the massacre, and his familiar features haunted Daniel. "Your own as well."

"I won't believe we're defeated before we've even begun," said Daniel. "All things are possible if you're on the right side."

Albrecht de Veer, a wool agent from the canton of Uri, raised an eyebrow. "That doesn't sound like the Raven. When did you become so idealistic, my friend?"

Since Lorelei.

Daniel stared down into his cup to hide his expression. Conquering sentiment, he faced the Swiss men again. "We've known all along that it wasn't Jean who took the gold."

"But until we find out who did, he's considered guilty."

"Josephine has it," said Daniel.

Stockalper gave a low whistle. "Are you sure?"

He nodded. "I had a rather interesting meeting with Josephine's chief clerk. It set me back a good piece of my reward, but I found out where the money is. It's in a bank trust in Geneva." His lips twisted in an ironic smile. "Under the name of Hippolyte Charles."

De Veer slapped his palms on the table. "There we have it, by God. We just need to petition the minister of justice, and Meuron will be free."

"It's not that simple," Daniel confessed. "We need proof, a positive link between that trust and the stolen gold."

"We're Swiss," said de Veer. "We've patience bred into us."

"We can't afford to be patient," said Stockalper. "Josephine and Fouché could arrange Meuron's execution very quickly."

Daniel's throat tightened. "Josephine won't dare make a move so soon after Bonaparte's march through the Alps. Destroying Meuron would be too much of a slap in the face after Switzerland cooperated in the campaign."

"Will Bonaparte's assault on Italy succeed?"

Daniel envisioned the French army, outnumbered and outprovisioned by the Austrian forces. Then he thought of the first consul's implacable confidence and desperate political need for a victory.

"He'll win. He knows he must bring home a prize. Genoa capitulated to the Austrians, but on the ninth, the French took Montebello. We'll have to wait for further word on his progress."

"So what do we do now?"

Daniel drummed his fingers on the plank table. "We send someone to Geneva to investigate that trust."

A man in the corner rose and brushed off his thighs.

"I'll go." It was Bayens, a banker from Zurich and a fast friend of the Meuron family.

Daniel scribbled the name of the trust on a scrap of paper and handed it to him. "I wish you luck, my friend. And be careful."

Bayens jammed an odd red top hat on his head and left the wineshop.

"I still think we should break Meuron out of prison and spirit him home to Switzerland."

A chorus of splutters and sneers rose from the men. "You think we haven't tried?" said de Veer. "Last month we broke into the Hôtel du Midi. The guards killed Brenner and transported Meuron to the Saint Lazare prison. Every time we come close, they move him."

"Where is Meuron now?" Daniel asked.

"At the Feydeaux," said Stockalper.

"I think you made a big mistake, Daniel, goading Josephine," said de Veer, but he grinned. "Pushed her into the bath, did you?"

"She had it coming."

"And what's this about a new wife?"

The sour smells of wine and burned tallow suddenly seemed oppressive to Daniel. "How did you find out about Lorelei?"

A man stepped from the shadows at the back of the cramped room. "I told them. I knew you'd take my advice."

Daniel's astonished gaze took in the man's rough clothes, his shock of dull, unwashed hair, and the new hardness in his once boyish eyes. So the lad had made it to Paris.

"Sylvain." Daniel kept his voice expressionless. *How much did you tell them?* He tried to convey the silent question across the room.

"Your friends were surprised to hear you'd lost your heart to a Swiss country lass," Sylvain said. He tugged at the faint strings of a beard that sprouted sparsely on his chin. "Seems everyone thought you preferred the women of Paris."

"All of them," Stockalper added, and laughter rippled through the group.

Daniel covered his chagrin and called for more wine. Evening yielded to night as the Swiss patriots discussed their plans. They had no answers as to how their nation could survive in the world of Bonaparte's all-encompassing vision. But one thing was certain: they needed Meuron, the one man with enough influence to unite the splintered factions of Switzerland and stand firm for independence. They had to liberate him and take him to their mountain homeland.

A heated sense of mission seized Daniel, surprising him. Not long ago his interest in Meuron had been purely personal. Now he found himself thinking like a patriot rather than a mercenary; now the sanctity of Switzerland mattered to him.

The city bells tolled midnight as Daniel and two companions returned to the Tuileries. Sylvain and de Veer's daughter, a young, soft-spoken woman called Greta, would join Daniel's ménage as footman and maid to Madame Severin. But their secret duty was to watch over her, for Josephine's jealousy could still turn lethal.

After lodging Sylvain in quarters at the Riding

School behind the palace, and Greta in a dressing room below their suite, Daniel made his way up a winding staircase. His eyes burned from studying maps; his throat ached from talking. As he walked by sleepy palace guards, the past leaped out at him with fresh vigor. Would he never be shed of the screams of his brothers-in-arms, the rage at his own impotence on that bloody day? He thrust aside the question and trudged toward the suite of guest rooms on the second floor.

He made his way across the darkened sitting room. Draped over a brocaded divan worth a fortune, Barry looked up and thumped his tail. Daniel paused in front of the door to Lorelei's chamber. He smiled slightly, remembering her indignation at their being given separate bedrooms. Convention dictated that husbands and wives sleep apart, visiting each other by invitation only.

He pushed at the door. The well-oiled hinges made no sound as he entered. An ormulu clock ticked quietly on the mantel. Heavy Gobelin curtains enclosed the bed. Misty moonlight streamed in through the tall, narrow windows. From outside came the never-ceasing sounds of Paris: the shouts of river pilots, the clopping of hooves on cobblestones, the hoarse songs of men whose revelry lasted late into the night.

Bandboxes, glovers' parcels, and huge cartons littered the floor. Interesting smells pervaded the air: perfumes and pomatums, the crisp scent of new silk and lace. But something was missing: the faint, ineffable fragrance that was the essence of Lorelei. He missed it.

As he approached the draped bed, an iron fist of foreboding clutched at him. The room was too empty, too quiet. He couldn't even hear her breathing. He drew back the curtain.

The bed was still perfectly made. She was gone.

Panic hissed in his ears. He leaped over the parcels and bundles, heading toward the door. His boot caught in a length of gauzy white cloth, and he nearly stumbled, stopping himself by grasping the brass door handle.

He found a candle, fumbled a few seconds lighting it, and ran to the bathing chamber.

Her boar-bristle brush from Father Emile lay on the table. Perfume bottles and sachets were lined up like an infantry regiment.

Wax spilled on his wrist. He swore under his breath. Tense and breathing quickly, he hurried to check his own room.

The bed-curtains gaped wide. The counterpane made a large mound in the middle of the bed.

Relief, welcome as a spring breeze, drifted over him. On light feet he went to the bedside and let the candlelight creep over the small, still form. He should have known his wife wouldn't stand on convention.

She slept as sweetly as a child, her curls scattered over the pillow and one hand lying palm up beside her face. Her lips were moist and slightly bowed in a dreamy smile. Poor mite, he thought, tenderness prodding his heart. She had no inkling of the danger her existence wrought. Time after time he'd grappled with the problem of telling her who her father was. And time after time he'd backed away from the task. He'd stolen enough of her innocence as it was.

He imagined her traipsing from dressmakers' salons to jewelers' shops, from glovers to bootmakers, from perfumeurs to coiffeurs. He pictured her in a closed coach fighting its way across crowded bridges and through narrow streets. How different this glittering, artificial world must seem compared to the quiet majesty of her mountain home.

"Oh, princess," he whispered to the sleeping girl, "Paris is no place for you."

Lorelei's eyes snapped open. From the window came the deep indigo tones of *l'heure bleue,* the first flush of light heralding the dawn. The maid who'd brought her supper yesterday evening had sworn no lady rose before noon.

What a waste of the morning, thought Lorelei, bracing her hands behind her and sitting up. Something solid and warm stirred beside her.

Daniel. His hair darkened the pillow like spilled ink. His face, unmarred by the lines of care that creased it during his waking hours, was turned toward her. He looked young, impossibly handsome, curiously vulnerable. And more relaxed than she'd ever seen him.

*I'm good for him.* The thought wrapped itself like sunshine around her heart. Smiling, she had to force herself not to touch him, to wake him. He had probably come in quite late from his errands and needed his rest.

Carefully she drew her leg from beneath his and slipped out of the bed. He groaned softly and hugged her pillow.

Dressed in a long shirt Madame de Remusat called

a shift, Lorelei padded out of the room, closing the door behind her.

Barry trotted to her side, the sinfully thick carpet muffling his footfalls.

"Good boy," she whispered. "I'll take you out for a run in just a moment." Her gaze shifted to a spot on the carpet. "Oh, Barry. You disgraced yourself again."

The dog tucked his tail in shame and went to the door.

She made hasty ablutions in the bathing chamber, sparing a few seconds to gape in awe at the massive bath with its magical steam geysers. Daniel's razor had fallen to the floor several feet from the tub. She placed it in his shaving cup.

She considered wearing one of the garments Madame de Remusat had chosen yesterday but decided against it. She couldn't tell back from front, and Barry was in a hurry.

She removed the shift and pulled on her shirt, breeches, and boots; then she left the palace through the grand rear entrance Claire had shown her yesterday.

Barry galloped over pebbled walkways and across neatly scythed lawns still sopping with dew. A pair of ornamental pools, their surfaces still as glass, reflected the peach-colored dawn. Larks and swallows chirped in the arbors.

Barry lifted his leg on a statue of Gambrinus. Though tempted to savor the quiet dawn, Lorelei knew she should return to her rooms. Daniel would worry if he awoke and found her gone. He worried too much. Besides, Claire de Remusat had arranged for a small army of seamstresses, glovers, milliners, shoemakers, and even a dancing master to visit today. And very soon Lorelei hoped to get to the business of meeting Josephine and consulting with her physicians. She had little hope of discovering the cause of Madame Bonaparte's affliction, but the first consul expected her to try.

A few yards away, Barry pricked his ears and froze in a listening stance. Then he gave a joyous yelp and started running toward the end of the sprawling park.

"Barry, come back this instant." She hurried after him. He looked back for a moment, hesitated, then bounded forward in defiance.

"Crazy beast," she muttered. "You'd best not be after Madame Bonaparte's dog again."

Flagrantly disobdient, he led her to the old Riding School. Here the Swiss had been forced to lay down their arms. Here the French had rewarded them with slaughter.

All except one. The last royal guard lay sleeping in the palace. She shivered, imagining Daniel's horror and pain.

A faint rhythmic sound intruded on her thoughts. Nose to the ground, Barry hurried onward. As Lorelei drew closer to the sound, her throat tightened.

Smooth, rapt chanting came from the Convent of the Feuillants at the rear of the Riding School. The palace prefect had told Lorelei of it. The Revolution had banned clerics; Bonaparte had brought them back—on his terms, of course, giving them no political power.

The tiny chapel, shadowed by willow trees that

swished in the morning breeze, beckoned to a place in Lorelei that hungered for the familiar in this alien city. Barry sat on the chapel porch and whined softly.

*"Attends,"* she ordered and stepped inside. Two tiny points of flame at either side of the altar added to the light streaking in through small, high windows. She took out her rosary and fingered the smooth beads while her eyes adjusted to the dimness.

Whispering, she joined in the Agnus Dei. During the service, she counted a dozen robed figures. Her eyes lingered on three who stood in the shadows of an ancient Romanesque pillar.

The service came to an end, and the clerics turned to leave. Lorelei inclined her head to acknowledge their curious stares.

A sibilant gasp brought her head up sharply. Astonishment, delight, and apprehension collided in her heart as she found herself gazing at three very familiar faces.

# Chapter 16

A leaden weight dropped on Daniel's chest. Jerked out of a sound sleep, he coiled his arms to defend himself. Low laughter tickled his ear, and the feeling of alarm melted. His arms relaxed to encircle his wife.

"Idiot," he murmured, too befuddled to be annoyed. "Don't you know it's dangerous to attack a man in his sleep?"

"I couldn't resist." She brushed her lips against his stubbled chin. "You looked so handsome lying there."

He savored the milky texture of her cheek, the fresh morning smell of her, the welcome pressure of her body on his. He yearned to make slow, sweet love to her, to lie abed for hours holding her close. Then his gaze fastened on the Gobelin bed hangings, and he let go of the wish.

It did no good to pretend they were an ordinary husband and wife, beginning an ordinary day together. He was a mercenary, she was the bastard princess, and both were under the hate-filled eye of Josephine Bonaparte.

"You're soaking wet," he said, squinting through the morning light. "What have you been doing?"

She propped an elbow on either side of his head. Her smile was a small miracle, one of those little things about her that he would carry with him long after he unraveled the mess they were in and they went their separate ways.

"I took Barry for a run in the garden."

Alarm raced through him. "I told you not to go out alone."

"Alone?" From the sitting room came the sound of Barry devouring his breakfast. "I had a one-hundred-fifty-pound dog with me."

"Next time I want you to wake me."

"But you were sleeping so nicely. Where did you go last night, Daniel?"

"I had some business to take care of."

"It was about that Jean Meuron, wasn't it?" she asked.

He didn't want to discuss Meuron with her. The less she knew, the better. Besides, she was too distracting for rational thought.

Mist clung to her chestnut curls and eyelashes. Her lips were moist and open, innocently alluring. He tried to look away, tried to think. He should see that Sylvain and Greta were prepared to protect her; he should set in motion the plan for freeing Meuron; he should—

She kissed him soundly, her lips cool against his mouth. His thoughts scattering, he drank the dew from her lips while his hands slid up under her shirt to caress her smooth flesh.

A sound of delight escaped her; then she held her breath, waiting, her heart pulsing against his. A feeling of intense joy slipped over Daniel. He'd expected her to change as the newness faded from their marriage, to become more practiced, less spontaneous. But she still had not lost her sense of wonder.

"You behave," he whispered, "as if you've never done this before."

She shivered, the delicate motion rippling like warm water over him. "I'd hoped," she breathed against his mouth, "that I was getting better at it."

How could she get better at something she already did with a magic an enchantress would envy? Laughing softly, he extracted his hands to unbutton her vest.

"I have something to tell you," she said, sitting up. Her backside settled provocatively upon him.

"What's that?" he asked, only half attending.

She shrugged out of the vest and lifted the hem of her shirt. Her arms tangled in the full sleeves, and the fabric muffled her voice. He lay transfixed by the sight of her breasts, painted a delicate peach-gold by the early sun.

". . . are here," she finished, wrestling free of the shirt.

His hands slid up her torso. "What?"

"I said, Father Julian, Father Anselme, and Father Emile are here."

Daniel reared off the bed, dumping her into the rumpled folds of the counterpane. His desire evaporated, burned away by hot flames of suspicion.

"Where?" he demanded. "Here? In Paris?"

"Yes. At the Convent of the Feuillants. Does this mean you're not going to make love to me now?"

He took her face between his hands and gave her a lingering kiss. "Later, my sweet."

"Remind me to keep my mouth shut until after we've made love," she said.

He began jerking on his clothes. "You saw them? Spoke to them?"

"Yes." She put her shirt back over her head. Her curly mop emerged from the neckline. "Barry led me to them this morning. It seems Bonaparte was so grateful for their aid that he pledged a generous grant to the hospice. Father Julian and the others came to accept the honor in person."

"I see," Daniel murmured. "Did you ask them?"

She nodded. Pain crept into her eyes. "It was Gaston. Father Julian said he turned up missing the very day we left. I never dreamed that Father Gaston was capable of harming anyone."

Daniel's mind raced. Gaston was dead. But could more than one of the canons be involved?

She bit her lip. "Father Droz and the dogs found the body, but they couldn't recover it from that canyon. They believe his death was an accident, Daniel." She lifted her agonized gaze to him. "I didn't tell them otherwise."

He didn't know what to say. He'd taught her to deceive on his behalf. "Did you tell them about us?"

"Of course."

He wished he'd seen their faces. "How did they react?"

"Father Anselme burst into tears. I would've been in for a scolding from Father Julian if there hadn't been others present. But I'm a married woman now. He can't direct my life."

"They're staying at the convent?"

"Yes. They said Madame Bonaparte was most insistent."

I'll wager she was, Daniel thought. Now he was certain that she'd lied yesterday about her contact with one of the canons.

Barry wandered into the room and nuzzled Daniel's hand. Absently stroking the dog, he said, "Lorelei, there's someone else from Saint Bernard's at the Tuileries."

She laughed. "Who? Barry?"

"Sylvain."

Her face went pale and stiff, and her hands clenched into the richly worked fabric of the counterpane. "Why is he here?"

"He's to be your footman."

"That's not an answer."

"I told him to come to Paris. To help with Meuron, and now to watch over you. This city's a dangerous place."

"Daniel." She hugged her knees to her chest. "I couldn't bear to face him. Why didn't you ask me before you hired him?"

"Because I'm your husband." He forced out the hard truth. "Father Julian can't direct your life, but I can."

Her chin came up stubbornly. "He killed Belle."

"That was an accident," Daniel said.

"Sylvain's a crack shot. He doesn't have accidents, in spite of what he confessed to Father Julian."

"Damn it, Lorelei, he's just a youth. Can't you forgive him? The man loves you, for Christ's sake."

She blinked, her eyes wide and startled. "How easily you say that of Sylvain. But it's odd you've never said that *you* love me."

He couldn't. Pain shimmered behind his eyes as he recognized the limits of the man he was. He had no right. "You'll accept Sylvain as your footman and that's final."

"That doesn't mean I have to forgive him."

Feeling bleak, Daniel bent to pull on his boots. There was a time when her spirit had been light and free, when forgiveness had come as easily to her as her smile. At his hands she'd learned to distrust, to grieve, to hate. If she couldn't forgive Sylvain, what would she think of Daniel when the snarl of lies was unraveled and his blackness lay revealed at her feet? The prospect made him feel nauseated.

"I hired a maid, too," he said. "A Swiss girl named Greta de Veer. I think you'll like her."

"I hope she knows her business," Lorelei snapped. "Because I don't."

A knock sounded at the outer door. He opened it to let in a servant bearing a tray of chocolate and rolls.

Lorelei fell on her breakfast ravenously. Daniel watched, reminded of the first time he'd breakfasted with her. On that day four months ago it had never occurred to him that he'd find the sight of her spilling crumbs on a rumpled bed impossibly desirable. He smiled at the irony of it.

But when she filled a dainty china cup with steaming chocolate, his smile disappeared. A faint warning called from the back of his mind. She raised the cup to her lips.

"Don't drink it!" He lunged toward her.

She looked up, her brow puckered. "Does it need sugar?"

He grabbed the cup and emptied it into a potted fern.

"Daniel? What's the matter?"

"They're back," he said. "The canons are here."

"Oh, Daniel. It's over. It was Father Gaston. You can't think—"

"I must, damn it."

The three canons sat at a long table in the chapter house of the convent. With their dark robes and self-righteous scowls, they resembled an inquisitional tribunal. Standing before the table, Daniel told himself he had no reason to feel defensive.

"You took that child from her home, from the people who love her." Father Julian's voice shook with fury.

"She's a grown woman, and she came willingly."

"So she said," Father Emile said. "No doubt you lured her with promises you don't intend to keep."

"Marriage to me," said Daniel to the prior, "was preferable to your plan for her."

"What plan?" Father Anselme asked, turning to Julian.

Father Emile frowned. "You never discussed—"

"I am prior," Father Julian cut in. "My plan for Lorelei was not a matter for discussion." With a visible effort to keep a tight grip on his temper, he went on, "I was going to send her to a convent. She could have lived and worked there in complete safety. She *knew* I had the means to care for her."

Father Anselme removed his spectacles. "She knew? Then you told her about—"

"It can't matter now," Father Julian said testily.

"True," said Daniel. He watched the canons closely. Julian and Anselme glared at each other while Emile studied both with keen interest. "Lorelei chose me, not a nunnery."

"One of our brothers died trying to save her from you," said Father Anselme. His gnarled hands clenched. His flesh appeared waxy in the pale light from a small window.

Daniel planted his hands on the table and leaned forward, his gaze moving from one angry face to the next. "One of your brothers died," he said slowly, "because I killed him."

Emile's face flushed red while Julian's drained to white. Father Anselme's lips moved in a silent prayer. Was their surprise feigned or genuine? He couldn't be sure.

"Gaston stole a musket from the Army of Reserve," Daniel said. "He fired at us, and I shot him with an arrow." A shadow passed over his heart as he remembered the robed figure plummeting like a wounded bird into the gully.

Father Emile's eyes narrowed. "How do we know you're telling the truth? Gaston was no killer."

A sudden flash of insight struck Daniel. "The prior knows."

Father Julian's eyes blazed with fury. "By God—"

"Gaston killed Junot, didn't he?" Daniel demanded.

"Who the devil is Junot?" asked Father Anselme.

"An assassin," the prior stated, his accusing stare fixed on Daniel. "He would have killed Lorelei, just as—"

"Lorelei's my wife now." His suspicions confirmed, Daniel stepped back and placed his hands on his hips. "She's under my protection. Stay away from—"

An explosion shook the small chapter house. Father Julian shot to his feet. Father Emile plunged his hand into his sleeve. Daniel bolted from the room and raced toward the Riding School. Nightmare memories swept him like hellfire. It was happening again, the salvos of artillery, the howls of the mob—

"Long live Bonaparte!"

He skidded to a halt. People poured across the Tuileries gardens, waving hats and handkerchiefs, not to riot, but to cheer victory. More cannonades came from the Invalides. A palace footman grasped Daniel by the shoulders and kissed him soundly on both cheeks. "Have you heard, citizen? Bonaparte has defeated the Austrians. He signed the peace at Marengo!"

That evening Daniel glared at the mirror over the hearth in his bedroom. He adjusted his cravat, then plucked a thread from the sleeve of his tobacco-colored redingote. Chafing beneath the stiffness of new fabric, he reflected on the tidings from Italy. From the jaws of defeat, Bonaparte had wrested a stunning victory. To celebrate the news, Josephine had organized a concert on the terrace of the Tuileries.

Behind him, a door opened and closed. The thick mirror reflected an image of Sylvain in his new footman's livery.

"Have you told Lorelei about me?" the youth asked, his face taut and anxious.

"Yes. I wouldn't expect a warm welcome from her."

Sylvain hung his head. "I don't know what to say to her."

"It's not Lorelei you should be worrying about." Turning from the mirror, Daniel explained, "Bonaparte has decided to make a generous offering to the hospice. Father Julian, Father Emile, and Father Anselme have come to accept the endowment."

Sylvain's head jerked up. "They're here?"

"They're at a convent nearby."

"Daniel?" Sylvain's voice shook.

"Yes?"

"I'm scared. Scared for us all. All these men—this court full of intrigue—it's like a noose tightening around us."

Daniel looked away from Sylvain's light, clear gaze, eyes that had once glowed with innocence. "You'd be a fool if you weren't afraid," he muttered. He glanced through the half-open door. From Lorelei's room came the sound of female conversation as the maids readied her for the evening.

"Just keep your eyes and ears open," said Daniel. "And a weapon up your sleeve."

Sylvain went to take up his post on the landing outside the suite. Daniel glanced at the clock. Five minutes to nine.

He hesitated, staring absently at the wide buckles on his shoes. His thoughts drifted to his first gala, a fête celebrating the liberation of the prisoners at the Carmes. Josephine had still called herself Viscountess de Beauharnais. Daniel had still believed in honor. He'd been young then. Young and stupid and hopelessly smitten. She'd been at the peak of her sultry beauty, her web of deception as light and subtle as spider's silk, trapping him in its gossamer bonds.

Jesus, what would she do to Lorelei?

The door to her room stood ajar. Boxes and parcels were scattered on the floor. A dressmaker's dummy, draped in beautiful gauzy stuff, occupied one corner.

A young woman stood looking out the window at the winking lights of Paris. A single candle fanned its glow over her, gilding the elegant column of her neck and winking in the garland of upswept curls that crowned her head. Her face was a study in shadow and light, her familiar features rendered mysterious by the uncertain glow.

My God, he thought, drawing in a quick breath. My God, she's beautiful.

She turned in a gentle drift of pale skirts. "Hello, Daniel."

Had it not been for her lovely low voice, he would have sworn she was a stranger.

In a nervous flutter, her hands smoothed the wispy

fabric of her dress. Gathered softly beneath her breasts, the long skirt fell in a graceful shimmer to her slippered feet. The effect of the sheer iridescent fabric was one of impalpable lightness and subtle charm.

"I'm not angry about this morning anymore," she said.

"Thank God for that," he said, weak with the truth of it.

"Do I look presentable?" she asked.

"Presentable?" He licked his dry lips. "By God . . ." Somewhere beneath her pearly skin, her beautiful chestnut curls, her fashionable dress, was the scruffy hoyden who'd pulled him from an avalanche four months earlier. But he could see no trace of her now. He regarded a creature touched by pagan gods, lovelier than the Lorelei of legend whose shattering beauty lured men to their death.

"Daniel?" She stared at him inquiringly.

"Yes," he said. "You look quite presentable." He offered his arm and escorted her to the terrace.

The fading hiss of a descending rocket knifed the balmy night air. The placid garden ponds reflected a trailing plume of pink sparks, eliciting murmurs of pleasure from the huge crowd gathered below the terrace.

Josephine Bonaparte nibbled at a crème de marron, then reluctantly fed the rest of the sweet to Fortuné. Five years ago she would have devoured the whole thing and two more like it, but now she had to be careful. Though she'd admit it to no one, she no longer had a young girl's constitution, could no longer indulge without restraint her taste for rich foods.

She slid a glance at the banquet table where Hippolyte Charles stood with a group of men. She could always indulge other desires, other ambitions.

Looking at her lover, who cut a fine figure in his double-breasted redingote and breeches adorned at the knees with tiny bells, she felt no hot stab of desire. Her liaison with Charles was more complex than animal lust. He gave her a feeling of power, a sense of ownership. He was good at making money, which was more important than being good at making love. Together they'd made a small fortune in army contracts, and a bigger one from the Bern treasury. There was a delicious irony in the fact that her lover profited from the military excesses of her husband.

Yet worries niggled at her. Daniel knew about the Swiss gold. Hippolyte had sworn he could render the trust untraceable, but she shuddered at the thought of her husband finding out.

Bonaparte. She didn't know precisely when he'd slipped from her control. In the early days of their marriage he'd been as eager as a love-starved dog, flopping at her feet and offering his heart on a gilt platter. His lovemaking had been as avid and sloppy as that of a green youth. When on campaign, he'd sent her letters overripe with embarrassing passion.

But now, four years later, their relationship had changed. No longer blind to her indiscretions, no longer uncertain of his power to lead a nation, her Corsican swain had grown into a man of limitless potential—and left her behind.

She hadn't loved him then but, perversely, she did now. Desperately.

Suave and unfailingly courteous, Charles Maurice de Talleyrand-Périgord bowed deeply before Josephine. "Madame," he said. "A great victory. Remarkable, truly."

"Indeed, Monsieur Talleyrand." She gave the minister of foreign affairs a gracious smile and extended her hand. "Bonaparte's work is over. Yours is only beginning."

Talleyrand's thin eyebrows slashed upward, and a trace of wickedness tightened his smile. "I assure you, madame, I'll negotiate a treaty that will leave the heads of Europe spinning."

"No doubt you will, monsieur."

He bent over her hand, his warm breath fanning her wrist. In truth, she was a little afraid of Talleyrand. A silk stocking filled with mud, Bonaparte privately called him. Talleyrand had not only survived all the regimes of the past ten years but had risen to the top of each.

"What begins," he said smoothly, "is your husband's finest hour." He gestured at the surging crowd, some of them dancing to the concert music, others drinking toasts to Bonaparte.

"Rabble, the lot of them," grumbled a familiar voice. Joseph Fouché, minister of police, joined them. "Probably hatching plots even as we speak."

Talleyrand's nostrils thinned. "And a good evening to you, too, Citizen Fouché."

Fouché made an awkward bow, his badly tailored frock coat bunching at the waist. Josephine pondered the contrast between the smooth, erudite Talleyrand

and the coarse, brutal Fouché. They hated each other, yet both were firmly bound to her husband.

Talleyrand moved off to join Madame Grand, his beautiful mistress. Fouché tugged at his lopsided mustache and stepped closer to Josephine.

"The plan's thwarted," he murmured, his garlic breath hot against her face. "Severin outfoxed you, madame."

"How could I have foreseen this?" she hissed, waving her fan. "Not in my wildest imaginings did I ever suppose he'd marry her."

"He's done us all a favor by making a princess into a nobody. We've nothing more to worry about from her."

"You fool," said Josephine. "Severin could be killed. Then she'd be a desirable commodity again. And what of the cleric?" she demanded, smiling falsely as her brother-in-law, Lucien Bonaparte, waved to her from the dais several feet away. "The fact that she's married makes no difference to *him*."

"He must be stopped from taking any action," said Fouché. His tone and the expression on his face chilled her. The simple statement was a death warrant.

"Do as you see fit," she said. "Now, what about Meuron?"

"I'll see to him as well," said Fouché.

Josephine swallowed uncomfortably. "He's not to be harmed until I say so. If something happens to him, Severin is likely to broadcast his suspicions about the Bern gold."

"Leave them both to me. You've other worries, madame." He turned to study the swelling crowd, the fireworks blossoming overhead. "Your husband is soaring to a height no mere monarch ever reached."

"And I should be worried about that?"

"Indeed you should. It makes him vulnerable to assassination."

"That's your problem, monsieur."

"But one that you share. If we lose him, civil war will consume this nation. The people crave stability, and we can't give them that until Bonaparte has a successor." Fouché walked away, his sharp nose seeking out plotters.

Josephine gripped her champagne flute until the crystal bit into her palm. She cursed her barren womb, cursed the fruitless pilgrimages she'd made to Plombières, swallowing the stinking waters, covering herself with mud, all in the hope of getting her womb to quicken. Bonaparte's latest plan was a direct slap in the face. Imagine, ordering her to consult with that little Swiss sheep about so private a problem.

Fury swam like a red haze before her eyes. She should have been in her glory this night. She should have presided like a queen at court. Instead, worries bombarded her.

As if to drive home her frustration, Daniel and his young wife stepped onto the terrace. Across the length of the veranda Josephine couldn't quite make out the features of Louis's bastard. Josephine's vision wasn't as acute as it had once been, but never would she submit to the indignity of wearing spectacles.

As the couple moved slowly toward her to pay the obligatory respects, she tried not to admire the easy, economical grace with which Daniel Severin moved.

He was another man she'd once owned. Recalling his earnest proposal on bended knee, she regretted the loss. Remembering the soft moonlit hours they'd spent making love, she felt a warm spasm of latent pleasure.

She'd lost his untrammeled devotion. Then, through Meuron, she'd found a way to control Daniel. Now he'd defied her. If their encounter in the bath was any indication, Daniel had found new strength and the confidence to resist her.

The fool. She still had the power to squash him like a cockroach beneath a boot heel.

"Good evening, citizeness." Rich as melted butter, his voice poured over her.

She smiled carefully. "Ah, I didn't see you come in."

His cool gaze acknowledged the lie. "May I present my wife, Lorelei."

At last Josephine gave her full attention to the woman. Like a wave of nausea, horror broke over her. Her hand clenched convulsively around the arm of her chair.

Good God. The bastard princess was a beauty. Damn Claire for not warning her.

"It's an honor to meet you," said Lorelei, her voice low and lovely.

"Charmed, I'm sure," Josephine murmured. She searched feverishly for some flaw, some latent hint of Louis's skinny neck, his grotesque nose, his too-wide mouth. The dead French king's features were all present in his daughter, but with a difference. Her neck was slim but swanlike, her nose well defined but beautifully proportioned, her mouth full but maddeningly sensual.

A well-sculpted face was common, Josephine told herself. Yet there was something else about the girl—an aura, a radiance that arrested the eye. An air of wistfulness clung to her, but at the same time a remarkable intelligence lit her eyes. Her smile was as natural and warm as a sunbeam.

Josephine had expected coarseness from a mountain-bred girl. Yet when Lorelei dropped into a curtsy, she seemed to float to the graceful rhythm that drifted from the musicians' gallery.

"I've been eager to meet the woman who finally brought the Raven to roost," said Josephine. "Daniel is such a . . . demanding man. I always wondered what sort of woman could answer his needs. He has so many, you know." Josephine sipped her champagne and waited for Lorelei to squirm.

Instead, the chit grinned and nodded, her shining curls bobbing. Virgin hair, Josephine surmised. The chestnut locks hadn't seen a drop of henna.

"And talents, too. He's a wonderful man." Her low-pitched voice gave one the urge to lean forward and listen. "How wise of you to understand his character so well."

Daniel said nothing. He didn't need to speak at all. Josephine glanced at his dark blue eyes and realized that inside, he was howling with laughter.

A servant offered a tray laden with flutes of champagne and a variety of sweets. Josephine looked longingly at the crèmes de marron, but settled for another glass of champagne.

Slim as a budding sapling, the bastard princess devoured three rich crèmes. Josephine's hatred swelled like a fresh bruise. "I do hope I can be of service to you," said Lorelei.

The reminder of Bonaparte's plan cut into Josephine. "We shall see." She forced out the words.

"Our congratulations on your husband's victory," said Daniel, obviously as eager as she to abandon the topic. His gaze flicked briefly to Hippolyte Charles. With a polite bow, he took Lorelei's hand and led her down the wide steps to join the dancing couples. A bouquet of sheer, drifting gowns and smart military uniforms blossomed on the lower terraces.

"A handsome couple, aren't they?"

Josephine's head snapped around. "Claire! Why didn't you tell me?"

Claire gave a guileless smile. "Tell you what, my dear?"

"Damn you, you said she was a plain girl of simple manners."

"But that was before Tournon got her hands—and her gowns—on her."

"Tournon?" Josephine's voice rose, and she struggled to recapture her usual soft Creole lisp. "But she's *my* couturiere."

"And Marie Antoinette's before you."

Josephine absorbed the remark as living tissue absorbed poison. "Damn you, Claire, you go too far—"

"Nonsense. You're silly to feel threatened by a Swiss commoner. Even a beautiful one."

Josephine watched Lorelei move lightly on Daniel's arm. "She can dance."

"Yes, that was a pleasant surprise," said Claire. "She said one of the canons at the hospice taught her."

"Which one?"

"I didn't ask. Could he be one of the clerics who's here?"

"Perhaps." The canon was Fouché's problem. The blundering cleric had made a mess of things; now he was dangerous. He'd outlived his usefulness.

She turned cold eyes to the couple. The expression on Daniel's face struck her like a blow. Even five years ago, when he'd been foolish enough to believe she, the Viscountess de Beauharnais, would marry him, he hadn't looked at her with tenderness, amused affection, and quiet pride. This was not the infatuation of a smitten youth, Josephine realized, but a man's deep adoration, a love that promised to last an eternity.

A weakness she could exploit.

"They're quite taken with each other, aren't they?" mused Claire.

Josephine said nothing. Her mind was already leaping ahead. She couldn't eliminate Lorelei; the chit lived under her roof, and Bonaparte had sent explicit instructions to see to her comfort and safety.

But murder was only one way to cope with an enemy. Josephine knew another means to destroy the bastard princess.

Lorelei sensed a difference in Daniel when he drew her into his chamber that night. He was always tender when making love to her, always solicitous, and the present moment was no different. Yet as his fingers moved expertly over the row of pearly buttons down her back, she felt that his usual wariness had softened, and she saw in his eyes a lightness that might have been joy, might have been love.

The idea bore with it a flood of need. She grew ever more eager to touch him, to caress him, to unlock the secrets he kept hidden in his soul.

Beneath the gown she wore a frail tunic, nothing more. He slid the wispy garment off her shoulders. The motion invaded her every pore: thin fabric skimming down her torso, sliding over her thighs, pooling at her feet. Breathless, she felt him reach for the shell combs in her hair, felt her curls spill over the nape of her neck, just brushing her shoulders.

She saw herself reflected, naked, in his eyes. The knowledge that she pleased him made her giddy, yet steadied her hands as she helped him remove his clothes. As always, the sight of him caught at her heart and brought urgent heat to the center of her.

He laid her back on the bed, on a counterpane that had probably been bought for a price that could have fed the canons of Saint Bernard's for years. Yet the opulence seemed paltry compared to the rich beauty of Daniel's body and the luxurious splendor of his kisses.

She felt as if she were gorging herself at a banquet laid solely for her pleasure. The simple angle of his head as he bent to kiss her, the subtle shift of his hand on her leg filled her with a hunger that burned like fire inside her.

On a gasp of yearning, she spoke his name.

"Mmm?" The light, quick movements of his mouth over her throat and neck, the lush rhythm of his fingers, never ceased.

"You're too good at this," she said.

He laughed low in his throat. "Is that a complaint?"

"It just doesn't seem fair."

"Nothing's fair in this world, Lorelei." His tongue traced the shape of her ear.

"That's exactly what I mean," she said, shuddering. "These little things you do—touching me here, kissing me there. And all the while I just lie here like a trout."

"You're my wife, not a trout, Lorelei."

She cupped her palms around his shoulders. "I just feel I should be . . . doing something. Touching you in some way—"

His eyes grew stony. "Stop trying so hard, Lorelei."

"But couldn't you show me, teach me—"

"Whores' tricks? That's what you're asking me. Ways to use your body to pleasure a man."

"To love you," she insisted, her cheeks flooding with color.

A smile softened his lips. "Idiot. Don't you understand? You've touched me in a way no woman ever has before, and it's got nothing to do with kisses or body parts or bedroom gymnastics." He shook his head in wonderment. "You fill me so full of—" He broke off and frowned, at a loss.

"Full of what?" she prompted.

His palm traced the curve of her backside. "Lust, Madame Severin."

"Lust? That's all?"

"Delight. Affection. And a lot of other things. Powerful things. It can't be healthy."

Frustrated, she struck him on the shoulder. "How

do you do it, Daniel? You manage to talk and talk, and yet you say nothing!"

"You're right. We both talk too much." He kissed her, his tongue plundering a response from her.

She moved her fingers through the dark hair on his chest and over the ridges of muscle on his stomach. His breath caught, and beneath her hands his skin contracted and he held himself rigid.

"Don't . . . stop," he said through clenched teeth.

Surprised, Lorelei pulled away slightly. His words filled her with a heady sense of purpose. A tiny bead of sweat glinted in the space above his heart. She leaned over and drew the moistness into her mouth, fascinated by the strange salty taste. Her hands mapped the contours of his body; then she drew back again to study his astonished face.

"Lorelei." Yearning and awe roughened his voice. He pressed her back against the bed.

"Wait," she said. "Just lie there."

"Like a trout?"

"You're much more warm-blooded." Her curls fell forward as she bent to touch, to taste, to lose herself in the precious task of loving him. Her own body responded with a drenching need. She loomed above him, enthralled by the sight of his midnight hair spread across the pillow, his blue eyes deep with their untold secrets.

For the first time she controlled the rhythm of their love. It gave her a strangely exhilarating sense of both power and abandonment. Her kisses dragged groans from his throat and wove a spell of enchantment around them. She learned the potency of one small movement, one whispered word. There was a sublime selflessness in loving him that had somehow become as essential to her as breathing.

The bond between them tightened, and the new closeness wove itself like a spell around them. Something inside Daniel was changing and reaching, warmed by alien feelings he dared not name. Simple lovemaking had been transformed into an act that shifted the foundations of his life. In the deepest moments of the night he buried himself in her precious softness and felt a rapture that was dangerously close to worship. He could not tell the precise moment it had begun, but the darkness within him had started to fade.

In the confused aftermath of their shattering pleasure, he glanced around the dimly lit chamber. The room had once been overrun by militant sansculottes. He waited to feel the remembered waves of terror and guilt, but Lorelei's presence seemed to shield him from nightmares. He held her close, wishing he could deny her blood ties to the Old Regime.

She settled into the lee of his shoulder. By turning his head, he could just make out her profile. Candlelight suffused her face, making her appear mystical, angelic.

A staggering affection welled inside Daniel. What a wonder she was, at once childlike and womanly, wise and naive, accessible and distant.

"Will there be time to visit the Louvre tomorrow?" she asked, stirring him from his thoughts.

"No," said Daniel. "I have other plans."

"What other plans?"

He touched her beneath the chin and lifted her gaze to meet his. "Making love to you."

When Lorelei slept that night it was with the knowledge that a new bond had been forged between them, a powerful bond that had the force of eternity.

But when she awoke the next morning, she found herself alone, the hollowed-out spot where Daniel had slept long cold.

Bleary-eyed, her body still pulsing pleasantly from their love, she draped a sheet around herself and pushed open the door. Barry scrambled up to greet her, but she petted him distractedly, her attention snared by a note in the salver on the table by the door.

The letter *N* circled by laurel leaves graced the heavy cream stock. Lorelei broke the seal.

It was a summons from Josephine.

# Chapter 17

Daniel smelled a trap.

He leaned against a wrought-iron fence in front of a fountain. Water trickled sluggishly from a fish's mouth into a murky basin with a skin of green slime. He could not pinpoint the precise source of his awareness, but the morning sky seemed suddenly ominous and a summer wind rippled the hairs on the back of his neck. The air crackled with unease.

At dawn Sylvain had come with a whispered message. A Swiss partisan who'd been watching the Feydeaux had seen Fouché arrive in a swift coach. The minister of police had disappeared into the building while an armed guard assembled at the rear alleyway entrance.

Angling the brim of his bateau hat to conceal his face, Daniel loitered at the head of the alley. Moments dragged by as the police guards joked among themselves, and Daniel's thoughts drifted to Lorelei. An image of her face, as clear and lovely as morning in the mountains, formed in his mind.

*"Attention!"* The order rang from the alleyway. The police guards formed two lines between the prison door and the black coach harnessed to a pair of matched bays. Fouché dashed from the building, followed by a tall man flanked by guards.

Jean Meuron.

It took all of Daniel's restraint not to fly to the prisoner's side, dagger drawn to carve him away from his captors. But he was too heavily guarded. Daniel had only a glimpse of dark hair and a wrenchingly familiar face smeared with grime before Meuron was shoved into the coach.

The police guards mounted and followed the conveyance out of the alley. Daniel joined the shoppers and soldiers who crowded the avenue. He shuddered to think what would become of Switzerland if Meuron died.

Although he traveled on foot, he had no trouble keeping pace with the vehicle. Piles of refuse, jutting milestones, and crowds of people slowed the police caravan. The snapping of the coachman's whip failed to clear the way.

Daniel followed the party over the bridge between Ile de Louvier and Ile Saint Louis to the left bank of the river. They traveled along the quays of the Seine to a high-walled building of smoke-blackened stone. The coach drew to a halt. The guards dismounted, and Meuron was hustled inside.

Daniel struck his fist against the thick wall of the fortress. The Chantereine was the most impenetrable stronghold of Paris. It had once imprisoned the most notorious outlaws of the Revolution. Jacques Sommelier had died here; René Saint Jean had babbled state secrets in these chambers. Now the building housed only a few incorrigibles and a plethora of paper. The Chantereine had become an unofficial archive of revolutionary printed matter: tons of pamphlets, books, and documents from the turbulent years of the Terror.

Today the Chantereine became the home of a Swiss patriot wrongly accused of crimes against the state.

This was Josephine's doing, Daniel reflected furiously. Josephine working with Fouché. A display of her power. Revenge for Daniel's defiance. He wondered what the devil she'd do next.

Lorelei stood in the yellow drawing room on the ground floor of the palace, awaiting Josephine Bonaparte. Outside, she heard Sylvain's boots ringing through the corridor as he paced. He had behaved as if the summons were a disaster of the first order, but she refused to be infected by his nervousness. Bonaparte wished her to consult with his wife. He knew better than to expect a miracle.

She eyed the elegant furnishings, her gaze traveling over a brocatelle wing chair and the beautiful sweep of Lyons silk hangings that graced the tall windows.

She thought the first consul's wife must be a great lady indeed to command this sort of luxury. Bonaparte's "incomparable Josephine" had been younger than Lorelei when she came to Paris to wed a French nobleman. Widowed by the guillotine, she had been imprisoned at the Carmes, the very place where Daniel had spent two hellish years. Lorelei had no doubt that he and Josephine had met there, forming a bond of their misery and of their mutual determination to survive.

Although he tried to hide them, Daniel bore the scars of the ordeal. She couldn't help but wonder if Josephine, too, was haunted by the shadows of a turbulent past.

A light step drew her attention to an arched doorway. Josephine paused there while the sunlight streamed like a mantle of gold over her. She wore a white gown, her womanly curves apparent through the wispy muslin. The little dog called Fortuné cavorted at her feet.

"There you are," said Josephine, her voice as smooth as warm oil. "Come, sit with me."

"Thank you, madame," said Lorelei.

Josephine glided to a settle and arranged herself on the white upholstering. "We've much to talk about."

Lorelei seated herself across from Madame Bonaparte. A coffee tray and a leather folio lay on the rosewood table between them. For a moment she studied Josephine frankly. Her face was compelling, the gray eyes deep, the mouth mobile and expressive.

"You're staring."

"I'm sorry. Father Julian was forever accusing me of

gawking. I was just thinking that Daniel was wrong. He once said—" She broke off, mortified by her carelessness.

"What did he say? I'd be most interested to hear."

"It's not important, madame."

"If Daniel said it, then it's important."

For the first time in her life, Lorelei wished she knew how to lie smoothly. "He said you weren't beautiful, that your attractiveness is an illusion, the result of artifice."

Madame Bonaparte smiled coldly. "I see."

"But he was wrong, that's clear. You're a beautiful woman."

Josephine's hand faltered almost imperceptibly as she reached for a tiny cup of coffee in a gold-rimmed saucer. "So I've been told. But a woman in my position hears many lies."

"I never lie, madame."

"Indeed," Josephine said. "Now. As to the business my husband wishes us to discuss. In his letter to me he speaks very highly of your skills as a midwife."

"A physician, madame," said Lorelei. "I confess, midwifery is not an area in which I'm experienced. But I suppose my being a woman led him to believe I might be of help." She searched Josephine's face for a trace of resentment, for failure to conceive a child was often considered a poor reflection on the woman. But Josephine's expression remained carefully blank.

"Would it be convenient to discuss your case now, madame?"

"We can discuss my barrenness until the Austrians take Paris," Josephine snapped. "I bore my first husband two healthy children. The last was seventeen years ago. Neither Bonaparte's will nor you can simply wish a babe into my womb."

"But you've been married only four years, and your husband has been off campaigning much of the time. Is it possible that prolonged abstinence could account for the lack of a child?"

Josephine laughed, a sound like rustling silk. "My dear girl, I think we can rule out abstinence as a cause."

"I see. Well, with your permission, I'll consult with your doctors. But there is no reason to hope that I can discover something they don't already know."

"If you insist, you may introduce yourself to the physicians at the Hôtel Dieu. Josephine waved a milk-white hand. "Now. Your frankness seems to be contagious." A wistful regret played around her mouth. Yet her eyes held a hard avidity that was disturbing in its intensity. "I didn't invite you here today to wring a miracle from you, but to rectify a gross injustice. You've been lied to, my dear, abominably, for over twenty years."

Mystified, Lorelei said, "I can't imagine what you mean."

Josephine picked up the leather folio and opened the flap. "These documents concern your birth."

"Father Julian brought them?" Anticipation thudded in Lorelei's chest. The folio contained something startling, something important. Something that had been hidden from her, she thought with rising anger.

"I didn't get them from Father Julian," said Josephine.

"Then who—"

"That's not important." She held out a yellowed document, the ink faded, the lower portion pockmarked by official stamps and seals. "This is the true story of your parentage, Lorelei."

With shaking hands, Lorelei took the papers. "Oh, madame." Impulsively she leaned across the table and hugged Josephine. The first consul's wife gasped in surprise; she smelled sweetly of *muguet*, and her body was soft and pliant.

Josephine looked startled. "Good Lord," she murmured.

"Have I done something wrong?"

"It's just that . . . I didn't expect to like you. Read the paper, Lorelei," Josephine said unsteadily. "And then decide whether or not to thank me."

Her heart tripping, she let her gaze devour the page.

She froze, then closed her eyes. She opened them only to discover the incredible name still there. "Oh, sweet Jesus," she whispered at last. "It can't be true."

"I'm afraid it is," said Josephine. "Your mother was Thérèse Chambrai. She was the king's lover for a short time."

"I don't believe it," Lorelei said in a tortured whisper. "I won't! It's impossible! King Louis disliked . . . Father Emile claims the royal marriage went unconsummated for seven years."

Josephine's mouth turned down in distaste. "Louis never kept his mistresses for long. He had an . . . affliction that made amorous liaisons unpleasant for him."

"Then—"

"You must accept the truth, Lorelei. But tell me, did you never ask questions about your parentage?"

"Of course." People lie, Daniel had told her. Get used to it. "But no one saw fit to answer me truthfully."

"Surely you must have had some clue, some hint?"

"No, but . . ." Lorelei dipped her hand into her new reticule and brought forth her rosary. She turned over the silver crucifix and stared at the letters engraved there: LPB.

"I always thought this was a jeweler's mark." The beads turned icy cold in her hand. She dropped them to the floor.

Josephine retrieved the rosary and gave it back. "The letters stand for Louis Philippe de Bourbon, King Louis XVI of France. I realize it's a shock, my dear. A dreadful shock to find yourself the spawn of a despot and a court whore. I should have found a gentler way to tell you. Pity."

Lorelei stared down at the vile paper. She handled it with tenderness when she longed to hurl it into a fire and deny everything. "May I keep this?"

"Of course. It's yours by right."

She started to fold the page; then a phrase caught her eye. Her head jerked up. "I was born at a convent in Yverdon!"

"Yes," said Josephine. "It was common in those days for genteel women to retire and hide their indiscretions."

Horror poured through Lorelei. Of course! Father Gaston had been trying to kill her, not Daniel! He'd known; he'd found out last summer when he went to Yverdon. But it didn't make sense, she thought feverishly. Father Gaston was a Royalist; he believed in the divine right of kings.

But not their bastards, a voice in her mind whispered.

She had an urge to confess her thoughts, but hesitated. She had no right to burden Madame Bonaparte with her fears.

Lorelei remembered the brigand, too. He hadn't tried to rob her; he simply wanted her dead. She shuddered. If Daniel hadn't come along . . .

"I must find Daniel," she said, sliding the document into her reticule. "I must tell him." Her hands shook. King Louis—her father—was responsible for the massacre of '92. Could Daniel ever look at her and not see the man whose cowardice had led to the murder of eight hundred Swiss?

"Good God," said Josephine. "You don't understand, do you?" She took Lorelei's hands in hers. "Daniel already knows."

"He can't. He would have told me."

"Clearly Daniel Severin sought to serve his own selfish interests by aligning himself with a woman of royal blood."

"No, Daniel wouldn't—" Lorelei bit her lip. *People lie. Get used to it.*

"Can you be certain, Lorelei? He can be most convincing."

"He was so reluctant to marry me," Lorelei said, recalling his grim face on their wedding day. "If your husband hadn't commanded it—"

"Daniel's reluctance was obviously part of the pretense."

*You must marry me because you love me.* Her own naive words echoed across the weeks.

*I never said that.* His answer reverberated in her head.

Then it came to her. Her eyes cleared, and she leaned toward Josephine. "I have proof that Daniel's motives were pure."

Josephine's beautifully groomed eyebrows arched in skepticism. "What sort of proof?"

"He was buried in an avalanche in the Great Pass and suffered from memory loss. He couldn't tell us his name or his purpose in being there." Warmth spread through her as she recalled the hours they'd spent together, the moments of passion that neither could deny. "He started to love me *before* he remembered who he was."

"Preposterous. This memory loss must have been a pretense."

"But it couldn't have been; he—"

*People lie. Get used to it.*

A small recollection niggled at her, breaking to the surface of her thoughts. He had slipped. Long before his "lost" memory returned, he'd mistakenly written the first three letters of his name on the last page of the treatise, then scratched them out. She remembered other things, little things. He'd once called her "princess." He'd queried her closely about her past, about Father Julian and the canons.

A wave of nausea struck her. "Dear God," she whispered. "He did know."

Josephine tilted her chin up. "So it's established. The scoundrel married you in order to raise his own status."

"He's made no move to do that," Lorelei said in desperation.

Josephine shot her a knowing look. "No doubt he's waiting for the right moment. Where does he go each day? Where is he now?"

She looked down at her hands. "I don't know. Madame, you speak as if you know Daniel very well."

"I do, my dear."

"How is that?" The horrible truth was closing in on her. "Was it at the Carmes?"

Josephine nodded. "And after. My dear, there is no kind way to put this. We both expected the world to end any day. Is it any wonder we clung together in those desperate times?"

"You were lovers," Lorelei stated, feeling a depthless emptiness open inside her.

Josephine neither confirmed nor denied it. "That's all in the past. We must plan what to do now."

"Do? There isn't anything I can—"

"Nonsense. We're friends now. Leave the plans to me."

"Please, Sylvain, don't question me now." Lorelei ran out of the palace, Sylvain at her heels. Perfectly trimmed box hedges and ornamental orange trees streaked past. The garden held no enchantment for her, not now, not when her soul had been ripped to tatters by betrayal.

"You're as pale as snow. What did she say to you?" Sylvain panted. "Lorelei, please."

The heavy scent of roses choked her. "I'm going to Father Julian."

He grabbed her arm. "I can't let you do that."

She wrenched away, wondering wildly if Sylvain, too, had been in on the secret. "You can't stop me."

Frustration twisted his features. "I'm going with you."

"This is a private matter." She hurried toward the old convent. Let Sylvain follow. Father Julian would banish him anyway, for he'd left the hospice in disgrace. But no one could banish the pain tearing through her soul.

The convent was quiet except for bees humming in an ancient arbor of yew trees at the center of the cloister. She made her way to the monks' cells. A brown-clad figure sat on a bench outside the room Father Julian occupied.

The man looked up, his cowl falling back.

She heard the sharp intake of Sylvain's breath. He touched his sleeve nervously. His gaze darted over the men working in the garden, and he seemed to relax.

"Father Emile," said Lorelei. Good God, how could she look at his kindly face and not let him see her heart was breaking?

"Hello, my dear." He stood and took her hands. His gaze flicked coldly to Sylvain. "What are you doing here?"

Sylvain planted his fists on his hips. "I'm in Daniel Severin's employ."

"Leave it to him to employ the likes of you."

"I must speak to Father Julian," Lorelei broke in. "It's urgent."

Father Emile's eyes widened briefly; then he shook his head. "I'm afraid the prior's not feeling well."

Alarmed, she said, "Then he needs me."

"Father Anselme's with him. It's just a mild stomach complaint. He's resting now."

"I'll look in on him." Giving him no chance to object, she pushed the door open. She felt Sylvain's presence behind her as she peered through the gloom at the figure on the bed. Father Julian's face was as pale as moonstone and etched by haggard lines.

Father Anselme looked up from a stool beside the cot and adjusted his spectacles. "Lorelei, my dear girl—"

She closed the door on Father Emile and Sylvain. Immediately, they fell into rapid, angry conversation. "What's the matter with Father Julian?" She touched the prior's wrist. His pulse was normal.

"A stomach complaint, not serious. It's sleep he needs."

She bit her lip in frustration. "Is he eating well?"

"He had a bowl of cabbage soup only an hour ago. Emile and I take turns tending to him." Father Anselme set aside the book he'd been reading. "You seem upset. Is there anything I can do to help?"

"I must speak to Father Julian. In private."

"But—"

"Leave us, Father," said a faint voice from the bed. The prior lifted his hand in a dismissive gesture.

Father Anselme frowned, but levered himself up from the chair. "As you wish, Father. I'll be outside."

Lorelei sank to her knees beside the prior. "I'm sorry you're ill, Father Julian."

"Pour me a glass of water, Lorelei. I've been so thirsty."

She fetched a goblet of water from a pitcher by the

door and watched him drink. His movements were steady as he drank.

"Why didn't you tell me who my parents were?" she demanded.

With exaggerated care, he set the goblet on the table by the bed. His face was pale and taut with shock. "I hoped I'd never have to. Who told you?"

"Madame Bonaparte."

His pallor suddenly darkened to rage. "That woman."

She extracted the document from the folio. "Where did she get this?"

His eyes widened in recognition, but he said nothing.

"It wasn't fair, Father. You had no right to keep the truth from me." She pressed her fists to her eyes. "I'm a bastard," she whispered. "My father was a despot, and my mother was a court whore." She felt as dirty and corrupt as they. She had a foolish urge to run, to flee, but the taint would always be with her, as much a part of her as her unruly chestnut curls, her brown eyes, the shape of her fingernails.

"No, no," said Father Julian. "Your father wasn't a bad man, but an incompetent governor. And your mother . . ." He paused and sipped his water.

"Tell me about her, Father Julian. Did you know her?"

"Briefly. She lay on her deathbed when I was called to Yverdon. She'd turned very bitter. It was she who named you Lorelei, for a woman who was invincible to males. It was her determined wish that you never succumb to any man."

"She'd be disappointed, then." Lorelei paced the room, unable to look at the man she'd respected and obeyed for years. "You planned to send me into exile," she said accusingly. "To lock me away from all men as if I were a treasure you could own."

A look of guilt and terror crossed his face. He began to cough and gestured weakly for the basin. Father Anselme hurried in; obviously he'd been listening at the door.

Something inside Lorelei seemed to splinter, the shining pieces of the past nothing but rubble now. With the sound of Father Julian's retching echoing in her ears, she stalked from the room and slammed the door behind her. Without looking at Sylvain or Father Emile, she marched out of the cloister.

"Where are you going?" Sylvain demanded, hurrying after her.

"To the Hôtel Dieu to meet with other physicians. That's the reason I came to Paris in the first place." She owed Madame Bonaparte her efforts, no matter how hopeless. And perhaps a hospital tour was just the thing to keep herself from shattering under the burden of her new knowledge. An angry determination seethed inside her. She had to get on with her life.

"I'm coming with you," said Sylvain.

Father Emile joined them. "So am I."

"Please yourselves," she replied.

The surface of the river glittered through an archway. Lighter boats scudded past barges and bathing houses. Lorelei and her two companions headed east toward the hospital.

As they walked along a wide avenue shaded by

spreading chestnut trees, none of them noticed a shadowy figure slither from an alleyway and fall into step behind them.

Daniel stepped into their suite at the Tuileries. It had taken him the better part of the day to summon a meeting of the Swiss partisans and re-form their plan to free Meuron. They'd all agreed that it was too risky simply to wait for Bayens, the banker, to trace the Geneva trust. Josephine and Fouché were getting desperate.

But for now Daniel wanted nothing more than to spend the rest of the day and every moment of the night with Lorelei. The very thought of her had the power to smash through his frustration. She was not one to dwell on failure, to gnash her teeth at difficulty.

Absently greeting Barry, he called her name.

The door to her bedroom opened. Greta stepped out, her apple-cheeked face drawn with worry, her fingers twisting through a ropy blond braid.

"Greta, what is it?" Daniel demanded.

"Your wife, sir. I—I don't know where she is. But Sylvain's with her," she added quickly. "He didn't leave Madame Bonaparte's door the whole time Lorelei was with her."

Sweat drenched Daniel's brow, and fear burrowed into his gut. He seized the woman's plump arms. "Lorelei was with Josephine?"

"Yes. About three hours ago."

"And then?"

"I'm not sure. She left the palace."

Daniel bolted into action. His search took him first

to Josephine's rooms. A maid told him that Madame Bonaparte had gone out for the day. He raced through the palace and gardens to the old convent where the canons were staying and burst into Father Julian's room. The prior lay sleeping; Father Anselme dozed in a chair beside the cot.

Daniel touched the old man's shoulder. "Where's Lorelei?"

Father Anselme blinked and rubbed his eyes. "What's that?"

"Lorelei. Where did she go?"

A look of hatred flashed in Father Anselme's eyes. "To the Hôtel Dieu."

Daniel wondered about that look of loathing and about why Father Julian lay sleeping at this hour, but he had no time to spare. "Alone?" he asked.

"Sylvain and Father Emile are with her."

He ducked out of the room and raced toward the hospital.

On the Ile de la Cité in the middle of the river loomed the large rectangular building. The bridge was crammed with travelers and soldiers. Shops and stalls flanked the arched byway. Women trudged past, their market bags bulging with long loaves of bread, bulbs of garlic, soup greens, and wheels of cheese. Horses clopped along, harnesses jangling, drivers calling out to the slow-moving handcarts. In the middle of the bridge, a black berlin was stalled, the driver unable to carve a path through the tightly packed crowd. Paris had too few bridges, a matter Bonaparte had pledged to rectify.

Impatient, Daniel climbed up on the bridge rail to

survey the area. *Coches-d'eau* and rafts guided by *flotteurs* with poles glided beneath the bridge. Craning his neck, he was able to see the entrance to the hospital.

Lorelei stood with her companions on the grand staircase and spoke to a doctor robed in surgical dress. Dizzy with relief, Daniel decided to wait for them to fight their way back through the throng.

Lorelei spoke with unaffected animation, her hands making eloquent gestures. She wore a lovely loose dress of pale gold, a sweet bonnet crowning her chestnut hair. Pride and affection collided in Daniel's chest. She was adorable, she was remarkable, and she loved him. She was far more than a mercenary like Daniel Severin deserved.

They bade good-bye to the physician and started across the bridge. Very quickly, Sylvain became separated from Emile and Lorelei. The youth scowled and waved his arms at a fishmonger whose cart blocked his way. A cloaked man hurrying past nearly collided with the other two.

Then, above the babble of voices on the bridge, Daniel heard Lorelei's cry of alarm. Like a nightmare unfolding, he saw a knife blade in the stranger's raised hand.

Daniel lunged away from the building and dropped to the pavement. A cartload of crated live chickens trundled in front of him. Shouting Lorelei's name, he vaulted the cart and shoved through a sea of startled travelers.

Emile and the assailant struggled at the bridge rail. Lorelei cried out and waved desperately at Sylvain. Daniel plowed toward the struggling men.

He reached them as the assassin fell backwards into the river. The man's cloak billowed on the water; then he sank out of sight. Father Emile leaned against the rail, panting, his face gray and shining with sweat.

Shaken to his core, Daniel yanked Lorelei into his arms. Sylvain came running, his young face drawn taut with self-disgust. "I tried to get to her," he gasped out. "Damn!"

Daniel understood what he was feeling. Neither of them had been there when Lorelei's life was in danger.

The Parisians, hardened to violence by the excesses of the Terror, gathered at the bridge rail and looked on with mild interest. The body never surfaced.

Lorelei wrenched away from Daniel and stared into the murky water, then looked at the canon. "Are you all right?"

For a moment, hatred burned in Father Emile's eyes; then he composed himself and made the sign of the cross. "With God's blessing, we're all fine."

"Who was he?" Lorelei asked.

"Some ruffian. The city's crawling with them."

Daniel glanced at Emile. "Where did you learn to fight like that?"

"An unfortunate necessity. Paris was my home before I joined the hospice."

Daniel moved toward Lorelei; she jerked away, her face unreadable. A strange sense of foreboding intruded upon his relief. "Lorelei," he said, "what—"

"Leave me be, Daniel. You and I—"

A shrill whistle split the air. Gendarmes arrived, scattering the crowd like leaves before a brisk wind. Daniel barely listened to the questioning, barely reacted when witnesses swore the good cleric had clearly acted in self-defense.

Daniel's entire being was centered on Lorelei, who kept her distance and regarded him with haunted eyes. Something vital had died inside her; she'd lost her sparkle. She no longer gazed at him in that adoring way. Did she think him responsible for the attack? he wondered anxiously.

She'd had a fright, he told himself. That was why she was so withdrawn.

She was silent during the walk back to the Tuileries, where she dismissed Greta from the suite with a curt order. When she swung to face Daniel, her eyes blazing with fury, he realized that something much deeper disturbed his wife.

# Chapter 18

Silence hung thick in the elegant room, punctuated by the quiet tick of the mantel clock and the thud of apprehension in Daniel's ears. He felt the pad of the carpet beneath his feet, smelled the fragrance of the freshly cut roses that graced a low table. Only a few feet separated him from Lorelei, but her expression was a wall built of betrayal and distrust.

"You were with Josephine today," he said.

"Yes."

"Because Bonaparte ordered you to consult with her?"

"Yes."

"Yet the two of you discussed other matters as well."

"Indeed we did." Her formal address and cool regard seemed alien, an early frost on a tender flower.

"What did Josephine say to you?" he forced himself to ask.

She clenched her hands into the fabric of her dress. "Things I should have been told long ago."

He backed up mentally, tripping over the lies and half-truths he'd told her over the months. So many of them. So damned many. "Tell me, Lorelei."

Her eyes emanated an inner pain so sharp that he wanted to look away. "You knew my true identity all along, didn't you?"

"Oh, Christ." So this was the way Josephine had chosen to take her revenge. Not as lethal as poison, but nearly as effective. He walked to the sideboard and poured a glass of wine. "So she told you, the bitch." How much had she revealed? he wondered feverishly. Everything? Even his purpose in going to the hospice last spring? He gulped the wine.

"Don't you dare insult her," Lorelei snapped. "She's the only one who didn't assume I'd fall to pieces on hearing that I'm Louis the Sixteenth's bastard."

The last word hissed between them like a dying flame.

He sucked in a deep breath as regrets washed over him. "I meant to tell you. There never seemed a good time—"

"Oh, but there couldn't be a good time for you. You deceived me. You came to the hospice intending to lure me into marriage."

So Josephine hadn't told the whole truth, probably because she couldn't have done so without implicating herself. "Bonaparte, at your request, forced the marriage," he countered.

"Then why did you come to the hospice? Tell me that."

The idea of more lies sickened him. Yet he couldn't tell her the truth, either. Turning away, he noticed a new edition of the *Moniteur* on a stand by the door. The front page proclaimed a ball tonight to celebrate Bonaparte's triumphal return to Paris.

"I had political reasons," he said. "Damn Josephine."

"You may curse her all you wish, Daniel, but I'm grateful to her. She told me because it's *my* life!"

"Don't endow her with so many principles," he said, pivoting back to face her. "She meant to shame you."

"Shame or not, I deserve to know who my father was."

He gazed at her shattered expression. "But has it occurred to you, Lorelei, that the truth was concealed for good reason? Your identity puts you in peril. Surely you understand that."

"Oh, do stop. You've gotten what you wanted—a wife with royal blood. No doubt you'll try to use that to your advantage."

"This is a republican court," he reminded her. "What good does royal blood do me?" Setting down his wineglass, he went to her and cupped his hands around her shoulders. "Have you seen me try to exploit you, Lorelei? Have you?"

Doubts flickered in her eyes. But then her expression hardened and she pulled away. "No, but then again,

I haven't seen all that much of you in Paris. Where do you go each day?"

"My meetings concern Jean Meuron. That's all I can tell you, Lorelei."

"More secrets?" she said acidly, stalking to the window and staring out through the gently blowing curtains. "How you must have been laughing as you pretended to have lost your memory."

The recollection of that first deception slapped him like a sluice of icy water.

"Yes, it was a pretense, wasn't it?" she accused, facing him again. "A way to gain my sympathy, my trust."

"I never meant to hurt you with my deception. I was injured; I couldn't walk. I had to protect myself—and you."

"Why would the famous Raven help me? What master bought your scruples?"

He swallowed slowly, framing a response. "The decision to protect you was entirely my own, Lorelei. I swear it."

"What made you so sure I was in trouble in the first place?"

"News of the confession of the abbess of Yverdon reached Paris," he said carefully.

"Who else knew?"

"Father Julian, of course. And Father Anselme. Gaston found out from the abbess."

She gazed dully at him. "I guessed that. No doubt he sent the news to Paris. And Sylvain was with him on that trip."

"He knows."

"And Father Emile?"

"Sylvain tells me he nursed Gaston through the typhus and might have heard the truth then."

"Damn you all."

"Lorelei—"

"I don't wish to speak of this anymore." She strode across the room and tugged the bellpull, summoning Greta and the other maids. "I shall make an appearance tonight in honor of Bonaparte's return, but you needn't concern yourself about escorting me." She went into her room and slammed the door.

Daniel finished the last of the wine. Then he grew angry with himself, for his thoughts became muddled when he should have been doing some clearheaded thinking. Certain pieces of the puzzle simply didn't fit. Gaston had revealed himself to be an assassin, but Daniel knew in his gut that the man hadn't acted alone. Someone had given the documents to Josephine. And King Louis's treasure still lay hidden somewhere at the hospice—if Father Julian hadn't helped himself to it already. There were too many loose threads still unraveling.

Sylvain came with a message from Stockalper and the other Swiss: tonight, as the city reveled in Bonaparte's return, Meuron's escape would take place.

Daniel felt two forces pulling him in opposite directions. His heart told him to stay with Lorelei, to repair the damage Josephine had wreaked. Yet he had a part to play in Meuron's deliverance. Another matter of the heart. Another secret.

Chandeliers threw spinning constellations against the vaulted ceiling of the Gallery of Diana. The hall was lined by busts of ancient Roman heroes. Here, Daniel recalled, Louis XVI had held court.

The idea triggered an agonized thought of Lorelei.

Napoleon and Josephine presided from a table on a dais. The captured battle flags of Marengo, tattered and bullet-shot, hung like trophies behind and above the dais. The first consul wore his impeccable consular uniform of red and gold; his wife was draped in a golden sheath and ropes of pearls that had once belonged to Marie Antoinette.

Bonaparte had staked everything for everything. And he'd won. To most of the attendees—from the illustrious Talleyrand to the shifty-eyed Fouché—they appeared the victor and his glittering ornament of a wife, both flush with Bonaparte's first triumph as consul of France.

Didn't they see? Daniel wondered. Bonaparte's support of republicanism was all empty show. He wouldn't be content for long with the title of first consul. Already he had shed the demeanor of a mere statesman and assumed the bearing of a sovereign. But none of the revelers seemed to realize that the republic they'd nurtured on blood was fast becoming an aristocratic court with a fixed etiquette. Bonaparte hadn't rewritten history. He'd merely switched the players.

Daniel tore his gaze from the sparkling panorama and watched the main door. What was keeping Lorelei?

He approached Sylvain, who stood like a sentinel at the entrance. "It's a night to fly free, no?" whispered Sylvain.

Daniel nodded. "If fate has its way, the stalwart will

quit the city by dawn." And who more steady and stalwart than Meuron?

He prayed Dominique Larrey would do his part. Bringing in the surgeon had been a gamble, for Daniel had been forced to confess nearly everything to Larrey. But his instincts had been correct. Larrey was far more concerned about Lorelei's well-being than about affairs of state, and he'd agreed to help. He was to come to the palace in the morning to offer Lorelei a tour of the Cochin hospital. Instead, he would drive her to the Port of Saint Paul east of the city, where Daniel would meet them and take Lorelei back—whether she was willing or not—to the safety of Coppet in Switzerland.

God, he was eager to leave Paris. He longed to take Lorelei away from the empty spectacle of Bonaparte's court and the city where assassins lurked around every corner.

The memory of the attack on the bridge chilled him anew. Yet one good thing had come of the incident. Daniel had learned he wasn't the only one dedicated to keeping Lorelei safe. Both Sylvain and Emile had defended her.

Again, his gaze roved the crowd. "Where the devil *is* Lorelei?" he asked Sylvain.

"Greta spoke of a new gown, a present from Josephine."

Daniel's hackles lifted at the idea of accepting gifts from the she-wolf who'd nearly eaten him alive. Her lupine temper had infected Lorelei, and he could only hope her influence would fade.

Restless with his thoughts, he strayed through the tall glass doors to the veranda. The perfume of roses and freshly mown grass hung in the air. In this very place eight years before, he'd fought off howling rioters; now he had the weird sensation of stepping in blood visible only in his troubled mind.

Yet, strangely, the image didn't sicken him as it once had. Because of Lorelei. Now when he thought of the Tuileries, he would remember her and not the eight hundred murdered Swiss. The discontent in his soul was beginning to ease.

An uncomfortable notion occurred to him. Now that he was in danger of losing her love, he realized that he was beginning to depend on it, to crave it as sustenance for his soul.

A stir in the middle of the ballroom drew him back inside. Feminine shrieks erupted, and the dancers fell back to make room. A glass dropped with a resounding crash.

Yapping sharply, Josephine's lapdog streaked across the floor. Ears and jowls flapping, Barry followed close behind. Clutching a large shawl around her, Lorelei rushed after them.

Josephine gripped the arms of her thronelike chair, her mouth forming an *O* of horror while Bonaparte laughed uproariously.

Spying his mistress, Fortuné made for the dais. Barry's jaws opened, and he bent his great head to seize his prey. Fortuné leaped up the steps, skittered across the table, and landed, trembling, in Josephine's lap.

Seconds later Lorelei skidded to a halt at the base of the dais and grabbed Barry's collar. Sweetly flustered, she gathered her shawl at her throat and bent in a curtsy. "Forgive me," she said, looking up at the first consul and his wife. "Barry escaped our apartments before I could stop him—"

"He's a beast," Josephine declared, her hands moving over Fortuné, seeking injuries. "He ought to be—"

"—commended for trying to rid the palace of a pest." Bonaparte chuckled, motioning for a footman. "Take my wife's little bonbon off to safety," he commanded, aiming a contemptuous look at the quivering dog. The footman left in one direction with Fortuné, Sylvain in another with Barry. Breathing a sigh of relief, Lorelei curtsied again.

"General," she said, her low voice drawing the guests closer around her. "Congratulations on your victory in Italy."

"Well," said the first consul, "a few more grand deeds like this campaign and I may yet be known to posterity."

"Indeed so, sir."

Craning his neck over a sea of bobbing heads, Daniel could see that she wore a strained smile: studiously beautiful, self-consciously provocative. A woman's smile, a stranger's smile.

Her perusal found Daniel. Their gazes locked. Her eyes shone with unnatural brightness as if glazed with ice. Her smile never faltered as she looked away.

A coldness seized him. He started forward, but Bonaparte rose and descended from the dais. "To the dance floor," he said, grinning at Josephine's daggerlike stare. "I'm more at home on the battlefield, but the musicians can adjust to my steps."

The honor paid to Lorelei set the onlookers to whispering. A footman carried away her shawl.

*"La belle,"* a man near Daniel murmured. "Can this be *la petite Suisse?"*

"Ah, that dress!" someone else remarked.

"I thought the Grecian style outmoded."

"She'll bring it back, see if she doesn't."

"Tournon will slay us all yet with her designs."

"And dear Josephine will slay *her."* This was from Lucien Bonaparte, who regarded his sister-in-law with malicious anticipation.

Lorelei and Bonaparte led the promenade. His senses thrumming with shock, Daniel groped blindly behind him, finding a balustrade for support. He, like the entire male population of the Tuileries, couldn't take his eyes off Lorelei.

He wanted to vomit. He wanted to scream. He wanted to rip off his coat and cover her with it.

Instead he stood motionless, betraying no sign of the violence roiling inside him.

A new gown, Sylvain had said, a present from Josephine. The word "gown," Daniel realized, could be only loosely applied to the wispy thing that draped Lorelei's supple body.

The fabric was of purest white; Bonaparte favored white for all women of his court. This particular shred of gossamer must have been woven by fairies—it was that sheer, that insubstantial.

In the manner of the true demimondaine, Lorelei had eschewed underclothes. It was blatantly, achingly, astoundingly clear she wore nothing underneath her gown.

A golden clasp gathered the sheath at one shoulder, leaving the other bare. The tips of her breasts moved subtly beneath. He could make out the shapes of her legs, her feet strapped into sandals, the erotic V-shaped shadow at the apex of her thighs.

The white misty thing was more provocative than stark nudity. She managed to retain an air of mystery, like a dream just out of reach, all but forgotten on waking.

He tore his gaze from Lorelei and glared at Josephine. Strain pulled at the corners of her mouth, but when she caught his eyes, she smiled brilliantly.

It was her doing, this shameful display of his wife. The gown would keep the gossipmongers in trade for weeks.

Barely able to check his fury, he strode toward the dais. Josephine graciously extended her hand. Daniel took it, his grip like steel. Her expression grew stony, but she refused to flinch.

"Your dear wife has made quite a sensation in her new dress," said Josephine.

"So I see," he drawled. "Your doing, I presume."

"Of course."

He forced himself to smile, not giving her the satisfaction of revealing his rage. "How kind of you," he murmured. "She's captured the fancy of every male present—including your husband." He couldn't resist adding, as he bent to kiss her hand, "It's backfired, my dear. True beauty simply cannot be mocked, but I wouldn't expect you to understand that. Far from making my wife look the fool, you've created a sensation." He dropped her hand and walked away.

Lorelei swept across the dance floor, her smile beautiful and false, her movements fluid and flamboyant.

A great sadness welled unexpectedly in Daniel, and he didn't understand why, until he caught another glimpse of her cold, knowing eyes.

She'd finally lost her innocence. Josephine, this court, this city, had stolen it.

His Lorelei, who'd survived assassins, healed the sick, and taught Daniel how to live again, had surrendered the one precious part of herself that had made her so wonderfully unique.

Sadness hardened into anger. The icy rage was new to him, and painful, a wound in a part of his body he didn't know he possessed and didn't expect to heal. As the bright rhythm of the music measured the moments, he recognized the feeling.

Jealousy. The Raven was jealous. Slobbering sick with it.

He'd never cared enough about a woman to fall victim to the acid emotion. Now suddenly he wanted to rip out every pair of gaping eyes and crush them into the floor. He wanted to sink his dagger into every chest and cut out every lusting heart.

This jealousy was making him a dangerous man.

But he made certain no one knew that as he strode into the midst of the dancers and closed his hand around Lorelei's wrist. She gasped; Bonaparte stopped and glared.

"Pray excuse us," said Daniel, a winning smile on his face. "My wife isn't well." He placed a solicitous hand at the small of her back. "Darling, we'd best go."

"I've only just arrived," she stated, thrusting up her chin. Light from the chandelier struck her beautiful naked throat.

Bonaparte shot Daniel an understanding look. "On the contrary, your wife is very well indeed. But I've caused enough suffering on the dance floor." He bent gallantly over her hand, kissed it, and turned to Daniel. *"A vous, monsieur."*

Pressing none too lightly with his hand, Daniel steered her toward the door.

"I intend to stay." Her husky voice had an edge of alarm.

"Oh, no," said Daniel, his hand skimming her bare shoulder. "I'm afraid not, darling." They left by way of the veranda, now peopled with strolling couples and groups of raucous military men. The illuminated gardens rolled out below them. He headed toward the palace entrance beneath a great clock.

Her body stiffened in resistance. "Don't you dare force me, Daniel Severin." The contempt in her voice turned the balmy breeze to an ice storm.

"Look," he said with exaggerated patience. "You can leave quietly with me now or balk and—"

"Yes. I'm balking." She twisted from his grasp and whirled, the wispy sheath clinging to interesting parts of her. She started to march back toward the ballroom.

He glared at her. He didn't need her stubbornness, not tonight of all nights. "Don't make me embarrass you, Lorelei." He counted silently to three. When she didn't turn, he closed the distance between them in two strides, took her arm, and spun her around to face him.

"You've been humiliated enough tonight. Don't make me add to it."

"Then stop acting as if you own me. I'm staying."

She stood with her feet planted, her stance combative, defiant. A band of soldiers stopped to stare.

"Come with me now," said Daniel, his voice hard with desperation. "Or I'll drag you, by God."

"Then you'd best be about it," she retorted, "for it's the only way you'll get me to leave."

"I'm sorry for this," he whispered, and truly he was. Picking her up, he slung her over one shoulder, her buttocks aimed at the night sky, her flailing legs held still with one strong arm.

As Daniel crossed the veranda with his wife, female voices tittered. *"Touché,* citizen," a man called. And then, as if the display were an act in an opera, people began to applaud.

"Parisians are so easily amused," Daniel muttered. The sound of clapping echoed in his ears as he chased the maids from the suite, kicked open the door to his chamber, and deposited Lorelei on the bed.

"You damned barbarian!" She bounced up and ran for the door, her dress ghostly pale in the moonlight.

He darted past her, slapped the door shut and turned the key. "Unless you relish a dead fall three stories down," he said, pocketing the key, "you'd best resign yourself to spending a bit of time with your husband. We're going to settle this, Lorelei. Now."

She retreated until her backside met a bedpost. Reaching behind, she gripped the post and stared at him with a stranger's eyes. "There is nothing to settle," she said. "You lied to me. I won't forgive you. What more is there to say?"

*That I love you.* The admission welled up in his heart

and screamed through his mind. *More than life, more than freedom.*

Yesterday she would have believed him. Tonight she'd think it yet another lie.

He went to the mantel and took up a tinderbox. Very slowly and deliberately, he lit a slim taper, then moved about the room, lighting every candle until the atmosphere glowed.

A strange excitement mingled with the rage inside him. He'd known her as a virgin, a partner in delightful lust, a tender, willing lover. But never like this, as a provocative woman fully aware of her sexual power.

She watched him, expressionless, her eyes wary. At last he swung back to face her.

His breath snagged in his throat.

The candles had been a mistake. Unwittingly he'd created the perfect setting for the outrageous gown. The fabric molded itself to her form, shining like molten gold and shadowed intriguingly, moving in a shimmer of light with every breath she took.

Drawn like a fly into a silken web, he came to stand in front of her, his hands locking around the bedpost, his arms imprisoning her.

"What the hell happened to you?" he demanded.

Defiance danced with the reflected candle flames in her eyes. "I grew up, Daniel. I grew wise."

He gave a short bark of laughter, though his eyes stayed riveted on her full, moist lips. Insolently he plucked at the translucent silk of her dress. "You call this grown up? I call it the gown of a whore. Is that what Josephine taught you?"

"*You* liked Josephine's lessons well enough, Daniel," she shot back.

His heart turned cold. So the bitch had told Lorelei that as well. "In God's name," he said softly, "what can you have been thinking of, parading yourself about in this?"

"I was thinking it might draw men's attention to the fact that I'm no longer some little Swiss sheep all moon-eyed over her husband."

"Oh, you got their attention all right." His gaze dipped to the rise of her breasts, the dusky shadows beneath the silk. "God help us, you've got mine, too."

"How vexing," she retorted, sinking down on the bed, out of the frame of his arms. "For I don't want yours. Leave me alone." Her voice was cold, each word a stone dropped into a dark well.

"Not until we have this out."

"Then you're in for a long wait."

Exasperated, he went down on one knee and took her by the shoulders. Her skin was smooth as cream beneath his fingers.

"It's me you're angry at, Lorelei. So why did you shame yourself, make yourself look like a woman of loose morals?"

"Ah," she said harshly. "Then I succeeded. I hope everyone present noted that fact."

"My God, why?"

"Because I must establish that to support my divorce suit."

Her naive, desperate plan struck him like a hammer. The fact that he'd driven her to it tore into his soul.

"There will be no suit," he vowed. "I can't let you go, Lorelei."

It was truer than she could know. Each time they were close he could feel himself fusing with her, sinking into her goodness. His mouth drew closer to hers. He could feel her breath, rapid and delicate against his face. One kiss, he told himself. One kiss would give him back his Lorelei, the openhearted, unpredictable girl he was fast learning he could not live without.

He pressed his lips to hers and tasted the familiar sweetness, the ripeness. . . .

She pulled back. "No. I don't want—"

"Liar," he countered. "You want me." He claimed her lips, and the pliancy of her mouth proved his point. He drew back to study the helpless dreamy look in her eyes.

"You taught me this game, Daniel," she said softly. "But I learned on my own how to win at it." She leaned forward and claimed his lips, making bold with her tongue, plunging it into his mouth with calculated precision.

His body reared in response. It was a kiss designed to leach a man's soul from his body, a practiced kiss, a courtesan's kiss.

He realized, to his utter shame, that she hadn't even moved her arms. He was that vulnerable to her, that desperate. A mere kiss reduced him to melted butter at her dainty feet.

He pulled away, his mouth watering with the taste of her, his body alert to her sensual assault.

"Do I shock you?" she asked with angry triumph in her voice.

"Was that your intent?" he demanded, leaning forward, finding himself engulfed in her scent of rosewater and new silk. "Because I warn you, it's a dangerous one."

"I'm used to danger by now." Laughter moved in her supple throat. "It's in my very blood."

"By God, you push me too far." He thrust her back on the bed. The impossibly thin fabric heightened his awareness of her taut body. He suckled her breast through the silk, drawing hard as if to devour the rancor between them. His hand slid up her thigh to the veiled nakedness she'd displayed before the first consul's court.

"Daniel," she gasped, "this is not what I—"

"I'm only giving you what you begged for, what you wore that dress for," he said. He took her mouth in a rough, biting kiss. She returned the kiss in fierce, wild defiance. His hand tunneled down between them to free himself of his constraining trousers and he claimed her with a savage mastery that left his senses spinning. She jolted beneath him, clasping him to her. The pulse of her response milked the last shred of control from him, and he exploded in a frenzy of angry passion.

The ruined gown rustled as he drew back and straightened his clothing. He sat on the edge of the bed, rested his elbows on his knees, and dug his trembling fingers into his hair.

He turned to look at her. She lay perfectly still, staring at the ceiling and making no attempt to cover herself.

The raw sense of power turned to shame. He jerked

the counterpane over her. "Why did you do it, Lorelei? Why did you provoke me?"

"I'm the daughter of King Louis's whore," she said matter-of-factly. "I simply meant to play the part." She shifted, her bare shoulder burnished by candlelight. There was a red imprint on her flesh where he'd clutched her hard. "You certainly played your part."

His heart lurched. "No. Oh, no. You can't think like that. Lorelei, you're the same person you were before you found out. Nothing's changed—"

"Everything's changed. I'm a creature of lust, my parents' daughter." Bitter laughter broke from her. "What a great joke on fate that a king's daughter should couple with a common mercenary."

The barb found a home in his heart. "Don't think like that, Lorelei. Please don't think like that."

"It's really quite simple. We must get a divorce."

His head snapped up. That had been his plan from the start, but somewhere, without acknowledging it to himself, he'd abandoned the scheme. "Lorelei, I told you, there will be no—"

"An annulment would probably be more appropriate, since the church forbids—"

"Damn it, I want to know—"

"Do you?" she demanded, sitting forward. "But that's just it, Daniel. You've known all along. What you don't know would fill a child's thimble."

"I'm sorry. I should have told you about your parents. I wish to God I had."

"It's too late for wishing, Daniel."

He glanced at the clock. He longed to spend the rest of the night unraveling the lies he'd told her, but within an hour he would be gone to the archival prison to free Meuron.

"Please don't do anything rash," he said, reaching for her.

"Like rape?" she flung at him, recoiling from his touch. She whipped back the covers and left the bed. The gown hung alluringly down her back, but he felt no desire, only a deep, uncomfortable regret.

"I'm going to get some sleep—alone." She stooped to retrieve the key from the pocket of his discarded coat. A crumpled bit of paper lay on the floor beside it, but the breeze blew it beneath the bed. She swung back and stared at him. "And after that, I'm going to put an end to this marriage and get on with my life."

Lorelei slammed the door to her chamber and turned the key in the lock. She stared for a long time at the door. She hated him for his driving strength. She hated him because old hurts still haunted his eyes and touched her heart. She hated him because, although he'd die before admitting it, he needed her.

She couldn't let that matter now. If she did, she'd find herself groveling at his feet and grasping at scraps. She'd be no better than her father, vacillating like a leaf on the wind, never committing himself to a single course.

She stripped off the beautiful sheath. She'd certainly gotten Daniel's attention with it. She cherished the instant he had first spied her in the gown. That stricken, disbelieving look on his face would live in her memory for years to come. Just for a moment she had felt truly beautiful, felt a power that didn't come from blood or birth or rank.

The crushed silk still held the scent of their love. Love? No. It had been lust and possession. Treading heedlessly on the fabric, she moved toward the bed. She would never wear such a dress again.

She threw back the counterpane to find a folded piece of paper. Frowning, she snatched it up and moved toward the window, angling the note to the torchlight from the gardens.

*Come at once*, she read. *Father Julian needs you*.

The note was signed by Father Anselme.

With a gasp of fear, she hastened to the armoire. Her trousers, shirt, and *bredzon,* freshly laundered and pressed, lay in the bottom drawer.

She wondered if she would always be at the whim of others. It was the nature of her profession. The doctor in her gave no thought to personal rancor. The prior was ill; he might have taken a turn for the worse.

She pulled on the familiar garments and eyed the locked door. No doubt Daniel would try to stop her, or at least insist on coming. She couldn't face him again tonight, and no doubt Sylvain was standing guard outside the suite.

Fine, she thought, glancing at the window. It was time she made a decision and acted on her own. God knew she could use the practice.

From her rucksack she took a rope that had survived the journey from the hospice. She secured one end around a wrought-iron window bar and squeezed out onto the ledge. The courtyard lay three stories below, but the distance didn't daunt her. She'd scaled cliffs a hundred times as high. She made a smooth, quiet descent into the darkened courtyard. Voices, bursts of laughter, and strains of a carol drifted from the Gallery of Diana.

Dewdrops wet her boots as she jogged across the gardens, darting from shadow to shadow. Moonlight silvered the ornamental ponds; a leaky fountain dripped steadily into the night quiet.

At the ancient convent, she found the door to Father Julian's cell and tapped gently.

Father Anselme opened it, his lined face gilded by the candle he held. "Lorelei! Come in, my child."

She tried to slay the affection that rose in her chest at the sight of the man who had been parent, teacher, and friend to her. She tried to remind herself that he was privy to a hideous deception that made a pawn of her.

"What is his condition?" Her voice was hard, alien.

Father Anselme adjusted his spectacles and peered at her sharply. "The stomach ailment has gotten worse."

Father Anselme set the taper on a stool beside the cot, and she gazed down at the prior. Shock and sympathy collided in her chest. He lay staring at the ceiling, his eyes glazed with pain, his sharp-featured face drawn and beaded with sweat. His thin, bloodless hands rested on his chest, which rose and fell jerkily.

"What is it?" she asked.

"I thought it might have been rancid food, but no one else has fallen ill."

She had a sudden image of Daniel lunging toward her cup of chocolate, snatching it from her hand. *Don't drink it. . . .*

"What has he eaten?"

"Some broth, some watered wine."

"Who prepared it?"

"The convent kitchens."

She touched her fingertips to Father Julian's wrist and winced at the threadiness of the pulse. "What are his symptoms?"

"He can't keep food down. He's passed virtually nothing for eight hours."

"It could be an ulcerated stomach."

"I thought of that. But he's vomited no blood."

"How long has he been like this?"

"He took a turn for the worst an hour after supper."

Guilt settled in for a long stay. While she was dancing and making love, the prior lay suffering.

"Father." It rattled her to see him so weak, this man who had been a tower of strength all her life. "Can you hear me?"

"Lor . . . elei." His voice rasped like a dead leaf scuttling over cold stone. He raised a trembling hand, pointed at Father Anselme. "Leave us. Please."

The old canon nodded and withdrew.

Father Julian took a convulsive breath. "Never meant . . . betray you. . . ."

"Hush," she said, "you're spending your strength. There's an apothecary not far from here. I'll send for a purgative."

"No! Must tell you about the treasure."

His words made little impression, for she was suddenly caught up in the frantic urgency of the field hospital, the helpless frustration of watching a man die.

She searched her mind. No fever. Accelerated pulse. She listened to his chest. Lungs clear.

His forehead was clammy. Cool already. His mouth worked soundlessly; then he spoke again. "My fault," he whispered. "My greed nearly killed you."

His words penetrated her alarm. "Father Julian, what are you saying?"

"The trea . . . sure."

"Treasure?"

"Your father. Louis the king. Left a fortune. I should have given it to you . . . rightfully yours."

Lorelei's heart raced. "My father left me a fortune?"

Father Julian nodded weakly. "It's . . . at the hospice."

At last she knew what it was all about—the attempts on her life, Father Julian's secrecy, all ploys so he could keep a legacy that should have been hers. She searched her heart for the rage of betrayal, but instead found only pity. The wages of his sin had come to nothing.

"Father Julian, how could you?" she whispered, sick with disillusionment. "You're a man of God."

"A man," he said, his eyelids fluttering. "Just a man."

A horrible thought struck her. "Father Julian, you must tell me. Did Daniel know of this treasure?"

He pressed his lips together, his eyes rolling with nausea. "I believe he did. Searched my office."

She buried her face in her hands. At last she knew what Daniel really wanted, why he'd married her.

"Must . . . get the treasure," said Father Julian. His throat rattled ominously. "It's in the monstrance."

The holy vessel was made of battered pewter, studded by paste jewels, hardly a treasure. "I don't understand."

"The jewels . . . belonged to Marie Antoinette."

She pictured the polished stones, large and clumsily mounted. "But they're paste."

"They're real. Uncut, polished by tumbling." His voice trailed off on a sigh; then he seemed to gather strength. "Tell no one. No one, do you hear?"

"Yes, Father." Even through her roiling emotions, she clung to practicalities. She was going to leave Daniel. She would need some way to live. The treasure could provide funds for setting up her own surgery somewhere far away.

"Promise me, Lorelei. Too dangerous."

"I promise, Father." And she meant it. She knew now what greed could make men do. "I'm going to fetch Dr. Larrey," she said, rising to her feet.

"Lorelei." She swung around to find that Father Anselme had entered the room again. When? Had he heard?

"It's too late." He reached into the folds of his robe. For a wild moment she expected to see a weapon in his hand. Good Lord, she suspected everyone now that her dreams and beliefs lay in pieces.

He brought out a vial of oil and stepped forward, his old face weary with grief. *"Per istam sanctam unctionem. . . ."*

The words soughed into the quiet cell. Father Julian gave no sign that he heard. A tiny sound burbled from between his lips. His chest stilled.

She dropped to her knees beside him and pressed her

hand to his throat. She found no pulse. He was dead. The prior of Saint Bernard's was dead.

"I didn't hear his last confession," said Father Anselme.

I did, thought Lorelei. She tried to think of him as he had been in life, stern yet caring, strong and implacable. Yet her grief, her memories, were corrupted by his final words.

Father Anselme fetched Father Emile. He joined their vigil, his face a taut mask, ascetic, betraying no emotion.

An hour passed, then two. Father Anselme levered himself up. "I must go see to . . . arrangements," he said.

Lorelei nodded. "Father Emile and I will stay."

Emile knelt and began searching under the cot.

"Father Emile, what are you doing?"

He looked up sharply. Perhaps it was a trick of the candlelight, but she fancied she saw a flash of ferocity in his pale eyes. Perhaps he, too, had guessed at Father Julian's treachery.

"Someone must do an accounting of the prior's effects." Father Emile drew from beneath the cot a stack of books, a wooden lap secretary with a leather top, and a large canvas rucksack.

She moved the candle closer. Light glinted off the insignia embroidered on the flap: a sheaf of black-fletched arrows.

Realization broke over her.

"Good heavens," she said, dropping to her knees beside Father Emile. "This is the rucksack Daniel lost in the avalanche."

* * *

"Christ, I can't find the damned thing." Daniel scowled into the night. "I must have left it in my coat." The stench of rotting vegetables filled the alleyway behind the Chantereine.

"It's not like the Raven to be careless," said Sylvain. Lamp glow from the windows of a wineshop struck his bright hair.

"I haven't been myself lately," Daniel muttered, thinking of the angry scene with Lorelei a few hours earlier. He winced at the memory of finding her door locked against him. How was he ever going to convince her that he'd changed, that he wasn't the man who'd come to the hospice with murder in his heart?

*You knew it would come to this. You knew she'd find out,* said an accusing voice at the back of his mind. *You should have told her.*

"We'll have to do without the floor plan," said Daniel. He and Sylvain crept along the alley toward the river. A gendarme peered down the length of the passage. Hearts pounding, hands on their weapons, they flattened themselves against the moldering wall. The gendarme passed on, whistling under his breath and swinging his lantern.

The Seine lapped at the ancient walls of the Chantereine. Paris never truly slept; even at this hour laughter rang across the water from an anchored barge. Daniel edged toward the bank, his quiver thudding against his back. The weapon seemed antique and out of place in this modern city where soldiers armed with pistols loitered on every street corner.

Sylvain leaned out over the horizontal bars at the

end of the alley. Drunk-catchers, they were called, designed to keep reeling men from falling into the river.

"The water stinks," said Sylvain.

"Just concentrate on keeping your bowstring dry."

A low shadow slipped down the river toward them. One of the occupants of the dory lifted an arm three times in succession.

"There's Stockalper," said Daniel.

"Right on time," said Sylvain, returning the signal. His eyes were sleek with excitement. Daniel tried to share the youth's anticipation. In a short while, they would deliver Meuron to the boat, to be borne downriver to the Port of Saint Paul, where Larrey would be waiting with Lorelei, and ultimately to Switzerland. There, backed by a united front, Meuron would force clemency from Bonaparte, keeping him from further plundering Swiss independence and the country's rich treasury.

Yet Daniel could summon only cold purpose. Before the night was out, he would kill again, darkening the stains on his soul.

They donned oilskin cloaks, leggings, and caps to protect themselves in the foul passageway they were about to enter. Gripping the iron loops protruding from the ancient stonework, Daniel lowered himself toward the water. Shiny bugs darted over the wall, weaving in and out of fetid moss. A rat slithered into the river and swam away, swill rippling in its wake.

Sylvain made sounds of disgust in his throat. They reached the drainage duct, a small rectangular hole which, only hours ago, had been barred. The Swiss partisans had filed the bars, leaving a space large enough for a slim man to fit through.

Daniel's boots filled with river water as he entered the hole. The smell of refuse slapped him in the face, and he nearly gagged. The duct was narrow, never meant to accommodate a man.

"All right?" he whispered to Sylvain.

"I feel sick."

"I'd be surprised if you felt otherwise. Just be glad this building's virtually uninhabited."

As if to give the lie to his words, a metallic grating sounded above, followed by a *swish.*

*"Merde,"* said Sylvain.

"Let's hope not." Daniel clung to the upper surface of the duct. Something slid past them and trickled out into the river.

"Maybe it's someone's shaving water," said Sylvain.

"You can always hope so."

The tunnel sloped dangerously upward. Daniel's hands and feet slipped on the stonework. His hands were scraped raw.

"Can you make it?" he asked Sylvain.

"Fingers hurt. Won't . . . be able to draw my bow."

"You'll make yourself, if you have to."

"Is that how you do it, Daniel? Is that how you kill?"

"I don't know anymore," he said with total honesty.

They climbed in silence until they reached a gray square of murky light slanting through bars of thick rusty iron. "That's it," Daniel breathed. "That's the grate." Peering up between the bars, he saw only empty blackness.

"Anyone there?" Sylvain whispered.

"I can't see much. Be ready the second I get this grate moved." Bracing his knees on either side of the drain, he grasped the iron bars and pushed upward with his shoulders, his neck, even the top of his head. Metal scraped against stone and slowly loosened. At last the grate came up. Daniel slid it to one side, raised his head, and glanced around. All dark. Quiet.

The large vaulted chamber was piled high with moldering papers and books and straw, sacks of refuse and glass bottles.

"Clear," he whispered. They exited the duct and gratefully shed their oilskins, burying them beneath a heap of straw. Sylvain took off his neckcloth and scrubbed his face.

Somewhere a door creaked. Sylvain dropped the cloth.

Daniel heard the snick of an arrow leaving a quiver. "I've got this one," said Sylvain.

He's good, thought Daniel, but he readied his weapon, too.

A shadow stepped into the cavernous room. Sylvain's bowstring snapped into the silence. The arrow thudded into living flesh.

The man cried out. Daniel and Sylvain rushed to him to stifle the sound. But after a few seconds it didn't matter; the man expired, shot through the chest.

"I feel sick," Sylvain whispered again.

As Daniel bent to check the body for keys, a wave of nausea struck him as well. He was tired of darkness and secret deeds. He longed for a clean battle fought in sunshine, an honest fight bought with honest sweat.

The guard must have been an underling, for he had

no keys. Grunting with effort, Daniel and Sylvain moved the body to a corner of the large chamber and covered it with layers of straw.

They slipped out the door and found themselves in a gloomy corridor. "He's two stories up," said Daniel, peering through the thick, damp darkness.

"How do you know?"

"De Veer greased some palms." Cursing again the loss of the floor plan, he groped his way to a narrow flight of stone steps. They climbed slowly, silently, pausing on the first landing to look down a long hallway lined with stacks of paper.

The place had changed since the days of the Terror. No longer were the cells crammed with desperate men and women, some of whom had committed a crime no more heinous than being born with the blood of an ancient noble house in their veins.

Like Lorelei.

The thought of her struck at him from out of nowhere. She hated him now, just as he'd always known she would.

And now that she knew the truth, he should be at her side. But it was too late for forgiveness. He pictured her lying in her opulent bed, despising him, planning a life without him.

He jerked his head, signaling for Sylvain to follow. At the second landing, dull yellow light glowed from a half-open door.

". . . beaten me again, Foulard," said a voice. "You've won the very supper from my babes' mouths." Coins clinked on a wooden table.

"Come on, Isambard, you can't play upon my sympathy. Your daughters eat like queens, you're so smitten with them."

"No more than you are with your own boy." Cards rippled as a deck was shuffled. "Tell me, is he still at the Sorbonne?"

"Yes, getting marks of highest distinction. Means a hard job for me, keeping him in books and doing without his wages."

Sylvain readied an arrow. As Daniel followed suit, he tried to empty his mind as he always did before a kill.

For the first time ever, the effort failed.

He couldn't wrap himself in the familiar cocoon of cold blackness. His mind was invaded by an indelible image of two working men at a game of cards, boasting about their children.

His knees trembled as he drew his bow, pivoted, and stepped into the guardroom. "Gentlemen," he said. "Pardon the intrusion."

The men raised startled eyes from their card game. The stout elder one was was leaning back in his chair, his feet hooked around the legs. When he saw Daniel, his chair thudded to the floor.

The younger one jerked to his feet, one hand on the hilt of his sword.

"Please don't," said Daniel. Sylvain stepped up beside him. "Our arrows are much quicker than your steel."

The older guard remained frozen, staring. "But you're—"

"—easily spooked," Daniel finished for him, flinching from the recognition in the man's eyes. "At this range I could skewer you to that wall."

The younger guard drew a deep breath, preparing to cry out.

"Isambard, stop," said the older one. He looked terrified. "You've come for Meuron?"

"Yes." Daniel moved aside so Sylvain could enter the guardroom. The youth swiftly disarmed the guards, tossing the swords and halberds out the door. Then he bound them hand and foot where they sat.

Daniel helped himself to Foulard's key ring. "I don't suppose you'd tell us where Meuron is?"

"Please, monsieur. This will cost me my job as it is."

"Get into the army contracting business. The first consul's wife earns fortunes that way," said Daniel.

Sylvain murmured apologies as he stuffed their mouths with rags and tied them in place. Daniel took the lamp, and they left, locking the door to the guardroom behind them.

"Now to find Meuron and get out of here," said Daniel.

They tried the first cell. The ring had four keys; the third one worked. The cell door swung open.

The musty smell of disuse struck Daniel in the face. "Jean?" he whispered to the darkness.

A faint, irritated squeaking sound answered him. They locked the guards' weapons in the cell.

Daniel tried four more doors and found only empty rooms. But in the fifth cell, the smell of old food and urine and wine hung in the air. A shadow slumped in one corner where the lamplight didn't penetrate.

Daniel's heart slammed into his throat. "Jean?"

Feet scuffled on the cold floor. Paper and straw rustled. "What the hell— Who's that?"

"It's Daniel," he said. "Daniel Severin."

A quick-drawn breath, and then silence. Tension, stretched by a multitude of misunderstandings, by years of rivalry, by Jean's ideals and Daniel's cynicism, thrummed between them.

*"Daniel."* The hoarse whisper shivered through the darkness.

"Are you well?"

"Well enough."

"Can you travel?"

"Yes."

"Then let's go. That's Sylvain with me, Jean. He's from the Valais, a patriot like you."

Jean hesitated. "And you, Daniel?"

"I'm here, am I not?"

The three walked toward the guardroom. Sylvain paused to raise the lamp high. From the guardroom came scuffling sounds, chair legs bumping the floor as the guards struggled to get free.

"Monsieur Meuron," Sylvain said in an awed voice. He rubbed his eyes and blinked. "Holy Mary Mother of God, you're—"

"Daniel's brother," said Jean.

"Half brother," Daniel said hastily.

"You're as alike as twins."

"Save Daniel's hair." Jean stared at Daniel, questions burning in his eyes.

"But you told no one," said Sylvain. "Why?"

"I didn't come to save him because he's my brother,"

said Daniel. "That's too selfish a reason to endanger you and the others. Let's go."

They descended to the room at the head of the drainage duct. Despite Jean's assurances, Daniel knew his brother was weak from the months of imprisonment. Lorelei will give him something for that cough, he thought with an absurd stab of hope.

"Jesus, we're going down there?" Jean asked, peering at the narrow shaft.

"You first, Sylvain," said Daniel.

The youth lowered himself into the opening.

"Now you, Jean," said Daniel. "I'll go last and replace the grate. That way they won't realize we're going by the river."

Jean took a deep breath and descended. From beyond the door came the muffled sound of voices and footsteps. Fighting panic, Daniel grasped the iron grate.

The footsteps drew closer, hurrying.

From the corner of his eye, Daniel spied a flash of white.

Sylvain's discarded neckcloth. It would give away the escape route.

"Don't wait for me," he whispered.

"What's that?" asked Jean.

"Trust me. Go on. There's something I have to do."

"But—"

*"Just go, Jean!"*

Daniel intended to grab the neckcloth and dive for the hole. But even as he snatched up the wisp of cloth, the door opened. It was all he could do to set the grate in place and crouch between two stacks of old books.

"I hate this place." It was the voice of Foulard. Torchlight glimmered from the doorway.

A scratching sound drifted from the drain.

"What's that?" asked someone else.

Isambard, Daniel recalled. They'd broken out of the guardroom. Damn his newfound sensitivity. He should have killed them.

"I don't know. Go check the drain."

"The drain? But they couldn't have—"

"Just check it."

More footsteps, then a long pause. The torchlight swung about the chamber. "I don't see anything. Damn, Foulard, we're in for it now."

Daniel held still, praying they'd hear no more from the drain, hoping they wouldn't notice the corpse beneath the straw. Endless seconds dragged by, each one an agony of apprehension.

Light from the swinging torch flickered over him. He caught a glimpse of Foulard's frowning face, the eyes narrowing with surprise and recognition.

"It's him!" Foulard shouted.

Daniel leaped up and sprinted for the door.

"Halt!" shouted Isambard.

Daniel pounded up the first flight of stairs and burst through a doorway on the landing. Racing blindly through a black hallway, he headed for a patch of gray light.

Shouts and footfalls nipped at his heels. He came to an unglazed window with a wide ledge. Vaulting through the narrow opening, he found himself on a crumbling wall walk. Torches bobbed at the far end of the walk. He threw a glance back at the window. Armed with a pike, Isambard squeezed through.

Knife in hand, Daniel prepared to kill his pursuer. The guard who'd boasted about his daughters was youthful. Lanky and scared, but brave enough. He aimed his pike at Daniel.

In a lightning bolt of memory, Daniel recalled other guards, other Swiss, other struggles.

He swatted the pike aside and drew his arm back, ready to dispatch Isambard in a flash of steel and blood.

But something made him hesitate.

*Don't kill him, Daniel.* Lorelei's voice reached across the weeks, the months, and touched a spot of mercy in him that had lain dormant for years. He thought of how she'd changed him, made him feel, made him care, made him believe something good existed in the dark void of his soul.

More footsteps rang behind him.

His hand shook. He swore. No more, he thought. Lowering the knife, he turned to run.

A wall of prison guards closed in to meet him.

# Chapter 19

Daniel's rucksack lay gutted like a carcass at Lorelei's feet. At either side of Father Julian's head, twin tapers burned into the silence.

Sick with shock and betrayal, Lorelei held the contents of the sack in her shaking hands. "Oh, sweet Jesus, help me," she whispered. "Tell me it's a mistake."

His face taut with regret, Father Emile said, "I wish I could. But you hold the evidence of your husband's treachery." He shook his head. "I had my doubts about the man, even from the very start. But you loved him well, so I didn't interfere."

She looked down at the two nearly empty vials. "Arsenic and calomel," she said, nearly choking. "But how futile. There's barely enough poison here to kill a cat."

Father Emile gently took the vials from her and put them in the folds of his robe. "But his intent was clear. I'd best get rid of this poison." He reached for his tall sugarloaf hat.

"We should notify someone," she said dully. "Perhaps Monsieur Fouché—"

"I think not," said Father Emile. "The prior is beyond punishing, and we dare not tarry to bring Severin to justice. His crimes will overtake him, just as Julian's did."

She picked up the letter they'd found sewn into the lining of the rucksack. Her gaze drifted over Josephine Bonaparte's careless scrawl. It was a promissory note in which Daniel was pledged to find and eliminate one Lorelei du Clerc, to earn the sum of two hundred thousand francs upon her death.

Her stomach twisted in torment. It was all for money. Every tender word, every kiss, every touch, had been a lie.

She raised tortured eyes to Father Emile. "I thought Madame Bonaparte was my friend. But she sent Daniel to murder me."

"They are both without hearts or souls. If I weren't a man of God, I'd call the scoundrel out."

"Still, one question nags at me. Daniel had plenty of chances to carry out the plan. Why didn't he?"

"No doubt he thought to profit even more greatly by marrying you. I wonder what his plan was."

Lorelei knew with sick certainty. Daniel was aware of the treasure kept at the hospice. "It doesn't matter now," she said, holding back the tears. She would not cry for him.

Emile glared at the corpse of Father Julian. "And this hypocrite knew of the plan. He was concealing the rucksack."

"He must have found it the day after the avalanche. I remember seeing footprints and signs of digging in the snow, but I never imagined—" She broke off and hugged herself.

Father Emile draped an arm around her shoulder. She breathed in his comforting scent of wool and church incense.

"You're not safe in Paris," he said. "Severin or some other assassin could be on his way here as we speak. You must leave. Now."

"But what about Father Anselme?"

"He knew, too, and made no move to protect you. Besides, he's too old to match the speed we must make."

The ache in her heart intensified. The man who had been her teacher, her mentor, her father, had by his silence betrayed her. Whom could she ever trust? "I must pack, then, and fetch Barry."

"Lorelei, child, there's no time. If Madame Bonaparte wishes you dead, you mustn't tarry even for a moment."

"But where will I go? I have no money, no—"

Father Julian's last words came back to her: *The jewels . . . belonged to Marie Antoinette.*

"I must go back to Saint Bernard's," she said. "There's something I must—" She bit her lip.

*Tell no one. . . .* Father Julian had sworn her to secrecy. She knew she had to honor a promise made to a dying man, even one who had betrayed her.

"I'll take you home, Lorelei." Father Emile spared her the decision to justify her secrecy. "I'll keep you safe." He turned to regard the waxen corpse, the eternally still hands folded on Julian's chest. "Anselme will see to the burial."

Julian had always wanted to be buried at his beloved mountain pass. But he'd loved King Louis's treasure more, and he was now condemned to rot in a Paris churchyard. Her heart in shreds, Lorelei made the sign of the cross and followed Father Emile out of the convent.

"She's gone?" Daniel glared through the bars of his cell at the robed and hooded figure. "Did she leave with Dr. Larrey?"

Josephine Bonaparte peered at him from the folds of the hood. She'd come in secret, disguised by the concealing cloak, and she was carrying a rolled book or pamphlet of age-yellowed paper. "Oh, no, my dear Monsieur Severin."

His heart sank to his knees. A torch burned outside the cell; spiders danced in the flickering light, and the smell of pitch, sharp as corruption, filled the air. A shadow moved in the outer doorway. Daniel had the impression of someone lurking there. Waiting for Josephine? Listening?

"Your wife cannot be found," said Josephine, her voice taut with triumph. "No one has seen her in two days."

He hurled himself at the bars, bruising his hands.

"By God, you bitch, if you've harmed so much as a hair on her—"

"You're quick to blame me, Daniel." A secret smile played about her lips. "It's my belief that she fled Paris to escape you." She shook her head. "You should have done my bidding and killed her, as I hired you to do."

With a furious curse, he turned and kicked at a stack of old pamphlets. He shared a cell in the archives with forgotten diatribes of the Revolution and a number of rodents.

His tormented mind tracked back over the past two days—the quarrel with Lorelei, the furious passion, the shattered look in her eyes as she hurled accusations at him. He shouldn't have left her that night. He should have begged her forgiveness—but there hadn't been time. While he was crawling through a sewer to free his brother, Lorelei had fled.

Very casually Josephine added, "One of the canons of Saint Bernard's is also missing."

He curled his fingers around the bars. The metal felt cold in his hands, as cold as the gust of suspicion that blew through his soul. "Which one?" he demanded.

Her tongue darted out to moisten her lips. "Oh, now, there's a question."

"Which one, damn you?"

"All in good time," she drawled. "But first we've a matter to settle between us."

"The gold," he muttered.

"I must have your assurance that the matter of the Bern gold will never be revealed."

"You'll have it," he said without hesitation. All the

gold in the world wasn't worth Lorelei's life. "Just get me out of here, and your secret will be safe."

"You make it sound so simple. And I could make it simpler still. Your death would put an end to my dilemma."

The shadow in the doorway stirred. Daniel tried not to look at it. He bared his teeth and wondered if the strength of his hatred could rip through the iron bars. "But that's not so easily achieved, is it, Josephine? Fouché needs me alive, for I'm the only one who knows what's become of Meuron."

She tapped the rolled paper on the bars. "You gave up your freedom for your brother. I wonder if he'd do the same for you."

"Don't count on it."

She laughed. "Ah, how noble you've become. Yet you've lost everything for the sake of a man who has turned his back on you." She lowered her voice to a hiss. "The minister of police has effective methods of gaining such information."

"He could probably torture a lot of talk out of me," Daniel agreed. "But I'd not say anything that would interest him." He yearned to reach through the bars and throttle her. "Who is with my wife?"

"It might be the devil himself, monsieur." Her fingers toyed with the edge of the booklet she held.

He resisted the urge to blurt out everything, to beg her to secure his release. His nerve-racking concern for Lorelei came face to face with his loyalty to his brother and the Swiss. But he knew he couldn't buy his freedom by capitulating to Josephine. He glared triumphantly. "Meuron is gone. When the time comes, he'll get Bonaparte to deal fairly with Switzerland."

"You think some puny Swiss patriot can halt my Bonaparte?" She laughed harshly. "You're a fool. Your precious brother will be hunted down like a common thief. You're in no position to bargain with me, Daniel."

"But indeed I am, Josephine. I'm sure your husband would be interested to learn what really happened to the Bern gold."

She stiffened. "You gave your word . . ." Then she seemed to relax and plunged her hand into her cloak, bringing out a familiar-looking hat. "But then again," she added, "I don't need your word now, do I?"

Daniel stared at the odd red hat that had belonged to Bayens, the banker. "Where did you get that?"

She dropped it on the floor. "Its owner drowned in the Seine, poor soul."

Bile pushed at Daniel's throat. He forced himself to think clearly, to fix her with his fiercest gaze, and to lie through his teeth. "Bayens wasn't the only 'poor soul' who was investigating your theft."

Her breath caught. "You're lying."

"I might be. Then again, I'm probably not. Tell me who's with my wife." He waited a few seconds. "Your lust for money is surpassed only by your terror that Bonaparte will grow disenchanted with you. And I have information that could make him *very* disenchanted."

"Damn you—"

"Talk, Josephine. Or I will."

"She left Paris with the cleric called Emile." The words came out in a venomous rush.

Relief washed over him as he envisioned Father Emile struggling with the assassin on the bridge. He had to believe the canon could keep her safe. Otherwise he'd go mad. Still, Josephine had given up the information too easily. His thoughts jerked ahead. Emile would probably take Lorelei to Switzerland. "What of the others, Father Anselme and Father Julian?"

Josephine's hands clutched at the pamphlet. "Father Anselme is still at the convent. The prior is dead."

Daniel blinked in disbelief. "Father Julian's dead?"

"Presumably of a stomach ailment."

"Presumably? Damn it, you can't afford to be coy."

"Dr. Larrey suspects poison."

Daniel's blood froze. "You're saying Father Julian was poisoned?"

"You see, it's dangerous for amateurs to play this game."

His mind racing, Daniel pivoted away from the bars and started to pace. Julian, murdered. "Your hand is in this."

"Not this time, Daniel."

Certain she was lying again, he rubbed his stubbled face. Father Julian must have been behind the intrigue from the start. Gaston was probably just a lackey. But why would the prior wait twenty-one years to do away with Lorelei?

Because she wasn't a threat until her identity became known. In his way, Julian had been fond of her. How could he not be?

But obviously greed had gotten the best of Julian and he'd decided to act, to secure the king's treasure for himself.

Then who, Daniel wondered, had poisoned the prior?

Josephine's low voice drifted through the silence. "I see I've given you much to ponder. And here's something more." She shoved the rolled pamphlet through the bars. "I thought this might relieve your boredom. And perhaps it will make you think twice about betraying our bargain." She turned to leave.

"Wait!"

She swung back, her face in shadow, but he could feel her sly smile like a sickness in his gut. "You've got to get me out of here," he stated.

"I have no further obligation to you, Daniel. I've given you what you asked—information about your wife."

Rage exploded in his chest. She was a master at exacting revenge. Leaving him to agonize over Lorelei's fate was a punishment far worse than death.

But he knew his adversary. He, too, could inflict wounds. "You're pathetic," he said softly. "I feel sorry for you."

"There's no need for that," she snapped.

"Pathetic," he repeated. "And scared."

"I fear nothing!" Her voice rose. The hood fell back, and torchlight glared over her face. "Nothing!"

"Oh, yes, you do. You have that special desperate fear of a woman who knows she's losing her hold on her youth, and on the husband who once adored her."

She gasped as if he'd struck her. "How dare you speak to me like that!"

"I'm a desperate man, Josephine. And a desperate man dares anything. You know, without face paint, you look your age. In another few years even cosmetics won't help you."

She bared her teeth, but he could see the tears in her eyes and knew his barb had sunk home. "You're beyond all help," she retorted. "I'm leaving." Her face haunted, she backed away.

A guard moved quickly to the doorway. The torchlight flickered off his face. Recognition stabbed at Daniel. It was Isambard, the man whose life he'd spared. It could have been a trick of the light, but Isambard seemed to fix him with a brief, penetrating stare. Then the door thumped closed.

Daniel walked to the low rope-sprung cot and sat down. The stench of moldering straw and mildewed paper thickened the air.

He dropped his head into his hands, his fingers sliding through his hair. "Oh, Lorelei," he whispered brokenly, "my love, where have you gone?"

With a wrenching sense of loss, he realized she was fleeing Paris, fleeing him.

As fresh and shining as a rose in springtime, her image came to haunt him.

*I can't heal you until you tell me where it hurts.*

I'm hurting now, Lorelei. Help me. Help me, please.

*It's odd, you've never said that you love me.*

I wanted to tell you, Lorelei. But I had no right. Not after all I did to you.

Seeking a diversion from his agonizing thoughts, he picked up the old faded pamphlet Josephine had left. The first few pages contained a collection of revolutionary ballads, the words full of innocent, lofty patriotism.

He shook his head. What would become of revolutionary ideals under Bonaparte? He was brilliant on the battlefield. He was the darling of Paris now. No one would gainsay him.

Except Meuron. At least Switzerland had a chance.

Daniel wished the thought could fill the grinding emptiness inside him.

He stood and paced the cell. Uncertainty nagged at him. He felt as if he were deciphering a puzzle in the dark. Father Julian had tried to murder Lorelei. Someone had killed Father Julian. Yet something didn't fit.

He paged through the booklet. Why had Josephine left it?

*Perhaps it will make you think twice about betraying our bargain.*

His chest tightened with dread. The bitch. Obviously she wasn't through with him yet.

A political cartoon caught his attention. He stared at an engraving of the sansculottes planting a tree of liberty in the breast of a dead Louis XVI. Thank God, he thought, that Lorelei never saw the hatred her father had inspired.

The mob scene in the drawing showed speech banners waving over a sea of distorted faces. Rubis, his earring exaggerated by the cartoonist, proclaimed victory. A gaunt Jacobin with a surgeon's wig crushed beneath his foot drew an oversized scalpel along the arm of a Royalist. The banner flowing from his mouth read, "Let the veins of France be purged of blue blood."

A woman representing the mother country suckled a litter of babies at her ample—

Daniel's gaze snapped back to the surgeon.

The artist had given him fanatical eyes, a twisted mouth. Yet something chillingly familiar lurked in the gross caricature.

"Oh . . . my . . . God," Daniel whispered. He crumpled the page in his hand. Stark terror iced his heart.

He knew who the killer was.

"Father Emile!" Lorelei leaned across the banquette of the posting chaise and jostled her companion. "Father Emile, look!"

The canon glanced up from his book, his features snapping to full alert and his hand plunging into the folds of his robe.

"I didn't mean to startle you," said Lorelei.

He pulled out his hand and smoothed his robe. "Quite all right. I was lost in thought."

"You've been that way since we left Paris, Father."

"I have preparations to make, devotions to say. My brothers at the hospice are in for a shock when they learn the sort of man their prior was. What was it you wanted, Lorelei?"

She pulled aside the leather curtain of the coach. "I can see the mountains at last, Father Emile. Look!"

Far in the distance, billowy clouds crowned the first thrusting peaks of the French Alps. Late summer foliage cloaked the mountains in a drapery of hard green and soft shadow creased by sparkling flows of water and patched in places by snow.

The very sight gave her a feeling of freedom and

openness, a poignant sense of homecoming. Yet at the same time loss twisted through her. How could the Alps, in all their majesty, ever be a home to her again when her heart and soul lay behind in Paris, at the feet of the man who had betrayed her?

Shuddering, she let go of the curtain and took out her rosary. An ache throbbed behind her eyes, but she could not cry. The tears that used to spill so easily were no balm to her shattered heart. Ironically, it was Daniel who'd taught her to face sorrow when, after Michel Toussaint's death, he'd shown her that no amount of weeping could repair a loss.

Yes, Daniel had taught her much: that people lie, that people hurt one another, that people will do anything for greed. Most unforgivable of all, he'd taught her that there was more to life than hiding at a mountain pass watching travelers cross, never to return. He'd made a permanent impression, but that would be her secret pain. Like her rosary, the memory of him was one to be taken out and agonized over in private.

She had to learn to live her life without him. In time the burden of loss would lighten.

Yet a feeling she couldn't deny pressed at her heart. She couldn't regret having known Daniel, couldn't regret having loved him. Whatever his motives, he'd made her feel love to the very depths of her soul, had opened her to a world of passion.

Damn you, she thought. I still love you.

She loved him because he'd taught her to believe in herself, to seek out the life she wanted. She loved him because, in the deepest moments of the night, he'd clasped her to him and murmured words of pain and joy in her ear.

She pulled her mind from the tormenting thoughts. "I hope Barry's all right. I wish we could have brought him."

"You have an entire pack of dogs awaiting you at the hospice. Bonaparte took a fancy to Barry. He'll treat the beast well."

She eyed him curiously. Lines of strain bracketed his mouth. "How did you know Bonaparte liked Barry?"

"Even men of the cloth are not insulated from Paris gossip." He checked the view again. "Geneva's two days' drive away. Bourg-Saint-Pierre's another two days farther." His pale eyes rested on her face. "After that, we'll travel on foot—alone."

# Chapter 20

The afternoon following Josephine's visit, Bonaparte appeared at the Chantereine. Flanked by his consular guards, he strode into the archival prison.

Maybe there is a God, thought Daniel, peering through the gloomy antechamber. The guards stepped outside while Bonaparte advanced. Clad in immaculate livery, the sash crossing his chest at a precise angle and his jackboots gleaming with a high sheen, the first consul emanated an aura of power and authority.

"You're a sorry sight," he said, tucking his bicorne hat beneath his arm and regarding Daniel's unkempt hair and clothes. "The Raven, caged like a songbird."

Daniel didn't rise to the taunt, for hope had begun

to carve an inroad into his desperation. "Sir, my wife—"

"Yes, let's talk of wives." Bonaparte's voice was a slash of anger. "My wife came to see you."

So he knew, thought Daniel. Isambard? Perhaps there was virtue in showing mercy. "She did," he said. But he had no time to discuss Josephine. "Lorelei is in danger. I must go to her."

"That's unfortunate. You shouldn't have broken the law."

Daniel studied the implacable face. It was time to call Josephine's bluff. "Meuron never took a sou from the Bern treasury. General, I can tell you where that gold is."

"The matter of the Bern gold is closed." The statement was slowly and deliberately spoken, Bonaparte's very tone an interdict against further discussion.

At that moment Daniel realized that the first consul knew the truth. And that—God curse Josephine's black soul—it made no difference. "I see," said Daniel. "But the matter of my wife, sir, is not."

"She has left Paris, which is best for all concerned." He shook his head. "Pity, she would have been an asset to the hospitals of the Republic. However, I assure you she's safe."

"No." Daniel reached into his soiled redingote, drew out the cartoon, and smoothed it against his thigh. "This was given to me by"—he hesitated, choosing his words carefully—"an individual who seems immune to the law."

"What's that?" Bonaparte squinted at the picture. "Who the devil is he?"

"He calls himself Father Emile, a canon of Saint Bernard. But clearly he's a Jacobin."

"A radical," Bonaparte spat.

Daniel detected a thrum of nervousness in the first consul's voice. "This radical has my wife, sir."

"Why did you not suspect him sooner?"

"He guarded his motives well. And I, like a blind fool, came to trust him after a certain incident."

Bonaparte lifted an eyebrow. "Go on."

"A ruffian tried to knife Lorelei, and Emile fought him off." Daniel shook his head in self-disgust. "I realize now the knife was meant for Emile. He was defending himself."

"Fouché's doing, no doubt. If Emile harbors Jacobin sympathies, Fouché would know about it. But what would he want with Lorelei? She's harmless. Married—for now, at least—to a commoner, and a foolish one at that."

"The man's dangerous." Daniel forced himself to speak calmly, though his every nerve burned with desperation. "Time hasn't cooled his hatred for the aristocracy. I've heard him air his views many times. Don't underestimate him, General. You've become a person of unparalleled importance. You can't afford to let radicals like Emile roam free, not even in Switzerland."

A tic started in Bonaparte's cheek. Absently he rubbed at it. He had a well-founded horror of assassination. "Fouché does his job well. No plot escapes him."

"Fouché's only one man. Your enemies are many."

Bonaparte grinned humorlessly, his mouth a dark slash in the gloom. "So I'm to believe you'll be my champion in this?"

"Was it Caesar who said, 'The enemy of my enemy is my friend?' "

Bonaparte shook his head. "I'm sorry for you, Daniel. If he means to kill Lorelei, he's had ample opportunity already."

Raw panic leaped in Daniel's stomach. Then a thought struck him. He remembered Emile's fastidious ways, his habit of cleaning and rearranging, as if he were looking for something. "Emile will take her back to the hospice first; I'm certain of it."

"Why?"

Daniel drew a deep breath. The time for keeping secrets was past. "Father Julian, the prior of Saint Bernard's, guarded a fortune in jewels, given to Lorelei by her father."

Bonaparte's eyes narrowed. "Louis left a treasure?"

Daniel nodded.

"How do you know of this?"

"I found mention of it in Father Julian's papers. I believe Emile intends to trick her into leading him to the treasure."

"Ah, greed. Now, there's something I can understand. Just where is this treasure?"

Daniel ground his teeth. "I don't know. Somewhere at the hospice." He glanced at the caricature, and his stomach clenched. His Lorelei was too fragile to combat the treachery of a man like Emile. "Look, once the treasure's found, it's yours. You can have it and everything else I possess—just let me go to her."

"You're quick to dispose of your wife's fortune, monsieur."

"As her husband, I have the right. All I want is Lorelei, General. Safe and sound."

"I don't need Louis Capet's money," said Bonaparte. "I have all of Europe at my feet. Besides, you're a prisoner of the Republic. You have no rights."

"So was Regulus a prisoner of the Carthaginians," Daniel shot back, an idea forming even as he spoke.

Bonaparte's eyes lit with interest. "He was indeed. Are you a student of the classics, then?"

Daniel raked a hand through his hair. "I'll play Regulus's part, and willingly."

"He made a costly bargain."

"One I'm prepared to make, sir." He swallowed past the dryness in his throat. "On my honor."

"Love," Bonaparte muttered, his mouth twisting with irony. "What fools it makes of us."

Daniel glanced up, frowning. "We are speaking not of love but of human decency. Lorelei is unique. She's a woman of great heart and a gifted healer. How can you sit by and let an outlaw like Emile rob the world of such a treasure?"

"It's love, pure and simple," said Bonaparte. "You'll argue the classics with me, make desperate bargains. Look at me, by God, and admit you love the girl."

His gaze met the first consul's stolid face. "I deceived her. I have no right—"

"Your rights be damned. You love the bastard princess. She loves you." Bonaparte squeezed his eyes shut and rubbed the bridge of his nose. Suddenly he looked older than his thirty years. Wiser. "Count yourself lucky you have her loyalty, her faith. For eight years you've wallowed in guilt over the massacre at the Tuileries. That guilt twisted you, my friend, and it will haunt you until you let it go."

Daniel braced himself. What else did Bonaparte know? That Daniel had been Josephine's lover? Was that why he refused to admit the truth about the stolen gold?

Bonaparte shook his head. "We know so little happiness in this life. You have a beautiful woman who loves you." His voice thickened and his eyes grew distant, and Daniel realized he was speaking of matters close to his own heart. "Aye, she loves you, and you love her. So simple is the binding of hearts. Know that the first consul of the Republic envies you."

Daniel blinked in surprise. This soldier, this conqueror, harbored the romantic nature of a poet. A nature that grappled with pain over the treachery of his wife.

"I do love her," Daniel whispered, pressing his forehead to the bars and uttering the words Lorelei had begged to hear. When? he wondered feverishly. When had he given his heart to her? He'd just pledged to give his own life for hers. This from the Raven, the soulless mercenary, the empty, wandering man. When had her life come to mean more to him than his own? And why did it no longer scare him to admit it?

The admission didn't matter, he conceded. She'd gently woven her way into his heart, sparked warmth in cold ashes, breathed life into a dead soul.

"What good does it do me?" he asked. "I face a death sentence."

"That's where you erred, my friend. A man was killed at the Chantereine. You're responsible for that crime."

A denial crowded into Daniel's throat, but he choked it off. To save his own life he would have to betray Sylvain.

"So you'll let a Jacobin do away with an innocent girl and help himself to King Louis's treasure?" Daniel demanded.

"You leap ahead too quickly. There are other matters to discuss before I make my decision. The old canon, Father Anselme, accuses you of having killed one of his brothers."

"In self-defense," Daniel stated. "Gaston was a Royalist. He was Lorelei's champion. I think he dreamed of seeing her make a marriage to a noble, restoring the royal luster to France."

Bonaparte scowled. "A fool's dream."

"Of course, but Gaston must have believed in it. He paid for it with his life." Daniel thought of the cleric toppling from the ridge, a raven-fletched arrow protruding from his breast. "By God, in the end we had the same purpose—to protect her life," he whispered. "Why could we not have worked together?"

"Secrets," muttered Bonaparte. "They kill like poison."

A silence drew out, Daniel in an agony of waiting. The first consul's stare pierced him like a surgeon's needle. "Regulus, you say?" he remarked at last. "I have not thought on that tale for a very long time. I should like to see if the Raven possesses such a sense of honor."

Two days and two hundred miles lay behind Daniel. Aching in every bone and joint, he melted from the saddle and tethered his rangy gray gelding near a stream. Evening light flickered off the ribbonlike surface of the narrow waterway. His senses buzzing with exhaustion, he stumbled down the bank, fell face first into the chilly water, and drank deeply.

Somewhat revived, he dragged himself up and loosened the horse's girth. The beast's thick neck, ridged with a huge windpipe, gave it uncommon stamina. The gelding had borne Daniel through faubourgs and forests, meadows and fens. They'd stopped only to snatch an hour of rest here and there.

But this evening he sensed the animal had reached its limit. Its long neck rippled as it drank. Daniel grabbed a handful of dry leaves, rubbed the tough, lathered hide, and reveled for a moment in the sharp, honest scent of sweat. He fetched a bag of sweetened oats from the saddlebag and placed it on the bank.

"Rest easy, my friend." He glanced at the fast-darkening sky. "But quickly. We can spare only a few hours." He lurched back up the bank and flung himself on the ground in the shade of a spreading alder. Blue flax and poppies rippled in a sea of color all around him; the heart-shaped leaves of the alder danced and shimmered before his eyes.

Through his exhaustion, he pondered the last forty-eight hours. It had been Isambard who had unlocked the door to his cell, Isambard who had, in whispers, let Daniel know that Josephine had been defeated at last.

"She's been banished to Malmaison, an obscure country estate," Isambard had said. "I've heard talk that a cache of Swiss gold has been recovered and returned to Bern."

Daniel knew Bonaparte would one day call her back, lavish her once again with his strange, consuming passion. But the incident had driven a wedge between them. Josephine would make more mistakes; Bonaparte's ambitions would broaden.

Daniel arranged his bow, arrows, and hunting knife—all given to him at the gates of Paris—close by.

The first stars of evening flickered through the leafy canopy. The horse made a contented grunting sound; then Daniel heard the quiet crunch of grain between the animal's teeth.

The incessant clamor of Paris lay far behind him. Here the quiet was deep and all-pervading, punctuated by the poignant trill of a nightingale and the chirp of a cricket. The smell of damp earth and fast-moving water surrounded him, and the cold purple sky glowed with a beauty that made his eyes ache.

Lorelei, he thought. I love you. I'm coming for you. . . . She filled his heart and mind with a soft sweetness. Love flowed through him like sap through trees in springtime. He wondered what he used to think about before her. He'd been nothing, no one. Loving her had given form and purpose to his life; it would give meaning to his death, if it came to that.

The thought wrapped him in a curious lassitude, and he drifted off, sucked into sleep by exhaustion.

Darkness lay thick when he awakened. An ominous noise had jarred him from sleep. He sat bolt upright.

A quarter-moon shone through the alder leaves. He cocked his head and listened.

Heavy panting and a shuffling of large feet sounded nearby. The horse's ears pricked. Daniel grabbed for his knife. His fingers were clumsy with sleep, but he managed to hold the blade low, the sharp edge up as he rolled into a crouch.

The snorting grew louder. A bear, perhaps, or a wolf. A chill touched the back of his neck. He'd bested a hungry bear once, but luck had played a part then. He wasn't feeling particularly lucky now.

Dry grass and leaves rustled, closer now. Daniel tensed.

The stalker burst through the underbrush. Moonlight glinted in yellow eyes. Black lips rolled back in a terrible grin.

The horse snorted and beat its hooves on the bank. The beast hurled itself at Daniel, huge paws slapping him to the ground.

Daniel's breath left him in a whoosh. His chest bucked beneath a leadlike weight. He stared up at the hot, slavering mouth, the teeth dripping with saliva. He smelled the beast's maw and grimaced.

"Christ," he muttered. "You're about as subtle as your mistress."

Barry yelped joyously and lapped at Daniel's face. Daniel scrubbed the slickness from his cheeks. "Enough," he commanded, thrusting the dog off his chest. "I'm happy to see you, too."

Bracing himself on his elbows, he stared at Barry and shook his head. "God, you're a wonder."

Barry bounded down to the stream. The horse looked on sharply, tense at the withers, tail snapping.

Barry waded into the stream. At its deepest, the

water only reached his chest. Undeterred, he plopped down full length in the water and drank enough to drown a pig.

Then, his brindled fur streaming, he pulled himself out and shook violently, subjecting Daniel, the horse, and everything within a radius of several yards to a thorough soaking.

Daniel wiped the water from his eyes. "By God," he said, "you've run two hundred miles."

Yet as astounding as Barry's unexpected appearance seemed, it was consistent with the dog's breeding and training. The mastiffs of Saint Bernard's were remarkable, and Barry embodied the best traits of all. It was no great task for a dog thus conditioned to follow Daniel's trail; his nose and his instinct had led him unerringly to his adopted master.

The dog flopped down beside Daniel and placed a huge wet paw in his lap. With a lurch of his heart, Daniel saw that the nails were worn to stubs, the pads cracked and red. He cleaned Barry's feet and gave him some meat and cheese from the saddlebag. The dog devoured the meal, then trotted eastward along the road and yelped impatiently.

Daniel bolted to his feet and tightened the cinch of the horse's saddle. He trusted the dog's instincts.

For three days they traveled at a punishing pace. On the fourth day, when dawn broke, the gilt rays spread over the thrusting, jagged line of the Alps.

At Bourg-Saint-Pierre Daniel inquired at the posting inn.

"A young girl and a cleric?" the proprietor repeated. "Of course I remember such a pair. You've just missed them, monsieur. They set out for the hospice an hour ago."

With Bourg-Saint-Pierre an hour behind her, Lorelei tilted her head back and regarded the clarion-clear morning sky. "The weather's perfect, Father," she said. "Sylvain once told me the climb takes eight hours. I wager we'll reach the hospice in seven."

Father Emile lifted an eyebrow. "A wager, you say? And just what have you to wager?"

Despite his teasing tone, she flushed with guilt. She really felt that she should tell him about Father Julian's last words, concerning the fortune held for her at the hospice. But the dying man had been adamant about keeping the treasure a secret. In those last moments, he might have been mistaken, too, the jewels a product of a sick man's ravings.

"Sylvain and I used to make outrageous wagers," she confessed, adjusting the buckle of her rucksack. "It was just a game we played. Of course, we never paid on any bets."

Father Emile's face creased with disapproval. "I always thought the boy an insincere novice. In fact, I advised against taking him on charity."

"Sylvain was—" She broke off and ducked her head. So much had changed. Hardening her resolve, she placed one foot firmly in front of the other. "Sylvain and I were the best of friends once," she finished lamely.

"You've been hurt. I see you're worldly-wise now," said Father Emile, his hand gripping her sleeve. "You'll find an end to your troubles at Saint Bernard's."

"Will I?" A chill passed over her skin. "I'm not sure." She continued up the sinuous path. "I used to be afraid of the world beyond the mountains. How childish that seems now. The only thing I have to fear is the greed and dishonesty of men." She thought of Josephine and added, "And women."

Much of the day passed without conversation. In distant meadows surrounded by glaciers, herds of goats grazed. From time to time a shepherd shouted or yodeled a greeting. Signs of the army's passage lay about: guideposts and sledge tracks, a swatch of cloth torn from a uniform, a chicken carcass picked clean, cigar butts ground flat by boot heels.

With a twist of inner pain, she remembered her journey with Daniel, sharing a meal with him while sitting on a gun sledge, flinging her arms around him when he agreed to bring Barry along. It all seemed like a dream now.

The air thinned, and the trees grew sparse. Father Emile's breath quickened. Lorelei exhorted him to slow his pace, but he pressed doggedly upward. They reached the line of eternal snow, where hard-packed patches of ice hid in the shadows and last season's snow overhung the path.

"I'd forgotten the silence," said Lorelei, sidestepping a small rockfall. "The blessed, lonely silence."

Farther up, more rockfalls blanketed a section of road that curved around the sheer face of the mountain. The very top of a guidepost poked above the pile of loose rubble. Father Emile came up short. Something that sounded like a curse escaped him.

Lorelei regarded him in surprise. "Father, I've never known you to swear."

"I fear a delay," he muttered, "and don't relish passing a night on the mountain."

She planted her hands on her hips. Her gaze followed the spill of rocks upward to its source, a precipice heavy with rock, ice, and snow.

"We can't climb over this," he said.

She scaled several feet up the mass of rubble. Pebbles rained down into the gorge that slashed through the mountains.

"Lorelei, be careful!" the canon said. "You could fall!"

But the loose gravel felt familiar beneath her booted feet. No danger served up by nature could equal the treachery she'd faced in Paris. She studied the terrain, then gave a shout of elation. "Father Emile, I've found a way!"

Moving cautiously, he climbed up beside her, and she pointed at a huge uprooted tree amid the rubble. Its great trunk slanted upward, nearly spanning the deep canyon. Large branches, thick with summer foliage, radiated out from the trunk. The topmost branches just brushed the next bend in the road, linking it with the section that had been covered by the avalanche.

"We'll use the tree as a bridge," she said.

Father Emile touched her shoulder. She felt the tension in his fingers. "It doesn't quite reach the road," he said glumly.

"We can climb the last bit." She handed a length of

rope to him. "Here. I don't want to see you fall into that gully."

They approached the fallen tree that spanned the deep gorge. An unseen waterfall crashed over rock far below.

"I'll go first," said Lorelei, securing the rope around her while Father Emile tied the other end to himself.

"I think not, my child. It's safer for you to follow."

She faced him solemnly. "Father Emile, I have great respect for the dangers of the mountains. But it's time I learned to get on by myself, don't you think?"

Without waiting for a reply, she pulled herself onto the tree trunk, then turned to see that he followed.

The canon surmounted the fan of muddy roots and straddled the thick trunk, his robes snagging on the dry bark.

She inched across, pausing now and then to glance back at Father Emile and to keep a safe length of rope between them. Great branches hampered the way and caught at the rope. Birds swooped through the canyon, caught on skirling updrafts of wind.

A sudden sense of exhilaration gripped her. She would carry on without Daniel, just as surely as she would cross this gorge.

Her boots were worn from the many miles she'd traveled in them. She prayed the thin soles wouldn't slip. Inch by precarious inch, she led the way across the makeshift bridge.

The wind howled through the canyon. Shadowy gullies spun ominously below her. She tore her gaze from the dizzying sight and grasped a stout vertical branch.

Their pace slowed as the girth of the tree trunk narrowed. Sticky sap tugged at the soles of her boots. The incessant breeze caught Father Emile's robes and raised a shimmer of sound amid the dying leaves of the tree.

The trunk sagged beneath their weight. Slender, supple branches whipped at Lorelei's face and hair. The road still lay several feet ahead of her, the gap wider than it had looked from the other end of the tree. Between the makeshift bridge and the road lay a drop too deep and treacherous to contemplate.

"I'll need more rope." She unfastened a second coil from her rucksack and edged forward. The tree bowed. Gasping, she held fast to a branch, then made a loop in the end of the rope and tossed it at the thick wooden supports beneath the road.

After several tries, the rope caught. She gave a tug, then started to climb.

"Be careful," said Father Emile.

She pulled herself closer and closer to the planked road. Her shoulders trembled with the effort. She could hear the wheeze of Father Emile's breath behind her. Loose rock crumbled beneath her feet, the sounds echoing across the yawning canyon.

The rough rope blistered her hands. As she whispered a disjointed prayer, an image of Daniel drifted unaccountably into her mind. She saw him clearly, the sharp blue of his eyes, his laughing mouth and thick black hair slashed by pure white. She shook her head. She should not be thinking of him at a time like this. She should not be thinking of him at all.

She leaped toward the rock face below the road.

The sheer stone raced to meet her. Putting out her

feet, she stopped the arc of motion. For a sickening moment, the rope went slack. She fell.

Gasping, she scrabbled for purchase. One hand found a stout support beneath the road. The weathered wood was slippery from snowmelt. Splinters dug into her palm, but she ignored the pain and heaved herself up onto the road.

"It's not quite as easy as I thought it would be," she called to Father Emile. "Do be careful."

He swung across on the rope and thudded against the rock. Lorelei held her breath as loose earth swished down into the gorge. An ominous creak sounded, followed by a loud snap.

"Lorelei!"

She grabbed his wrist. His legs dangled over the bottomless canyon. A hiss of terror escaped his lips.

"No!" she said through gritted teeth. "I won't lose you, too." She pulled, dragging him over the edge to the surface of the road. The wooden support plummeted into the canyon so far below that she couldn't hear it land. A sound of relief burst from him. He lay trembling while he caught his breath.

"We're even now, Father Emile," she said, grinning weakly.

He gave her an odd look.

"You saved me from the ruffian in Paris," she reminded him. "And now I've returned the favor."

"Thank God for that," he muttered.

"I'll make you an infusion of sassafras tea when we get to the hospice. It's good for the nerves."

"That would be most agreeable." He heaved himself up and began coiling the ropes.

She rose to her feet and brushed the mud from his robe. "Look, your cincture has come unknotted." She reached for his scourge.

He pushed her hands away. "It's quite all—"

"Father Emile?" She stared through a gap in the homespun fabric. A dull metallic gleam had caught her eye. "You're carrying a pistol. Why?"

A flush rose in his cheeks. "Because," he said, tightening the knot of his scourge, "travel is dangerous, even for a man of the cloth. Thank the Lord I haven't had to use it."

As they resumed their trek, unease niggled at her. Hospice rules forbade the canons to carry weapons. Still, Father Emile meant to protect her. She thought of the man with the ruby earring and shuddered. It was only sheer luck that they hadn't encountered any brigands this time.

Over the rising wind, a new sound drifted to her ears. She stopped. "What was that?"

He shrugged. "Probably falling rock. We loosened it on our climb."

"No, it's—" The sound came again. A smile broke over her face. "I hear barking. It must be one of the dogs from the hospice."

Father Emile looked at the rising road and scratched his head. "I see nothing."

"Not in that direction." She rushed to the edge of the path and gazed down at the rocky terrain and Alpine meadows. A flock of goats, so distant they resembled grains of sand against a field of green, grazed far below. The goatherd's dog? she wondered.

A streak of brown and white flashed through the trees.

"Barry," she said.

"Absurd," said Father Emile. "It can't be, the animal's in Paris."

"And Daniel!" She clenched her hands to her heart. The tall man hurrying behind Barry was unmistakable, the white in his hair flying like a banner amid the black locks. Unbearable emotion rose in her chest. "Oh, Father, he's come for me, it must mean—"

A dull click stopped her. She swung back to see Father Emile cocking the pistol.

Confusion broke over her, swiftly followed by dread. "No!" She lunged for the weapon.

"Stay back," he ordered, holding the weapon away from her. "The bastard came to murder you once. Do you think I'll let him try again?"

He raised the pistol and laid it expertly across his wrist. Daniel and Barry moved in and out among the trees. Emile swore, the words sounding alien on a cleric's tongue.

She tugged at his sleeve. "Please, Father. You're a man of God."

"And Severin's the devil himself!" He shook off her hand.

She bit her lip. She knew the canon could be right. But images of Daniel swam through her mind, unchecked by the bitterness she'd nurtured during the long journey from Paris.

She couldn't believe he was the same man who'd set out to hunt her down. He'd risked his life to protect her. He'd taught her to love deeply, desperately, in a way no murderer could have. The fact that he'd come after her sparked a feeling of unconditional joy. She wanted to hear him declare that he'd changed, that he'd turned from his mercenary ways.

"I beg you," she said, "give him a chance."

He lowered the gun, but kept his finger on the trigger. "A chance to kill you?"

"To explain. Perhaps I was wrong to leave Paris so hastily. Perhaps he changed—"

"Or perhaps he saw another way to use you." Father Emile squinted through the trees. Daniel and Barry had reached the rockfall that blocked the road. As sure-footed as a goat, the dog leaped unhesitatingly over the loose rock. Daniel began crossing the uprooted tree.

The canon sighted down the barrel of the pistol.

Lorelei grabbed his arm. "Father Emile, I love him!" She reached for the gun, felt the cold black metal in her fingers. Father Emile's face was very close. His eyes burned with fury, and his lips were drawn back in a snarl.

Terrified, she wrenched the pistol from his hand. It dropped to the ground with a thud. Shoving her back, Father Emile dived for the weapon, seized it, then whirled on her.

"Don't be a fool, my child," he said, breathing hard. "The man coerced you into marriage and hid the truth of your birth from you. How can you love him?"

She threw a desperate glance at the fallen tree. Daniel was halfway across. His lips moved, but the words were lost to the wail of the wind, the echoes of the rockfall, the sounds folding over one another.

"Because he protected me when he could have lined

his pockets with Josephine's gold," she whispered. "Because he believed in me when Father Julian forbade me to pursue my medical studies." The wind lashed her face, bringing tears to her eyes. "And because he touched my heart, Father. I can't explain it any better than that."

His eyes narrowed. "What would you give to spare his worthless life?"

"Anything. My own life."

"The secret Father Julian left with you?"

"What does Father Julian's deathbed confession have to—"

"Deathbed?" Emile's eyebrows shot up. "You mean he didn't tell you until he lay dying?" He stiffened, seeming to conquer his surprise, and muttered, "Stupid of me. I should have made certain . . . Just tell me where the treasure is, and you can have your mercenary."

Daniel faltered on the tree trunk, grabbing at a branch to steady himself. Lorelei had no time to wonder how Emile had guessed about the treasure. "In the sacristy," she blurted. "The jewels set in the pewter monstrance aren't paste; they're diamonds and rubies that once belonged to Marie Antoinette. Now, please, Father, put the gun—"

He gave her a look of wonder. "You mean it's been in plain sight all these years? My God, that's an irony. I've handled it myself a hundred times. . . ."

She stopped listening. Daniel had nearly reached the topmost part of the tree. He moved with frantic speed in and out among the leafy branches.

"Lorelei!" His voice echoed across the canyon. "Run! Get away from him. He's the—"

The pistol jerked and exploded. Loose gravel and old snow pelted her from above. Daniel dropped from sight.

Horror burst in her chest. A scream ripped from her throat, and she lunged at Father Emile. His wiry strength resisted her pummeling fists.

"Monster!" she shrieked at him. "You promised—"

"I promised nothing to you." His arm swung out. The gun clubbed her across the face. She reeled back. A shattering pain numbed her cheek.

Calmly Emile reloaded the pistol.

Disbelief swirled like a fog around her. Daniel was gone. The realization filled her with an agony that promised to last an eternity. Her Daniel, her fierce, vital husband, was lost to her forever. She would never hear what he'd come to tell her.

"Oh, Daniel," she whispered, staring at the fallen tree and pressing her cold hand to her cheek. The wind jerked at the branches. The bottom of the canyon lay out of sight, but she pictured him lying broken and bleeding in the icy black shadows. "My love, what have I done?"

"You won't have long to grieve, princess." Emile's mouth made an ugly twist of irony. She stared at him over the black barrel of the pistol.

"F-father Emile? What are you doing?"

"What men who love liberty have been doing for ten years."

The wind stung her eyes, her lips. "I don't understand."

"I have what I want now. Control of the hospice. And Louis Capet's treasure."

Daniel's last words echoed back to her. *Run! Get away from him. He's the—*

Her face drained of color. "It was you, wasn't it?" she asked. "You tried to kill me. Father Emile, why?"

"The world must be rid of Louis's bastard. You're a threat to liberty."

She trembled like a leaf on the wind. Oh, God, a moment ago she'd saved his life. Only to let him take Daniel from her. Grief and horror tumbled through her mind. "But—but it was Father Gaston. He tried to murder me!"

"Not him." Emile snorted in disgust. "He revered you. He had grandiose visions of seeing you royally wed and the dynasty carried on. He was your champion. Foolish girl. It was the Raven he was trying to kill." Emile's lips thinned in a humorless grin. "Gaston's idiocy played right into my hands."

She saw a distant movement over his shoulder.

Barry. The mastiff had climbed the rockfall and was above them now, bounding down toward the road.

Instinct kept her from betraying what she'd seen, from revealing the sudden sick hope that charged through her.

"But you've known who I am since last summer," she said. Slowly, carefully, she got to her feet.

"So I have," he admitted. "Gaston again. How I wish he could know how much he helped the cause of liberty."

She took a tentative step forward. The man was nervous. She observed the shifting gaze, the unsteady hand. If she could keep him talking, perhaps she could find a way out. "Why didn't you simply murder me as soon as you learned my identity?"

With each second Barry was coming closer, leaping over the rockfall.

She drew a shaky breath. Perhaps someone at the hospice had heard the gunshot. The shot that had killed Daniel. Soon she would join him, she thought. Then her indifference changed to icy rage. Not like this. Not at the hands of a fanatic like Emile.

"I had no success finding the treasure," he said. "Besides, you were no threat so long as you remained at the hospice. In truth, it amused me to see a royal princess cleaning bedpans, soiling her hands on other people's running sores." His voice slashed through the wail of the wind.

She prayed he couldn't hear Barry's approach. The dog reached another rockfall and scaled it with ease, reappearing on the slope above.

"Your royal soul was mired in tasks befitting a slave. I only wish your father could have witnessed your debasement." Emile's mouth contracted. He seemed to savor his victory like fine wine. "Tell me, did you love the court as Louis did?"

"I prefer the mountains of Switzerland," she stated, keeping her eyes from the small approaching figure. "But that day in Paris . . . you saved my life when that ruffian attacked me."

He shook his head. "A mistaken perception. He was after me, my dear. Sent by Fouché. Prior Julian started to have fits of conscience about the treasure. That was why I had to eliminate him, too."

"Poison," she said, the bile rising in her throat. "You poisoned him with the arsenic in Daniel's rucksack. That's why there was so little left in those vials." She took a step back. Bits of ice and rock, loosened by the gunshot, still rained from above. "God help me, I accused Father Julian on his deathbed of betraying me for the sake of the treasure."

"I'm sure he's forgiven you. The idiot was as blindly devoted to you as Gaston—and every other fool at Saint Bernard's."

Emile cocked the pistol. "Good-bye, princess. Take comfort in this: Marie Antoinette's jewels will fuel my cause, and your blue blood will water the tree of liberty."

Lorelei held her breath. Daniel, she thought. She would die with his image in her heart.

Emile's eyes burned with self-righteous fire. His finger tightened on the trigger.

A scrabbling sound broke from above. From the bank behind Emile a blaze of white and brown flew downward.

Barry's jaws closed around the canon's extended arm. With a rough cry of surprise, Emile fell sideways. The pistol thumped to the ground.

Lorelei stumbled forward. Emile made a gurgling noise that mingled with Barry's growls. A knife flashed. Emile jabbed the wicked point at Barry. The blade made an arc toward the snarling dog and came away slick with blood.

Hatred invaded Lorelei's heart. This man had killed Father Julian and Daniel, the two people she loved most in the world. He would not kill again.

"No more!" she screamed, snatching up the pistol. It felt curiously hard and heavy in her shaking hand. She aimed at Emile's head and fired.

His skull exploded in a hail of red. Shock broke over Lorelei. Never had she believed herself capable of acting so quickly, so coldly.

Thunder sounded above, punctuated by a storm of rock and snow. She looked up to see a vast shelf of snow loosen and come hurtling toward her.

The second gunshot reverberated through the canyon. His hands raw from grasping the hanging limb, Daniel jerked as if he'd been hit.

"Lorelei!" He shouted her name, but the sound was lost to the unearthly noise of the avalanche. He strained to see through the thick leaves, but could make out only patches of sky and a rising cloud of dust. The tree shuddered violently, and debris pounded at the branches. Gravel poured into the chasm.

Grim determination and cold horror firmed his tenuous hold on the limb. Instinctively seeking cover, he'd dropped from the tree, barely managing to grab a branch and avoid plummeting to his death.

His feet kicked at empty air. He looked down, saw a cloud of dust rising from the shadows at the bottom of the gorge. An urge to let go prodded him. Go ahead, said a voice in his mind. Rid the world of your worthless soul.

He could think of no good reason to live, for if the shot hadn't killed Lorelei, the avalanche surely had.

Still, hope flickered in his aching heart. She'd taught him to hope. As long as there was a chance that she lived, he would risk a lifetime of loneliness and torment to get to her.

With the sheer strength of his arms, he pulled himself up along the branch. The limb bent and cracked. His heart jolted with fear, but he climbed doggedly on, knotting the muscles of his arms, sucking air between his clenched teeth.

Swinging his legs, he wrapped them around the main trunk. The air vibrated with the lingering aftershocks of the avalanche.

From some point above, Barry yelped frantically.

Daniel's hopes flared higher, almost blinding him in their intensity.

The tree trunk narrowed as he reached the end. Two yards lay between the makeshift bridge and the supports beneath the road. Without a second's hesitation, he jumped. Sailing through cold, empty air, he discovered that he very much wanted to live. The realization charged through him with a power that took his breath away.

He slammed into the broken wooden structure beneath the road and clambered to the surface. Pain tore through his side, but he ignored it, his senses focused on reaching Lorelei.

He found the dog digging at a huge mound of rock and snow.

"Oh, God, no." He dropped to his knees beside the dog and plunged his hands into the rubble. The snow stung his blistered palms. "Please, God," he murmured over and over, his cheeks hot with alien tears. "Please, God."

Barry gave a muffled woof. Daniel dug deeper. He

found a limb. An arm, perhaps. Something wet. Blood.

Oh, Jesus, he thought. He wasn't an experienced rescuer. Should he pull her out quickly and risk further injury? Or should he excavate slowly and risk suffocating her?

He grasped the limb and hauled with all his might. The body emerged. Barry whined and shrank back.

Vomit burned Daniel's throat. It was Emile. His head was shot through, his mouth open in a silent scream.

She killed him, thought Daniel. Dear God, I made her kill.

Barry erupted into motion again, snow and dirt flying between his powerful legs. Thrusting away the murderer's body, Daniel threw himself down to help.

As the moments passed, panic scoured his guts. She'd been under tons of snow and ice too long to have survived.

Barry woofed three times in succession. Daniel's hand encountered something. A fabric-clad arm or leg. Cold as the snow that entombed her.

He pulled her from the rubble and brushed the dust from her pale face. It was lovely still, but tragically empty of the glowing animation that had made Lorelei so unique, so wonderful.

Barry stretched out beside her and lapped at her cheeks.

Daniel bent his face to hers, trying to discern the warmth of her breath. He felt only the icy blast of the Alpine wind.

# Chapter 21

"We've done everything we can, Daniel," said Father Droz. "But with Father Anselme away . . ." He gazed sadly at the still figure on the cot. A glow from the new infirmary stove bathed Lorelei's waxen face in a warm gold and tinged her curls to deep ruby. Beneath a layer of blankets, her chest rose and fell faintly.

The rasp of a sled drifted through the window. The men were bringing Emile's body up from the pass. The dogs barked in the kennel yard. Daniel knew the canons deserved news of Father Julian, but in the hours since he'd arrived with his precious burden, he hadn't had the heart to speak.

Father Clivaz placed his hand on Daniel's shoulder. "Come. You should eat something. You need to rest."

"No." Daniel's voice grated hollowly in the quiet room. "I'm staying with my wife."

"Your wife?" Father Clivaz and Father Droz spoke as one. Murmurs erupted from the others in the doorway.

Daniel flung them a challenging look. But he saw no dour accusation on their faces, only approval tinged with sadness.

Dropping to his knees, he leaned over Lorelei and buried his face in the fragrant silk of her hair. "Please don't go," he begged. "Please." Loving her had been such a struggle. To lose now would tear the heart from him.

His pleas whispered through the infirmary. Father Clivaz and Father Droz moved to the door, where the others pressed close, silent and waiting. After a time they withdrew to say a mass for Lorelei, leaving Daniel with his fear and his pain.

He felt helpless, shackled by his own ignorance. They had examined Lorelei for broken bones and bleeding. They'd found minor bruises, but the cause of her unconsciousness eluded them. It was possible, he knew, for a person to bleed to death from the inside. He wished desperately for a fraction of the knowledge stored in Lorelei's wonderful mind. She would have known what to do. He knew only how to take lives, not how to restore them. Enveloped in a cloud of hopelessness, he bowed his head again.

"Please, I love her so. I beg you, don't take her from me."

Lorelei heard the familiar voice whispering to her. She thought she must be dreaming. Daniel was dead. She'd seen him fall.

She forced her eyes open. His haggard face came into hazy focus. Love and wonderment spilled through her, pushing past her doubts and fears. The man beside her, his eyes squeezed shut and his hands clasped in prayer, was no dream.

"I'm not . . . going anywhere," she said faintly.

His head jerked up. "Lorelei?" A deep sweetness she had never seen before radiated from his face. "My God, I was afraid you'd . . . Are you all right?"

She lay still, mentally examining herself. Her cheek throbbed, and her limbs ached, but she sensed strongly that her injuries were slight. "I think so. I'm hungry."

Elation flashed in his eyes. "I'll call for food. Yes. You'll need food." He sprang up, ran to the door, and bellowed an order to Mauricio. Shouts of gratitude came in answer.

Lorelei trembled inside. She was home. These were her lifelong friends, and yet the idea of facing them now filled her with trepidation. She was no longer the child they'd loved and cared for. There were so many explanations to make; she didn't know where to begin.

"Tell someone to bring the monstrance from the sacristy," she said to Daniel. He glanced back at her and frowned. "Just do it," she said. "I'll explain later. But . . . tell them to give me a little time to . . . I'm still not ready to see them."

He relayed the request to a lay brother. Then he pulled a stool to the bedside and sat down. Still his eyes held that unaccustomed brightness, as if sunlight had banished the shadows that had haunted them.

She pushed herself up on her elbows. Spots danced before her eyes. Sick guilt gripped her heart. "I killed Emile."

"I know. It was my fault. I should have—"

"No, Daniel. He died by my hand."

She wished he would touch her, but he remained still, watching her, his eyes full of pain now.

"I thought he'd killed you," she said. "I saw you fall."

"I fell, but the bullet missed."

Still, the ugliness lingered like an incurable disease. "I killed a man," she repeated.

He leaned forward. After a moment's hesitation, he laid his palm on the back of her hand. His skin was rough, broken.

"You killed a monster," he said. "He was no man of the cloth but a notorious Jacobin, a murderer."

"He wanted to be prior. And he wanted my fath—King Louis's legacy."

"Father Julian told you of the treasure?"

"Just before he died. That was why Emile took me away from Paris. I thought—" She bit her lip, took a deep breath, and continued. "I thought he meant to protect me—from you."

Daniel's mouth twisted in a grimace. "I've made so many mistakes in my life. So many of them. But the worst was deceiving you and denying what was in my heart."

She barely listened, for ghastly memories pounded

at her. "I should have thought of another way to stop him—"

"No," he said, his voice harsh. "Life is precious. You know that better than I. But Emile forfeited his right to live. If you'd spared him, he'd have killed again and again. You must believe that, Lorelei."

She shuddered. "So many have died because of who I am."

He took both her hands, holding them tightly in his. "Don't Lorelei," he said, his voice low and fierce. "Don't you dare blame yourself or feel guilty for anything that's happened."

She pondered his words, and a measure of peace invaded her soul. She knew then that she would be able to live with what she'd done.

"My God," said Daniel, "in all of this you've been a victim, blameless, while I—" Abruptly he let go of her hands as if afraid of infecting her with some sickness.

There was so much to say, so much she had to know, even if it meant laying them both open to unspeakable pain. "I found your rucksack among Father Julian's effects," she said.

He swallowed. His face grew paler. "Oh, God."

"Daniel, why did you agree to Josephine's plan?"

He ran his fingers through his hair. "I thought she owned me."

"Owned you? You mean, because of what the two of you—" She broke off and looked away, unable to continue.

"Because we'd been lovers." He spat the words. "That was part of it. But telling Bonaparte would have been worse for her than for me. It was her threats against Jean Meuron that lured me into her trap. A word from her, and he'd have been executed."

"What is Meuron to you?"

"It's not what he is to me that's important," said Daniel, "but what he is to Switzerland."

"Another secret you kept from me." Her voice was ragged with pain. "Just as you have so many things from the very start. Why did you pretend you'd lost your memory after the avalanche?"

He hunched his shoulders with guilt. "It was a way to buy time while I recovered. My guess is that Gaston realized why I had come to the hospice. He tried to stop me before I could . . ." His voice trailed off, and he hung his head.

"Kill me," she finished for him. With bitter shame she recalled the hours she'd spent confiding her hopes and dreams to "Wilhelm," hungering for his touch, his kisses, conniving to be alone with him. "You had ample chances to do away with me. What made you decide not to?"

"You," he confessed. "You, my darling. Even I wasn't so hardened that I could have harmed a single hair on your head."

She sighed and rested her chin on her knees. "But you knew my father was responsible for the death of eight hundred Swiss Guards. How could you look at me and not remember that?"

"How can I look at you and not love you?" He reached for her hand again, cradling it in his raw, blistered palm.

His declaration of love left her feeling dazed. She'd

waited so long to hear him say it, but she couldn't let herself believe him. Not yet.

"You've healed me of those memories, Lorelei. Now when I think of Paris, I remember dancing with you in the Tuileries gardens, making love to you. . . ." He gave a crooked half smile. "Seeing you and Barry terrorizing Josephine's rug louse."

Shivering, she gazed out the narrow window. The sky held a purplish tinge, and the wind carried the first crisp hint of twilight. "You say Josephine can use her influence against Meuron. What's to stop her from having him executed now?"

His mouth tautened, not with a smile but with grim satisfaction. "Meuron is free. He's in Switzerland."

She blinked in surprise. "How do you know?"

"I helped liberate him."

"You brought him to Switzerland?"

"No. I was caught during the escape."

"You were imprisoned?" She tried to picture him cornered, threatened by armed guards. The picture wouldn't form, for Daniel was nothing if not wholly committed to his own freedom.

"I was imprisoned," he said. "Charged with treasonous conspiracy . . . and murder."

She bit her lip. "You killed again."

"Not this time. But Bonaparte holds me responsible."

"Yet here you are. You, too, must have escaped."

He shook his head. "Not for want of trying. But it was Bonaparte who let me come after you."

At last all came clear in her mind. "You deny being

a man of honor. Yet you gave up your freedom for Meuron."

"I'm willing to give my very life to keep you safe, Lorelei," he said quietly.

The words rolled over her like a fresh wind off the mountains, making her feel light and clean and airy. She realized that this was a new Daniel, not the mercenary who'd come to the hospice with murder in his heart. She grasped his hand and held it tightly. Steady warmth thrummed across the bond, but it wasn't enough. "Hold me, Daniel," she pleaded.

He eyed her warily. "I don't want to hurt you."

"I won't break. Just hold me."

"You should hate me," he said in a tortured voice.

"I tried." She smiled weakly. "I found it impossible." His thumb moved over her wrist; then his arms settled gently around her.

"No, really hold me," she pleaded, "as if you'll never let me go."

He moved to the edge of the cot and buried his face in her hair. He wished the moment could go on forever, that he could bask in her love until he died.

But he couldn't. He'd given his word to Bonaparte that he would return to Paris to answer the charges. He had no doubt about the outcome. He'd be executed. What an inconvenient time, he thought wryly, to discover a sense of honor in himself.

But Lorelei had given him the gift of her forgiveness. At least now he could go with a peaceful heart.

A knock sounded at the door. Reluctantly he moved away from her sweet embrace and went to open it. In walked Mauricio bearing a tray with enough food fo a small army. Father Clivaz carried the monstrance. Behind them were the canons and novices, their faces wreathed in smiles when they saw Lorelei sitting up, her cheeks now flooding with color. The affection these men felt for her was tangible, like thick smoke in the air.

"Please, sit down, all of you," she said, her level gaze touching each man in turn. Typically, she paid no heed to her mussed hair or her rumpled shirt, which gaped open at the neck. She took a deep breath, then said, "Father Julian died in Paris. Father Emile poisoned him."

A chorus of gasps rose. Hands fluttered as the men swiftly crossed themselves. "But why? What would make our brother do such a thing?" asked Father Droz.

"He was not your brother, but an impostor," said Lorelei. "Hand me the monstrance, Father Clivaz." He gave her the big pewter vessel. Its tumbled jewels caught the light, casting deep ruby and emerald prisms on the plank floor.

Suddenly Daniel realized what she was holding. Her father's treasure. All these years it had been hidden in plain sight.

She weighed the battered vessel in her hands, then slowly turned it over, rubbing her finger across the mark stamped on the bottom. Daniel was unprepared for the utter desolation that haunted her face. He moved to her side and placed his hand on her stiff shoulder. A light from Father Droz's lantern picked out the markings: LPB. Louis Philippe de Bourbon. Her father.

"The jewels in this piece," Lorelei said in a shaky

voice, "are all genuine. They were sent by King Louis the Sixteenth to Father Julian for safekeeping."

Robes swished and stools scraped as the men edged closer.

She regarded them sadly. "The treasure was left to me, although I didn't know it until Father Julian confessed the truth on his deathbed. You see, I am King Louis's bastard daughter."

A babble of voices rose. Daniel yearned to gather her into his arms, but she held up her hand for silence and he knew she needed to continue. Whispers and gasps punctuated her speech as she told of her birth at Yverdon and how Julian and Father Anselme had kept her secret. Then she spoke of Emile and Gaston, the attempts on her life, her adventures in Italy and Paris.

Never once did she mention that Daniel had been at the very center of all the plots. He felt such an outpouring of love and gratitude that tears stung his eyes.

Having finished her tale, Lorelei thrust the monstrance at Father Droz. "The fortune is mine, but I will use only what I need to pursue my studies. The rest belongs to the hospice."

Father Droz moved to take the heavy vessel, handling it as if it were contaminated.

"Visitors coming!" called Timon, skidding into the room.

Daniel held his breath, then burst out: "Who?"

Timon grinned. "Just wait, monsieur. You'll see." From outside came the clamor of voices, the stamping of boots.

Christ, thought Daniel, has Bonaparte no faith at all in my word? He got up and rushed to the door.

Lorelei watched a group of men push into the infirmary. At the front was a familiar stooped figure.

"Father Anselme," she whispered.

"Lorelei, my dear child, thank God you're safe." He hugged her briefly. His woolly scent enveloped her, and she wondered how she'd ever suspected him of betraying her.

"You know about Emile?" she asked.

"I know what that impostor tried to do to you," said the old canon, gesturing at his companions. "We all do." He eyed the monstrance in Father Droz's hands. "And you've found your legacy as well. God forgive Julian for waiting so long to tell you about it. Child, you should have come to me before leaving Paris. I could have told you, spared you—"

"I didn't know whom to trust," she said. "But I never should have doubted you, Father."

"It's done," said Daniel quietly, "and you're safe."

She nodded, then looked up to study the men who had come in with Father Anselme. Everard, the courier, gave her a broad grin. Eyeing her uncertainly, Sylvain stepped forward. "It's good to see you, Lorelei," he said. "God, I'm sorry. So sorry for all—"

"Hush," she said, tears pricking her eyes. "I know now what necessity makes men do."

Another man moved from the doorway to stand beside Daniel.

The breath caught in her throat. She blinked twice, three times, but the astonishing vision remained. Though painfully thin, the man had Daniel's proud bearing. He had the same handsome face, softer, perhaps, than Daniel's, but the same blue eyes and black hair, lacking only Daniel's streak of white.

"Sweet holy Mary," said Lorelei, clutching the bedclothes. "You're brothers."

Daniel and the stranger moved close to her. "This is Jean Meuron," said Daniel. "My half brother."

At last she understood. His blood brother had been in peril. Josephine had given him no choice but to do her bidding.

"I'm pleased to meet you," she said slowly.

"Not as pleased as I am to meet my sister-in-law," said Meuron. Even his voice echoed Daniel's: deep, seductive, compelling. "I've heard nothing but praise for your talents as a doctor." His gaze drifted appreciatively from her to Daniel. "I see your greater skill lies in the taming of mercenary hearts."

"Daniel, why didn't you tell me?"

"I— We never acknowledged the relationship."

The simple words touched her heart. For the sake of Meuron's respected family, Daniel had stayed in the background, making his own way in the world.

"That was a mistake," said Jean. "How did you escape from Paris, Daniel?"

A half grin lifted a corner of Daniel's mouth. "I daresay my escape was easier than yours."

Still in the grip of amazement, Lorelei stared from one brother to the other. One important difference set them apart: in Daniel's eyes she recognized a deep and shattering love for her alone. The last of her doubts vanished like clouds before a burning sun.

Elation spilled through her and must have blossomed on her face, for there was a tangible easing of tension in the room. Men began to speak and laugh together.

"Will you go to Coppet?" asked Sylvain.

"I . . ." She looked at Daniel. Love and pride shone in his eyes, and yet a curious sadness lingered in his regard. "We'll speak of that soon. I need time to get used to all that's happened."

Tactfully, the men began filing out of the room. Mauricio thrust the tray at her. "Your supper's cold," he grumbled.

"It doesn't matter. I'll eat it anyway."

But she didn't. Daniel sat by her side, murmuring love words and drawing slow, soothing circles over her shoulders and back. Wrapped like a precious keepsake in his love, she drifted off to sleep.

It was dark when she awoke. Yet Daniel sat watching her, his features bathed by fire glow from the new stove.

"How do you feel?" he asked.

"Wonderful." She stretched her arms above her head. "Never better."

"Liar. You're probably sore to your bones from that avalanche. Are you hungry?"

"Oh, yes." She smiled broadly. "For your love."

He moved to the side of the bed. "My darling, I'll serve you a banquet of that." They kissed deeply, his tongue gently rimming the softness of her lips, his hands moving with exquisite care over her shoulders and down her arms.

"I love you," he said.

"Yes," she whispered. "Yes, I know."

"But you're going to have something to eat." She

opened her mouth to protest, but he said, "No arguments."

He brought the tray, and she snatched up a hunk of bread slathered with soft cheese. He moved to the end of the bed, grinning.

She scowled. "You're laughing at me."

"You're a royal princess, and now probably one of the wealthiest women in Europe. Yet still you eat like a peasant."

"And I always will."

"Lorelei." He grew serious. "Please believe this. I never wanted you to change."

She finished her supper, drinking from a mug of good Aosta wine and wiping her mouth with her sleeve. "Come here, Daniel," she said. "Come sit by me."

The cot creaked as he lowered himself beside her. He smelled of the woods and of crisp mountain air. Her hands crept up to cradle his face, and she smiled softly. "Now, about that banquet you promised me . . ."

He drew back and studied her with concern. "Believe me, I'm tempted. But after all you've been through, you should rest."

She lifted her hand to his shoulder and with her thumb found the warm, steady pulse in his throat. "The body heals, Daniel. Much more quickly than the spirit. I need you," she stated simply, pressing herself against him, feeling the taut contours of his body. "More than food, more than rest, more than jewels."

Dizzy with tenderness and passion, Daniel gathered her in his arms. The slippery silk of her hair stung his lips as he bent to kiss her brow, her temple, her cheek, and finally her mouth. God, how he'd missed the taste of her, the sweet, moist warmth that spilled through him each time he kissed her.

With unsteady hands he unbuttoned her shirt and drew it down over her shoulders; then he shed his own clothes. A tender smile played about his lips. "I often dreamed of making love to you here," he confessed. "But I never reckoned on the size of this damned cot."

Lifting her and the bedclothes to his chest, he made a nest on the floor in front of the stove, and they lay together, their bodies heated by the glowing embers and by love-driven passion, and by warm, sweet joy.

"I loved you," he whispered, making a trail of kisses along her jawline, "from the very start, but I was too blind and too scared to admit it."

"You should have listened to me," she said, gently chiding. "I tried to tell you many times." Her hand slid down his torso, bringing his flesh to vibrant life.

Desire, as raw and painful as a fresh wound, stabbed at him. His hands tightened in her curls; then he forced his fingers to relax. Gently, he told himself. She's been hurt enough. He took the mug of wine from the tray and held it to her lips. She drank slowly, the luxurious motion of her throat mesmerizing him. A droplet rolled down between her breasts. He caught it with his mouth, and the taste of it, heated by her flesh, nearly caused him to jump out of his skin. He reminded himself of her bruises—those he could see, and those she hid.

She set aside the wine. "I don't want you to hold

anything back, Daniel," she whispered. "You can't hurt me, not now. And never again."

Her soft plea freed him from restraint. They came together in a joyous clash, with life-affirming abandon. No shadows from the past lay between them now, and the knowledge sharpened every sensation. He felt himself rising to a place that was cleaner and lighter and more sparkling than an unscaled mountain peak. Heaven seemed to lie within his grasp, a shimmering gift, misty and exquisite, rolling out in shining waves before him.

The sweet tremors of her response enveloped him, and her name burst from his lips. They lay entwined for long moments, drifting down from the heights, staring into each other's eyes with wonder and love.

She folded her hands on his chest. "I'm going to enjoy being your wife," she said.

He forced a smile. "Are you, now?"

"Yes. We'll live at Coppet, won't we?"

"Coppet is the perfect place for you."

"And you, too, Daniel," she said quickly. "Don't you remember how well we worked together on the treatise? We'll study and write. And when the baby comes—"

"Baby?" He reared back, horror crashing in his ears. It was bad enough knowing he had to leave Lorelei. The thought of having to abandon both her and their child nearly drove him insane. "You're pregnant?"

Unaware of his fate, she giggled. "I'm sure I wasn't earlier today," she said teasingly. "But after the way you just loved me . . . who knows?" With a dreamy smile playing about her lips, she curled against him and drifted into contented slumber.

He pulled the covers over them both. Throughout their lovemaking, he hadn't allowed himself to think of the future, for to envision life without Lorelei was to open himself to an agony beyond bearing. But now, in the deep quiet of the Alpine night, he remembered his promise to Bonaparte and knew that, one last time, he would hurt her, hurt them both.

He lay making feverish plans. Father Anselme would have to go to Coppet with her. The canon was old and would soon retire from the rugged life at the hospice. Jean and Sylvain would see them safely to Baron Necker's castle. She would be safe there. He had to believe that.

The idea tore at his guts until, at last, exhaustion overcame him and he slept.

At midday, a knock sounded at the door. Daniel came instantly awake, his arms tightening around Lorelei. His breath made misty puffs in the cold air, for the fire in the stove had died. But beneath the covers their bodies, pressed intimately together, had stayed warm.

"What is it?" he called softly. Lorelei stirred, but didn't awaken.

"It's me, Sylvain. Party of soldiers coming."

Daniel's heart thumped with sickening force. "What sort of soldiers?"

"Consular Guard."

"I'll be out shortly."

Daniel rested his cheek on Lorelei's soft hair. Seductive heat emanated from her small, precious body, and he savored the moment, the scent of her, the smooth texture of her skin against his. Agony seemed to invade him like a rampant fever, for he'd found her only to lose her again.

"Lorelei, wake up."

Her eyes fluttered open; she smiled.

He wished he had her facility with words of the heart. "Lorelei, I love you," he said.

"I know." She kissed his chin. "I love you, too."

"I have to go back to Paris."

She pulled back, fully awake now. "But why? We're here, Meuron is free—"

"That's why." He brushed a curl from her cheek. He knew he would always remember the shape of her face, beautiful bones beneath beautiful skin, a visage that contrasted with the inbred awkwardness of her royal kin.

"But Bonaparte let you go free. The charges—"

He shook his head. "I had to give my parole, Lorelei. I swore to return to Paris and face sentencing."

"Sentencing? But the sentence for treasonous conspiracy and murder is—" She clapped her hand over her mouth.

"Death," said Daniel as gently as he could.

She clung to him fiercely, her fingers digging into his shoulders. "No! I won't let you go. We'll run away, find a place where no one will ever come looking for you."

Smiling sadly, he toyed with the idea of going with her into hiding. But he couldn't subject her to the uncertain life of an outlaw. After all he'd dragged her through, he vowed to give her a life of security. She could work and study at Coppet among scholars and poets. In time she would forget the man who had died with her image enshrined in his heart.

"Lorelei, listen to me. I won't have you living with a wanted man, always looking over your shoulder, waking up each morning to wonder if we've been betrayed."

"We could sail to America or—"

"I gave my word, darling. The Raven would have broken his promise remorselessly. But I'm no longer that man." He pressed his lips to her temple. "You yourself said I've changed. I won't disregard a vow I made on my honor."

"Even at the cost of our happiness, of your life?" she asked brokenly.

"Look, there's always a chance I'll be found innocent."

"I'm not foolish enough to believe that."

"Father Anselme and Jean and Sylvain will see you safely to Coppet. They and Baron Necker will care for you."

She stared deep into his eyes. "But who will care for my heart, Daniel? Tell me that."

"You're strong, my love, and you have important work to do. You'll carry on."

He stood and drew her up, pulling a blanket around her trembling shoulders. Her hair was mussed, her eyes wide and drenched with sorrow. "Get dressed, love. A Consular Guard is on its way. Bonaparte doesn't share your conviction that I've changed. He's sent a small army to ensure that I keep my word."

* * *

Her limbs bruised from the crush of the avalanche, her heart aching with the thought of losing Daniel, Lorelei stepped into the hospice yard.

He stood apart from a knot of canons and novices. In his chamois breeches and thick *bredzon,* his blazed hair streaming over his back, her husband looked as rugged and splendid as the glacial peaks that rose in a bowl around the Great Pass. Yet at the same time, he had never looked more alone, more vulnerable. He carried no weapon, only the shield of his hard, indifferent regard as he watched a line of six red-clad soldiers, mounted on mules, rounding the path to the west of the lake.

She pressed her hand to her heart. Oh, Daniel. Had she turned him into a man of honor only to send him to his death?

Meuron and his confederates were nowhere in sight. They would take no chances on being caught by the Consular Guard.

The soldiers reached the yard. Gaston had been the almoner; now that he was gone, Father Droz accepted the task of welcoming the visitors. His face was grave beneath his towering sugarloaf hat, but he planted his alpenstock and lifted his hand, palm out, in the customary greeting.

His cheeks bitten red by the cold, the captain of the Consular Guard dismounted. The sharp breeze ruffled the tiered capelets of his Garrick coat and tugged at his bicorne hat.

Lorelei hurried to Daniel's side. "Please don't go with them," she pleaded softly, putting her hand on his sleeve. His tense muscles beneath the woolen fabric were as solid as granite.

"I have to," he said, gazing at her with eyes full of tenderness. "Lorelei, this is the hardest thing I've ever done." Leaning down, he kissed her quickly, his lips as cool as his eyes were warm. He approached the French captain, Lorelei following close behind. The clerics stepped aside to let them pass.

Daniel faced the captain. "I am Daniel Severin."

The soldier nodded. "Captain Rémy Boitsfort." He held out a folded and sealed parchment. "This is from the first consul."

Daniel took the letter and stepped away from the group. Just for a moment longer he wanted to shield Lorelei from the dread words. With numb fingers, he unfolded the letter and squinted at Bonaparte's tight scrawl.

# Epilogue

*Château Coppet*
*August 1801*

Rubbing the small of her aching back, Lorelei paused in her writing and set down her pen. "What's the Latin for 'false echo'?" she called to the men in the next room.

She heard no reply, although the partly open door admitted a murmur of masculine voices. As always, the men were deep in debate about the new Swiss Confederation.

She decided to abandon her work for the day. The Academy at Bern had invited her to lecture on her listening device. In accordance with tradition, the lecture would be delivered in Latin.

Today the words wouldn't come. Her unborn child

stirred gently, the flutter of a promise to be fulfilled in just a few more weeks. I'm thinking for two, she thought, scowling at the ink-smudged paper.

She stood and gazed about the opulent study in her residence at Coppet. Over her desk hung a framed document: the Necker Prize. Baron Necker had thought her ideas on typhus so promising that he'd granted her a lifelong stipend to pursue her medical studies in his salon at the Château Coppet.

Lorelei hugged herself. Never, on her own, would she have had the courage to submit her ideas to the great man of letters. It was her name on the prize, but she would never discount Daniel's role in winning it.

A pair of tall mullioned windows framed a view of Lake Geneva and the snowy peaks beyond. In the garden, roses bloomed like multicolored sunbursts. Germaine de Staël walked there, deep in conversation with a half-grown Alpine mastiff. The dog was as handsome as Barry, his sire, and Germaine had declared a marked preference for his company over that of human males.

Lorelei walked to the adjacent room. Four men sat facing a blazing fire, their heads bent, a half-empty bottle of brandy on a table nearby, maps and documents scattered at their feet.

She cleared her throat. The men stood. Baron Necker bowed, his cloud of white hair brilliant against his crimson redingote. "Madame. How is the lecture coming?"

"It's not," said Lorelei.

Jean Meuron, looking less like Daniel now that he'd cropped his black hair, grinned at her. "Then come have a drink with us." He pretended to scowl at Father

Anselme, who glared implacably back. "The good cleric is argumentative today. We need you to soothe his temper."

She smiled fondly at Father Anselme. The milder climate and opulent luxury of Coppet suited him well, adding to his girth and opening his mind to the world of Swiss politics. "My temper's as mild as a lamb's," he said. "But I'll take the soothing anyway."

The fourth man walked to her side and bent to kiss her cheek. As always, his smile made her heart skip a beat and the brush of his lips awakened a tender throb of desire.

"You've spilled ink on my son," Daniel chided, indicating her smudged apron.

"Daughter," she corrected, smoothing a hand over the mound of her belly. "And she's keeping me from my work."

Daniel tucked her head against his shoulder. "Good for her. You work too hard."

"What are you arguing about?"

Daniel's gaze slid away, but Baron Necker said, "The militia. It's still without a leader."

Lorelei tugged on Daniel's sleeve. "You mean you haven't told them yet?"

"Told us what?" asked Jean.

With a sigh that was part exasperation, part affection, she fetched a letter from her desk and returned. "This is Bonaparte's letter—the one he sent to the hospice with the Consular Guard."

Daniel flushed. "I didn't know you'd kept that."

"Neither did I," said Meuron. "What the devil does it say?" He snatched the letter and read aloud: " 'I always thought the Carthaginians' treatment of Regulus was rather shabby. Still, he was as good as his word, as I don't doubt you would be. You opened the way to victory at Marengo. You opened my eyes to the needs of our loyal republic of Switzerland as well. For that I thank you.

" 'By order of the first consul of the Republic, the charges against you have been dropped. The Swiss need the Raven, a man who is, in his own way, a true patriot, as grand marshal of Switzerland, dedicated to preserving Swiss neutrality. I know the Raven will not fail me in this.' "

Jean looked up from the letter. "Christ, Daniel," he said. "I never knew a man to be so shy of glory. With a word, you could have ended our argument. And what's this about Regulus?"

Daniel shrugged. Lorelei knew he was still uncomfortable with personal honor. "It's a long story."

Then he drew her into her private study, saying over his shoulder, "Regulus was my brother, too, for a little while. But things didn't turn out for him half so well as they have for me."

He closed the door quietly behind him. The smile he gave her filled her heart with a love that was at once fierce and soft, wild and gentle, and as lasting as the mountains of Switzerland.

"Oh, Daniel," she said, "then you're not angry that I showed them the letter."

"No more secrets, Lorelei," he replied, his mouth moving down to caress hers, as light as the touch of dew on a rose petal. Then his kiss deepened, ripe with the promise of eternity. "Only this, my love, and years of it."

# Afterword

In 1801 Napoleon Bonaparte drafted the Constitution of Malmaison, and it became the governing document of Switzerland. His later Act of Mediation initiated the Swiss Confederation essentially as it exists today, and the cantons gave Napoleon the title of Restorer of Liberty.

Barry, the Alpine mastiff, actually existed. From 1800 to 1812 he rescued some forty travelers. Today a statue of him stands in Paris, and the handsomest male of each litter born at the Hospice of Saint Bernard is called Barry in his honor. The breed came to be called Saint Bernard in 1882.

Josephine's lapdog, Fortuné, lived—to Bonaparte's great annoyance—to a ripe old age.